PENGUIN BOOKS

PRITHVIRAJ CHAUHAN

Anuja Chandramouli is a bestselling Indian author. She is widely regarded as one of the finest writers in mythological fiction and fantasy. Chandramouli followed up her highly acclaimed debut novel, *Arjuna: Saga of a Pandava Warrior-Prince*, with *Kamadeva: The God of Desire*, *Shakti: The Divine Feminine* and *Yama's Lieutenant*. Her articles, short stories and book reviews appear in various publications like the *New Indian Express*, *The Hindu* and *Femina*.

An accomplished orator and storyteller, Chandramouli regularly conducts workshops on creative writing, mythology and empowerment in schools and colleges across the country. This happily married mother of two little girls credits caffeine and cake for her writing prowess. Currently, she is trying to raise awareness about 'writer's bum', which she insists is a very real thing.

You can get in touch with her at:

Email: anujamouli@gmail.com
Twitter: @anujamouli
Facebook: www.facebook.com/authoranujachandramouli/
Website: www.anujachandramouli.com

PRITHVIRAJ CHAUHAN

✽The Emperor of Hearts✽

ANUJA CHANDRAMOULI

PENGUIN BOOKS

An imprint of Penguin Random House

PENGUIN BOOKS

USA | Canada | UK | Ireland | Australia
New Zealand | India | South Africa | China | Singapore

Penguin Books is part of the Penguin Random House group of companies
whose addresses can be found at global.penguinrandomhouse.com

Published by Penguin Random House India Pvt. Ltd
4th Floor, Capital Tower 1, MG Road,
Gurugram 122 002, Haryana, India

Penguin
Random House
India

First published in Penguin Books by Penguin Random House India 2017

Copyright © Anuja Chandramouli 2017

All rights reserved

10 9 8 7 6 5 4 3 2

This is a work of fiction. All situations, incidents, dialogue and characters,
with the exception of some well-known historical and public figures mentioned
in this novel, are products of the author's imagination and are not to be
construed as real. They are not intended to depict actual events or people or to
change the entirely fictional nature of the work. In all other respects, any
resemblance to persons living or dead is entirely coincidental.

ISBN 9780143441199

Typeset in Sabon by Manipal Digital Systems, Manipal
Printed at Repro India Limited

This book is sold subject to the condition that it shall not, by way of trade
or otherwise, be lent, resold, hired out, or otherwise circulated without the
publisher's prior consent in any form of binding or cover other than that in
which it is published and without a similar condition including this condition
being imposed on the subsequent purchaser.

www.penguin.co.in

MIX
Paper from
responsible sources
FSC® C047271

This is a legitimate digitally printed version of the book and therefore might not
have certain extra finishing on the cover.

For my husband, Chandramouli Vidyasaghar, who gave me my very own weird and wonderful love story

Fever Dream

The queen tossed and turned; her sweat-streaked body caused the soft sheets to cling to her contours as she stifled a scream that fought to burst from her lips. *A good girl must be seen not heard*, she had been taught since childhood.

Silently she pleaded with she knew not whom, begging to escape the terror that was engulfing her. When that failed, she tried to wake up. Her efforts were entirely futile. No matter how much she tried, a force she could not withstand tore her apart, dragging her along the serpentine alleys of her simmering subconscious.

Propelled along a rocky slope, she felt the flesh scraped off her delicate feet, which were decorated with intricate henna patterns, leaving them battered and bloodied. Dragged along sandy plains, under a blazing sun, her skin, softened with milk and honey, caught fire. She wrapped her burning arms protectively around her tender belly and snarled savagely at the elements.

Then she was swimming against the currents of a raging river as predators with serrated teeth and spiked tails pursued her ruthlessly. The wind snatched her from their jaws as they were about to swallow her and lifted her high up in the air. Shrieking its terrible intent into her ears, it ripped off her garments before releasing her in endless space.

As she plunged into the depths below, she could not hold back the primeval screams of agony from bursting out in a shrill cacophony. Then she was falling through emptiness, plummeting towards certain death. Shutting her eyes tight, her arms flailing, she forced her leaden legs to move, desperate to arrest her fall.

Then with a suddenness that made her dizzy, everything went still. Holding her swollen belly in her arms, she opened her eyes. She was standing at the threshold of a stone temple. Before her, was an altar where a smokeless fire was burning. Vigorous and strong, it was brighter than her eyes could bear.

Shining with divine vehemence, it beckoned her forward. Helpless in front of the hypnotic pull of those ancient flames, she stood before it, so close that the heat scoured her clean even as her heart grew hot. And yet, she could not draw back.

Enraptured, she stared into its depths. She watched the mesmerizing dance of the flames as they swayed in discord to the crackling cadence of the age-old rhythms, orchestrated by the divine father out of his deep love for the sacred mother. The sky and the earth—always together; forever apart.

Tears sprang into her eyes and she clasped her hands in prayer as the earth mother addressed her throbbing heart.

What is it that you would know of me?

'Tell me of the child I bear in my womb.'

A mother always knows. A mother must.

'My boy will be the greatest of kings. A mighty warrior. A lion among men and as such will be entitled to the king's share of success, prosperity and happiness. He will shine with the brilliance of a thousand suns. His name will live forever.'

So it shall be. The flame in his soul is destined to burn for as long as his lion's heart can bear it. Blessed as he is with the tejas of the divine, he will shine brightest when he makes the ascent to the pinnacle of glory, just before his swift descent to darkness and the depths of abject failure. For so it must be.

'Never! I will never allow such fate to befall my son.'

A mother is a fool! He was never yours alone. And never will be. Prepare yourself for the reign of the king of the earth. For fame and fortune, love and death, glory and grief!

The flames rose higher and higher, oblivious to the mother who wailed in misery. Blinded by the all-encompassing radiance, magnified by the strength of her tears, she was ill-prepared for the darkness that descended without warning, snuffing out every trace of the sacred fire.

The silence was broken only by infernal howls of abject sorrow—a mother's terrible lament—amid the hushed murmur of a premonition, repeated over and over.

Prithviraj! Prithviraj! Prithviraj! King of the earth!

All around there was nothing but darkness. And the memory of light.

1

Karpuradevi, the Chedi princess from Tripuri and wife of Someshwar, scion of the Chahamanas, was filled with anxious expectancy and an almost unbearable excitement as she awaited the birth of her son. Ever since she had discovered that she was pregnant, her world, which had precious little she cared for, had transformed. Even as she grew big with her baby, she could feel her heart filling with fresh hope. Already her son was a hero who had come to slay the personal demons that had held her captive for so long.

During his conquest of Tripuri, Maharaj Siddharaj Jaisingh—king of the Chalukyas and her husband's maternal grandfather—had arranged her marriage. That is how she found herself in Patan instead of Ajmer. Maharaj Jaisingh had insisted on his grandsons being brought up under his care. Patan was a beautiful place and had prospered greatly under the reign of Maharaj Jaisingh. The palaces and temples were unmatched in splendour, while the parks, groves and gardens were aesthetic marvels.

She loved to bedeck herself in her finest clothes and ornaments, weave her thick hair into a braid and set out on a visit to the magnificent Sahasralinga Thala, a lake with a thousand shrines dedicated to Lord Shiva. Maharaj Jaisingh had performed the dedication shortly before mounting an expedition against Yashovarma of Malwa. Sahasralinga Thala filled her with peace and strength.

Yet, she could not love Patan the way her mother-in-law, Kanchanadevi, did. For Karpuradevi, it would always be the place where her wings had been clipped. She longed for the day when her wings would grow back and she could soar away across the infinite sky and endless ocean to whatever awaited her. Something told her that her wish was about to be granted; she truly believed that her son would make her life better and brighter.

While he grew in her womb, the limestone-bleached walls of the harem with its formidably arched entrance no longer felt like a prison or like one of Yama's hells. For the first time since her marriage, Karpuradevi defied Kanchanadevi's express commands and stepped out of her chambers during the period of her confinement to go on long walks, exploring the courtyards and the enclosed gardens of the harem.

She could even admire the rich mosaics and the elaborately engraved archways without feeling oppressed. Feeling quite courageous, she even cooled off by lifting the hem of her ghagra and lowering her legs into one of the numerous pools that dotted the harem. She spent many a happy hour there, allowing the fish to nibble at the hennaed soles of her feet or gathering lotuses and listening to the birds sing.

To everybody's shock, the formidable Kanchanadevi—daughter of the heirless Maharaj Jaisingh—expressed no outrage at the indecorous behaviour of her formerly meek daughter-in-law. In fact, she actually voiced her approval by declaring that the show of boldness made by the mother-to-be was incontrovertible evidence that she was indeed bearing a son, who in turn clearly showed the marks of a great warrior. After all a sheep could not deliver a lion, could it?

Having reached this gratifying conclusion, Kanchanadevi slackened her vice-like grip on her son's wife, though she still watched over her like a hawk. There were moments when her trademark glower directed at Karpuradevi was replaced with the slightest upward curving of her lips. Karpuradevi could not make up her mind as to what was more alarming—her mother-in-law's approval or her disapproval.

The good news, of course, was that for once they were in agreement. It *was* going to be a boy. Karpuradevi was certain. A mother could tell. Just like she knew that he was going to be a king. And a good one. She was going to make sure of it.

In their world beset with strife, endless political machinations and senseless bloodshed, weakness was the only crime and she would no longer be held guilty of it. So Karpuradevi, who had been sheltered all her life and knew little beyond the walls of the palace, decided that it was time to educate herself for her son's sake. She hated being so thoroughly dependent on her husband, who unlike her father enjoyed rubbing it in her face, and she had no desire to be a burden on her son. She would rather be his rock.

To her surprise, Kanchanadevi fully approved of her new-found resolve and took up the mantle of tutoring her. Unlike the vast majority of ladies in the harem, both of them could read and write. It was upon her insistence that Karpuradevi began to instruct herself on the political treatises, the rules of law, logic, warfare and political administration. She even started brushing up on her knowledge of omens. She particularly enjoyed Kautilya's Arthashastra.

Someshwar disapproved of excessive learning but didn't say anything. His mother was unpredictable and he did not wish to risk a tongue-lashing. He had a lot of merits but strength and bravery weren't on that list and both his mother and his wife had resigned themselves to the fact that Someshwar would never make a good king.

Not that he had much of a chance to sit on the throne. He was the third son of King Arnoraj, the ruler of Ajmer, born to his Chalukyan wife Kanchanadevi. His second son, Vigraharaj-IV, born to his chief queen Johiyani Sadhava of Maroth, sat on the throne of the Chauhans at Ajmer. If the martial exploits of Vigraharaj—the one people already referred to as 'Maharajadhiraja'—were of any indication, he would have a long and a glorious reign.

Needless to say there was not a lot of warmth between Vigraharaj and his half-brother, which in turn could be traced down to the outright hostility that existed between their mothers and to the more obvious fact that they both had a claim to the throne. Johiyani had the reputation of being fiercely protective of the rights of her young sons and even Kanchanadevi had fled pell-mell from her baleful influence. The image of her mother-in-law running for her life never ceased to amuse Karpuradevi, even though it made her feel disloyal.

'That woman,' Kanchanadevi had told her through pursed lips, 'is a she-devil. I have it on excellent authority that her father, noting that his precious daughter's face resembled the hindquarters of a monkey, hired disreputable women from dens of inequity to impart their skills of harlotry to her so she might ensnare her future husband. If that were not bad enough, she later brought in young girls trained in the same arts from her father's kingdom for my lord Arnoraj's amusement. Exploiting his weakness for the pleasures of the flesh, she became his chief queen. I would never stoop so low!'

Karpuradevi loved her mother-in-law's tirades, especially when they were not directed at her. They were rich in detail and full of dirt on the most powerful men and women of the age. She listened rapt as ever. She had heard the stories many times before; flattered, despite herself, Kanchanadevi resumed her narrative.

'It was brought to my notice repeatedly that she consorted with practitioners of the occult arts and fed her sons—Jaggadeva and Vigraharaj—the milk of man-eating tigresses so that they could grow up to be bloodthirsty brutes! Small wonder they both turned out the way they did. Even then, I knew that

Jaggadeva was a black-hearted villain and warned my husband about him. But he only laughed at my suspicions. If my husband had paid attention to my words, his life would not have been cut short so tragically by the monster raised by that she-devil!

'My father at least paid heed to my fears. Even his detractors would admit that Maharaj Jaisingh was blessed with sagacity and was the canniest of them all. He knew that she-devil was plotting to kill my boys, Someshwar and Kanha, so he summoned us to Patan while they were still babies and saved all our lives in the process.'

Kanchanadevi's aged bosom heaved with red-hot anger. Her daughter-in-law watched her with fascination. While she couldn't claim excessive fondness for her mother-in-law, it had to be admitted that Kanchanadevi had done the right thing.

Even here in Patan, they had heard dark tales of Johiyani's savagery and the things she had done to Maharaj Arnoraj's children by his other wives and concubines. It was rumoured that Kanchanadevi had stabbed an unidentified assassin who had ambushed them en route to Patan. She would have loved to verify the story but Kanchanadevi did not appreciate questions, preferring instead being listened to. What a king she would have made! She was very much her father's daughter after all.

Maharaj Jaisingh had ruled Patan, one of the most powerful kingdoms in *aryavarta,* and was a legend in his lifetime. He cut his teeth in the revered sport of war by subduing Laat and Khambat, where his rival kings had long struggled to establish their supremacy in Gurjardesa. Having established his prowess, Jaisingh went on to defeat the Paramars of Marwar before going on to conquer Chittor and Kathiawar, thereby establishing himself as the greatest ruler of his dynasty. As such, he had enjoyed the love of his subjects and the respect of his enemies.

The Chalukyas and the Chauhans had long been rivals and it was Prithviraj-I who handed Jaisingh his first major defeat and drove him out of Pushkar. Later, he would establish a truce with the Chauhans by giving his daughter Kanchanadevi's hand in marriage to Prithviraj's grandson, Arnoraj. Even this move earned him the admiration of friend and foe alike. There were not many among the Kshatriyas who had the acuity to stay their hand when the time called for it. By calmly going against the grain, the wise old monarch was able to consolidate his wins while making an ally out of the Chauhans.

By summoning his daughter and grandsons to Anhilwara Patan, his heavily fortified capital, Jaisingh proved his foresight and uncanny ability to predict which way the political winds would blow. Having managed to protect them from hostile forces, who would not hesitate to curry favour with the king of Ajmer by presenting him with the corpses of his half-brothers, he made his plans for the future.

'Father used to monitor the situation at Ajmer constantly,' Kanchanadevi informed her daughter-in-law. 'He told me that a throne could be secured in many ways and outright force wasn't always the best way to go about it. The rewards are many for those who wait patiently, gathering intelligence and planning how best to use the right opportunity when it presents itself, he would say.

'Had he been alive, the throne of Ajmer would have been claimed in the name of Someshwar. But while I'm still alive, I will not rest till his wish is fulfilled. One day, his descendants will lay claim to Sapadalaksha and from their ancient seat of power will carve out a mighty kingdom that will rival that of Indra's!'

Karpuradevi was moved by the passion in the grand old lady's voice and felt her own excitement rise. Her son clearly loved these stories too, for at that moment he gave her a hard little kick that made her wince a bit. Night and day, he kept her up these days, moving restlessly in her womb as if he couldn't wait to escape its confines and begin his conquest for glory and gain!

Ever since Karpuradevi had come to reside in Patan, she had resigned herself to the fact that her son would be raised here, the way Someshwar and Kanha had. But it was only a matter of time before they made their way back to Ajmer.

Her husband saw her only once after being informed that she was pregnant. He had found some time from whichever fanciful pursuit he was currently engaged in to pay her a visit. As always they had precious little to say to each other.

'Remember to visit the temple every day and say the prescribed prayers. Bear me a son, an heir worthy of the noble dynasty of the Chahamanas. If your womb proves incapable, strangle whatever it spits out!'

Her gut clenched and she placed her hands, which were twitching to strangle him, on her bulging belly. The baby she carried, unlike her husband, would be wise enough to realize that a daughter was the most precious gift on earth, an incarnation of Mahalakshmi, the goddess of prosperity.

On his orders, several pieces of precious jewellery, family heirlooms worn by his mother and grandmother, fine silks and skilfully carved idols of the gods and goddesses were carefully laid out in front of Karpuradevi. He showed her a particularly beautiful talisman bearing the ten avatars of Vishnu, set in solid gold and decorated with the *navaratnas*.

'I wanted you to see these! They are the gifts for my new bride, Ruka Devi. She is a beauty and a scion of our vassals, the Tomars, who as you know were the former rulers of Dillika till I broke their spine in battle and snuffed out the last of their futile efforts at resistance. The talisman, though, will be for my firstborn son, whichever one of you delivers him first.'

Karpuradevi arranged her features in what she hoped was a gracious smile. She was itching to remind her lord husband that his half-brother, Vigraharaj-IV, had taken Dillika from the Tomars and not him. It was not the first time Someshwar had taken credit for the actions of others and it wouldn't be the last.

Mercifully, he left soon after. That was the last she saw of him till her boy was born. Not that she was complaining. Someshwar had been with Maharaj Jaisingh during his war against her own Chedi. He had claimed credit for the death of her valiant uncle and Chedi king Mallikarjun, but there were those who swore that it was the brave Ambad, one of Jaisingh's vassals, who had dealt the fatal blow.

Some claimed it was Kumarpal, now Maharaj Kumarpal, who had taken his life. Everybody agreed that Someshwar had fought well but it wasn't his hand that had slain the fierce Mallikarjun, which, however, did not stop him from commissioning an epic saga in celebration of his fictitious victory. It was boorish of him, especially since they were currently living on the largesse of Maharaj Kumarpal.

She wished it was possible to understand why her husband did such things. The truth would be revealed once Hemachandra, the great Jain teacher who enjoyed the patronage of the king, completed his *Kumarapala Charitra* and her own husband would end up looking foolish.

Someshwar was Kanchanadevi's favourite and in Maharaj Jaisingh's kingdom, she made it clear that those who trained with him in the martial arts risked her implacable wrath if they dared best her boy in combat. And so he remained undefeated and singularly unskilled in the science of arms, yet utterly unaware of it, thanks to his rampaging ego that he lovingly nurtured with the help of his mother and the sycophants he surrounded himself with.

While it was easy to understand a mother's excessive love, Kumarpal's tendency to allow Someshwar such latitude was even harder to comprehend. More so in light of the fact that Arnoraj had taken the pretender Chahad's side against

Kumarpal when they were fighting over the right to succeed Maharaj Jaisingh. He had been a constant thorn in his side. Kumarpal had exacted his vengeance upon Arnoraj and made him pay a dear price for his actions. There were those who felt it would have been kinder of the victor to simply strike his head off!

Some murmured that Kumarpal had always been in love with Kanchanadevi as they were distantly related and had known each other a long time. He had supposedly been devastated when Maharaj Jaisingh had married off Kanchanadevi to Arnoraj. Others said that he hoped to claim the throne of Ajmer in Someshwar's name and bring the vast domain of the Chauhans under his sway.

Despite her advanced years, Kanchanadevi was a good-looking woman and it was not hard to imagine a man like Kumarpal finding her irresistible in her heyday. But it was hard to imagine them carrying on now!

Karpuradevi could not possibly ask Kanchanadevi about her purported romance with Kumarpal but her brother-in-law, Kanha, had given her an insight into the relationship they had shared. 'I know for a fact that when Mother talks he listens. Even his ministers follow his cue and agree that it is truly a shame and perverse of the gods to put all that fierce determination and sharp political acumen in a woman's body. During the war for succession, Mother took his side, very circumspectly, of course, against Chahad even though my own father fought against him. Maharaj Jaisingh's daughter has an unmatched ability for picking the winner!

'Moreover, she was furious with Father for ignoring her council and risking the safety of her own person and his flesh and blood by going to war against Kumarpal. She held the fort at Patan with the help of her father's trusted advisers, who had long been prepared for such an eventuality. It was their job to ensure that the administration did not suffer when dynastic misfortunes befell them and all around the jackals and vultures circled, fighting each other for the juiciest chunks of a kingdom without a strong leader.

'It was thanks to her that a relatively smooth transition to power was possible for Maharaj Kumarpal. Siddharaj Jaisingh's name carries a lot of weight here and many of his trusted advisers and generals acting on her wishes were assimilated into the new king's council, giving it the sheen of legitimacy. He has never forgotten the service Mother did for him.'

Karpuradevi did not doubt that this was her mother-in-law's way of punishing Arnoraj for making a hated rival, his chief queen. Kanchanadevi was not one to suffer such slights lightly! Kanha also told her about Kumarpal's plans for installing a puppet on the Ajmer throne. His mother would be complicit if it meant thwarting her stepson Vigraharaj. Her heart beat a little faster at the thought. Her boy unlike his father would be a lion and he would rule not only Ajmer, but Dillika, Patan and the whole of Bharat one day.

Cradling the swollen mound of her belly in her arms, she trembled with excitement. She could not wait to hold her baby. He was destined to do great things. Change the very course of history . . . Yet cold fear fluttered in her heart, an irksome presence in the midst of her exuberance and expectations and she fought might and main to suppress it. But it would not go away.

The labour pains began just as the sun was going down. Lakshmibai had assured her that women with wide, 'child-bearing' hips had an easier time during birthing, even as she sent for the *dai* and the vaidya. An attendant was sent to inform Kanchanadevi and Someshwar.

The royal physician had always been present to attend to the scions of the Chalukyas, born within and without the bonds of holy matrimony, for many years now. He would wait outside in case of complications and if the newborn needed his care. Men and women of high birth did not defile themselves by entering the birthing chambers. However, the presence of the vaidya and Kanchanadevi was crucial as both would bear witness to the fact that the child was legitimate and free of imperfections.

The dai had been waiting in readiness for days knowing that Karpuradevi's time was near and she appeared at once, bearing the tools of her trade. Lamps were hurriedly lit, water was heated and clean clothes were laid nearby. The air was thick with excitement as quick and efficient preparations were made for the birth.

They can tell, Karpuradevi thought with fierce pride, even as waves of pain hit her being and her heart hammered in her chest, *that my boy is destined to be the king of the earth*.

Lakshmibai was bustling around, seeming to be everywhere at once—a calm and a reassuring presence. She had been her nurse since Karpuradevi was a wee one and had accompanied her from Tripuri. The years had not left a mark on her smooth face, broad hips and heavyset, relatively firm bosom. Lakshmibai was made from good, sturdy stock and she would not let even time take its toll on her.

She had pampered her silly throughout the course of her pregnancy insisting that she take warm baths and had the maids massage her back, shoulders and limbs with sponges soaked in rose water. The chefs had been bullied into maximizing their culinary efforts to produce an array of delicious dishes to tempt the expecting mother to eat properly in order to ensure that the child was healthy and strong.

Now Lakshmibai wiped her brow and knelt by her side, ready to accompany her on the perilous journey to motherhood. It was a lot longer, more difficult and painful than Karpuradevi had been led to believe. But she bore it all with a grace and serenity that astounded the women who waited on her.

They were more used to the royal broodmares' neighing loud enough to bring the roof down on their heads.

At times the pain grew so fierce that Karpuradevi nearly passed out. There were moments when the dai and Lakshmibai exchanged worried looks. The baby was giving his mother a lot of trouble. But if he did not succeed in killing himself and his mother, they both knew that the ruddy constitution this evinced would stand him in good stead as the scion of a powerful warrior lineage.

Through it all, Karpuradevi showed the same strength that goddess Durga had when she had slain the evil Mahishasura. She seemed secure in the notion that nothing untoward would happen to her or to the baby. She never doubted it through the long watches of the night as she floated on a sea of pain. Finally, after what felt like an eternity of struggle and a tremendous push, she gave birth. The sun was just rising. The baby opened his little mouth and howled in protest at being forced to vacate the cosy premises of his mother's womb. Later, everyone who had heard him swore that his cries had sounded like the roaring of a lion.

'It is a boy!' Lakshmibai told her with a broad smile. 'He is the most beautiful thing I have ever laid eyes upon.'

The dai quickly tied and cut the cord, removed it and kept it aside for disposal. Lakshmibai began cleaning the baby, wiping his mother's bodily juices off him with a soft cloth dipped in warm oil. Her experienced fingers washed his hair and wiped it dry, before wrapping him in a swaddling cloth, exclaiming all the while, 'He is as handsome as a god! A precious little *Manmadha*!' and 'What a magnificent head of hair! So rare in newborns!' After what felt like an eternity, she held him up for her to see.

Although she was weak and tired, Karpuradevi raised herself up on an elbow, eager for the first glimpse of her baby. He was beautiful. Extraordinarily so. Clear-eyed, he gazed steadily at her while she took in his little pink lips and delicate features. His hair was black with streaks of deep brown that glinted as it caught the rays of the rising sun.

She tried to reach out for the baby but the dai forced her back on the bed. Lakshmibai had taken the baby to the vaidya, who was waiting in the chamber outside with Kanchanadevi. He examined the baby closely and his grandmother scrutinized him as well. Having checked him thoroughly for birth defects, the physician proclaimed that he was perfect in every way. Kanchanadevi nodded and her tone was sharp to mask the relief she felt. 'Of course, he is. My father, Maharaj Jaisingh, wished him to be called Prithviraj, third of the name, king of the earth. Destined to be *samrat* one day!'

Maharaj Jaisingh had been most insistent about that. He had wanted a great grandson named Prithviraj, who would perform such tremendous deeds that he would eclipse his namesake who had managed to defeat him. History must remember only your grandson, he had told her half in jest, while the other would be relegated to the dustheap, to be utterly forgotten!

The new mother was bleeding a little and the dai attended to her, applying cold compresses and a crushed herb poultice till it stopped completely. Once she was out of danger, the dai and her attendants wasted no time in changing the sheets and divesting the mother of her birthing robes, which would be burnt along with the afterbirth. Others rubbed her with turmeric-infused water to stave off infection, before wiping it dry gently as her body was still raw and tender from her recent labours. Then they clothed her in fresh garments.

Karpuradevi was not hungry but they made her drink a potion made with coconut milk and sweetened with *jaggery*. She was impatient to hold her son and wished they would stop fussing over her. Though she was completely drained, she would not lie back to rest, her eyes wandering restlessly, searching for the precious bundle of joy she had just delivered.

Kanchanadevi walked in then bearing the little prince. The harsh lines of her face softened and she seemed dangerously close to smiling. She accepted the small dish of solid gold that Lakshmibai held out to her, pouring a few drops of sugary water into his mouth, watching with approval when he stuck out a little pink tongue in search of more. The boy had a ferocious appetite.

'You have done well,' she told her daughter-in-law, 'his grip is strong. This baby was born to wield a sword and a bow. His name suits him too! It is . . .'

' . . . Prithviraj!' Karpuradevi finished the sentence, startling her unflappable mother-in-law slightly. She could not be sure, but the name had been whispered to her in a dream or a passing god had breathed it in her ear. *Prithviraj. Prithviraj Chauhan.*

The baby lay drowsily on the bed next to her, where she could drink in her fill of his beauty. He had just been fed and it seemed to her that he looked a little intoxicated. It made her want to laugh. She could look at him forever.

Karpuradevi had refused the services of a wet nurse, insisting on feeding him with her own milk. 'You will ruin your breasts if you carry on like this! They will lose their shape and elasticity and before the year is over, they will look like mine!' Lakshmibai had chided her. But she did not care. Being beautiful and desirable weren't everything. Besides, she already loved her son more than she could bear and hated the thought of him suckling at another's breasts!

The baby's nurses were on hand and they carried the baby away to burp him and change his tiny soiled clothes, since she was still far too weak to attend to his every need the way she would have liked to. Karpuradevi cursed her delicate constitution and grudged them every second for keeping her son away from her.

Although Kanchanadevi found it highly irregular, she chose to be amused about it since she was in high spirits over the birth of her grandson. Maharaj Kumarpal's rajguru had declared that the omens surrounding his birth had been most propitious. The young prince's birth chart indicated that his fame would overshadow even that of his namesake Prithviraj and his uncle Vigraharaj-IV.

For that alone, Maharaj Jaisingh would have loved the boy, Kanchanadevi thought to herself. Had she been the crying sort, she would have got all teary-eyed at this point. But she wasn't, so she sent word to the *jyotishis* instead.

Having examined Prithviraj's horoscope at the behest of Kanchanadevi in greater detail, the jyotishis assured them that the boy was destined for greatness, 'The prince was born on the twelfth day of *Jyestha* and his auspices could not be more favourable. He is blessed with martial skills worthy of a true conqueror and a thirst for power. It is only a matter of time before he eclipses every one of his illustrious ancestors!'

'It is the bold of heart who are favoured by the gods when they make their bid for glory. The lion cub born on this day enjoys the favour of fate and fortune.

'He will be a great king. Of that there is no doubt. His physical prowess will be extraordinary in the manner of Arjuna, the Pandava. In addition to that he will be very intelligent, good-looking and charismatic like our lord Krishna. Even the rashness and recklessness that are typical traits of those born under Jyestha will serve him in good stead when he drives the accursed *mlecchas* from our land!

'The prince is beloved of our earth mother Vasumati and she will shower him with riches enough to fuel his endeavours in building a mighty empire! In addition to that the lad will have the love of his subjects on account of his innate nobility and strength. Men will admire and respect him; his brave *samants* will be so loyal that they will fight to death for him; women will give their hearts unabashedly to him.'

'A horoscope like this is very rare. Even with all of Kubera's treasure and with all the force in the world, it will be impossible to procure the qualities he was born with. His name will live forever! Men and women will remember Prithviraj Chauhan long after we perish and they will tell tales of his greatness to their children. May he be forever blessed!'

These extraordinary pronouncements from the traditionally reticent Jyesthas, given to predictions of gloom and doom even at the risk of execution, sent the royal household into paroxysms of utmost glee. Maharaj Kumarpal, who had no children of his own, was in such good humour that he immediately had the heralds proclaim the news of the birth of Prithviraj-III across the length and breadth of the kingdom.

Messengers were sent to Ajmer to inform Vigraharaj-IV of the fortuitous birth and the predictions that had followed. Later, Kanchanadevi's spies told her that he had listened to the messengers with a strange smile and given orders that fabulous presents for the baby be taken at once to Patan. He had even taken off his heavy lion pendant and given it to the baby as a mark of goodwill. Kanchanadevi had not quite hated the magnanimous gesture but even she could not resist remarking that Johiyani Sadhava's son was well trained in the art of making himself look good.

Special pujas were held in the temples to honour the prince and there was feasting and celebrations held all over the land. Prisoners were released and Brahmins were presented with cash and cows.

Even Someshwar became less dour than was his wont on witnessing the grand celebrations that had unfurled to mark the birth of his son, thanks to the generosity of Maharaj Kumarpal. He was so gratified that he joined in the celebrations with uncharacteristic gusto and presented everyone who crossed his path with gold coins and freshly prepared sweets. The thought of feasting and drinking till dawn put him in even better spirits.

Kanchanadevi had been so pleased with the jyotishis that she had made sure they were rewarded with gold, silver, fine silks and rich presents and treated to a royal feast. As they began to depart, a lone member of that order hung back to talk to her in confidence. Discreetly, she ushered him into a private chamber where they might converse far from prying eyes, wagging tongues and hearts that bore nothing but ill will.

The man had eyes that watered constantly and liver spots on seemingly every bit of his exposed skin. He had the self-satisfied air of one who delighted in using a few well-chosen words to destroy a life mercilessly. Kanchanadevi found him repugnant but she gave nothing of her thoughts away.

He cleared his throat repeatedly and took his time getting to the point. 'Allow me to offer my congratulations on the birth of your grandson. If I am not mistaken, he takes after his uncle Vigraharaj-IV and his paternal grandmother. It is a fine horoscope, one of the finest I have ever laid eyes upon.'

He went on in this vein for a bit, reiterating all the things that had already been said before spitting out his piece. 'While his auspices seem to indicate nothing but an abundance of perfection, there is something I must tell you. The others noticed it too but they were too cowardly to give voice to their findings.'

A few more seconds were wasted while he searched in vain for the discomfiture he was sure she was feeling. To his disappointment, there was nothing but steel in that unflinching gaze. However, he still persisted, lowering his voice to a whisper. 'Jyestha was the oldest of the twenty-seven sisters married to Soma, the moon god. Her husband loved her younger sister, Rohini, the best of them all and Jyestha became increasingly embittered over the alienation of Soma's affection and was filled with anger and jealousy. There is a spiteful side to her as a result of her resentment over the happiness of others.

'Which is why those of this birth star must beware, especially when they are blessed with plenty. There is always a very distinct possibility of sudden, irrevocable loss. Once this child has reached the zenith of glory, there will be nowhere for him to go but down and the odds are he will be plunged into the depths of profound sorrow. I tell you this so that care and prudence is exercised in his upbringing to help him control his tempestuous passions and an effort is made to employ his prodigious skills wisely, in a manner that does not provoke envy in others. He must not allow success to go to his head if he wishes to avoid abject failure.'

Kanchanadevi listened in stony silence. The rascal had pocketed his fee before giving voice to such dire tidings. How dare he mar the perfection of the day with his ill-omened talk of defeat and loss? She had a good mind to take it all back and reward him with a thousand lashes instead.

But she listened with politeness to his unwanted advice before sending him on his way. More disturbed than she cared to admit, Kanchanadevi decided to go and take another look at her grandson.

Her daughter-in-law's refusal to use a wet nurse had been reported to her. Whatever was the world coming to when women felt free to behave exactly how they pleased, ignoring tried-and-tested traditions? These young mothers really tried her patience! They behaved as if they had accomplished something phenomenal by pushing out a boy from between their legs. She blamed the mothers for this lamentable state of affairs. They spoiled their daughters, failing to beat some sense into their empty heads. Husbands who did not do the same were equally reprehensible.

Still, her heart softened when she laid her eyes on the baby. He looked sweet as he reposed in the engraved cradle that she had had made for her own son, Someshwar. What high hopes she had had then! But now she had more reason than ever before to hope. Prithviraj-III would reverse Someshwar's fortune as well, she knew.

As for Karpuradevi, she was aglow with happiness and looked so radiant it was positively vulgar. Even so, her disapproving mother-in-law decided to be magnanimous and informed her about the wonderful things the jyotishis had predicted for Prithviraj, leaving out the prattle of the fool who had counted on her good humour to spill his poison.

The new mother brightened even more. Someshwar hadn't come to see the boy yet. Kanchanadevi sighed. She should have brought him personally, if only to dampen the excess ardour of his wife, who had given all the love that could possibly be contained in her heart to the prince, leaving nothing for her husband. Foolish girl!

Hadn't her useless Chedi mother told her that it was a wife's love that safeguarded a husband from his enemies and the caprices of fate? Kanchanadevi at least had had the good sense to love neither her husband nor her sons. Love was a fool's game that she had always refused to play. In fact, she could not even claim to love her grandson, she merely approved of him. As she approved of her own dear father. And Maharaj Kumarpal, of course. He at least had the good sense to give her the only thing she had ever wanted in a man—respect. Nothing more. Nothing less.

Seeing the new mother's eyes on the sleeping prince, Kanchanadevi could not restrain herself any more. 'You are his mother and yet you behave like a besotted lover! You know what that means, don't you?'

Karpuradevi did not reply but she didn't have to. It was obvious that she did not care for whatever her mother-in-law was going to tell her.

'When a mother chooses to love her son too much instead of giving him just the right amount of care, free from cloying emotions, it is a personal invitation to misfortune. In due course, your son will allow his heart to be stolen by one possessing the same attributes as yourself but younger, of course. And then he will cast you aside to follow the filly wherever she chooses to lead him, even if it is to doom and destruction!'

Seeing the stricken look on her face, Kanchanadevi was almost sorry, but then again, she reflected as she made her departure, excessive happiness always drew the baleful influence of the evil eye as that foul-tongued jyotishi had warned her. In fact, the way she saw it, her daughter-in-law should be thanking her.

Someshwar went to see his son when dusk had fallen. The baby and his mother were fast asleep. It annoyed him that his wife was not ready to receive him and considered having her attendants shake her awake. But he stood for a long time beside his son's crib in silence, watching the rise and fall of his chest. Here was living proof to his detractors and vicious rumour-mongers who had questioned his virility and cast aspersions on his manhood.

It had annoyed him just a little bit that the jyotishis had predicted that his son would perform marvellous deeds and his fame would exceed that of his ancestors. It was hard to believe that this wrinkled, shrivelled-up little thing would go on to become a great warrior. Why, even his male organ was no bigger than his little finger. While it was bad enough that he had to live in his half-brother Vigraharaj's shadow, it was even worse to think that in future, his only claim to fame would be that he was Prithviraj-III's father.

Someshwar clenched his fist. There was a sour taste in his mouth, his good humour from earlier that day had evaporated completely. The baby whimpered softly. It certainly did not sound like the roaring of a lion! Sometimes people said the most foolish things.

Motherhood suited his wife. She looked more desirable than she had in a long time. Clumsily, he tried to place the talisman around Prithviraj's neck but it was hard to do so when the baby was little more than a blob of flesh with folds of skin in place of a neck. Finally, he gave up and just placed it by his side. Karpuradevi woke up with a start, spearing him with a look that seemed to suggest that he were an *asura* who had meant to steal their son and drop him into the sea or bash his brains in with a rock. The sudden fierceness suited her even better, Someshwar decided.

He made up his mind. Ruka Devi could wait. Now that her fertility was properly established, he would have to visit her bed more often and god willing she would gift him with many more sons. Not lions though.

'You did well. Let us make another soon. A boy.' His words were met with silence. He repeated himself just to make sure that she had understood and walked away to join his companions for a night of revelry. At least in their company there would be no need to put up with the silent reproach of a wounded wife.

But he was willing to forgive her that day. After all, she had delivered his son—Prithviraj Chauhan. Perhaps the boy would make him proud one day and make his infuriating half-brother, Vigraharaj-IV, look like a fool in comparison. There was comfort to be had from that at least.

2

The early years of motherhood would turn out to be the happiest time in Karpuradevi's life. Within a year, she delivered another boy and her status was enhanced considerably. They named him Hariraj. His birth was a joyous but a quieter affair. He was a sweet-looking child though he did not possess the extraordinary good looks of his elder brother.

Prithviraj, who had started walking by then, was allowed to take a look at his younger brother a few days after his birth. Oblivious to the anxious eyes on him, he leaned over the crib for a better look. Hariraj began to bawl. Quickly, the older boy handed over his silver rattle (a gift from his maternal grandmother), instead of attacking him with it in a fit of jealousy as some people had feared. The baby stopped crying at once and Prithviraj smiled and so did everybody around him who had been watching avidly. Grown women had tears in their eyes.

When told about the incident, Kanchanadevi remarked that she hoped this unlikely camaraderie would last, especially given the chequered history of their ancestors who had not balked at fratricide when a crown and throne were at stake. Added to that was the fact that not one of them had died of natural causes. It seemed to her that no amount of sentiment could eliminate the very distinct possibility that brothers may turn on brothers and sons against fathers.

Determined to prove her point to Karpuradevi, who seemed mightily put out over her remark, she related a gory story from their family history. 'As you know, there was a clash between Maharaj Kumarpal and the pretender Chahad after the passing away of my dear father. The latter was the son of one of Maharaj Jaisingh's ministers and had the temerity to claim that my father had named him the successor to the throne. Naturally, I could not support such a spurious claim!

'However, my husband did not care for my views and supported him. Maharaj Kumarpal smashed Chahad and his supporters, including the Chauhans, at Abu. Determined to avenge his humiliation, my lord joined hands with Bhallal, the chief of Malwa, and tried yet again to instal Chahad on the throne of Anhilwara Patan, unmindful that his life had been spared by the man he sought to destroy and that he was putting Someshwar at peril with his ill-conceived schemes.

'Needless to say, it was a disaster and Maharaj Arnoraj was bested by Maharaj Kumarpal in single combat. Gracious in victory, he spared your father-in-law's life.'

Karpuradevi wondered if her mother-in-law had implored Maharaj Kumarpal to stay his hand for the love he bore her and restrain himself from killing Maharaj Arnoraj. On second thought, it seemed likelier that she had urged him to strike off her husband's head then and there. After all she was not one to suffer being scorned lightly! If only she had the guts to give voice to the questions that hovered on her lips . . .

Kanchanadevi was staring coldly at her almost as if she had read her thoughts. 'Maharaj Kumarpal is as noble as he is wise and has proved so on many occasions. Though a staunch Saivite, he has always shown tolerance for those belonging to other faiths like my father before him. Why, they have even allowed safe passage for the mleccha traders though their people have vowed to destroy our religion and burn our temples! The king is a good man and pays heed to the tenets of Jainism taught to him by the sainted Hemachandra, who as you know endorses non-violence in thought and deed. It was at the urging of his teacher that he made the decision to let a hated adversary walk away.'

Of course, Kumarpal's tolerance did not extend to Chahad, whose short but eventful life came to a bloody conclusion, Karpuradevi thought to herself. Besides, the terms set for Maharaj Arnoraj's release had been inordinately harsh in her opinion and she said as much.

'Maharaj Kumarpal insisted that Jalana, Maharaj Arnoraj's daughter, be given to him in marriage, though she was but a slip of a girl and he was over fifty,' she paused, hoping for a reaction but got none. 'And he nearly beggared the Chauhans by relieving them of all the gold and riches in their treasury. And in a final act of humiliation, he let the king of Ajmer leave, making it clear that he did not consider him a threat to his sovereignty. The crown prince, Jaggadeva, was helpless to act with his father being held hostage.' It had been quite the scandal—Arnoraj's humiliation as well as Kumarpal's insistence on marrying a girl who was much younger than him!

Kanchanadevi nodded. Jaggadeva was no match for Kumarpal but his brother had been a different story. She had heard that Vigraharaj had been away fighting the Turushkas, who had sent raiding parties to harass the Sapadalaksha subjects. He had scorned the suggestion of his father's advisers to pay ransom to the raiding Turks. Instead he had chosen to fight the mleccha hordes, successfully repelling them and preventing their advance in Baverak.

As for her husband Arnoraj, his military successes in his youth had been impressive. He had fought the Turushkas near Ajmer and forced them out of Sapadalaksha. In doing so, he had secured peace for his subjects and ensured their prosperity by protecting the treasures of the land from the Turks' grasping, avaricious paws. If that were not enough, he had mounted successful campaigns against Naravarman of Malwa and Haritanaka.

However, by embarking on this foolhardy expedition against the Chalukyas, he had tarnished his legacy and disgraced himself. If only he had listened to her instead of trying so desperately to give the bards something to sing about! She could have forgiven him for his infidelity or even his failure to recognize her true worth but it was impossible for her to forgive weakness or a man who had courted and known defeat. Thanks to his perfidy, history would never forget the extent of his foolhardiness or stop singing about it!

Rousing herself, she snapped at Karpuradevi, 'You know what happened next . . . Jaggadeva blamed his father for besmirching the reputation of the Chauhans. Being a treacherous brute, he murdered his father, unmindful that such a heinous crime would drag the noble name of his ancient family through the mud. Vigraharaj swore vengeance on his brother and declared that he would not rest till he had avenged his father's death and cleansed the throne of the Chahamanas with the blood of his evil brother.'

Kanchanadevi fell silent again, lost in memories. She still remembered the messenger who had brought her the dire tidings of her husband's death and Johiyani's decision to immolate herself on his pyre. She had no doubt that Jaggadeva must have forced her to enter the flames after dosing her with a particularly potent drug to prevent her going to her end kicking and screaming.

To her surprise, she had been aggrieved to hear the news though a part of her could not help hoping that Johiyani's badly brought up brats would kill each other, paving the way for Someshwar. But Jaggadeva and Vigraharaj both had male heirs. They were still children though. A lot could change before they grew up. Hopefully, they too would go to an early grave.

She knew Someshwar mirrored her thoughts and wished they could will the darkest desires of their hearts into being.

Feeling that she had made her views known quite adequately on the propensity of the Chauhans to commit regicide, patricide and fratricide whenever it suited their ambition, Kanchanadevi rose, leaving her daughter-in-law to her thoughts.

Karpuradevi felt that Kanha's version of the events, which had created quite the furore in the tumultuous times they lived in, was more interesting, especially since he did not mind sharing the dirty details with her unlike his mother. As one of the palace wags had put it, 'Maharaj Kumarpal treated his new wife, the Chauhan princess Jalana, most cruelly. It is said that she bore his savagery with courage and fortitude till her flower-like body could take no more.'

Karpuradevi had wondered if it was her mother-in-law who was responsible for the ill usage of Maharani Johiyani's dear daughter. Everybody knew that she had the run of the harem and at the time, Karpuradevi would have liked to meet the Chauhan princess but she had not been around and seemed rather suspiciously to be suffering from some ailment or the other.

'On hearing of the ill treatment meted out to his sister,' the wag had said in hushed tones, forcing her to strain her ears in order to hear the juicy details, 'Yuvaraj Jaggadeva's temper was a fearsome thing to behold, for Jala, as he referred to the princess, had been immeasurably dear to him. Later, there were those who felt he should have vented his fury on the Chalukyan king whose behaviour towards his own wife had been most ungallant, but he had grown too powerful and was beyond the reach of Prince Jaggadeva. Like a wounded animal, which attacks everyone in its vicinity, he turned his wrath on Maharaj Arnoraj.'

Kanha thought this version of events was too fanciful. 'Maharaj Kumarpal may be condemned for his savagery on the battlefield but the truth is there is no way of knowing what happened between our princess and her consort. I heard conflicting reports . . . Some say that Kumarpal was smitten by her beauty but she refused to allow him his conjugal rights with her on account of his callous treatment of her father. Having been refused once too often, he tried to force himself on her and accidentally throttled her to death. This seems unlikely because he has passed many edicts forbidding the ill-treatment of animals at the urging of his teacher and is gentle and courteous outside the battlefield. But that said, I can't claim to know how the man treats his wife in the privacy of his boudoir.'

Karpuradevi blushed hearing the last remark but she lowered her veil with a delicate movement of her graceful fingers, hoping he would not notice. She liked that he treated her as an equal and was comfortable saying all sorts of things in her presence.

Kanha, meanwhile, was still speaking, although it was hard to ignore the rising colour in his sister-in-law's cheeks. 'Still others claim that she killed herself because her heart belonged to another. The vaidya, on the other hand, told me that she was cursed with a weak constitution and was sick on most days. Who knows what the truth is?' He decided not to tell her another rumour, according to which, the princess had been suffering from a stomach ailment and was found doubled over and bleeding in the privy.

Instead he said, 'What matters is that Jaggadeva, from what I have heard of him, is not the sentimental type and merely used his sister's death to justify his actions in murdering his father when he refused to oblige him by going to the grave early. Similarly, Vigraharaj used his father's death as a pretext to get rid of the pesky elder brother with the stronger claim to the throne and to bolster popular support in his favour. And being Vigraharaj, he did it without any fuss. Some say he hired assassins who despatched Jaggadeva to Yama's abode during the civil war that was fought to determine who was worthy of the throne. Either way, Vigraharaj managed to keep his hands clean and his spotless reputation intact in his determined quest to secure the crown.'

'May he live long and usher in an era of peace,' Karpuradevi said, knowing that Kanha admired his half-brother, the king of Ajmer.

Kanha shrugged, 'Don't say that to mother or to my brother. If I weren't so loyal to them, I would have said that they are not as large-hearted as you, and are plotting the demise of Vigraharaj and his sons even as we speak. They won't take kindly to your wishing for his longevity!'

Whatever the truth was, Karpuradevi prayed that such a terrible fate should not befall her boys, who mercifully remained blissfully unaware of what it meant to be born into a royal family. Instead they played joyfully in the paradise that was childhood, content to catch frogs and fishes from the ponds in the harem, pleading with the kitchen staff to cook them or competing to see whose farts smelled worse. She wished they could remain her little boys forever.

While alive, not a day elapsed without Karpuradevi addressing a fervent prayer to the gods, pleading that her sons should never feel anything but love and affection for each other. Her plea did not go unheard and everybody remarked how Prithvi and Hari never fought nor engaged in the minor tiffs without which childhood, and later adulthood, was complete.

In all likelihood, the gods acceded to the first half of her prayer because they would not, could not, grant the next part, which was to keep her sons safe from harm and bless them with a long life, free from strife.

From the time he had started walking, Hari had become Prithvi's shadow and the latter did not seem to mind. Even at that age, he was used to adulation. There was a certain something about him which drew others to him in droves. A natural leader, even the older boys tended to defer to him, especially since he could outrun and out-think them even if he couldn't match them in terms of strength. In addition to that, he was a good sport and never told on them to Kanchanadevi if he happened to be at the receiving end of a bit of roughhousing.

As for the little girls in the harem, they were besotted with Prithvi and were crushed when he firmly refused to join them in games that usually required him to carry them away one at a time so they could take turns marrying him. Playing at conjugal bliss or whatever it was the silly girls enjoyed so much, never held any interest for him.

'Unlike his father and paternal grandfather, Prithvi knows enough to steer clear of the wiles of women,' Karpuradevi had murmured to Lakshmibai. Unfortunately for her, Kanchanadevi, scourge of the harem, had crept up on them and heard the last bit. Despite her recent approval of her daughter-in-law, who had produced two boys and seemed to have a head that wasn't entirely bereft of brains, she saw no reason to refrain from pulling her up every chance she got.

'At that age, his father no doubt like *his* father found girls thoroughly repellent too,' she said in her most quelling voice, 'but then he grew up and the one-eyed monster nestled between his legs stirred to life and he began to chase after thankless little chippies who did not love him half as much as his mother!'

Whatever did Maharaj Kumarpal see in her? Karpuradevi thought grouchily to herself, eyes lowered in a manner befitting an obedient daughter-in-law. Prithvi charged in just then and demanded a story from his grandmother. Disarmed, Kanchanadevi took his hand in hers and they walked away together but not before she had admonished his mother for not completing her reading of some of the more tedious prescriptive treatises among the *sastras*. It was mind-numbing material and Karpuradevi was determined to master it, if only to prove that she was smarter than her mother-in-law.

As for the other ladies in the harem, they couldn't resist Prithvi either. They were deeply enamoured of his good looks and shamelessly doted on him, plying him with sweets and presenting him with more toys than he could possibly need.

Prithvi shared all his toys and sweets with Hari and the other children. There was one exception though. His mother had given him a set of terracotta soldiers, made specifically for him, and this alone he insisted on playing with all by himself for hours at a time. If anybody tried to pick up one of his toy soldiers, he would throw an unholy tantrum and anything within his reach would be hurled at and smashed, giving a hint of an unpredictable temper that could strike like lightning. Hari and Lakshmibai appointed themselves as guardians of his precious collection and dissuaded anybody from provoking the wrath of Prithviraj Chauhan.

Prithvi liked to show off by performing cartwheels all over their chambers, scaling the pillars like a little monkey or hanging upside down from windows, scaring the ladies witless.

Their admonishments only spurred him to greater heights of daredevilry. Even Maharaj Kumarpal and his grizzled courtiers had taken to him in a big way. Prithvi liked escaping the confines of the harem, eager to be a part of the exciting world of men. He would sneak into the courtroom where Maharaj Kumarpal sat with members of his council. Slowly, he would move closer and closer, an inch at a time, until he had squeezed himself into the tiny space available on the king's throne.

Without missing a beat and cognizant that the boy was born to rule, Maharaj Kumarpal would carry on with his discourse, placing an arm around the child's shoulders without pausing his speech. Prithvi liked observing the powerful king of the Chalukyas, who carried himself with so much inherent strength and grace. But he never overstayed his welcome, creeping away as quietly as he had come.

Later, he and Hari would mimic his royal bearing, the powerful strides he took while walking, his strong voice that could threaten and assure with equal conviction, his ability to inspire fear and affection in equal measure. They even twirled their non-existent moustaches the way he did. To them, Maharaj Kumarpal was like one of the gods from the stories Lakshmibai told them. Hari wanted to be just like him. But Prithvi insisted that he would be greater by far and never that old. He would even be greater than his uncle, Maharaj Vigraharaj, the one they said was the finest warrior alive.

Both of them were presented to their father whenever he wished and they would dutifully give an account of their activities. However, he did not seem to care much for frogs and looked shocked when told about the time they had stolen a guard's sword and tried to chop off a horse's tail. He was a taciturn man and did not have the easy manner of his brother, Kanha.

Entirely unsure about how best to handle their extreme youth, he usually made a hash of it and remained a distant stranger to his sons, who cleaved to their mother instead. Seeing them in the thrall of Maharaj Kumarpal disturbed him and his inability to do anything about it bothered him even more. And so the space between the father and the sons widened considerably and the clumsy attempts of the former to bridge the gap only made things worse.

Worst of all though, were the rumours about the paternity of Prithviraj.

'Did you notice how extraordinarily good-looking he is? And so talented! Surely he must be the son of a god! It is hard to believe that he is the son of Someshwar, who is unfortunate enough to have a face that is so ugly only his mother could love it!'

'They say that Prithviraj is the spitting image of his uncle, Kanha!'

'*Niyoga* is an ancient practice and a respectable one. A chaste wife and a virtuous woman may cohabit with a man who by blood or status is the equal of her husband during his lifetime in order to beget worthy male heirs if her own overlord proves unequal to such an onerous task.'

Someshwar wished he could strangle every one of the rumour-mongers who spread such ugly lies. As for his wife, it infuriated him that she got on so famously with Kanha. Even the boys seemed to love him better than their own father! How dare they all carry on in this manner and make him look bad? Someshwar was determined to make them pay.

Ruka Devi had just given him a daughter. She was named Pritha. Useless little thing! Feckless females served only one useful purpose and that was entertaining a man in the boudoir. Hopefully, Ruka would give him a son soon and then he would feed Karpuradevi, Kanha, Prithviraj and Hariraj to the dogs!

Meanwhile, the boys did love their Uncle Kanha best of all. He wasn't an awesome personage like Maharaj Kumarpal or a remote curiosity like their father, rather he was their dearest friend and a willing partner in crime. Uncle Kanha visited them whenever possible, bearing gifts and good things to eat. He took them horse riding and even let Prithvi take the reins. They were allowed to watch as he cleaned and sharpened his sword and dagger till they both shone and could shave the thick hair clean off his arms. They took it in turns to hold the scabbard, which had monsters embossed on it with rubies that glittered in place of their eyes. More importantly, Uncle Kanha was never too tired to run around and play.

Sometimes, he took them hunting and had the smith make small bows and arrows for the boys to practise with. Prithvi was a natural and could easily bring down small game and the odd bird that flew within shooting range. Uncle Kanha would get so excited his celebrations would be even more rambunctious than the boys'.

Almost as good as the hunting, were the stories he told of his travels. There were places farther north where it was so cold, a man's snot would freeze in his nostrils and he could die from it, he informed them. And mountains so big and high, their peaks poked Lord Indra's bum up in heaven. The boys snorted with laughter but there was more. He told them of deserts so vast and hot, a man would be cooked alive even as he walked! Of wild beasts with sharp claws and wicked curved horns that could rend and tear; mighty rivers that were home to sea monsters with armoured hides and serrated teeth that lurked in the depths, hungry for the taste of human flesh.

Uncle Kanha told them about beautiful dancing girls in the south with skin the colour of honey, who could dance on swords and spears. He stopped midway when he saw Karpuradevi adjusting her veil. The boys were surprised but did not mind too much. Girls and their activities were not particularly interesting. Besides, it was silly of them to use swords for dancing instead of fighting.

Karpuradevi wasn't sure how she felt about Hari and Prithvi getting along so well with Kanha. For reasons she could not fathom, it bothered her a little. She supposed that the crux of it was that she felt left out from their world. A man's world that would never have much use or space for her.

Maharaj Vigraharaj-IV had claimed the throne of the Chauhans in a blaze of glory and was determined not to let the humiliation of his father at the hands of Kumarpal go unavenged. In a series of blistering attacks, he took on the might of the Chalukyas. He struck first in Saurashtra and vanquished Kumarpal's feudatory Sajjana. Word reached them in Patan that he seemed determined to annexe all of Mewar.

At Maharaj Kumarpal's war council meeting, the decision was made to attack Nagore, a Chauhan stronghold, as a retaliatory measure. Preparations began in earnest for the expedition. Someshwar and Kanha were to go there as well.

None of them said it, but Vigraharaj was living up to his reputation as a warrior par excellence. Rather than forcing a direct confrontation, he was chipping away at the limbs of the sprawling Chalukyan empire. He had made mincemeat of Nadol, Pali and Jalore and even if these were minimal gains he had done just enough to exact his retribution and enhance his legacy without sacrificing too many of his men.

In his heyday, Kumarpal would have dealt with the threat more aggressively but he was getting on in years and favoured a more cautious approach without risking a crushing defeat, of the sort he had meted out to Arnoraj many years ago, that might come to define him and tarnish his legacy. Besides, even Vigraharaj dare not strike at the heart of the Chalukyan territory.

Prithvi and Hari were devastated when told gently but firmly that they were too young to go to war. It was just too unfair! 'You are growing up fast!' Someshwar summoned Prithvi and told him gravely, 'It is time to begin your education. I expect you to be obedient and disciplined. As a scion of the Chahamanas, you are better than the others. Don't ever let them forget it! Don't ever forget who you are!'

He had nodded solemnly and in an uncharacteristic gesture of affection, Someshwar patted his shoulder, genuinely sorry that they would never be close. But that was no reason for him not to do his best by his son and heir, since Ruka Devi's womb remained recalcitrant. While there was life left to him he would do everything possible to ensure that Prithviraj-III inherited a mighty realm.

Uncle Kanha refused to take them along but to make up for his inexplicable cruelty he took them to the glorious armoury of Maharaj Kumarpal. Wonder-struck by the marvels on display, Prithvi and Hari forgave him for his sins.

Sharp spears with golden handles, heavy swords with pommels shaped to resemble lions or snarling tigers, bronze armour and shields of silver emblazoned with fantastic images of gods and monsters, javelins, huge curved bows, quivers and arrows used by famous Chalukyan heroes of Gurjardesa were displayed in a dazzling array. Prithvi and Hari were awestruck, hardly able to contain their excitement.

'Many of these weapons are no doubt stained with the blood of Chauhans,' Uncle Kanha told them. 'Our ancestors have clashed with the Chalukyans for a long time now and now we will no doubt see more of the same.'

Prithvi, who had begun to have an inkling of his place in the world, thanks to his grandmother's rousing tales of his ancestry, was appalled and his thick eyebrows became a single unbroken line when he frowned. 'But why? I thought we were all friends!'

Uncle Kanha shrugged, 'We are good enough friends and even married into each other's families when we were not hell-bent on fighting each other to death. Vigraharaj-II of the Chahamanas rose to fame when he defeated the Chalukyan Mularaj. Even your great grandfather Jaisingh fought the Chauhans and managed to draw blood before making up with them.' He decided not to go into the details of the clash between Arnoraj and Kumarpal with the lamentable consequences that followed, the reverberations of which were felt to this very day. Besides, his mother had no doubt told Prithvi her version of the events.

The frown deepened. 'Then why are we living here with them? Shouldn't we be avenging the dead Chauhans?' At least, the boy had little doubt about where his allegiance lay, even though everybody knew of his admiration for Maharaj Kumarpal, Kanha mused with wry amusement.

'You are a fierce one, aren't you?' he said, wagging a finger at Prithvi. 'It's like this . . . Circumstances dictate that it is safer for Arnoraj's sons by his second wife to be in Patan. Your uncle, Vigraharaj-IV, is a good man and an even better king but I am not sure he will be welcoming of those whose claim to the throne is every bit as valid as his. As for Maharaj Kumarpal, he did try to sack Ajmer once, though he did not quite manage it but he has proved himself a good friend to all of us, if not to your paternal grandfather.'

Prithvi was not sure if he understood what sacking meant but he rightly assumed that it was not anything good. 'If Maharaj Kumarpal does not like the Chauhans then why is he a good friend to all of us? And why are we friends with him if he has hurt our family? I know that he is a better man than most of the men I know but it is all very confusing. There must be a reason he is being nice to grandmother after he defeated grandfather.'

Kanchanadevi had indeed told the little boy most of it, though she had left out the part about the old king raping his child bride and putting some sort of monster in her belly that eventually killed her. He had heard or rather overheard Lakshmibai talking about it with someone. Raping like sacking had to be something bad, he surmised. Prithvi had assured his grandmother that he was determined to never ever be defeated.

Kanha, meanwhile, was smiling with approval. Why, the boy's powers of comprehension were well beyond his years! Perhaps the jyotishis had been right about him after all. 'Kings, even the good ones, are different from ordinary men. Their actions must be in keeping with the interests of the kingdom and the people entrusted to their care. It is why they have to fight wars, beggar another land to enrich their own, marry and then break the hearts of their wives to marry again and again in the interest of making powerful alliances. They have to betray friends and brothers, kill children to protect their own . . . It must all be done for the greater good, or so one hopes.

'Maharaj Kumarpal must have his reasons for affording us his protection. And Vigraharaj must have his reasons for keeping us at arm's length . . . But all that can change within a heartbeat if the need of the hour dictates as much.'

Prithvi looked thoughtful and there was a sudden intensity in his gaze when he asked, 'You said the throne of Ajmer belongs as much to us as Uncle Vigraharaj. Tell me, Uncle Kanha, who deserves it the most? My father or my uncle? What about you? When you people are no more, will it be my cousins or me who will deserve the throne?'

Kanha took his time replying. 'The answer to that question is simple. In the mad scramble for a crown, it is only the worthiest who deserve to wear it. However, life is hardly if ever that uncomplicated and reality can always be counted upon to throw up a few unpleasant surprises. Sometimes it is the unworthy, tyrannical and the cowardly who win the prize, if you can call it that. In the end, it may come down to chance as much as strength and the inviolate dictates of destiny, which remains obscure until the moment you are face to face with it.'

'I am not afraid of anything, not even destiny. I will play the game of chance. And I am going to win, Uncle Kanha. My kingdom will be bigger than my uncle's as well as Maharaj Kumarpal's,' Prithvi told him solemnly. Kanha never forgot that moment. It was when he realized that he was in the presence of a king.

'Of that there can be no doubt. The day will come when you would have established your valour and I will be by your side when you claim the throne of the Chahamanas!' Kanha told him, determined to be there for this boy who meant so much to him.

'We will be like Arjuna and Krishna, Uncle Kanha,' Prithvi enthused. 'Nobody will be able to defeat us in battle. Grandmother said that it would take the destructive power of Lord Shiva to stop them but he loved them both too much to do it. It will be the same with us, you will see.'

'Nobody can win all the time . . .' Kanha cautioned, wishing with all his heart that it wasn't so.

'I know that,' Prithvi replied with the cockiness of his youth, 'it is enough for me if I win as long as I am alive.' They were big words for a child but when the solemn boy uttered them, somehow it felt right.

Prithviraj never forgot that memorable conversation that left a deep impression on him.

Maharaj Kumarpal sent for Prithviraj, who seized the chance to put forth his demand to be taken along to the battlefield. 'I am afraid, there will be plenty of battles for you to fight in the future . . . too many in fact. But in the meantime, I need you to look after the kingdom, my people, your mother and grandmother. Can you do that for me?'

Prithvi wanted to put forth his arguments for letting him and Hari accompany them to the battle but he sensed it would be futile and couldn't mask his disappointment.

Sensing it, the king sought to comfort him. 'Governing a kingdom is even more difficult than waging a war. You will find that preserving something is hard, whereas destroying something is far too easy. I need to leave someone behind when I am far away. You are the one I trust and I will rest easier knowing that you are in charge.'

'They are all in good hands with me!' Prithvi replied gravely, glad that the king had said he trusted him, even though he was perfectly aware that Maharaj Kumarpal was only being kind and it was the mahamantri who would govern in his absence. Why did people insist on treating him like a little boy of five just because he was a little boy of five?

To everyone's surprise, he removed the tiger claw set in gold from around his own neck and placed it around Prithviraj's neck. The entire court stood up to applaud the munificent gesture. Cries of 'Maharajadhiraja', 'Maharaj Kumarpal ki jai' and 'Prithviraj!' rent the air.

Kanchanadevi was momentarily speechless when she heard about it. It was a talisman of great power to ward off the evil eye and it had been in Maharaj Kumarpal's family for many generations. It was a beautiful gesture and people would remember his acknowledgement of Prithvi's greatness in the future.

Prithvi and Hari watched from the ramparts as the soldiers marched past with the impressive paraphernalia of war— bronzed armour, swords and shields that glinted in the sun. There were elephants and war horses. Women showered them with flowers and rose water. They could hardly wait to grow up!

3

Prithvi began his studies shortly after his tonsure ceremony. Needless to say, he had not flinched nor shed a tear when the razor was repeatedly applied to his scalp and his beautiful hair shorn so it might be consecrated to the gods.

The little prince was bright and learning came easily to him but he showed scant interest in his lessons, driven to distraction by his restless energy and need for constant stimulation. Getting him to park his royal bottom in one place during the course of his lessons proved to be a tedious task as he was forever giving his tutors the slip.

Stories though were a different matter, particularly the ones with gods, demons, monsters, kings and wars. He could listen to them all day. Through the stories of the Ramayana and the Mahabharata, he was taught the iron code of honour that was suited to a royal prince of the Chahamanas.

These stirring sagas set his imagination on fire and with Hari listening avidly next to him, he visualized the grand adventures of a bygone era featuring swashbuckling heroes, epic struggles and glorious battles. It was a golden age where mighty men performed legendary feats for their land and for beautiful women who loved them. Even the gods and goddesses watched over them and played a part in their lives.

Prithviraj could not wait for the day when he would take his place in history. From his earliest days, he was taught that the only thing that mattered was heroism and the pursuit of glory. Courage was the only quality that defined a real man, who must resist pain and be willing to sacrifice everything, including his life for honour. These were lessons he took to his heart not just because it was the essence of what he was being taught but because such a model was very much in keeping with his own nature.

After his sacred thread investiture, the *upanayana* was performed, he was inducted into the household of Rajguru Bharadwaj and his formal education began. There was no more running away from lessons but Prithvi did not mind. It was the price to be paid before his martial training began in earnest.

Before his departure, Prithvi went to seek the blessings of his grandmother, who had prepared a feast in his honour. She had made sure that every one of his favourite dishes were served. There was safed mas, a spicy stew prepared with fresh wild boar, yoghurt, coconut and cream, and dal prepared with four different kinds of lentils, served with rotis soaked in ghee and so soft they crumbled in his mouth before he even began chewing. Sun-dried vegetables, skewered lamb and grilled fish were served as well.

Prithvi flung the *kaddu* under the ornate table and Kanchanadevi pretended not to notice as the maids discreetly removed the discarded pumpkin. He gorged on the sweets and pleased his grandmother by gulping down his mango *lassi* and asking for more.

'Tomorrow is an important day in your life,' she began, 'you must be pleased to leave the women and children behind. It is time for you to begin your journey into manhood. How do you feel about that?'

'I am a little sad to leave you all behind,' Prithvi told her, 'but mother said that whenever Guruji allows us, we may visit. And don't worry, I will not disappoint you.'

As if he ever could, Kanchanadevi thought to herself. He was going to be the king she herself would have been. Bold and daring, at the head of a mighty empire that stretched from the Himalayas to Lanka in the south. Perhaps he would travel to the ends of the earth and be the king of the world! There was so much she had wanted to tell him but in the end, she merely embraced him and fed him more sweets.

Karpuradevi cried a little. For some reason, all she could think of was an old dream, details of which had tormented her endlessly by remaining stubbornly elusive. Refusing to let him see her pain, she did her best to stay upbeat while he prattled on excitedly about learning to fight like Arjuna.

'I am going to work as hard as Arjuna, mother, and practise every single day. And soon I will be as good as he ever was and the poets will sing about me too! Just wait and see, one day they will argue about who was the greatest warrior—Arjuna or Prithviraj?'

Prithviraj Chauhan. King of the earth. She held him close to her bosom. Nowadays he was too energetic to keep still and let her hold him, but on that day she was grateful to him for not running away. They stayed that way for a long time, mother and son.

Hari's lips trembled but demonstrating remarkable restraint, he swore to guard Prithvi's toy soldiers with his life. Besides, he would be joining his brother soon.

Prithvi and the other youngsters would be leaving the royal residence at Patan and stay in a fortified residence constructed by Maharaj Kumarpal on the banks of Durlabh Sarovar for Guru Bharadwaj and his *shishyas*. It was a breathtakingly beautiful place with a spectacular view of the lake and was surrounded by woods of sturdy teak, acacia and bamboo.

Lessons were conducted outside on most days in the shade of a banyan tree with Guruji seated on a tiger skin. Prithvi never forgot his first lesson.

'All of you have gathered here with a common goal: the acquisition of knowledge that will mould your bodies and minds into finely honed instruments to carry out the diktats of your will and the ruling of destiny. You will learn to live your life in keeping with the rules of *dharma*, the moral compass that should be the guide man relies on as he journeys through the terrain of life; *artha*, which is the art of possessing without becoming possessed; and *kama*, the experience of pleasure with moderation. By adhering to *trivarga*—the three-fold path—it is to be hoped that you will someday achieve moksha, which is the path to enlightenment.'

Moksha sounded boring, Prithvi decided. But artha and kama, not so much. Suddenly he felt Bharadwaj's gaze on him. 'Some are born to rule, some among you will become powerful generals or ministers, while some will turn out to be scholars or poets. Whatever role the future has in store, it behoves you to play the part to the best of your ability for your conduct will be reflective not just of your parents and guru but of our age. Future generations will look to us for guidance and whether they will choose to emulate the best our legacy has to offer or treat it as a cautionary tale will entirely be in your hands.'

Prithviraj looked straight back and in those open eyes, Bharadwaj saw a powerful life force filled with more longing for glory and passion than could possibly be contained in one soul. It moved him deeply. Later, when asked for his opinion on the scion of the Chahamanas, Bharadwaj said, 'Prithviraj Chauhan is an extraordinary individual blessed with the countenance of a god, has a fierce intellect and a good heart. There is strength and valour in him. This when combined with the unstoppable forces that drive him, will ensure that there is no limit to what he can achieve or the glory that lies fully within his grasp.'

And yet, there is a curious restlessness in him and far too much passion. If he allows these to get the better of him, then it is equally likely that ruination will be his lot. Bharadwaj did not say the last part aloud. He knew that the words of a guru had the potency of a prophecy that may not just predict the future but also determine it.

Prithvi could not wait for his martial arts training to begin. His companions included the sons of the king's ministers, his generals and of powerful chieftains belonging to families of high standing who had rendered service to their sovereign for generations. Most had known each other since they were children.

It was a system designed to bring together various factions under the direct influence of the king as a means of promoting loyalty to the crown and the throne. In addition to that, an entire generation of noblemen—future ministers, warriors, scholars, poets—were raised together to serve the interests of the kingdom. Some would be companions of the king and accompany him on conquests while those with an aptitude for statecraft would devote themselves to governance after serving under existing administrative officials.

Given the tumultuous nature of their times when power changed hands with lightning speed, these were traditional measures to ensure the smooth functioning of the kingdom in times of peace and war or when misfortunes brought on by royal machinations brought them all to the brink of calamity.

At the time, Prithvi did not appreciate the finer points of the system but he did enjoy spending time with the youngsters and grew closer to them. There were representatives from the Chalukyan, Dahima, Kucchumbha and Mohil clans as well as Prithviraj's own, Chauhans.

Nahar and Padhri Ray were cousins, carrying in their veins the blood of the imperial Pratihara dynasty. With the advent of the Chauhans and the Chalukyas, their formerly vast empire had shrunk into insignificance. Nahar was smaller and wiry, though by the time they finished their studies he towered over the rest of them. He was good at his lessons and Guruji liked him for the speed at which he could do calculations. But he had the rare quality of not annoying his fellow students despite being studious and managed to get along just fine with the others.

Padhri was big and strong for his age and had a ferocious appetite. He lived for a good fight and was known to prefer games and the training field to lessons where he was constantly berated for being dim-witted. But no one laughed at his shortcomings for that would have meant that they were amenable to getting the wind knocked out of them.

Kanak was from the Kacchwaha clan and the others made fun of him for having ears that were a little too big for his small head. He always responded to those who laughed at him by promising to pin their ears back. Blessed with a shrewd mind as well as a marked proficiency in the use of arms, he would be a great general someday, thought his guru.

The boys tended to mock Jayanaka the most. He had come all the way from Kashmir and was a diminutive boy, with a hint of pink in his fair cheeks. Unlike the others, he did not consider being wrestled to the ground good sport. Though he acquitted himself reasonably well in the training field, it was clear that his heart was not in it. Jaya genuinely preferred reading and writing to fighting, excelled in his studies, recited snatches of poetry and tended to wander around with his head in the clouds, dreamy as you please.

Naturally the other boys felt he needed to have some sense pounded into his head. Padhri took it upon himself to do the honours and when the senseless fisticuffs had wound down, Jaya's lip was bleeding. To his credit, he remained defiant. Noticing this, Padhri aimed a kick at his gut. 'Someday you can tell your grandchildren that Padhri Ray beat you senseless and tried unsuccessfully to make a man out of you.'

'I don't think so . . .' he responded, spitting out a gob of blood and wiping his lips with the back of his hand. 'Someday I will write a drama about a fat bastard named Padhri Ray, who was born to a concubine and beggared the kingdom by eating all the food in the land. Having been chased out, he prostrated himself at the feet of Maharaj Prithviraj Chauhan, accompanying him like a dog, hoping for some reflected glory. Padhri's desperation to prove himself a worthy Kshatriya and not merely the son of a jumped-up whore, who was good for nothing but eating, would be great material for a comedy. Your character will be the butt of ridicule and people will fall over themselves, laughing at the bumptious, bullying boor!'

At the end of the little speech, there was shell-shocked silence for a few moments. Jaya assumed that he would depart the world of the living, hastened by Padhri's unforgiving fists. Prithvi was the first to burst into laughter and with that chortle he saved the budding poet's life. The others joined him.

Padhri's cheeks flushed with shame and he would have followed through on his original intention to beat Jaya to within an inch of his life had Prithvi had not intervened. Drawing himself up to his full height, he stared him down, though he was still dwarfed by the bulk of Padhri. 'Leave him be! You should know better than to pick on someone who isn't your own size. He could have tattled to Guruji and you would have been punished. How would you like to be deprived of your favourite meals and made to practise meditation when we are down in the training field?'

Padhri held his ground for a moment longer. But by then, they all knew Prithvi's nature. He could charm the birds off the trees but there was a violent streak in him and a fierce temper that could incinerate everything in its path. Besides, it was unheard of for him to back down from a fight. He would sooner die than embrace defeat, even if his adversary was twice his size. Grunting in disgust, Padhri stalked off skewering Jaya with a baleful glare.

'Someday, I'll write about you too,' a grateful Jaya told his rescuer. 'Long after we are gone, they will remember the kindness of Prithviraj Chauhan and his endless triumphs, more numerous than the stars in the sky!'

Prithvi said nothing but was pleased. So pleased that they were inseparable after that.

Life with their guru was governed by a rigid routine and the years rolled by. In the blink of an eye, they were no longer little boys but sturdy youngsters, chafing at the bit to go into the real world and make their mark. Every day, they woke up at the crack of dawn. They would be given a simple nourishing rice gruel sweetened with honey or buttermilk to break their fast before being led through exercise drills by the military instructors, handpicked from the armies of Maharaj Kumarpal. This would be followed by riding lessons.

Prithvi was good with animals and they loved him. He loved riding and was a natural horseman. The horse master informed his superiors that the Chauhan prince constantly urged his steed into a full gallop, even as his companions were struggling to hold steady when the rocking motion in the course of a trot or a canter caused their buttocks to bounce painfully on the beasts' backs.

At night, when Jaya and the others complained of aching thighs, saddle sores and painful blisters, Prithvi could hardly wait to be atop a horse again. 'It feels like riding the wind or having the river undulate under you,' he told Jaya, his eyes shining with joy. 'It makes me feel that I can travel the length and breadth of this very aryavarta, wild and free as the wind and see all the wonders there are to see and experience every pleasure that is to be had!'

'It is a good dream,' Jaya responded. He would have liked to add that it was an impossible one because he was going to be a king and would be expected to bring all of aryavarta under his yoke. But then again, that too was an impossible dream. For too long their land had been divided by warring kings, some of whom had proved stronger than others but none had ever managed to be strong enough to unite the whole land. But he held his tongue, because he genuinely hoped that Prithvi would be the great ruler Bharata so desperately needed if she were to prevail over those who lusted after her treasures.

After Prithvi was pried away from his beloved horses, they would take instruction in the science of arms. They would be drilled hard on a daily basis till they could throw a javelin with unerring accuracy or string a bow and bring down a bird while on horseback. They were schooled in swordplay, wielding a mace and hefting an axe, throwing daggers and darts, as well as wrestling. They were taught how to fasten their armour and use their shields. Later, they progressed to chariots.

Kanak always won when they raced their chariots. He seemed to have an uncanny ability to make the chariot an extension of himself and extract the maximum speed and efficiency from it. There seemed to be no manoeuvre on a chariot that he was incapable of performing. He teamed up with Prithvi for obstacle courses designed to test their javelin throwing and archery skills from a moving chariot. They made a formidable duo.

Padhri was a formidable wrestler while Prithvi was the best swordsman among them and nothing short of a magician with the bow. Already his skills were legendary and it was said that he never missed a target. Like Arjuna, he practised for hours after sundown and even in pitch darkness could bring down his target every single time.

Every day, they ran for what felt like hours to increase their speed and stamina. Prithvi was the fastest and it galled Padhri no end. So he kept running after they were given the command to halt in the hope that he would eventually beat his rival.

While he kept at his exertions, Nahar and Kanak chased him, pretending to be enemy soldiers under whose onslaught Padhri was fleeing, eliciting guffaws from all around.

Under the rigours of training and endless practice, their bodies became stronger, shoulders broadened while their arms and legs bulged with muscle. They started looking more like the fierce warriors that they were training to become.

On some days, their arms instructors would take them hunting. The surrounding woods were rich in game—elephants, gaur, stags, wild boar, leopards and panthers. Bharadwaj's chefs would prepare their fresh kills and they would feast on the venison. The skins would be dried, cured and returned to the hunter who claimed the kill so he could use it to make leather guards and proudly wear them on his forearms to protect them from the whip of a bowstring.

On other days, they would be taught how to care for and groom the horses and elephants. Occasionally, they tripped each other and laughed at the one who wound up with a face full of dung. Mostly it was Nahar who was the neatest of them all and objected most vociferously to having to wash animal wastes off his person.

They were taught to treat their weapons with infinite care—cleaning and polishing their swords and daggers till they shone, burnishing the edges till they were so sharp that they could shave the hair off their forearms. All of them cured and tested the bowstrings, cleaned out the arrowheads and kept them ready for use.

When it grew too hot for physical activity, they would have lessons with Bharadwaj and his assistants. In addition to reading and writing, they were taught logic, law and royal policy. Sanskrit was the main language used for instruction. Most of them were already familiar with Prakrit. Prithvi had an aptitude for languages and became fluent in Magadhi, Pisachi, Suraseni and Apabhransh as well.

He continued to be fond of tales from the Itihasas and the Puranas. Thanks to Jaya, he was able to appreciate poetry as well. Even Padhri who had got over his dislike for the little poet after being tutored by Jaya, which helped him escape the wrath of Guruji, said poems were tolerable provided they dealt with erotica.

Chafing under the enforced celibacy, the boys found themselves increasingly fascinated by the illustrations in the *Kama Sutra* that fired up their imagination and kept them up at nights, exploring the myriad means of pleasuring themselves. While they pored over the scrolls with rapturous attention to the details, Nahar commented, 'How come they make us do drills every day only to perfect our throwing skills and riding manoeuvres? Not that it isn't preferable to a discourse on living a virtuous life by avoiding the six *doshas*, but surely we need to practise those tricky looking positions since none of us are contortionists! Imagine trying some of this with a real girl and winding up with a broken neck! It is a grievous lapse in our syllabus.'

'There will be plenty of time to practise when you have something to practise with. Irrespective of all the training in the world, a man equipped with a needle cannot be called a swordsman,' Kanak retorted. It led to a heated argument about the length and girth of their individual equipment. Jaya turned away in mock horror when Nahar threatened to prove his shouted declaration of exceptional endowment.

He noticed that Prithvi was distracted, though he enjoyed the illustrations in the *Kama Sutra* every bit as the rest of them. He seemed far away. It was hard to say what he was thinking. He could be imagining himself astride a horse and galloping away into the great unknown or fancy himself at the receiving end of the amorous attention of an *apsara*, who had successfully transported him to the realm of pure ecstasy.

4

The old man had been waiting for the momentous event of his passing for a while now. But Yama seemed to take a perverse pleasure in making him wait interminably. It felt like only yesterday when Chakradatta, vaidya and confidant of the royal house of the Chahamanas had informed him with a doleful air that he did not have much longer to live.

He had been astounded that all he had felt was a little surprise. Given the many lives he had claimed and the fact that none of his ancestors had died from natural causes, he had always assumed that he would die with a sword in hand and a curse on his lips. His body, honed to perfection by war and personal effort, had stood him in good stead but alas! It had turned traitor condemning a mighty warrior to an ignominious death in the sick chamber. But if the vaidya was right, the illness would ravage his treacherous body and it would all be over soon.

The ancient quack had been mistaken. Years later, he still had one weak, trembling leg in the land of the living, with all the time in the world to rue at leisure the hasty decisions he had taken both in life and when he had believed himself to be a dead man. Chakradatta, the occasionally effective but mostly inept physician, was gone too. He had been informed that the old lecher's heart had given out while examining the breasts of the venerable treasurer's young wife, no doubt while doing his best to find a cure for the stomach ailment she had been complaining about.

He would have chuckled at the image but that sort of thing hurt his chest nowadays. Even so, he was not entirely unhappy. Comfortably settled in a small hunting lodge that he had ordered to be built in a remote tract of land on the lower levels of his beloved Aravalli range and with all his requirements taken care of, he lived a relatively simple life for one of his stature.

Besides, the location was ideal for a dying man. The rocky, inhospitable terrain discouraged habitation and spared him the attention of the unduly inquisitive. If that were not enough, the view had to be seen to be believed! Rolling hills that seemed to kiss the sky, fertile valleys and the mirrored sheen of lakes below. If he squinted into the distance, he fancied he could make out the ancient ruins and glorious temples raised by his own ancestors.

Most importantly, it was not too far from the sacred lake Pushkar that was dear to his family and people. A young man could make the trip within a day but for someone of advanced years, who had been dying for too long now, knowledge of its proximity was enough.

Sometimes, when dusk had fallen, if his failing legs were up for it, he enjoyed walking a little to catch a glimpse of the one thousand lamps that were lit at the Sahasralinga temple, which was built thanks to the largesse of Rudrani, royal consort of Chandan Chauhan. Their son and his namesake, Vigraharaj, had built the immense Panch-Vakra-Shiv, which many likened to Kailash, Shiva's abode, and whose massive outline was visible even at a distance. He himself had built the Gokarneshwar temple in that hallowed spot. But for a while now, he had contented himself with only the fleeting images afforded by his memory of the architectural wonders.

As the last rays of the setting sun were chased away by the gathering gloom, Vigraharaj, fourth of the name, mightiest of warriors and vanquisher of foes, whose empire extended from the Vindyas in the south to the Himalayas in the north, found his thoughts taking flight as they delved deep into his past as was their wont.

It was said of the Chahamanas of Shakhambhari, rulers of the Sapadalaksha, that the sun god, Surya, had been their progenitor, having acceded to Brahma's request for a troop of noble, strong and courageous men to protect the grand *yagna* he was conducting on the banks of Pushkar. And so, the Chauhans had emerged, proud and powerful, protectors of the people and demolishers of evil.

He laughed aloud at that even as violent spasms racked his body. No wonder they had bestowed the title 'Kavindra Bandhu' on him! When fanciful, he was every bit as bad as Somadeva, his court poet and partner in literary crime. He thought of *Harikoli*, the drama he had composed all by himself. Of all his many achievements, *Harikoli* had given him the most satisfaction. He wished there had been time to compose a few more . . . but there was only so much a king could do.

Since the time of the great Vasudeva, who had ruled from the vicinity of Sambhar lake, their line had thrown up mighty monarchs. His namesake Vigraharaj-II had invaded Gujarat and repelled their enemies in addition to erecting a beautiful temple to goddess Asapuri. His personal favourite though was Parama Bhattarka Maharajadhiraja Prithviraj-I, who had annexed Nagaur, Hamir and had been the scourge of the Chalukyas, successfully throwing them out of Sapadalaksha territory.

It was his grandfather, Ajayraj, who had founded Ajmer, that glittering jewel amongst cities, and heaped glory on their clan by inflicting a crushing defeat on Paramar Naravarma. If legend was to be believed, he had installed his son on the throne and given his life while fighting off the threat of the pestilential Turushkas, who with their insatiable appetite for booty had proved to be a persistent thorn.

Thinking of the thrice-damned Turks dampened his spirit and he sighed. His body was a constant reminder that nothing lasts forever. His beloved subjects had called him 'Maharajadhiraja' and 'Parameshwar' when he had emerged victorious in the battle for Dillika against the Tomars and conquered Pali as well as Jalore. He had disdained the council of his father's advisers who had favoured paying ransom to the raiding Turks. Instead he had fought the Turushkas and their mleccha hordes, preventing their advance past Baverak.

On that occasion, many were the paeans showered on him and there were those who believed that he was an incarnation of Vishnu. But his joy had been short-lived in light of the tragedy that had followed. The former king coughed and expelled a gob of phlegm that missed the muslin-lined spittoon, the way it did more often than not, though it had been discreetly placed at arm's length. He wondered if Rama and Krishna, other avatars of Vishnu, had ever been enslaved by the demands of their mortal bodies.

And while he was letting his thoughts run amok, the old man wished he had devoted more time and effort towards hunting down the pestilential raiding parties of the foreign invaders and put an end to the menace they had posed once and for all. They were little more than mosquitoes and he had swatted all he could before turning his attention to threats closer to home. Instinct warned him that the barbarians were very much in thrall to their blessed land overflowing as it was with milk, honey and gold. They would never be content with the occasional plunder and would keep coming back for more.

But that was hardly the worst of his mistakes. Restlessly he stirred, running his fingers over the few scraggly strands of woolly white, which were all that remained of a once luxuriant crop of hair, wishing to be rescued from his gloomy thoughts. But fresh grief and anger roiled through his insides when he thought of the accursed tragedy he had lived long enough to see.

If only his own dear son Amaragangeya, who had shown so much promise, had not been slain by the treacherous Prithviraj-II, the toxic effluent that had sprung forth from the loins of Jaggadeva, his dear departed brother and slayer of their father, Maharaj Arnoraj. If only he had stayed around to protect him instead of installing the youth on the throne and crawling away secretly in the dead of the night with a handful of his chosen men to die . . . There was no point dwelling upon all this, Vigraharaj knew. But an old dying man could still live long enough to exact revenge on the one responsible for spilling his son's blood.

Atreya ought to be here any moment, Vigraharaj told himself. He would bring tidings to gladden the heart. No sooner had he thought of him than Atreya was admitted to his presence. *Good*, he thought, *a king must not be kept waiting*.

Chakradatta's grandson looked exactly like him. But he reportedly did not possess the same erratic genius as his grandfather. However, he made up for it by genuinely caring for those in his care. Moreover, his conduct with the ladies was most proper.

Atreya was deferential to his royal presence, yet vaguely pompous, which was typical of those in his profession. Immaculately clothed, with every fold of his white raiment in place but not quite managing to hide the protuberant belly that clearly signified prosperity, white woollen shawl draped neatly across bony shoulders, his tightly turbaned head bobbed slightly as he brought his palms together in the age-old symbol of greeting and respect, murmuring, 'Namaste Maharaj! May you live forever!'

Taking note of the vicious scowl that followed his pronouncement, the vaidya hastened to give his report. 'Prithviraj-II, the slayer of the righteous king, does not enjoy the love or respect of his subjects. Instead they spit on his name, claiming that he is every bit the blood traitor his father, Jaggadeva, was.'

Vigraharaj snorted impatiently. 'Has my decree been conveyed to those who owe me a great debt and have sworn to be loyal while I am still breathing? Answer me!'

Atreya looked troubled. 'My best man has been sent, Maharaj, and he is fully capable of carrying out the perilous mission he has been entrusted with to your satisfaction. Your message will reach the Khokars and they will give their lives to do what they have been ordered to. But as your highness knows, it is not going to be an easy task.

'Prithviraj-II is moving fast to consolidate his position. He struck against the ageing Maharaj Vasantapala, subdued him and exacted a massive tribute from him. The chief of Panchpura has surrendered to him as well. Encouraged by these victories, even as we speak, he readies an expedition to check the advance of the Mussulmen. On his orders, the fort of Hansi is being fortified and it is his uncle Kilhana who has been appointed the governor of the province.'

Vigraharaj was apoplectic with rage. Vasantapala was the father of his dear wife Desaladevi. At least, his chief queen was not alive to experience first-hand the horror that had overtaken them.

'If Jagga's son thinks he can remain on the throne that by right should have been Gangeya's, he is sorely mistaken!' His voice choked with rage and grief. 'My boy was dutiful and capable. I trained him well. He would have been a fine king and ushered in a glorious age of peace and prosperity for the Chahamanas. After Jagga's death, I was advised to put his accursed son to death, but I chose to do the right thing never suspecting that my act of mercy would be the secret weapon, the vengeful spirit of my brother would use to destroy mine!'

Atreya having long been privy to the secrets of those in his care was a good listener and did not interrupt the grand old monarch. It was not his place to point out that there were many who would say that Prithviraj-II was guilty of exactly the same sin as Vigraharaj himself was—fratricide—though both men had been careful to avoid Jagga's mistake and ensured that it was not their hands that struck the fatal blow. It was an endless circle of violence from which there seemed to be no escape.

Vigraharaj's voice had given out and he leaned back, eyes closed as he relived his own installation and the many triumphs the gods had seen fit to bless him with. Yet they offered him no solace from the spectre of failure that haunted him night and day. If that were not enough, he had set in motion a chain of events that may just decimate his lineage.

Chakradatta had once told his grandson that Vigraharaj had been the best of kings—strong yet fair. It gave Atreya the courage to speak his mind. 'If I may be so bold as to speak my mind, sire . . .'

'Spit it out . . .' Vigraharaj ordered, even as a bout of vicious coughing took hold of him. An attendant placed a jewelled cup filled with a heated infusion of honey, ginger and tulsi leaves, which Atreya himself had prescribed, by the old king's side and withdrew as silently and swiftly as he had appeared. Vigraharaj reached for the cup and fortified himself with a few sips.

Determined to say his piece, Atreya composed his thoughts. 'Prithviraj believed that his claim to the throne was greater than Amaragangeya's since he was the heir of Jaggadeva, the elder son of Maharaj Arnoraj. Since then, he seems determined to prove himself worthy of the throne of the Chahamanas and has taken the first step in the right direction by vowing to eliminate the threat of the Turushkas.

'You have fought them, sire, and you know that they are dangerous and the threat they pose is real and not something we can afford to ignore. Every battle fought amongst ourselves weakens us even as they grow increasingly bolder. We should have put an end to them once and for all. Let us not forget the outrages perpetrated by Mahmud of Ghazni. If anything were to happen to Prithviraj-II, the empire of the Chauhans, which you so painstakingly built, will run the risk of being destroyed from within as new claimants to the throne will engage in fresh power struggles. Civil war is the last thing we need. Our enemies on the other hand will no doubt be hoping that it comes down to that so they can circle us like vultures.

'As things stand now, Amaragangeya does not have a son, so his younger brother is his heir. But Nagaraj is still a child and Prithviraj has sworn not to harm him, the way you yourself spared his life after the death of his father. Since he and his devout wife, Suhava Devi, are childless, in good time, it will be your other son who inherits the kingdom of the Chahamanas.'

He expected the old king to explode with rage. Instead Vigraharaj remained silent for a long time. Atreya felt the stirring of hope in his heart.

'You are a wise and brave man, Atreya. Everything you say is true. It may not be in the best interest of my kingdom if vengeance were allowed to claim the life of Jagga's son. But even so, the pretender made a mistake. He should have made sure that the old lion was well and truly dead before he made his bid for power. Now the slayer of my son will burn in hell for all of eternity with my final roar ringing in his ears.'

Atreya left with tears in his eyes. There was nothing left to do now. For better or worse, in life or death, he had given his word that he would serve Maharaj Vigraharaj-IV. The old lion had issued a death sentence and it fell on him to carry it out.

His man would get in touch with the Khokars and make sure they received the royal decree of Vigraharaj-IV, signed with his seal. And those fanatical assassins would move heaven and earth to carry out the instructions, no matter how much time it took or how many lives were claimed. They would not fail. As a vaidya, his hands had been used solely for purposes of healing but now they would be stained with the blood of a king.

He remembered everything his grandfather had told him about the Khokars and the assassins they harboured in their midst. 'They had originally been loyal subjects of the Shahi kingdom,' Chakradatta had told him, 'which comprised Kabul, Lamaghan and the region surrounding the river Chenab—Multan, Poonch, Lahore and Punjab. The capital was Waihind, a city of extraordinary beauty in southern Kashmir. The original rulers claimed descent from Kanishka, the Kushan king who embraced Buddhism, but as you know one can never know with absolute certainty when it is a question of ancestry or paternity. Kanishka's so-called descendants certainly had his penchant for renouncing their faith in favour of a new one; they were called the Turkishahis and were followers of Islam. The last ruler in this line was one Lagaturman and he was supposedly dethroned by his Brahmin vizier, Kallar. Hinduism returned with force, though there are some who insist, probably for the sake of convenience, that they were Kshatriyas.'

The old physician paused as he lovingly rolled his paan, spreading the white *chunam* and lime over the betel leaf before adding crushed betel nuts and his favourite spices, folding it up and popping it into his mouth with the air of a man who was feeding his very soul. He chewed with great gusto and relish for a few moments before he went on with his narrative. 'One of the Shahi kings, Maharaj Jaipal, fought against Sabuktigan, the mleccha brute who sired that abominable creature known to you as Mahmud of Ghazni. Unfortunately, Jaipal was defeated by the Turushkas when he launched an offensive and tried to attack Ghazni. If only the goddess of victory had smiled on him then, everything would have been different now.'

'Why do these stories always end with the Turushkas winning and our people losing? I do not like it when that happens!' Atreya had grumbled to his grandfather.

Chakradatta laughed and red paan juice spattered his white robes. It was a bitter sound. 'Ah! But that is because we never learn and keep making the same mistakes over and over again. Jaipal sued for peace and promised to pay Sabuktigan an indemnity but later when he returned safely to his capital city, he reneged on his promise and compounded his act of defiance by having Sabuktigan's amirs tortured and killed.'

He stopped talking and chewing long enough to spit. 'Jaipal was no doubt a brave man, blessed with a noble bearing and a burning desire to do the right thing, unlike the Ghaznavid whose countenance was so unfortunate that only his mother could look upon it without fleeing in terror. But the Shahi king's actions on that occasion were foolish in the extreme. He provoked the wrath of the Turushkas who turned east intending to teach him a lesson. They advanced on his land, helping themselves to entire chunks of it, forcing him to retreat step by step. His people had the worst of it.

'The mujahideen gave no quarter to the "infidels" and the "idolaters" as they see us, butchering every living thing in Jaipal's land, setting fire to the temples but not before helping themselves to the gold, of course! Finally after years of struggle, Jaipal committed suicide after his crushing defeat in the battle of Peshawar at the hands of Sabuktigan's son Mahmud. They say that the valiant Shahi king built a funeral pyre and climbed into it! This was the second of Mahmud's seventeen incursions into aryavarta to enrich himself at our expense!

'His successor, Anandpal, continued the struggle against Mahmud by bringing together a confederacy that included the rulers of Ujjain, Gwalior, Kalinjar, Kannauj, Delhi, Ajmer and the Khokars of Punjab. The Chauhan king Govindaraj-III joined hands with Anandpal. Oh, it was a glorious undertaking!'

He laughed bitterly again. 'You are not going to like what happened next . . . the mlecchas for all their barbaric ways were well organized and their foot soldiers and cavalry were more disciplined than and superior to our forces. Despite having a bigger army and the dreaded elephant cavalcade, the alliance was defeated. Ironically, it was probably on account of the fact that the elephants panicked and began to run amok crushing many soldiers. After this embarrassing defeat, Mahmud gained control of the northwest regions, including Punjab.'

Atreya had had tears in his eyes and Chakradatta told him kindly, 'Our men fought bravely but not very cleverly. Later, Govindaraj-III fought the barbarians with more success but selfishly chose to protect his own borders, refusing to go to the aid of his neighbours while Mahmud conducted seventeen raids, enriching himself considerably by tearing down temples and slaughtering innocents. There is a lesson there but not many of us bothered to learn it . . .'

'What was the lesson, grandfather? I promise to learn it by heart!' he had said with a child's sincerity.

'Their weapons were superior to ours. They had huge war bows made from a sort of composite material that gave them a much better range and increased power. The bowmen had thumb rings that allowed them protection from undue strain while enhancing the ability to draw the string much farther as well as ensure a quicker release. In close combat, the curved swords they used had more reach than our straight ones. Their horses were better. We should have made it our business to learn and improve our weapons but in these parts we are stubborn and insist on doing things the way they always have been even when proved ineffectual.'

The old man looked angry but seeing the effect on his grandson, calmed down. He continued. 'Even worse was our lack of discipline and unity. Their religion brings them together whereas ours creates rifts. The constant infighting and conflicts between our people seldom make sense as petty rulers turn against each other for next to no reason.

'Those who are defeated in this internecine struggle ally themselves with the victor's worst enemies simply out of spite . . . Did you know that a number of our people have given their support to the Turushkas and have agreed to fight in their armies simply because they can't let go of their enmity? Still others betray their own people lured by filthy lucre or because in our land it is your birth alone that determines who you will be as opposed to your worth. Perhaps the fools have the measure of it and we would all do well to ally ourselves with our *phoren* foes if only to be on the winning side! Make no mistake lad, defeat is staring us in the face and will swallow us whole if we refuse to learn!'

Atreya had felt helpless then and he felt even more so now. The Shahi kingdom had been annihilated and its rulers dead and gone. Some had fled and sought refuge with the Khokars and there they lived to this day, keeping alive in their hearts the hatred they bore the Mussulmen, having sworn to dedicate their lives to killing as many of them as possible.

Vigraharaj-IV had freed their leaders who had been taken captive by the Turushkas. They had hailed him as a champion of their cause and promised to repay him for his kindness. The old king was holding them to it and now ironically, they were bound by honour to obey his will, even at the cost of claiming the life of a king who had vowed to eliminate the Mussulmen!

Atreya shook his head with abject dejection. His grandfather had been right. *We never learn the lessons from the past and insist on making them over and over again,* he mused disconsolately to himself, which is why these stories always end with them winning and us losing everything.

5

Messengers conveying matters of great import and urgency arrived at Patan. Karpuradevi heard the sound of thundering hooves all the way in her remote chambers in the harem and felt the vibrations of the tremendous tidings they bore.

They conferred in secrecy with Kanchanadevi at length. Change was in the air, Karpuradevi could feel it. She could hardly keep still as she waited for her mother-in-law's summons. The matriarch's eyesight was no longer what it used to be so she was called upon daily to assist Kanchanadevi while she worked with Maharaj Kumarpal's council of ministers. The grand old dame had been trained by her father and Karpuradevi felt it was wise of the Chalukyas to recognize her potential. The last man who had failed to do so was her late husband, Maharaj Arnoraj, and look where it had got him.

She found the work itself fascinating. It involved the drafting of royal charters and despatches, listening to learned exchanges between the leading scholars of the day and reports from the treasurer on the state of finances throughout the kingdom. Karpuradevi had grown to love it, even when it was mind-numbingly tedious and required her to sit still behind the uncomfortable confines of her veil for hours without falling asleep as the *purohits* argued the finer points of theology or the account-keepers droned on endlessly about taxation.

Even so she would not have given it up for the world. With her Prithvi and Hari gone, she would have lost her mind sitting in the harem, chewing the fat with a gaggle of giggling, gossipy women. She loved that the door to a man's world from which she had been excluded had suddenly been thrown open to her and for that alone she owed Kanchanadevi an enormous debt of gratitude. It compensated somewhat for the fact that she had given birth to Someshwar and spoilt him rotten.

The object of her thoughts sent for her then and Karpuradevi hurried to her presence.

'Prithviraj-II is no more. The throne of the Chahamanas has been offered to Someshwar,' Kanchanadevi told her without preamble and with none of the emotion that such momentous tidings warranted. 'The council of ministers have ratified the decree. A delegation comprising the highest-ranking officials is making its way towards us even as we speak to escort their new king back to Ajmer. Messengers have been sent to inform Maharaj Kumarpal and my son as well.'

Karpuradevi nodded in wordless wonder. The events of the past few years had been tumultuous to say the least and seemed to be unfolding with a rapidity that made her feel giddy. Vigraharaj-IV had abdicated in favour of his son, Amaragangeya, or so they had been told. The mysterious disappearance of the old king promptly after the installation had resulted in a furore of speculation that had not quite died down before news reached them that the young monarch was no more.

Jaggadeva's son, Prithviraj-II, had claimed the throne, insisting that since he was older than Amaragangeya, it was his right. All attempts to find a diplomatic solution had failed and the cousins had gone to war. In the middle of the ensuing turmoil and strife, Gangeya had been cut down by his rival's soldiers, clearing the path to Prithviraj's ascension to the throne of the Chahamanas.

It had been barely two years—and now they were being informed that Maharaj Prithviraj, a man in his prime who was beginning to gain renown as an able administrator and warrior, was no more! 'What happened to him?' Karpuradevi queried. There was a chill in her heart. The deceased monarch had been her own son's namesake and hearing about his demise filled her with dread and an abiding sorrow.

'Does it even matter? My son is going to take his rightful place on the throne of the Chahamanas and you are concerned about his fallen rival?' the matriarch boomed at her. However, she relented after a full minute of making her disapproval felt. 'All the reports are confused and incoherent in the extreme. Spies are no longer what they used to be. I am convinced that we will do much better if we were to hire monkeys to do the job. At least, they will know enough to steer clear of taverns and every cheap brothel there is!'

Karpuradevi had nothing to say to that. Her mother-in-laws's grousing notwithstanding, the vast sprawling network of informers and clandestine agents she employed had its tentacles everywhere. The woman's ambition had always been boundless and she made no bones about the fact that she belonged in the heart of Sapadalaksha territory, helping her son rule.

Given the circumstances under which the great Vigraharaj-IV had simply vanished and the relative youth of Amaragangeya and Prithviraj-II when their burgeoning careers as the supreme ruler of Sapadalaksha territory had been cut short, it made sense to point an accusing finger at Someshwar and his mother. Karpuradevi wondered if her mother-in-law had indeed had a hand to play in the events that had culminated with the sudden ascent of her son.

Kanchanadevi glared at her. 'I refuse to address the base accusations of evil-minded people. I have said it before and I'll say it again—bad blood will always tell. That brood came from very bad stock indeed. I wouldn't trust that Johiyani to empty the contents of my chamber pot, let alone place the future of the Chahamanas in the hands of whatever abominations she had brought forth from her womb.

'A father-killer and a bloodthirsty savage who drenched the land in blood before dying of some unspeakably foul disease, both of whom in turn produced heirs every bit as unworthy as they themselves had been. Amaragangeya is the fool who had all the power in the world at his disposal and did not know how to wield it in order to keep his sorry self alive. As for Prithviraj-II . . .'

Karpuradevi held her breath, feeling sorrier than she could express for Johiyani Sadhava's unfortunate sons and grandsons.

' . . . if the informers have their facts straight, we can conclude that his demise is the result of a lover's tiff. His wife Suhava was a pious woman and an ardent devotee of Lord Shiva. She was so busy with worship that the woman forgot to keep her husband's affections from straying. He wandered right into the lascivious embrace of some common courtesan and got himself killed by one of the rival claimants to her venereal disease-fraught favours. That is all there is to it!'

Even as she made her little speech with great emphasis, Karpuradevi knew that the grand old woman did not believe a word of it.

Kanha was standing behind the fence on a raised bit of grassy land. He watched with his arms clasped behind his back while Prithviraj was receiving instruction from the master swordsman. His name was Harshit and he had heard of him. They said the grizzled veteran of Maharaj Jaisingh's infantry had once cut his way past dozens of enemy soldiers to take his king to safety.

A hard taskmaster, the old warrior made Prithvi practise his cuts and thrusts repeatedly. Over and over, the young prince went through the repertoire of swordplay, his stamina seemingly inexhaustible. It was only when Prithvi was drenched in perspiration that Harshit called on him to engage.

Instantly alert, Prithvi stood ready, his sword raised in readiness. Their blades clashed and they broke apart, circling, looking for an exposed part. Harshit feinted at his shoulder and Prithvi managed to turn the blade aside and responded with a counterstroke that would one day land with the force of a thunderbolt. But that day was not today, for Prithvi lacked the strength of an adult in his forearms and tired from his exertions could not manage the requisite speed, with the result that his tutor's blade came to an abrupt halt an inch from his chest.

'You need to be faster!' Harshit chided him. 'No enemy is ever going to cut you slack because you are tired, bleeding and dead on your feet! On the battlefield, king or pauper, there can be no room for error. The smallest mistake can cost you your life!'

Prithvi recovered with characteristic smoothness but even at a distance, Kanha sensed his fury at being bested, indicated by the slight scowl that distorted his features. His eyes narrowed suddenly when he spotted the opening. His opponent was going for his shoulder again and had exposed his hip.

Kanha had to restrain himself from shouting out a warning. The sly old warrior was setting the young prince up for another hit, having positioned himself just beyond the reach of his blade, no doubt to teach the prince a lesson about what happened to those who thought too highly of their own as yet burgeoning skills. Kanha clapped in amazement when Prithvi feinted a blow to the hip, then with a sudden burst of speed and remarkable dexterity changed the angle mid-attack and hit his master just beneath the ribs.

The veteran broke the engagement and drew back with just the hint of a smile tugging at his scarred lips. 'Good work!

Once your training is complete, your enemies will find that defeating you in straight combat will prove nigh impossible.'

All smiles now that he had acquitted himself, he fell at the feet of his master, received his blessings and made way for Padhri with a grin. Harshit Kinasariya did not take kindly to having his student best him even in mock engagements and in all likelihood, Padhri would retire with severe bruising that would have him tossing and turning all night long, cursing enough to make the ears bleed. The thought made Prithvi smile.

Excusing himself, he left the training grounds and ran all the way to the fence which he cleared with a single bound and stood before Kanha, a wide smile on his flushed face. So the youngster had been aware of his presence all along, his uncle noted with a smile. They embraced briefly and Prithvi stepped back to take a look at his uncle. The most recent campaign had taken a toll on him. He was burnt brown by the sun, there was a fresh scar across his eyebrow and a little more grey in his hair. Several days of hard riding had left him begrimed, sore and weary. But he was as irrepressible and full of vitality as ever.

Guru Bharadwaj had heard of his coming and sent his servants to attend to Prince Kanha personally. Prithvi kept him company in the bathing chambers where the attendants scrubbed him clean and massaged his shoulders with medicinal oils prepared under Bharadwaj's supervision.

When he was presentable, Kanha paid his respects to Bharadwaj, who had been his guru as well. Prithvi ran ahead to the kitchen to make sure that a hot meal was waiting for his uncle and made arrangements to ensure that they could dine in private. Lastly, he sent word to Hari so his little brother could join them. Everything was ready when Kanha re-emerged.

'What is there to eat?' Kanha enquired, 'I am ravenous!'

Prithvi himself was too excited to eat. The boys bombarded their uncle with questions about the adversaries he had been fighting. What kind of weapons and fighting techniques did they use? How heavily fortified were their cities? Did he despatch the man who had given him that scar to Yama's abode?

Kanha did his best to address himself to his nephews' questions between mouthfuls of food, enjoying their company immensely. Life worked in remarkable ways. It was not his lot to start a family and have sons of his own and yet he was closer to these boys than most parents were with their own children! He waited till the servants had cleared away the dishes so they could address more pressing issues.

'What news, uncle?' Prithvi enquired. 'I appreciate the visit but it is unlikely that it was affection for me that dragged you away from Maharaj Kumarpal's interminable wars.'

He knows, Kanha realized, most of it anyway. It always amazed him how quickly news travelled. Pausing only to quaff from his goblet filled with his favourite spiced wine, Kanha told them everything while Prithvi and Hari grew increasingly solemn as the full import of his words struck them.

'That is the long and the short of it,' he finished. 'Someshwar is on his way to Naharvala and Maharaj Jaisingh's old palace to meet with the delegation from Ajmer and I am to escort you two there. You are to be anointed as the yuvaraj, Prithvi. My mother insisted on it and the ministers were in perfect accord as it is supposedly a good idea to establish a clear line of succession.'

Hari whooped with genuine delight and clapped his brother on the shoulder. Watching him, Kanha was moved. The youngster did not have an envious bone in his body. He could not help envying his youth and the innocence which could derive happiness from the twin tragedies that had claimed the lives of the two kings who also happened to be their kin. Prithvi did not share Hari's excitement. It was not an act, Kanha realized; he is a wise soul, strangely aware that his inheritance was one that was drenched in blood.

'I have been singled out by Guru Bharadwaj for separate lessons on kingship,' Prithvi began. Sensing his tone, Hari quietened down. 'Sometimes during these lessons, he asks me to take notes while he listens to the reports of his spies. It was in this manner that it came to my attention that my namesake and relative, Prithviraj-II, the king of the Chahamanas, was slain by mounted assassins. He had been engaged in making preparations for war—a grand undertaking on a hitherto unprecedented scale. Apparently, he wanted to deal with the threat posed by the Mussulmen once and for all, chasing them away from our land and all the way to their barbaric abode, tear down their fortresses and raze their cities to the ground. He dreamed of teaching them a lesson so harsh they would never even think of setting foot in these parts again. At the time he was killed, the king was dealing with the logistics and figuring out how to raise enough money to outfit such a large army and feed them.'

Kanha was looking at him intently but Prithvi did not seem to notice. In his eyes, there was a melancholy so profound it frightened his uncle, who hadn't flinched when an enemy soldier's blade had grazed his brow, barely missing the eyeball. He wanted to reassure the boy but instead drank some more wine.

'The assailants seemed familiar with his movements,' Prithvi went on. 'They were waiting when the king attended evening worship at a small shrine that was dear to him. His bodyguards were mowed down within seconds though they were elite soldiers, chosen for their skills and bravery, and the assassins made short work of the king as well, cutting him in a dozen places before making their escape on swift Arabian steeds, finer by far than anything we have in these parts.'

Prithvi paused and Kanha picked up where he had left off, 'I am familiar with the reports too. Maharaj Kumarpal thinks it is the work of the Mussulmen. Ever since Mahmud of Ghazni came here with his thrice-cursed raiding parties, his people can't resist the urge to return, believing that there is rich scope for loot and plunder. But even so, this is the first time they have been bold enough to plan and pull off such a dastardly attack that claimed the life of a Chauhan king, no less!'

His laugh was bitter. 'You would think there would be outrage across the length and the breadth of the land. That the Hindus, who have proudly believed that their faith is the true one and in their religious fervour have been known to persecute those who worship other gods, nevertheless prefer to look away in the wake of such an atrocity! But the death of a Chahamanas king caters to the petty political interests of too many in this divided land of ours!'

Prithviraj was looking more solemn by the second. 'What you said makes sense, Uncle Kanha, and the Mussulmen have a lot to answer for! Almost as much as we do for fleeing before their advance!' He was breathing heavily, his eyes burning bright with furious resolve. 'On this day I swear to you, uncle, that I, Prithviraj Chauhan, the third of the name, will never retreat from a battle against the Mussulmen. I will fight them and drive them from aryavarta or die trying!'

'I will fight by your side, brother, and swear to resist the Turushkas while there is life in my body!' Hari reiterated quietly. Kanha supposed he should be moved by so much idealism but it only depressed him so he drank some more and kept his thoughts to himself.

Prithvi clapped his brother on the shoulder, before picking up the thread of the discussion again: 'Getting back to the matter of the murdered king, Guruji thinks, and I agree, that placing the blame squarely on the shoulders of the Mussulmen is a tad simplistic not to mention convenient. The way things stand now, they are merely dacoits who harry us like pestilential flies though that may change at any moment. However, the fact remains that they have neither the skills nor the funds for a high-risk plot like this . . .'

Kanha was silent; the thought had crossed his mind too. It was hard to believe that Prithvi was still a boy. 'According to a report from one of the spies, the death of the king was an act of revenge. As you know, there are some who blame him for the death of my uncle Vigraharaj's son and successor, Amaragangeya. The fact that he followed him to an early grave has prompted some to conclude that the assassins were paid by relatives or well-wishers of Vigraharaj. Perhaps even Vigraharaj himself . . .'

'I'll admit it is possible but the truth is that we will never know for certain,' Kanha replied thoughtfully.

Prithvi smiled but it was the most sorrowful sight Kanha had ever seen. 'But we do know, don't we? When I walked out after my session with Guruji, I went for a ride and told myself that a crown and a throne are simply not worth the price in blood that it exacts. Then I realized that Arjuna would have preferred to beg for alms rather than fight so many of his kith and kin. It did not stop him from spilling oceans of blood in Kurukshetra. The same holds true for me at this moment. I would have preferred to take my horse and travel to the ends of the earth but now that I am to be king one day, it feels like my hands are tied. There is every possibility that I will do things that are every bit as terrible, perhaps worse . . .'

At that moment, Kanha understood the boy's loneliness like never before. He had his friends who were with him all the time and yet they could never get close to him. Every action of his was conducted openly and without artifice, yet none could claim to know that subtle, passionate mind or predict his next move.

'It is also possible that you will be the great king this land so desperately needs,' Hari told his brother stoutly. 'With you at the helm, I have no doubt that we will see an era where our people are united under a strong ruler. It will usher in a golden period of peace and prosperity.'

Kanha saw that the words which were intended to comfort, pained Prithvi and he ignored his brother. 'You would make a good king, Uncle Kanha,' he told him instead. 'You have absolutely no interest in ruling and very little ambition. You don't seem interested in making strategic alliances by marrying into a powerful family, bringing forth war-like sons or engaging in petty politics. Yet, whatever you do, you do well. There can be no doubt that you would be an ideal ruler.'

Kanha grinned at that. 'I don't think so. My brother, your father, can keep his crown and the throne. He has nothing to fear from the likes of me.'

'If you don't mind my asking, Uncle Kanha, why haven't you taken a wife? Don't you want to have children? Everybody else acts as though nothing is more important than having as many wives as you can possibly afford to and more children than you can count. Guruji says that a man is bound by dharma to have sons who will perform his last rites, say prayers for his immortal soul, take care of his unfinished work and atone for his sins. He was your teacher too and yet you don't seem to set much store by that sort of thing . . .'

Kanha took his time before framing a response but this was neither the time nor place for dissembling. Anyone else in his place when told about the sudden change in his fortunes would be celebrating all night long. Someshwar had done just that. There had been feasting, drinking and dozens of dancing girls who had been all too willing to engage in every act of debauchery the new king and his followers had come up with. Prithvi, meanwhile, looked for all the world like an ancient soul determined to figure out the solution to the conundrum that was life.

'As a prince of the Chahamanas, a suitable girl would have to be found from a similar background . . .' he began, 'that would mean that even if I lacked ambition, her family wouldn't. Any children we bring forth, would be more pieces to be used and manipulated in the game for power. It is not something I care to be involved in. At the time, it was my belief that by turning my back on convention, my freedom would be complete, my life would be more to my choosing . . .'

'But it wasn't, was it, Uncle Kanha?' When the Prince said it with a searching look in his eyes, it sounded more like a statement.

Kanha nodded in affirmation. 'I remain very much a piece to be used and manipulated. My mother in her wisdom had decided that it was in the best interests of her firstborn for me to be employed in his service. I fight by his side, clean up after him and help fulfil their plans. It is hardly something to get worked up about since within these constraints I can still be whatever I choose to be . . .'

Prithvi smiled, 'You have the right idea, Uncle Kanha. Everybody should have the freedom to make their choices. But Guruji would say that not even the gods have that kind of control over their own destinies. So perhaps it is best to take the path that lies ahead and do the best I can . . . There is nothing else left for me to do, is there?'

They chatted for a bit longer before retiring to bed. Neither of them felt like celebrating that night. Not that it mattered when Prithvi returned to his chambers. His companions had been waiting up for him, eager to celebrate his good fortune.

'Consider me your loyal servant, your majesty,' Padhri prostrated himself at his feet, the solemnity of the declaration marred by his tipsiness. He had sneaked in some liquor to mark the occasion and had helped himself to it rather liberally. 'I will protect you from your enemies and watch out for your royal behind in battle!'

'You will no doubt have the pick of all the beauties in the land,' Nahar wisecracked. 'I will vet them thoroughly and sample their goodies first just to make sure that they aren't those notorious *vishakanyas* Guruji told us about! See? I am willing to die for you! Especially since it is the only way I want to go . . .'

'Shut up, you bloody pimp . . .' Prithvi roared, 'I will have your hands chopped off if you so much as lay a finger on the ladies in my land!'

As their revels continued till the wee hours of dawn, there wasn't a hint of Prithvi's melancholia from earlier that evening. He was every bit as high-spirited as his friends if not more.

6

It was the moment the queen mother had long dreamed of. She looked resplendent in a grand cream-and-gold pattamsuka silk sari. Elegant *kundalas* studded with diamonds and a pearl necklace adorned her ears and neck respectively. She wore her silvery hair in a bun befitting her advanced years. Standing proud and tall, she awaited the dignitaries from Ajmer.

Someshwar, who was to be anointed the king, waited with her. He seemed a little stiff and ill at ease, Kanchanadevi noted. His costly raiment, golden armour and fine accoutrements appeared to weigh him down. That was not the case with her grandson though.

Prithviraj, who was to be named yuvaraj, had also donned a golden armour and stood on a raised dais by his father's side, looking every bit the king he would someday be. The cynosure of all eyes, he was comfortable with the attention and so majestic that his grandmother could not help thinking that not even her dear father, Maharaj Jaisingh, had possessed such a dazzling aura.

Karpuradevi, the chief queen of Maharaj Someshwar, stood next to her husband, a picture of grace and elegance. The distance between them was palpable even though they stood close to each other. She wore a red-and-gold devamsuka sari and a kamcholi blouse embroidered with rubies and pearls.

The heavy pallu was draped around her shoulder and over her head and allowed to fall loosely on her left arm.

Her hair had been parted in the centre and braided, with flowers and ornaments woven in. A *maang tika* of gold and pearls adorned her forehead. She wore heavy, ornate chains and necklaces, rings of solid gold on every one of her fingers, ivory and gold bangles from wrists to elbows, a nose ring that had been fastened above her ear and anklets on her feet. A heavy gold girdle had been tied around her waist.

Camphor powder and saffron had been used to render her skin flawless and brighten it. Collyrium darkened her eyes and red dye had been artfully applied to her lips. She was a vision of feminine beauty and many commented that she looked every bit as auspicious as goddess Lakshmi.

Kanchanadevi wasn't displeased with her daughter-in-law's appearance. It was she herself after all who had chosen her garments and the jewellery. Still, she could not approve of the way she barely looked at her husband. Her son was the sole recipient of her adoring smiles. A stern talking to was required, she supposed, but at least the woman had applied herself with due diligence to her studies and had made good progress. She noticed Kanha standing unobtrusively, far enough not to draw attention to himself but close enough to respond should the need arise. All was in accordance with her plans.

Even fate had acceded to her iron will and the timing for this happy occasion could not have been better. Maharaj Kumarpal's health was failing but he refused to slow down, opting instead to go to war against the Paramar king, Daravarsha. Someshwar and Kanha had been fighting by his side when the glad tidings of Prithviraj-II's demise had been received at Patan.

Gracious as ever, Maharaj Kumarpal had blessed her son, whom the ministers at Ajmer had decided would be named the king of the Chahamanas, and sent him and Kanha with an armed escort and rich presents while he himself stayed back to secure his borders.

The fanfare sounded as the delegates made their entrance into the ornate chamber that had been readied for their coming. Maharaj Kumarpal had grown to rely heavily on Kanchanadevi and while he was away it was understood that she spoke with his voice. It was what her father, Maharaj Jaisingh, would have wanted. The council of ministers in Patan had been most cooperative when it came to obeying her orders and everything was prepared to receive the dignitaries in Naharvala, at her father's residence. Her father had been in the habit of retreating to Naharvala whenever he wished to get away from the endless demands of looking after his kingdom.

She loved the beauty and tranquillity of the place. Maharaj Jaisingh's palace was a marvellous edifice. The surrounding grounds were lush and green. There were fields, dear little houses, livestock, gardens and orchards. Gorgeous peacocks had made themselves completely at home as had the deer, who accepted tid-bits from the citizens, tame as you please.

One of Kanchanadevi's fondest memories was of the time when her father had killed a lion armed only with his spear. Its pelt was gifted to her and she always carried it wherever she went in order to remind herself to be worthy of the lion among men who had raised her to be a queen.

Maharaj Jaisingh had a wonderful collection of exquisitely wrought sculptures that were displayed in the garden. Inside the palace were wonderfully sculpted marble figures, exquisite statues in bronze and beautiful paintings done with natural dyes that remained as bright as they were the day they had been done. Kanchanadevi had taken good care of the place and was proud of it.

Mahamantri Sallakshanapal, who had long served the Chauhans, including Maharaj Vigraharaj-IV and Prithviraj-II, led the delegates. He was flanked by Pandit Padmanabh and Senapati

Sinhabala. They represented the old guard of the administrative arm of the Chahamanas and were determined to carry out the most important mission of their lives before retirement.

Everyone wore traditional dhotis with an *angarkhah*, the fitted long shirts and jackets embroidered with gold and silver. The most arresting feature of the grand vestment was the head-dress, which sparkled with gems, and the antelope-skin shoes that curved upwards at the toe.

The sudden, unexpected passing of Prithviraj-II had left them shaken and the throne empty. The late king had been without issue and Amaragangeya's brother was too young. Their enemies were already circling and they had no choice but to turn towards Arnoraj's second wife, the redoubtable Kanchanadevi, and place their hope in Someshwar.

Ten armed guards from the imperial army escorted them. They had been chosen on the basis of their daunting physique, years of impeccable service and formidable bearing. They wore ceremonial armour and everyone present couldn't help gawping at their long swords, which fit snugly into engraved scabbards with only the golden pommel visible. Gold-tipped bows were slung over their shoulders and quivers inlaid with ivory and silver were fastened to the back of the armour.

The dignitaries offered presents to the queen mother and Maharani Karpuradevi. A sapphire necklace set in silver with matching *jhumkas* for the former and a girdle of solid gold studded with diamonds and a tiara decorated with rubies for the latter. Prithviraj received a breastplate and Someshwar was offered the ancient crown of the Chahamanas.

Once the formalities and lengthy speechifying were completed, they all trooped outside and the ten-thousand-strong Chauhan crack troops, who would accompany Maharaj Someshwar to his capital city, were presented. They were all well-built and smartly turned out, encased in their bronze armour, holding up their emblazoned shields and spears. Bronze helmets polished to a mirror sheen shone under the sun. As Someshwar inspected his men, they hailed and saluted him.

Kanchanadevi had felt that a demonstration of Prithviraj and his companions' skills before Maharaj Someshwar's new troops might be in order. Their guests were escorted to pavilions where they were seated comfortably and served refreshments while attendants fanned them with *chamaras* made with peacock feathers.

With strident notes from the bugle and the pounding of drums, the exhibition started. Led by Kanak, Prithvi's companions charged into the arena as if they were galloping into battle and at his signal executed a series of wide turns and tricky manoeuvres with spectacular precision. At its conclusion, they set their steeds to a full gallop and rode shoulder to shoulder in unison before coming to a dramatic halt a short distance from where Maharaj Someshwar was seated. 'Hail, Maharaj Someshwar! May you live long!' they cried out.

The headlong charge and thundering hooves had made the king a wee bit alarmed but regaining his composure he accepted the salutation and dismissed his son's brave companions. In unison, they made their retreat and positioned themselves at one side of the arena.

There was anticipation in the air and it rose to a crescendo as the bugles and drums sounded again, heralding the arrival of the handsome young prince.

Prithviraj rode in on a majestically caparisoned war elephant to riotous cheering from the crowd. Already, he was a legend. 'That elephant's name is Udayagri, a dangerous beast!' people murmured to each other, retelling a tale that had already been repeated hundreds of times. 'He was in rut and had already claimed many lives!'

'The bull elephant gored his victims with those wicked tusks and ripped their bodies asunder, scattering them for miles around!'

'He liked to pierce them through and toss them aside or over his back!'

'The prince stood like a young lion straight in its path, not even batting an eyelid when it charged at him! They say the great beast dropped to its knees, tame as you please, in deference to the fire in the prince's eyes, its tusk a whisker away from his heart, paying obeisance as if to a god!'

'Now he is loyal to the prince and pines like a lover when they are separated.'

Kanchanadevi had heard the wild tales. In truth, the elephant had been gifted to Prithvi by Maharaj Kumarpal when word of his skill with the sword and the bow had reached him. Reckless as ever, Prithvi had insisted on breaking in the beast himself and succeeded in the very first attempt. And the legend in all its exaggerated glory had been born. She did not mind whichever version of the story was told and retold as long as it made her grandson look good. The gods favoured the bold and there was none more so than Prithviraj Chauhan.

He made an impressive figure, lean and hard-bodied. His face was framed by longish dark hair, which glinted under the sun, and his trademark sunny smile made the women swoon. He had refused to use a helmet and the men pointed out the fact to each other, commenting that his reputation for bravery despite his youth was full deserved.

'Why, he looks like a young god! And for one of his years, he has a commanding presence and exudes a certain magnetism that is clearly irresistible. Listen to the crowd roar! His men will follow him into the thick of battle, towards the very gates of hell without batting an eyelid!' It was Mahamantri Sallakshanapal who had spoken. He seemed very much taken with the yuvaraj.

At his side, Sinhabala nodded in agreement, stroking his luxurious white moustache of which he was inordinately proud, especially since he was completely bald. 'We have heard wonderful things about the young prince in Ajmer and Delhi, rajmata. They say that he is a fine rider and an excellent swordsman and archer.'

Kanchanadevi couldn't conceal her pleasure at such lavish praise. 'You will be the judge of that yourselves . . .' she murmured. Maharaj Someshwar watched impassively as his son waved at the crowd. Karpuradevi did her best to remember that she was a queen now and it would never do to clap her hands with gay abandon, the way the commoners did. 'Though still a lad, he is nevertheless twice the man his father is!' she thought with savage satisfaction.

Covertly, she sneaked a glance at her husband. Judging by the sour look on his face, it seemed as if he had somehow read her thoughts. Served him right too! Their marriage, if it could be called that, was on the rocks and had been for a long time. Any interaction between them was limited solely to the public sphere and occasions demanded by social protocol.

Karpuradevi was careful to mask the extent of her disdain, making sure that their exchanges were always exceedingly polite. As he grew older, his virility had suffered and she had been told that it took more and more effort to arouse him and necessitated acts of depravity that usually left him drained, humiliated and furious.

In recent times, she wielded a lot of power thanks to Kanchanadevi, who had taken her under her wing, and to the fact that she was the mother of Someshwar's only two sons. Her position made her feel secure but she knew better than to rub it in his face. She made sure that the boys visited him whenever possible and had Lakshmibai tell them wildly exaggerated stories of their father's valour, knowing that his spies would carry the news back to him. She hated having to stroke his ego but it had to be done. Determined to ignore the unpleasant taste her husband always left in her mouth, she turned her gaze back on the young hero.

Prithvi, ever the daredevil and showman, slid down the elephant's trunk, launched himself into the air and as the entire audience held their breath, landed lightly on his feet. The spectators were in a mad frenzy by then.

The opponents who would cross swords with the prince had been carefully selected. All were prime fighters—big, muscular and strong. They had limbered up and held their swords in readiness for the exhibition match.

When the signal was given by Guru Bharadwaj, Prithvi sprang into action. Within moments, he had proved that his vaunted victories had not been orchestrated by the royal family. When the song of steel began, he moved with a fluid grace, keeping in time to a beat only he seemed to hear. Next to him, some of the best swordsmen in the land seemed almost as awkward and clumsy as children wielding sticks. The prince moved with lightning speed and seemed to be everywhere at once, kicking up clouds of dust from the earthen floor of the arena. His opponents struggled in vain to find an opening.

He blocked, thrust and parried, leaping lightly over the exposed blades, even balancing on one before forcing his opponents to surrender with his sword pointed at their throats. It was a dazzling display, which had the crowd on its feet.

Karpuradevi exhaled slowly. There had been ugly rumours that Kanchanadevi had issued a warning that if any among the swordsmen dared to best the prince it would be the last thing he ever did. Surely after that exhibition, nobody would dare to dispute the fact that her son was the best in the land.

Prithvi had retreated to a tent where his attendants were waiting to wipe him and straighten his garments. While they were engaged thus, workers scurried around the arena placing target drums. Prithvi reappeared, mounted on his horse and wielded his bow. Performing a quick circuit of the arena, he hit the targets with dead accuracy at 500 paces.

What followed was even more thrilling. Prithvi was blindfolded and goose feathers were tossed into the wind and he brought them all down, releasing arrows in a steady torrent. They seemed to come alive as he shot them, flitting into the crowds as his admirers tried to grab them, eager to keep them as souvenirs.

One impossible stunt followed another, firing up the crowd. With a final flourish, Prithvi rode towards the pavilion where the royal family and the guests of honour were watching him equally spellbound. In quick succession, he released his arrows—each one of which soared through the air and landed at the feet of his father and the royal dignitaries—in a warrior's salute, mimicking the actions of Arjuna before the battle of Kurukshetra.

A final arrow sailed through Karpuradevi's four-inch-long nose ring before landing at the feet of his grandmother. She frowned at the irrepressible youth. This had not been part of the original programme but Prithvi would not be Prithvi if the wild and untamed beast in his breast did not struggle to break free.

In the resulting chaos, his companions rushed to him, all decorum forgotten, hoisting him on their shoulders and carrying him around the arena while the spectators showered flowers on him with deafening cries of *Prithviraj! Prithviraj! Prithviraj!* Only Karpuradevi felt, rather than noticed, the envy in her husband's breast. She would summon Prithvi to her and perform the *aarati* to ward off the evil eye herself.

Their guests were ushered to a large hall for the feasting and revelry that was to follow. Good-looking members of both sexes, dressed in alluring silks, served them the elaborate meal: grilled kebabs of wild boar, roasted quail, hard-boiled eggs and a wide assortment of flavoured rice and flatbreads, accompanied by rich gravies, fresh vegetables, lassi, sweetmeats and spiced wine.

Musicians, dancers and acrobats enlivened the proceedings considerably. While mostly everybody else busied themselves with eating and drinking their fill, mesmerized by the sinuous movements and rhythmic grace of the dancers, Mahamantri Sallakshanapal and Kanchanadevi talked quietly about the imminent departure on the morrow. The young prince responded to the command in his grandmother's eyes and joined them.

'We will be joined by 10,000 soldiers as we make the journey back to Ajmer where the king will be crowned again before his subjects. The people will be happy that there has been a smooth transition to power following the demise of the late king and will look forward to the coronation of Maharaj Someshwar as well as that of the yuvaraj, who has already won their hearts,' the mahamantri informed them, beaming at the young prince.

Kanchanadevi nodded, 'The prince and his companions will accompany us. He must get to know his people and they, him. His education will be continued in Pushkar with the wise men who have made it their home. My younger son, Kanha, will return to Maharaj Kumarpal's side. It is important for the moment at least that a cordial relationship be maintained with the Chalukyas.'

Sallakshanapal seemed pleased to hear that. 'The young prince will have the best education money can buy, rajmata, you have my assurance. As for Maharaj Someshwar, we are happy that his allies are powerful and loyal.' *Especially since he does not have the military genius and strength of a Vigraharaj to crush his enemies when they come to his borders,* the mahamantri mused. *Hopefully, in the time left to the ageing Chalukyan monarch, Someshwar, which was to say his mother, would strengthen their position considerably.*

'I look forward to it,' Prithviraj told him. 'This will be my first journey out of Gurjardesa. Only in my dreams has the Sapadalaksha territory been shown to me and it will be glorious to return to my land and see it with my own eyes: every village, lake and temple that witnessed the footfalls of my ancestors.'

The mahamantri allowed himself a small smile, charmed by the enthusiasm of his new yuvaraj. Someday he would make a great king! He would not be around then, thanks to his failing health, which according to his fool of a physician was the result of a steady diet of excessive eating and drinking when clearly the man's incompetence was to blame. But he had a feeling that the boy he was conversing with was fortune's chosen one and it would have been a joy to see him take the Chahamanas to the zenith of glory. His belly was uncomfortably full with the excellent food and drink that idiot of a vaidya had expressly asked him to avoid, his senses pleasurably lulled by the exquisite music and dance. Everything had gone smoothly under the circumstances.

'So tell me, mahamantri . . . how goes the investigation to find and punish the killers of Johiyani Sadhava's grandson?' Kanchanadevi interrupted his reverie.

His smile disappeared and the mahamantri felt decidedly queasy. 'We are doing our best to hunt down the killers, my queen. But it has proved to be an uphill task. Maharaj was readying an expedition to root out the Turushkas and recover the territory lost to them. He sent emissaries to all the neighbouring kingdoms inviting the young and the bold to join him and make his vision a grand success.'

There were real tears in his eyes, Kanchanadevi noticed dispassionately. Prithvi was watching the exchange intently.

'We will not rest till his assassins are captured and made to answer for their sins!' he concluded, his voice thick with emotion.

It was not the reassurance his grandmother was looking for, Prithvi knew. And he understood something else: she would not rest till she had punished the one who had killed her husband's grandsons. Not that she had loved either of them but because it had set a dangerous precedent and endangered the safety of her own son and grandson. That she could never allow.

7

'I come bearing news of great import, maharaj. Prithviraj-II is no more! His uncle, your half-brother Someshwar, will be placed on the throne. May his reign be blessed with prosperity, victory and a strong successor!' Atreya informed his king. His chest felt tight and he had trouble breathing.

The news did not seem entirely to Vigraharaj's liking though his orders had been carried out to the last letter and his scowl deepened with that pronouncement. 'Well, it is truly rare for kings in our line to die of natural causes, so that's that I suppose. But why has Someshwar been chosen to be the king? The gods know the ministers could not have made a more unworthy choice if they had tried! He is spineless, shallow and completely unfit to rule. Why haven't they named my other son, Nagarjun, the king and established a regency council to help him rule?'

Atreya had the troubled air of one who wished he did not know as much as he did, 'You know the reason, maharaj! Nagarjun is still a boy. Besides, the ministers have reposed their faith in Kanchanadevi more than the new king. She is an able and experienced administrator trained by Maharaj Jaisingh, who as you know did not have any sons and in a mad moment, decided to raise his daughter as if she were one.'

So this was what it had come to, Vigraharaj thought bitterly—the honour of the Chauhans and the fate of the mighty kingdom he himself had carved out were in the hands of a woman!

The same Kanchanadevi his sainted mother had claimed was a degenerate, unnatural creature without the feminine graces, and her libertine son, he had been told, was a molester of young girls. They may as well have offered the throne on a silver platter to the Chalukyas! Everybody knew that Kumarpal would be pulling the strings of the puppet on the throne who may not even be a legitimate Chauhan. The thought that his successors were doing such a shoddy job of keeping the family honour intact was infinitely more painful than the numerous aches, pains and burning joints that made up his failing body.

When he spoke again, his voice was steady. 'Tell me more . . . Someshwar has two sons, doesn't he? And a younger brother, Kanha I think, who is supposedly a fine warrior. I wonder if he has an eye on the throne. He can't be a worse king than his brother at any rate! Don't they say that Kanha is carrying on with his brother's wife? Perhaps the war for succession has not been concluded just yet.'

Atreya blinked; infirm or not the old man missed nothing and if he wasn't mistaken there was a hopeful note in his voice. He was no doubt wishing that a brother would kill a brother all over again, vacating the throne for his own son.

'Kanha is every bit the faithful hound his mother trained him to be,' he said, trying to moderate his tone. 'I just don't see him making a claim for the throne now or in the event of his brother's passing. Prithviraj, the third of the name, has been named the heir and successor to the throne. Prince Kanha seems content to serve and follow orders. They say he has taken young Prithviraj, who shows a lot of promise, under his tutelage, determined to educate and train him to be the best and most valiant of kings.'

He thought the invalid's eyes gleamed but it could have been a trick of the light. His grandfather might have been comfortable discussing the seamier aspects of the troubled relationship between King Someshwar and his wife, but he was

a cautious man and dared not give voice to the things he knew.
Or thought he did.

Thanks to a certain delicate condition that afflicted the
male of the species, Someshwar had been unable to assert
his marital rights with the many wives and concubines that
adorned his harem with the unhappy result that they remained
mostly virginal and entirely barren. When the murmurs began
in earnest, he had looked to drink all manner of intoxicants to
restore his flagging self-esteem.

High on *kushumba*, he would give free rein to his temper and
violent tendencies with the result that the vaidya who served in the
royal household had found himself being called upon to treat the
ill-used ladies of the harem for broken bones, burns and assorted
mutilations of the flesh. Or so it was said. Then Karpuradevi had
gotten pregnant and delivered two boys in quick succession.

That should have put to rest the vile rumours, but if
anything, the tongues began to wag faster and more viciously
than ever. According to the scandalmongers, it was Kanha,
the king's younger brother, who had successfully cohabited
with the queen and it was their union that had yielded such a
healthy crop of progeny.

Atreya had never cared for rumour or harsh truths. He
refused even to discuss the issue with friend and foe alike. After
all, men had their tongues ripped out or their throats slit open
for far less grievous offences.

'Tell me more about the lioness's cub. Does he take after
his father?'

'He takes after you, maharaj!' Atreya said without
hesitation. 'Everyone says so. The young prince has been blessed
with a ferocious intellect and can speak in six languages. His
skill as an archer is unmatched and some say even Arjuna pales
in comparison. Even blindfolded, he never misses a target, so
acute are his senses. Why, he likes nothing better than to send
an arrow through the nose rings of poor, unsuspecting maidens

as they go about their work! Most importantly, he is a born leader and a charismatic one.'

'My nephew reminds me of Prithviraj-I and god willing, his legacy will be even greater!' Atreya was pleased to note that the old king's attitude had softened. At least, he was not thinking of instructing assassins to kill Maharaj Someshwar and his heir.

It was time for Atreya to leave. Bidding the old king farewell, he was on his way out when a frail voice stopped him in his tracks. 'Thank you for your service, Atreya. You are a better man than your grandfather. I know that you dream of the day when our land will be free of those who seek to destroy our religion and enslave our people. It may be that my actions thwarted its realization, but don't give up hope just yet. If Someshwar's son is wise enough to learn from the mistakes of his ancestors, perhaps he will more than make up for them . . .'

His voice faded away. When Atreya stepped into the darkness outside, his heart was full with grief. It was too late, he was thinking, when the shadows detached themselves from the inky blackness and surrounded him. Mercifully, the first blow of the dagger was to his heart, killing him instantly. He felt nothing when they continued hacking his body into pieces.

Vigraharaj felt a band tighten around his chest. It was Yama's noose tightening around his body, he knew and exulted. At last! In the final moments left to him, his thoughts turned to Prithviraj—the boy Atreya had said took after him. He uttered a final blessing soundlessly as the faceless emissary of the god of death pressed a cushion over his face, holding it in place. *May you live forever!* Then his thoughts went still. And silent. Vigraharaj-IV, greatest of the Chahamanas, was no more.

8

They left for Ajmer at dawn. It was an impressive sight—the serpentine train comprised men, women, horses, elephants, camels and wooden wagons drawn by teams of oxen. The roofs of the wagons were covered with reeds to provide shelter from the rain. This was the baggage train, heavily laden with saris and other garments, rolls of silk and spare clothes, thread, needles, bed linen, combs, brushes and jewellery.

In addition to this, the wagons were tightly packed with medicinal potions and herbs, food and provisions for their journey. Chests filled with sugar, salt and spices were crammed in, lending their delicious aromas. There were sacks of rice, maize and flour, bottles of wine and strong spirits, cured meats hung from hooks driven into the roof of the wagons, dried fruit and sun-dried vegetables. These were rounded out by an assortment of pots, pans, ladles, banana leaves and everything needed to cater to the culinary requirements of such a large party.

Weapons and tools needed to make repairs along the way were carried in cloth pockets affixed to the sides of the wagons. The royal ladies travelled in *palakis* lined with colourful silks edged in gold and they sipped on coconut water or chilled sherbet to take the edge off the blistering heat. Five treasure carts with their wheels chained together had an armed escort of formidable-looking troops of proven loyalty to deter even the most foolhardy and greedy of the bandits.

Kanchanadevi's thoughts were in the past, when she had fled Ajmer under perilous circumstances. Now she would make a triumphant return. It was the last journey she would undertake before it was time to meet her father on the other side. Maharaj Jaisingh would be so proud. And how mawkish she was getting in her old age!

Her daughter-in-law watched her circumspectly. Every movement of the palaki was hard on the grand old woman's weakened joints but she never once gave the faintest indication of the pain she must be feeling, holding herself proud and erect. Truly Maharaj Jaisingh's daughter was a legend and made of stern material. Karpuradevi had never thought that such a day would come when she would grow genuinely fond of the woman, who had once made her life hell. But now she only remembered the valuable lessons she had generously and painstakingly been taught on how to be a king's mother. And wife, though even she would admit that it was the one thing she had not learnt very well.

Her heart was full of mixed feelings as she looked out for a glimpse of her son. Prithvi was astride his favourite horse and from where she sat he looked tiny but there was no mistaking his painstakingly polished armour. She sensed his excitement and her heart lifted, filled with so much love for this special son of hers, it hurt a little.

Maharaj Someshwar was inspecting the armed troops gathered at the outskirts to escort him back to Ajmer. There were 40,000 foot soldiers, each division carrying its own flag and insignia, wearing the traditional heavy armour and helmets. The 5000-strong cavalry flanked them on either side.

They were all brave men and fierce fighters. 'When they are not performing feats of valour on the battlefield, they are in training for battle,' Senapati Sinhabala told his new king. 'You will find they have incredible stamina and are capable of travelling long distances on minimal rations and bearing extreme temperatures with equanimity, sire!'

The procession wound its way northward through the countryside. Prithvi was thoroughly enamoured of the landscape. He was having the time of his life, seeming to have overthrown the darkness that would sometimes enshroud his spirit. Hari and Jaya were by his side as he paused to observe and comment on almost every village, shrine and local attraction they passed by. For him and his companions, this was their first trip out of Gurjardesa and they were enchanted by the little temples that cropped up frequently by the wayside, the swaying stalks in the fields that dotted the countryside and the thorny scrub.

Though Prithvi had been schooled on the history of the Chahamanas, Pandit Padmanabh was convinced that no teacher employed by the Chalukyans could do justice to their rich heritage and felt there was a gaping hole in his education. He took it upon himself to enlighten the young prince about his roots. 'Vasudeva, who was of divine birth, is said to be the first ruler of Shakambari, what you now know as Sapadalaksha territory. The Sambhar salt lake, which sustained so many generations of his people, was gifted to him by Lord Vishnu in recognition of the services of his ancestors, who had emerged from the Agnikula at Mount Abu to rid mother earth of the *daitya* menace.

'Among the early rulers of Shakambari, Vakpathiraja-I proved his mettle by remaining undefeated in as many as 108 battles,' the pandit said expansively. 'He gave the imperial Pratiharas and the Rashtrakutas a taste of Chauhan might and humbled their pride. Vigraharaj-II is a personal favourite of mine and the title "Khurarajondhakara" was bestowed on him in honour of his unmatched valour after he crushed the spine of the Chalukyans. Even now his name is enough to give nightmares to the people of Gurjardesa!

'His nephew Govindaraja-III took after him and it is with pride that we can claim that it was a Chauhan who was the only one who had the temerity to prevail against Mahmud of Ghazni. They called Govindaraja, "Vairigharatta" because he ground his enemies to dust!'

'And because the ladies he had taken to bed ground their teeth in frustration every time he took his pleasure with them . . .' Nahar murmured to his companions leaving them guffawing.

The pandit shot them a reproving glare before launching into a long story about the pious queen Rudrani, who was acclaimed as 'Atma Prabha' after she successfully lit thousands of lamps with her yogic powers. 'Jaya! When you write her story, if you do not wish your reader to fall asleep, be sure to mention how she lit fires in the loins of her admirers!' Kanak whispered.

'There were a few bad apples in the history of the Chauhans. You know about Jaggadeva but there were others. Bisala was stricken with a deadly disease when he violated the chastity of a good woman. He died vomiting blood and with his body covered in festering sores and pus-filled boils!' Padmanabh informed them.

Noting with satisfaction the expression on their faces, he continued, 'Prithviraj-I was a fine example of everything a good king should be and I have no doubt that you will follow in his footsteps, my prince!'

Noting the ingratiating look on his face with amusement, Jaya commented, 'I have no doubt Padhri and Nahar will follow in the footsteps of Bisala and die of some unspeakable disease!' Padhri looked like he wanted to punch him but restrained himself when he saw Prithvi's warning glare. Instead he vented his feelings by aiming a kick stealthily at the pandit's horse and felt better when the beast bolted, taking the esteemed personage, screaming till he was blue in the face, on a wild gallop, sending the boys into paroxysms of laughter.

Galvanized by the pandit's tales, Prithvi decided to visit the sites of battle and temples raised by his ancestors by taking the circuitous and long route to Ajmer.

Someshwar balked even more than Pandit Padmanabh at the suggestion. 'There are too many dacoits in these parts who seem to do nothing but prey on travellers. It would never do for a prince of the realm to spill his blood so wastefully at the hands of n'er-do-wells!'

Besides, if anything happened to Prithvi or Hari, he was not sure he had the time or inclination to make any more worthy heirs.

Kanchanadevi was more amenable to the idea. 'It will be very educational no doubt and it will do Prithvi good to see for himself the kingdom he will someday inherit as well as his subjects. Provided you make arrangements for a contingent of guards to see to his safety, there is no reason he shouldn't go.'

The new king had never won an argument with his mother and his improved status did nothing to change that record. He gave in with ill grace and made a proclamation before his ministers. 'The prince wishes to familiarize himself with the Sapadalaksha territory and after due consideration, I have decided to permit him to do so. It will be very educational, I am sure, and he will go on a tour of the kingdom on my behalf and will resume his studies upon his return.'

Even Someshwar was somehow mollified when he beheld the joy that lit up Prithvi's face, spreading like sunshine and lifting the spirits of everyone around. He hated how much he envied his son his easy charm but there was no denying that it was there.

Kadambavas, a man vouchsafed for by Mahamantri Sallakshanapal, together with a selection of handpicked soldiers, would accompany Prithviraj and his companions on their adventure.

He was a middle-aged man but already the hair above his temples was showing a touch of grey. Quiet and taciturn, everything about him, from his piercingly dark eyes and muscular arms to his neatly trimmed beard, bespoke supreme competence. It was small wonder that it was being said that Kadambavas would replace Sallakshanapal as the mahamantri soon. Even Kanchanadevi had been impressed. She had taken one look at him and decided that he must accompany the prince on his jaunt across Sapadalaksha.

Their first stop was Kantha Fort, located atop a hill. It was the only one within 200 miles of Anhilwara Patan. It was the scene of a great Chauhan victory over the Chalukyan Mularaj. Prithvi remembered that memorable day in the treasury when Uncle Kanha had told them about the bloody history between his ancestors and the Chalukyans.

Kadambavas tended to keep to himself but Prithvi sought him out while the others were exploring.

'It was Vigraharaj-II who took the attack to the Chalukyas,' Kadambavas replied to his barrage of questions, 'and Mularaj fled, barricading himself behind the doors of Kantha Fort. He was hoping that since it was Navratri, Vigraharaj would be forced to return to the shores of Sambhar lake with his troops to offer worship to his family deity. But the king chose instead to build a shrine to goddess Asapuri at Bhrgukachchha, thus fulfilling his religious duties as well as continuing with the siege. Finally, Mularaj had no choice but to approach Vigraharaj in person and negotiate a peace treaty.'

Together they circled around the fort, taking in the main entrance with its arch, the watch stations, deep moat and brackets for torches. It seemed formidable but a closer look made Prithvi realize that parts of the walls were in ruins and the jungle growth was creeping over it, reclaiming stone and mortar.

'But that wasn't the first time a cowardly Chalukyan ruler had sought refuge in Kantha,' Kadambavas went on. 'When Mahmud of Ghazni blazed through this way, with his camels and cavalry moving so fast people thought they were the daityas come back for vengeance, Bhimdev-I hid in the fort while his capital city and subjects burned. There was virtually no resistance as Mahmud made his way to the great Somnath temple. Did you know that there were no troops there to repel his advance? There were thousands of Brahmins, dancers, musicians and devotees though . . .'

'Tell me what happened,' Prithvi demanded with morbid fascination. 'Why is Somnath alone considered a tragedy of such epic proportions? Guruji told me that Mahmud of Ghazni had swarmed over Punjab and destroyed the famous Kangra temple, helping himself to the treasure of the Shahis that was stored there. Mathura, on the banks of Yamuna, where thousands of pilgrims go daily hoping to draw closer to Krishna, met with the same fate. They say that the extent of booty plundered during his incursions amounts to thousands of kilos in gold, silver and precious stones. If that were not bad enough, he didn't let a single temple, city or even hut he rode past alone, burning it all down.

'Your guru seems to be a thorough man but he did leave out a few things,' Kadambavas said with uncharacteristic feeling. 'In addition to rubble, he left behind more dead bodies than could be counted and these included children and babies. Mahmud took with him not just all the wealth he could get his avaricious paws on but tens of thousands of slaves of both sexes and elephants. More importantly, he took our pride and left behind nothing but shame!'

He had fallen silent, so Prithvi prompted him, 'Tell me about Somnath . . .'

'What is there to say? The devotees placed their faith in the lingam, screaming themselves hoarse, and cried themselves a river of tears, begging the three-eyed god to despatch the demon hordes to Yama's abode. But he must have been preoccupied with making love to his wife or meditating or dancing the *tandav* while his devotees were butchered in droves. They say that Mahmud personally stripped the stone lingam gilded in gold bare before smashing it to smithereens. The pieces were then taken to Ghazni and added to the steps of a mosque so our sacred relics may be trod on forever . . . I am not a religious man as you may have noticed but nevertheless, it makes my blood boil.'

'I have heard of that lingam . . .' Prithvi said. 'They say it was a marvel of the known world, that it appeared to be floating in mid-air with no support from above or below and those who had the fortune to lay eyes upon it were truly blessed. What happened to Mahmud of Ghazni?' He was hoping that the man had died in agony. Slowly.

Kadambavas shrugged. 'You would think he got his comeuppance and he probably did. But it does not matter . . . in his country he is most certainly considered a hero. I am told he was very liberal when it came to distributing the wealth he stole. He built a magnificent capital city full of palaces, museums, places of learning, temples to his god and luxurious baths paved with marble for his people. That was nearly a century and a half ago. The Ghaznavid empire is no more, reduced to dust and rubble by conquerors more savage and bloodthirsty than Mahmud. The wrath of our gods and the curses called upon his head by his victims, both from here and elsewhere, seem to have caught up with him and his descendants and they disappeared screaming into the bowels of hell. Do you get satisfaction from the fate that overtook him, prince?'

'It is only the extraordinarily foolish who derive satisfaction from wanton destruction even if it is at the expense of one's enemies,' Prithvi replied. 'None of the things we lost were restored. But that said, there is one fact alone which provides a small measure of comfort . . .'

'What is that?' Kadambavas enquired with genuine curiosity.

'No matter how saddened I am by the unfortunate events of the past or with the shortcomings of the people of aryavarta, I am nevertheless proud of their ability to pick up the pieces of their shattered self-esteem, move on and find a way to survive. And no matter how much pain and humiliation we were subjected to, a hundred and fifty years later it doesn't sting as badly. Though we still remember and grieve, which is as it should be, life still goes on, doesn't it? And it will go on, long after our actions cease to matter.'

Kadambavas looked at him as if he was seeing him for the first time. 'That is a fine way of looking at it, yuvaraj.' He picked up his spear, raised it in salute and walked away. He did not say anything aloud, but Prithvi grinned when he heard his thoughts, clear as day. *Damn it all! This is the bastard who could win it all back for us or the moron who could lose everything.* It was hard to be offended with an honest man.

Prithvi and his companions never forgot that grand adventure. They rode their horses up the slopes of Mount Abu—the mountain of wisdom and home of the gods. Pandit Padmanabh had told them in his singularly dry manner about the demons, giants, monsters, beautiful apsaras and holy men who lived there. Bharadwaj had told them about it as well.

The people on these summits were wild and unrestrained, with bristly hair and bushy brows, armed with bamboo bows and arrows. However, they were warm and hospitable folk and offered them thick mares' milk. They even invited them into their humble homes to share a hot meal. Later, they brought mules to take them up the steep slopes. Prithvi insisted they be richly compensated and they blessed him, assuring the young prince that they would always include him in their prayers.

Prithvi caught the sardonic expression on Kadambavas' face. 'The goodwill of the people counts for something, doesn't it?'

'All I know, prince, is that the road to damnation is usually paved with good intentions . . .' That made Prithvi smile. He liked Kadambavas. He did not believe in mincing words when he uttered them. 'Besides, I couldn't help thinking that dacoits have slit throats for a lot less!'

Prithvi frowned. 'Robbers are men without honour and I will not suffer their presence in my kingdom! They will be rounded up and put to death immediately if not sooner. It is more than what they deserve.'

Kadambavas did not doubt it. The prince had quite the temper.

Majestic trees loomed over them. The air was crisp and bracing. Mist descended on them at times and they spurred their mounts to rush into its chilly embrace. They sat around a fire at night telling each other scary stories while Kadambavas and his men patrolled the neighbourhood.

'We were all meant to find each other,' Jaya began solemnly, after Kanak had wound up his tale about an evil spirit who used the guise of an attractive woman to lure young men into the woods and sucked out their blood through the male organ, leaving only the desiccated husk behind. 'In a former life, Prithvi's father abandoned his mother who was pregnant, allowing himself to be ensnared by the wiles of a sorceress. She maintained her youth and strength by dining on the flesh of newborns and convinced her husband to do the same. The wielder of black magic was eagerly waiting to partake of the life in the queen's womb. Kill two birds with one stone as it were.

'But the child she was carrying was a fierce one and imbued his mother with his own unstoppable ferocity. In the dead of night, she slew her rival and husband both, stripped off her clothes and bathed in their hearts' blood, singing and dancing with wild ecstasy. Her companions gathered the blood and imbibed it, believing it to be sanctified by her touch. They believed that she was an avenging goddess who had destroyed the evil that had nearly engulfed them. Immediately, they became impregnated and brought forth the brave samants who would protect the life of the divine child, forever more.'

Prithvi imagined the look on his mother's face when informed about her naked and bloodthirsty shenanigans in a former life and had to suppress the urge to laugh. No one else was laughing though and he could have sworn that Padhri had tears in his eyes while Kanak and Nahar looked solemn as priests performing an arcane ritual. They never forgot the story. And till their last days, Prithvi's companions retold it to all who would listen, provided they were far away from Maharaj Someshwar's presence, insisting that it was nothing but the whole truth.

As they journeyed farther, they saw many beautiful temples of the Hindu and Jain faith. Prithvi took an immense liking to a small rock temple dedicated to a strange goddess with an unpronounceable name. She reportedly fed her devotees with blood that oozed from her nipples. The temple itself was carved from the rock on the face of the mountain, surrounded by charming champa trees, and could be accessed only via the steps that had been hewn from the rocky terrain.

They visited the spot known as Agnikund, the fiery pit from which the four foremost Kshatriya clans had emerged.

The ascent was steep and it was a tortuous climb. But it seemed fitting for such a hallowed spot and they climbed up the rocky face like mountain goats.

Prithvi could feel the mountain breathing beneath his hands and hear the violent vibrations as its belly rumbled with an awful, insatiable hunger. When they approached the old stone basin, they saw that it was filled with the digested remains of every meal consumed by the fire god, Agni. They stood among the smouldering remains, overwhelmed by the splendour and the divine power they bore witness to.

Prithvi left the others behind to lean over a ridge and look into the depths below. The evening sky seemed to reflect the grand yagnas held in the days of yore. All around them were lofty peaks—Achalgarh, Shikar muni, Gaumukh and Dilwara—that seemed to reach up to the sky, slashing its cottony underbelly and splashing its scarlet blood across the clouds.

Jaya caught up with him. 'It was at this very spot that the Brahmins prayed to Shiva and Vishnu to rescue them from the outrages perpetuated by the daityas, since the warriors of the Kshatriya race were no longer around to protect them. Parashurama, an avatar of Vishnu, had vowed to exterminate them after one of the race had killed his father. Hara and Hari paid heed to the prayers of the Brahmins and combining their powers with Brahma, the supreme trinity brought forth from the sacrificial flames the four—Paramar, Chauhan, Chalukya and Pratihara. Together, they slew the daityas and then they went forth and were fruitful. It marked the rebirth of the Kshatriyas.'

They spent some more time there. The others wanted to take a look at a slab of granite housing the impress of Vishnu's feet housed in a cave temple. Prithvi preferred to stay where he was, looking down from his seat on the lofty summit, taking in the sweeping grandeur and serenity of all things in nature. It was Kadambavas who approached him in that quiet, unobtrusive manner of his. 'So what exactly did you think of the famous story of the origin of the Kshatriyas?'

'It does not matter what I think. You wished to come here and the question is whether you believe any of it . . .' Kadambavas replied, 'I was born in more humble circumstances. But there are some things I learnt growing up. One of them is that irrespective of his origins, the contents of every man's voided bowels stink as bad as everyone else's. Which is not to say that anybody is exempt from experiencing the pleasures many are foolish enough to believe are reserved entirely for the gods and the pain that is supposed to be the lot of the mortals. In case you are wondering about the specifics . . .'

'The former involves food, alcohol and women, not necessarily in that order, and the latter includes dying and an overflowing chamber pot!' Prithvi finished for him, with a full-throated chuckle. 'As for me, sometimes I believe and sometimes I don't. But I do know one thing for certain, of the fire-born, the Chauhans have always been the bravest and it is my intention to be the bravest of them all.' Prithvi knew Kadambavas believed that words were wind, but he would show them all!

The memorable journey made by the merry band passed by in a happy blur. They made it all the way to the Triveni Sangamam, the legendary spot that marked the confluence of the Ganga, Yamuna and the subterranean river, Saraswati. It was the very place where Durlabharaja-I had dipped his sword following his conquest of Gauda. They shoved Padhri in to cleanse him of his sins before jumping in themselves.

Their next stop was the temple of the Shakambhari family deity, Harshanatha, raised by Govindaraja-I. Since then, every

Chauhan had made it a point to make his own contribution to the hallowed spot with the result that the temple was a thing of beauty. Every inch of the stone edifices was covered with gold shells and intricate carvings depicting gods, demons, kings, warriors and dancing damsels so beautiful the boys couldn't resist touching their voluptuous curves. Through an arched doorway, they entered a spacious hall with life-size statues of the Pandavas and their brother-turned-enemy Karna. Prithvi stood in front of Arjuna trying to memorize every detail of his noble countenance.

'Art is tricky,' he told Jaya, 'and deceptive. The sculptor has captured so much detail that you can almost feel the breath of the Pandava hero on your face but then the illusion lifts. Wouldn't it be something if the statue contained within itself a small portion of the man he had once been? I would have liked to sit down and simply talk with him . . .'

The resident deities—a four-faced lingam, Vishnu, Brahma and Savitri—wore the finest garments and exquisite jewellery of real gold and precious stones. When the head priest got wind of their presence, he performed an elaborate puja asking the gods to shower blessings on the scions of the Chahamanas.

As they were leaving, the boys were assaulted by an *ikkhanika*. 'She speaks with the voice of god,' the head priest murmured to Prithvi. 'It has been months since we have laid eyes upon her for she spends all her time meditating in those caves yonder. Your divine tejas must have drawn her to you.'

Her act, if it was one, was very convincing. There was something feral, almost animalistic about her. She spun around like one possessed as convulsions wracked her body and her limbs contorted at impossible angles even as her female attendants tried to hold her down. Only the whites of her eyes were visible . . . It was quite the spectacle.

'*Vasumati* . . .' she shrieked in an unearthly voice. 'The earth mother has chosen you! Remain faithful to her and she will reward you with fame and victory beyond your wildest dreams!' By then the ikkhanika was out of control, frothing at the mouth and rolling on the floor, ripping her garments and scratching deep furrows into her face. Throwing her arms around Prithvi's legs, she held them tight, while words poured out of her in a wild, incoherent torrent, '*Buried treasure* . . . Take it! The goddess left it for youuuuu . . . only youuu . . . But beware, Prithviraj Chauhan! Her love alone is pure . . . the others . . . they will betray you . . . be the death of you!'

Prithvi may have been carved out of stone, so still and silent was he. All around, his companions stood frozen in shock. Kanak, who had once faced the charge of a tigress without blinking, looked positively petrified. Kadambavas placed his hand on the hilt of his sword. The slow movement caught the eye of the ikkhanika and she launched herself at him, throwing her arms around his waist. 'You too! A woman will be the death of you! Betrayal!' She went on ululating and prancing around, beating her chest with clenched fists as if to put out the fire there. And then she fell into a dead swoon.

When they rode towards Ajmer, past the dense woods and thick cover of vegetation and thorny trees, which had formerly deterred the advance of the Chalukyas under Maharaj Kumarpal, Prithviraj felt his heart soar. The capital city of the Chahamanas was beautiful and the citizens had turned out en masse to welcome their young prince, scattering rose petals and showering the procession with rose water. They were delighted to note that he was incredibly handsome and rode his horse masterfully.

Prithviraj fell deeply in love for the first time in his young life. It was clear that a great deal of love and care had been lavished on the city. His city. Thousands of people belonging to various races had laboured endlessly over it. The painstaking effort showed. The fort itself was massive with formidable-looking walls, turrets and deep moats filled with crocodiles.

Architects and builders renowned for their work had created marvels and the city shone like a brilliant gemstone. The Chahamanas were patrons of art and there were fine displays from the best sculptors in the land in the palaces, temples and parks across the city. Only the most talented weavers had been employed for the carpets, drapes and tapestries. The frescoes and murals lovingly installed by painters at the zenith of their talent were truly fit for the gods. They depicted scenes from the Ramayana and the Mahabharata, focusing on heroic deeds, romance and the code of chivalry the Kshatriyas were expected to follow.

Rare species of exotic blooms were in abundance in fountains and pools in the garden city. Kadambavas pointed out the finer features of Anasagar, the artificial lake eight miles in circumference with its decorated tunnels and sluiceways, which had been Ajayraj's pet project to ensure a steady water supply in the arid land. It was situated past a vast embankment between two hillocks, Bajrang Garh and Khobra Bherun, and two magnificent palaces rested on its shores.

Eager to emulate his grandfather, Vigraharaj-IV had built Vishalsagar lake, which was equally splendid. On its banks stood fascinating creatures carved in stone that sent forth jets of water from their mouths. 'Artists are silly creatures . . .' Nahar commented, 'another orifice would be far more suitable for conveying piddling streams of water.'

'I am pleased to note that the capital city has exceeded your expectations, prince!' Kadambavas murmured, ignoring Nahar's juvenile wit. 'What would you consider its most arresting feature?'

'I like that there are temples as well as *viharas* of equal magnificence. In fact, I noticed this particular feature in nearly every part of the kingdom,' came Prithvi's somewhat obscure reply.

'As you know, prince, your ancestors were staunch devotees of the three-eyed god but they have always been accepting of those who belong to other faiths. In fact those Jain viharas you noticed were built by Maharaj Ajayraj and later by Maharaj Vigraharaj-IV. The latter even used to participate in their religious ceremonies and out of deference to their practices forbade the killing of animals on the special occasions observed by those practising Jainism,' Kadambavas told him.

'Maharaj Jaisingh and Kumarpal were equally tolerant in Gurjardesa. And I will always strive to emulate them. If we can live so peaceably with the Jains then perhaps the day is not far when a similar rapport could be established with the Mussulmen.'

The idealism of the young never failed to depress Kadambavas. 'The Jains are not guilty of inhuman behaviour that includes plundering, razing and torching our temples and cities, torturing, raping, maiming and slaughtering our people . . .'

'Mahmud of Ghazni and his soldiers believed that our gods were demons and as their followers we were evil.' The prince had the dreamy cast he sometimes had. 'They felt their actions were perfectly justified because it was in keeping with *their* religious beliefs. Hopefully, the day will never come when we forget the wisdom of our ancestors and start seeing evil in others, prompting us to destroy the things dear to them.'

An army of palace attendants descended on them just then. Prithvi was to refresh himself immediately, pay his respects to his father and join his mother and grandmother.

Clasping Kadambavas's hand warmly, Prithvi thanked him and bid his farewell before departing.

'He will be a marvellous king,' Jaya opined in the rapturous tone of a love-struck girl. 'You think he is just a boy, but if the man he becomes is half as good-hearted as the boy he is, he will still be twice as great as any other ruler before him.'

To his surprise, Kadambavas found himself agreeing with the budding poet's exaggerated paean of praise. Over the last few days, he had grown rather fond of the moody youngster with the ebullient spirit. There was no denying that Prithviraj Chauhan had a noble heart but his passions ran deep, and when faced with marauding Mussulmen, there was little doubt that he would cast his lofty notions aside and drive them back to their hellholes with his spear lodged up their bungholes. Hope was always a fine thing. Till life and fate both shat on it.

9

Prithvi found it hard to believe that they were both gone. Maharaj Kumarpal had been the first to go. His health had been declining for a long time but he would not listen to his physicians who had the temerity to suggest that he spend a few weeks under their supervision, following a strict diet to cleanse his system, take medicated steam baths and get his body massaged with healing oils. They promised him that he would live for another hundred years if he was willing to place himself entirely in their care.

'I have lived a warrior's life—training, fighting, enduring the hardships of campaign. A man sees terrible things on a battlefield and his slumber is plagued with nightmares. And yet I would trade this life for nothing, not even for a crown and a kingdom. A warrior I was born and as a warrior I will die!

'The next man to suggest I subsist on goat feed and pamper myself with smelly oils and massages like a courtesan will be summarily executed!' he had thundered.

Maharaj Kumarpal's wish was granted. He spent his last days on the campaign trail, putting young warriors to shame with the skill he evinced while wielding his weapons. When the old warrior's heart finally gave out, they said it was while he was resisting attempts to evade arrest when Ajaypal, a distant relative of his, made a grab for power, tired of waiting for the old king to die.

Maharaj Jaisingh and Kumarpal had between them ushered in a glorious era for Gurjardesa and for nearly eight decades their subjects had thrived under their just rule. But after Kumarpal's death, violence rocked the land, even as his subjects mourned the loss of the king they had loved wholeheartedly.

Kumarpal's grandson Pratapamalla, born to his daughter, was brutally murdered by unknown assailants. One of Ajaypal's first decisions as the new king was to have his predecessor's minister, the virtuous Yashpal, and the famous Jain teacher Hemachandra's successor, executed, thereby undoing the peaceable effects of years of religious tolerance that had been the policy in Chalukyan territory. Unrest boiled over in the kingdom as Jain monks were persecuted and their places of worship torn down.

The news reached Sapadalaksha. Maharaj Someshwar delivered the news to his mother personally. 'At least, his life ended on his terms. It would have been worse if someone of his stature were to spend his last days in chains, languishing in a dungeon. Mark my words, the days of that scoundrel Ajaypal, who is already undoing the good work of my father and Maharaj Kumarpal, are numbered. When death comes for him, he will see the will of Yama enforced in the most violent manner imaginable!'

Kanchanadevi was trembling. Someshwar knew that it was not on account of age and infirmity but rage. 'Maharaj Kumarpal was the best of kings, Mother, and I owe a considerable debt to him!' he said somewhat awkwardly.

Kanchanadevi nodded and indicated that her son should leave. It had taken Maharaj Kumarpal's death to wrest a noble sentiment from her son. She supposed she ought not to be so harsh on him but he persisted in being a crushing disappointment. It bothered her no end that Someshwar did not possess the military genius and acumen his half-brother, the Sadhava woman's son, had been blessed with. In the early days, Someshwar had done his best and in campaigns against Gwalior, Hissar and Sarhind, he had acquitted himself reasonably well. However, these skirmishes did not do much towards expanding the kingdom.

It could have been worse, Kanchanadevi thought to herself. Nowadays he spent all his time wooing and marrying the young daughters of his feudatories and making a royal fool of himself. It was only a matter of time before one of his many wives cuckolded him and produced an 'heir' to rival Prithvi's claim to the throne. Not that it bothered her: if she were alive she would have such abominations taken care of immediately. If she weren't, it did not matter that much. She had trained Karpuradevi well. It pleased her that she had taken the callow girl, who had wept herself into a hysterical frenzy at the prospect of allowing her husband to take his conjugal rights with her, and transformed her into a queen. She had made her into someone who could manipulate and intrigue with the most nefarious and devious of power-hungry courtiers.

Prithvi came from Pushkar, where he was continuing his studies, to see his grandmother when he heard the news. She was pleased to see him and insisted that he dine with her. Belatedly, she noticed that Hariraj was there too and invited him to join in as well.

'I am sure you haven't had a decent meal in ages!' she groused, piling his plate high with food enough for three people. 'Some of these new-fangled notions about the merits of vegetarianism drive me to distraction! Maharaj Kumarpal used to argue with his Jain teacher that the dietary habits of a goat are hardly suitable for a Kshatriya warrior in training. It was the only point they disagreed upon, but I support his view entirely. A growing boy needs meat, eggs and milk!'

She rolled her eyes when he patted his emerging moustache meaningfully. 'You could live to be a thousand and you will still be a boy to me, so don't you give me any of that attitude, Prithviraj Chauhan! Have you paid your respects to the king, your father?'

Prithvi nodded, chewing his way through a mouthful of food. 'Yes grandmother, I did see him but he seemed rather busy.' He threw his younger brother a look, which his grandmother did not miss. Someshwar had been hopelessly drunk and was toying with the breasts of an indecently young female when he had received his sons.

On their way out, Prithvi and Hari argued over whether it was one of his umpteen new wives or new concubines. She had tossed an inviting look at Prithvi and his loins had responded immediately, so he was convinced she was a trained bed-slave. He was still thinking about that when his grandmother cleared her throat.

'Maharaj Kumarpal was one of the best men I knew, grandmother,' he told her sincerely, 'Hari and I used to mimic his mannerisms in the hope of becoming like him one day.' Kanchanadevi brightened up immediately.

'He was very fond of you . . .' she informed him, 'and it pleased me that he always treated you like the great king you were born to be. The greatest this land will ever see.'

Prithvi rolled his eyes at that and pushed his plate aside. Kanchanadevi wondered what had happened to put him in such a sour mood. 'Your mother must have been very happy to see you . . .' she began.

'Mother was meeting with an important trade delegation,' Prithvi told her. 'I am to see her later tonight. Apparently, the king is indisposed and mother is taking care of things.' He said it all with supreme nonchalance but the tiniest of frowns marred his perfect features.

Ah! So that was it, she mused triumphantly to herself. While her daughter-in-law had surprisingly turned out to be less of a disappointment than she had originally thought her to be, the truth was that she tried to do too much. Still, if it hadn't been for her and Kadambavas, administration would have ground to a standstill a long time ago, given that her son was otherwise occupied on most days.

She had warned Karpuradevi about this and it served her right for not paying heed. In his boyhood, she had doted on her firstborn excessively. He had been the beginning and end of her world. But now she was unable or unwilling to give him the same attention. Governing the kingdom took up all her time and she threw herself into it, intoxicated with the power, prestige and respect it had won her. Now, not even her precious son could give her the same satisfaction and when he responded with hurt at the negligence, Karpuradevi buried herself in even more work. Women these days simply had no idea about moderation.

'I have always meant to ask you, grandmother . . .' Prithvi's troubled voice broke into her thoughts. 'Why is it that you don't seem to care much for Uncle Kanha?'

Kanchanadevi was startled. Sometimes it was hard to know exactly what was going on in that head of his. 'Kanha?' she replied thoughtfully, 'he is a good boy and dutiful. Always has been and always will be.'

'Then why don't you like him?' Prithvi persisted.

'Everybody else likes him well enough,' Kanchanadevi told him exasperatedly. 'From the moment he was born, people started fussing over him because he was better-looking and more likeable than poor Someshwar. It was hard enough on my firstborn to grow up in the shadow of my father and later Maharaj Kumarpal, and then Kanha and Vigraharaj came along. Their achievements outshone his and it took its toll on Someshwar. Why, even Someshwar's wife and children get on better with Kanha! It fell to me to make amends for all this.'

Prithvi and Hari exchanged another look and she spoke to Prithvi sternly, 'Concentrate on your education, young man.

The future of Sapadalaksha is in your hands. Don't waste your time fretting over inanities and the endless stupidity your near and dear ones are engaged in. By obsessing over the never-ending propensity your flesh and blood have for engaging in foolish behaviour, you risk becoming a fool yourself.'

He grinned when he heard that, a sudden smile that brightened every inch of her large, airy chambers and her heart grew warm. 'There is no risk of that ever happening! For I am Kanchanadevi's grandson!' he told her with genuine feeling.

The stern matriarch waited till Prithvi had taken her blessings and left. Only then did she allow herself to cry. For the first and the only time in her long life.

It was the very last time Prithvi saw her alive.

Karpuradevi had hoped to see her son later that night but he had left for Pushkar after dining with his grandmother. It bothered her that he had left without saying goodbye. Had she hurt his feelings by being so preoccupied with affairs of the state? But somebody had to take care of the kingdom that would one day be his, while his father buried his head in every pair of pillowy tits that presented themselves when not trying to drown in liquor! Surely, Prithvi understood that?

Karpuradevi grew increasingly agitated. She had wanted to tell Prithvi that she was so proud of him. He was doing very well indeed in Pushkar, even better than he had under Guru Bharadwaj. Pandit Padmanabh placed a lot of emphasis on the fine arts and cultures, which she felt would balance his martial inclinations beautifully. Perhaps she should suggest that spiritual learning be incorporated into his syllabus, but if she were to do so, Pandit Padmanabh would listen with exquisite manners before doing exactly as he pleased. Sometimes, she hated all men equally. The mothers were to blame, of course!

She remembered the flash of temper that had flared up from the depths of Prithvi's eyes when she had failed to attend to him immediately, moments before he had bowed formally and taken his leave. Her heart had broken a little when she realized belatedly that the anger was directed at her, his mother! Surely he knew that she loved him so much that her heart and even the entire universe could not contain the full measure of it?

'When I grow up, the first thing I am going to do is marry you!' he used to say when he was just a wee boy. 'There is no one as beautiful, good and kind as my mother!'

His words had made her so happy! 'I am sure he will feel exactly the same way when he grows up and notices that his mother has become a toothless old crone!' Kanchanadevi had remarked irately.

Tears rolled down her cheeks and she wiped them hurriedly as Kanha entered the room. 'He is no longer your baby,' he told her kindly. 'Prithviraj is almost a man. And you no longer have the luxury of devoting all your time and thoughts to him. When he inherits a kingdom that you rescued from falling into a complete shambles, he will thank you.'

'You give me far too much credit,' Karpuradevi demurred. 'The credit goes entirely to our new Mahamantri Kadambavas. He is so clever and capable. I always feel like a bumbling child next to him, but he is a patient teacher. And you are nothing short of a godsend for the Chahamanas! Why, you are the reason we are not facing ruination even as we speak!'

'I suppose you are referring to the fact that I dissuaded my brother from waging war with the Chalukyas and their King Ajaypal?' Kanha stroked his beard absentmindedly. It was looking untidy. He needed a wife to take better care of him, Karpuradevi thought to herself. Most men did.

Kanha, meanwhile, was thinking about the unpleasant conversation he had had with his brother on the subject. A lot of harsh words had been bandied about and the entire episode had left a bad taste in his mouth.

'Have you no gratitude?' his brother had bellowed at him. 'Ajaypal has disrespected Maharaj Kumarpal's memory and it behoves us to avenge the insult. Let us march and show the Chalukyas the full extent of Chauhan might!'

'We cannot meddle in the affairs of the Chalukyas just yet and for reasons of foolish sentiment at that,' he had replied tiredly. 'The territories subjugated by Vigraharaj are testing our strength and trying to break free. Dillika is also a cause for concern with supporters of the Tomars raising their voices against us. We need to strengthen our position here before you run off to make war!'

'Do you know what the people are saying,' he had raged, eyes bloodshot with alcohol and spittle spraying from his mouth. 'They are saying that I was a puppet king controlled by Maharaj Kumarpal and that I am in cahoots with the Chalukyas. Out of respect to the late king, I stayed my hand though such slander makes my blood boil. But I will not take it any more!'

'They say other things as well, brother . . .' Kanha told him quietly, 'rumours so vile and vicious it makes my blood boil but that is hardly reason enough to race off into an ill-advised war leaving our kingdom in Sapadalaksha to crumble into dust.'

On and on they had argued through the long reaches of the night with a lot of shouting and crystal goblets being smashed. But ultimately, Kanha had prevailed and his brother had left to drown his sorrows in wine and women. It was his brother's pet subject and the door had certainly not been closed on that particular issue.

Karpuradevi was looking intently at him and Kanha smiled in reassurance. 'I will visit Pushkar one of these days and have a talk with Prithvi. It is going to be all right. You will see.'

She nodded gratefully, resisting the urge to go galloping after him that very minute. She didn't know what she would do without Kanha. And Kadambavas. If only she had been a man! Life would have been so much simpler for everybody!

10

Prithvi was pleasantly surprised to see the two visitors who had come to see him at Pandit Padmanabh's gurukul at Pushkar. It was a small palace raised on the banks of the sacred lake, discreetly tucked some distance away from the shrines that tended to crop up nearly every day in that area. It was said that it was here that Brahma performed his famous yagna. Since it was in Sapadalaksha territory, the prevailing belief was that Vishnu had created the first Chauhan right there to dissuade the irksome daityas after discovering that the Paramars, Pratiharas and Chalukyas were simply not up to such a daunting task.

It had to be admitted that the place itself was truly beautiful. It had a tranquil quality to it despite being teeming with pilgrims, who swarmed over the lovely valley nestled between the hills to bathe in the ghats or to offer worship at the famous temples dedicated to Brahma, Vishnu and Mahadev. Thanks to the generosity of the Chahamanas kings, the famed temples had silver doors and marble archways. The idols and statues were carved by sculptors, who seemed to have instilled the life-giving creative force in their art, which in turn resulted in the faithful feeling as if they were showered with divine benediction.

His new teacher was engaging and Prithvi enjoyed their private sessions. He was taught the finer points of *anviksiki*, meant to sharpen his powers of reflection, *trayi* or Vedic knowledge and the subtle art of *dandaniti* or political science, including the seven ways of dealing with an enemy.

Pandit Padmanabh was a corpulent man and the rolls of fat gathered at various parts of his pudgy body was an ample indicator of his insatiable appetite for milk, ghee and sweets. 'My head is too small to contain the full extent of my knowledge and so my belly proved most obliging!' he was fond of saying while rubbing the vast expanse of his midriff with filial pride.

The pandit possessed an extraordinary intellect and his mental powers were second to none in all the land. In addition to his religious duties, he employed a vast network of informers, who had their eyes and ears everywhere. 'If a rival king so much as belches or farts, the pandit is the first to know,' Kadambavas had told Prithvi and the latter did not doubt it for a moment.

His partiality for dairy products aside, the pandit would not touch a drop of alcohol and practised the strictest celibacy. 'A man's natural gifts are almost always diluted and rendered ineffective when he is enslaved by the demands of a raging libido,' he had told Prithvi. 'But since you are a king, celibacy is not an option for you, which is why you must learn to cater to the needs of your body without ever overindulging in the pleasures of the boudoir.'

Pandit Padmanabh received a lot of visitors and his residence was usually teeming with activity. There were people from every walk of life—soldiers, devotees, perfumers, food vendors, travelling mendicants, nuns, monks, jewellers, smiths, musicians and dancers—traipsing in at all times.

The pandit's students, who were bound to practise celibacy for the duration of their studies, were particularly happy when the dancing girls arrived in droves at Pushkar during major religious occasions to dance at the temples with pure hearts and the ardour of devotion in honour of the gods. The thoughts of their observers were far from pure when they took to frequenting the temples in the hope of seeing them rehearse.

A lot of them were exceedingly young, so young that only the promise of perky breasts showed. Some were fully flowered with flawless skin and thick, long hair, which they wore plaited. All were lithe and agile with the slim, elegant arms and legs characteristic of a dancer's body as they went through the entire repertoire of their dance pieces with terpsichorean precision. Every single one of them was exquisite.

'They may have narrow waists but have you noticed that their hips are full and rounded? Rather like wine jars and every bit as intoxicating as the contents of one . . .' Nahar gave his expert opinion.

'And they have ample bottoms, every single one of them, probably to make up for their tiny bosoms . . .' Kanak added.

Prithvi was disinterested in the dancers. Their lengthy performances with the exaggerated mannerisms bored him to tears. Besides, he could barely see their faces under the elaborate make-up they wore. As for the heavily kohled-eyes, they could scare children senseless, he confided in Jaya. He felt his time was better employed riding his horse or elephant, practising his sword play or archery skills.

Jaya found his indifference worrisome. His mother had told him that the men who resisted the charms of women were usually the ones who loved too deeply and painfully when they eventually, inevitably succumbed.

Prithvi was pleased when Uncle Kanha and Kadambavas arrived at Pushkar. He was happy enough studying under the pandit who despite his ponderous bulk and laidback manner had an incredibly sharp mind that missed nothing. But his trip across the country had changed him and he found himself chafing at the bit when forced to submit to the rigours of his education. The restlessness was becoming more than he could bear.

On most days, he wanted nothing more than to take his horse and disappear into the vast beyond that summoned him, going wherever his wild and implacable spirit led him. No amount of training could diminish the intensity of the energies that were burning inside him. Even Hari and Jaya dared not approach him when he was in one of his stormy moods. During their intense training bouts, when his ardour was inflamed to unmanageable levels, his opponents swore they saw the intention to kill writ large in his eyes, even when the tip of his sword stopped just short of slicing a throat or severing an artery.

'The young lion wants to be let loose but it isn't time yet,' the pandit told Kanha and Kadambavas. 'There are times when his disposition is placid and he seems content to draw or paint, both of which he does extremely well it must be said. However, there is something of the savage and implacable warrior in him. We tried to expose him to the soothing effects of music, but he gets impatient.

'There is a lot he still needs to learn. That impossibly high energy he possesses need to be channelized in a constructive way. The prince needs to find his way forward and the path he takes must be one of noble purpose. He has to be trained to acquire the discipline that is needed to do this for himself. Once it is done, I would have succeeded in giving aryavarta its greatest ruler and finest warrior, blessed with the countenance of a god, a body honed to withstand the violence of war and a brilliant mind capable of envisioning a better future and taking his people there safely.'

'With you as his teacher, the prince will truly excel and achieve his true potential,' Kanha told the pandit, who beamed with pleasure. Kadambavas wasn't as effusive because he was thinking that it would be better for all of them if Padmanabh spent less time speechifying and more time actually teaching.

Prithvi talked the pandit into letting him accompany the two men who had undertaken a quick tour of inspection across the countryside to ascertain for themselves if Maharaj Someshwar's subjects were happy and to check that his officers were not enriching themselves at the expense of their king. Dressed as commoners in rough-spun clothes divested of insignia and ornaments, swords concealed beneath their robes, the three of them got ready to leave. Three small steeds and food supplies had been arranged for them. A small unit from the royal cavalry would follow them at a discreet distance.

They rode for several days, making their way deep into Sapadalaksha territory, spending the night in humble lodging houses for travellers, partaking of simple and traditional local dishes. Prithvi was all ears as Kadambavas explained the inner workings of the kingdom to him.

'You know the main cities and towns of the kingdom—Ajmer, Sambhar, Nagaur, Pushkar, Narena, Mandalgarh, Bijoliya and Rewasa. These come under the direct administration of the king and there are magistrates appointed for each of these divisions, the *vishayas*. The *jagirs* are the king's feudal lords and they are given choice territories in return for loyal service rendered. They are entitled to the taxes otherwise owed to the state. In return, they maintain the king's peace, pay an annual tribute and keep the army supplied with well-trained troops. The smaller villages irrespective of whether they come under the vishayas or the jagirs are allowed local self-governance—*grama sabhas* and *panchakulas*—under the control of officials appointed by the king.'

'As for the conquered territories such as Dillika, they are ruled by the *mandaleshwar*. They are usually the descendants of the deposed monarchs, who have sworn fealty to our king,' Kanha added.

At the frontiers of the kingdom were forts such as Hansi, Tabarindah, Samana and Saraswati, given to the care of trusted relatives of the king. They stopped at each of these, since the two men had business there to take care of. All the forts were manned by a garrison of troops stationed there permanently. As they were strategic points of entry into the kingdom, they had to be regularly checked and fortified.

To Prithvi's eyes, the fortresses seemed impregnable and superbly maintained. The soldiers stationed there were valiant and disciplined. When he remarked on this, Kadambavas nodded. 'The credit, of course, goes to Maharaj Vigraharaj. He had a gift for administration and battle strategy. My father was a part of his council and he told me that there wasn't a single detail he overlooked. The king made it his business to know everything happening in his land. They say he never forgot a name or a face.'

'Why did he leave the kingdom to Amaragangeya, who was barely out of the gurukul from what I hear, and disappear to parts unknown?' Prithvi wanted to know.

Exchanging a dark look with Kanha, Kadambavas told him, 'His trusted physician, Chakradatta, had diagnosed him with a mysterious ailment. Vigraharaj, who had survived so many battles where the odds were stacked against him, found his courage abandoning him when told that it was a disease that would take his life and not an enemy's spear. Unable to face the prospect of dying slowly and in great agony, losing control of his senses and having to be cared for like a child, the king decided to retire from courtly life and spend his last days in prayer and meditation.'

'But he outlived Amaragangeya, didn't he?' Prithvi pressed.

'Where did you hear that?' Kanha asked sharply.

Prithvi shrugged. 'Pandit Padmanabh's network of informers is even more extensive that Guru Bharadwaj's. Sometimes, when bored, I study the scrolls inscribed by his assistants, who keep a meticulous record of the reports.'

'What have you learned from them?' Kadambavas wanted to know.

'Only that words are unreliable . . .' Prithvi said flippantly. 'The pandit is very particular about confidentiality and it is not like him to put state secrets down in writing where any bored student can find them if he chooses to apply himself diligently. It is probably one of those elaborate tests he keeps designing for me but even so, if one reads between the lines, one may just get an insight into or catch a glimpse of the truth.'

They travelled for a few moments in silence. 'I also learned that my uncle took certain measures to ensure the safety of his person. Four handpicked men, known to be fanatically loyal, guarded him at all times. They were known to promptly kill anyone who overstepped the accepted distance deemed safe by them and asked questions only after the deed was done. Some of his more persistent enemies tried to have him poisoned, but he had his food and drink tasted before he went anywhere near them.' Prithvi seemed to be speaking to himself; he was looking straight ahead as he was riding and his companions strained to hear what he was saying.

'The pandit, who had dabbled in the healing arts himself, knows of certain illnesses that can be caused by creatures that are so small that they cannot be seen. They can jump from the body of a sick person to one in the prime of his health . . . Maharaj Vigraharaj's trusted physician certainly knew about it too, because he appears to have studied it extensively. Couple that with the fact that he attended to the slain Jaggadeva who extracted a promise from him in his dying moments and you realize that this presents an array of extremely interesting possibilities . . .'

Uncle Kanha looked agitated, Prithvi noted. It was hardly surprising. The man was a straight arrow and simply did not have the stomach for this manner of devious devilry. Kadambavas, on the other hand, was chuckling. A dangerous man, Prithvi mused to himself. There was more information he had gleaned about Maharaj Vigraharaj's life and death but it would never do to be too forthcoming with sensitive information. However, someday Prithvi resolved to get in touch with that mysterious sect who lived among the Khokars.

The weather was clement and a light breeze had sprung up. Prithvi enjoyed the feel of it in his hair, which was unbound by the turban Kanha and Kadambavas wore. Entire tracts of land had been devoted to agriculture. As the three riders rode past fields with swaying stalks of wheat, barley, jowar and bajra, they could hear the field hands singing as they worked. Mostly they were folk songs with funny words and often cruel bits of doggerel about the members of royalty who lived off the fat of the land and the blood and sweat of the people.

'Clearly these people don't think the Chahamanas kings are gods sent to make their lives easier!' Prithvi observed drily.

'If you toiled endlessly in the field under the unforgiving sun, from the day you are old enough to hold a sickle to the day you die, yet barely made enough to keep body and soul together, you wouldn't think highly of those you blame for your predicament either,' Kadambavas replied.

'If they work so hard, why is it that they have so little to show for it?' Prithvi wanted to know as he looked at their listless faces and bony, emaciated frames. Some of the smaller children were playing under the trees. They were practically naked, so threadbare were their clothes: little urchins who rolled in the mud and wiped their noses on their arms.

'Because they have to pay taxes for the land on which they raise the crops,' Kadambavas replied. 'Because they have to borrow money to buy the seeds and equipment needed for a rich harvest, which thanks to the criminally high interest rates charged by unscrupulous moneylenders eats into whatever little they make. Because the *talarakshas* will whip them bloody if they don't pay up the taxes and the hired grunts of the moneylenders will beat them to an inch of their lives or kill them outright if they don't return the loans with interest. As my father used to say, it is not very fortunate for them that they were born under such unrewarding circumstances.'

Prithvi processed this information. Viewed from outside the lens of the comforts he had taken for granted most of his life, the world was a very different place. And not remotely beautiful. 'Is there any way to balance the scales?' he asked.

'We owe it to ourselves and to them to try,' the mahamantri said, 'but the truth is that when push comes to shove, we will not give up our wealth so easily. And they will fight to survive, for a better life, if not for themselves for their young ones. In the meantime, as long as it suits us, we will look away from their suffering. Someday, there will be change but you know what people like the pandit say . . . the more things change, the more they stay the same.'

Prithvi rode on, wanting to be alone with his thoughts. Uncle Kanha caught up with him and urged him to slow down and the latter obliged. 'Your mother worries about you,' he told the prince.

'There is no need for that, is there? As you can see, I am doing perfectly fine.' His lips were pursed.

As they made their way farther inland, the path became narrower, forking into twisting and turning lanes that became increasingly bereft of greenery or vegetation. There was something foul in the air—sulphurous fumes so thick Prithvi could taste it on his tongue and feel it burning his throat. They covered their mouths with their cloaks and went on.

Groups of people stood aside to let them pass. They were miserable specimens of humanity—painfully emaciated, clad in ragged clothing that seemed to be coming apart revealing half-naked bodies blackened by soot and grime. They shuffled along carrying baskets of something heavy that seemed to be breaking their backs.

Columns of dense smoke rose up in bilious gusts making it even harder to breathe. Prithvi heard a rhythmic pounding that seemed to emanate from the pits of hell—a relentless hammering that made him want to shut his ears. He spurred his horse, anxious to see where the sound was coming from. The heat was unbearable and sweat ran down his body in rivulets, making him long for a breath of fresh air or something cool to drink.

He saw the excavations from a little distance and the shafts that had been dug to allow access to the veins of mother earth rich with deposits of copper, silver and gold. Miners went down into the gaping maw, descending down the layers of steps that had been excavated into the rock, with the resigned air of those who knew that they might not make it back and didn't care either.

They carried their picks, chisels and hammers, the rudimentary tools used to cut into the rock, on belts around their waists. The ore was being hauled out in small woven baskets and lifted up with a rope-and-wheel contraption. Just looking at them, Prithvi knew that the painful toil had exacted a heavy toll on them.

Looking around he saw dead bodies dragged to one side and dumped like trash. 'What happened to them?' he demanded of the overseer, who knew enough of the world to know he was in the presence of somebody important.

'They died. The tunnel where they were working collapsed on them. Sometimes they just kill themselves with the picks or chisels, believing that death couldn't possibly be worse than this life,' he replied with a shrug.

Prithvi insisted on being taken into the tunnel. It was the voice of a king and there could be no denying him. Kadambavas shrugged. The overseer lit a small lamp and led them in. It was the unbearable heat that got to him first, slamming into him like a solid wall of acute discomfort making the blood boil in his veins. The near pitch darkness, which the flickering light barely dispelled, was almost as bad. And the smell! The stench of humans working, perspiring and urinating in confined quarters hit him hard along with the sour scent of misery and despair. It seeped into his bones, contaminating his very soul and a part of him wanted to flee from there without ever looking back.

They saw a group of men, stripped down to their loincloths, labouring with their picks in the dim glow of a lone lamp as they worked the mineral-bearing rocks. The flesh had melted off their backs revealing the skeleton beneath the skin down to the last detail. They worked mechanically, pausing occasionally to stare at the visitors.

Prithvi saw their faces and the hopelessness in their eyes. It was the worst thing he had seen in his young life. Never before had he encountered horror on such a gargantuan scale. Along with the terrible pity over their plight, there was profound gratitude that he felt knowing that he could get on his horse, leave the place and never come back. His secret thoughts made him feel deeply ashamed.

They climbed out of the tunnel on to the other side where more horror awaited them. Women and children, who resembled corpses awaiting the funeral pyre, worked in teams, gathering the heavy pieces of broken rock, pounding it some more with mortar and pestles, washing it in little streams, which had turned black with soot, to separate the ore. There was no singing or laughter here.

The prince was quiet for the longest time as they left the mines behind, lost in his own private thoughts. He used to do that even as a child, Kanha remembered. If he was daydreaming and thinking pleasant thoughts such as the prospect of victory and glory on a battlefield, his face would be the picture of good cheer and a pleasure to look upon.

But when he was brooding or contemplating something dreary, his features would darken like the skies before a storm, thick with menace and the promise of retribution. Kanha glared at Kadambavas as if chiding him for his lack of judgement in bringing the prince here. The latter looked back at him impassively.

'Who are these people?' Prithvi asked, breaking the doleful silence that had descended. 'What have they done to deserve this?'

'Some of them are criminals and mostly deserve to be here,' Kadambavas replied. 'As for the others, they are too poor, unlucky or just unfortunate. It is said that those who wind up here are being punished for their sins in former lives. Once fate decrees they have paid their dues, the lucky ones are granted the blessing of a merciful death.'

'Our grand dwellings, marvellous temples, the sumptuous meals, the mountains of gold, silver and copper coins in the treasury, all the finery, these people are paying for everything, aren't they?' Prithvi asked. His voice was agonized, thick with suppressed tears.

'They are not the only ones paying,' Kanha replied calmly. 'There are the taxes collected mercilessly by the agents of the king, remember? They have to be paid, willingly or unwillingly, in exchange for the safety and security offered by a good king. What matters though is that there is a price everybody pays for the life that is given to them. Some heavier than others.'

He paused for a moment to let that sink in, gathering his own thoughts. 'Fate is blind and nobody is exempt from its vagaries. Before they came here, these people could have been living a good life, chiefs of their tribes, nobility belonging to royal families even, before fate decreed that they should end their lives here. A lot of them are the victims of malice and envy directed at them by others more deserving of a fate like this. It is the way the world works. One moment you have everything good that life has to offer and it can be taken away in the next, leaving you with nothing.'

'Nothing is permanent . . . Destiny determines everything then, doesn't it? From the time of our birth to our death,' Prithvi asked, turning to Kadambavas.'

'That is so, prince . . .' the mahamantri conceded, 'but though the working of destiny is mysterious and unknown to us, there are still some things very much in our control in the time given to us. Think of it this way—the starting and ending of your journey has been decided but how you get there and the means employed must be decided by you alone. You will be king one day and you can choose to be a good one, capable of mercy and compassion, always aware that your every action affects the fate of all in your domain. It is an awesome responsibility and many have broken under its weight but you will not be one of them. You will learn to care enough to remain humane but not allow yourself to be overwhelmed by the plight of those whose condition is beyond your help and even the gods' for that matter.'

Prithvi nodded and rode ahead of them.

'His mother is not going to approve . . .' Kanha said in a low voice. 'His moods are unpredictable and increasingly dark.'

'The natural instinct of a mother is to protect her offspring from terrible things out there in the world, which is reasonable enough. However, we both know that hiding behind a mother's skirts is hardly appropriate for a Kshatriya warrior or any man for that matter,' he said unapologetically. 'Shielding a child from the world outside is not quite adequate to keep him safe from harm. It is far better to let him see and judge for himself how best to slay the monsters that will one day confront him. As for his depression, it is nothing that a woman and wine won't cure . . .'

Kadambavas himself seemed unaffected by the things they had seen as if he had seen far worse and got over it. 'Besides, this is the education the prince needs and has actively sought out for himself. Instead of locking them up with fat priests who put them to sleep every time they open their mouths, youngsters should know what the real world is like, not be kept out from it to the point where they can no longer function in it.'

Prithvi had caught up with the troops who were accompanying them. He was conversing with their leader and had ordered him to select a handful of men, his equanimity restored and his manner imperial as ever.

'You will take a bag of copper coins from the mahamantri,' he instructed, 'and proceed to load three carts with all the food and wine that you can procure. Be sure to buy sweets for the children. Once the carts are loaded to capacity, take them to the mines and tell the overseers that work will be suspended for today. Let the miners eat, drink their fill and rest tonight before they resume work. Everybody deserves a respite from misery. Once my orders have been carried out to the letter, I would like you to report back to me.'

Digging his heel into the flanks of his horse, the prince rode away without a backward glance while the troops hastened to obey. Kadambavas winked at Kanha. 'The world is a changed place now!' he said sarcastically.

'At least he is trying, and the little things count! You know they do . . .' Kanha insisted. The mahamantri shrugged and handed over a small purse of copper coins to the pair of hands stretched upwards towards him before setting off after Prithviraj Chauhan.

11

Dusk had almost fallen and the three of them were considering riding hard and making straight for Pushkar, when they heard a commotion up ahead. A wail of despair that broke off suddenly as if the person had run out of air. It was followed by the clatter of approaching hoofs and raucous shouting punctuated with the drunken jeering typical of ruffians.

A young girl tore into their line of vision, running as if the hounds of hell were in pursuit of her, trying to flee from the footpath and break for the cover of trees but riders flanked her on all sides, blocking her every time. What remained of her clothes hung in tatters, revealing the lush contours of her naked body. Ringlets of matted hair hung loosely all the way to the small of her back. Ugly, discoloured bruises marred her sweat-streaked face and body. Her feet were so bloodied that it defied belief that she was still running.

The dozen or so horsemen following closely at her heels were armoured and carried decorated shields. Some even wore spiked helmets. They were merely toying with her, laughing and urging her to greater exertions, secure in the notion that she was theirs to do with as they pleased. They were clearly enjoying the sport immensely. One had grown tired of the chase and reaching over grabbed that magnificent cascade of ringlets, yanking her head back. She screamed again, struggling violently, kicking and biting like a cornered wild beast. The man seemed most aroused by her struggles. It was there in his eyes.

Something snapped inside Prithvi. They were the chains holding back the lion in him. Unsheathing his weapon with a single, fluid motion and holding the point of his sword high, he spurred his own mount forward with a roar. The man who was holding the girl by the hair looked up in surprise and the expression froze on his face when the blade buried itself deep in his throat, killing him instantly. The moment she was free, the girl ducked and rolled out of the way, half hoping that she would be crushed underfoot and this would mercifully all be over.

For the briefest of moments, her eyes met her rescuer's. Surrounded by enemies on all sides, he was caught up in the savage exhilaration of bloodlust and made a fearsome sight. But even at the height of his killing frenzy, she saw concern for her own safety. It may have been her imagination, one of those tricks of the light, but it was the moment she came back to life. And hope.

With shouts of fury, the remaining riders had unloosed their steel. Kanha and Kadambavas had reacted reflexively, their years of battle training taking over at once as they narrowed the gap between them and the prince, barely pausing as they joined the melee. Positioning themselves on either side of Prithvi, they cut through the attackers, throwing them aside with practised ease.

The clash of swords rang out as the two unevenly matched groups hacked and slashed at each other, faces twisted with extreme fury. The trio had the skills but their opponents had the numbers. Prithvi was the youngest in the group but he made up for it with a killing fury and fought like a veteran. His sword was a blur of movements as it tore into the exposed parts of the throng of bodies, slicing through arteries, mercilessly inflicting mortal wounds with the unerring instincts of the born warrior.

Swinging his sword in an almighty arc, the biceps of his arms straining, he noticed that his opponent was a large, turbaned man with ugly warts on his neck just before his blade sliced cleanly into it. On the periphery of his vision, Kadambavas fought with consummate skill, surrounded though he was on all sides. On his other side, Uncle Kanha had succeeded in unhorsing many of the men.

Prithvi heard the reinforcements arriving at breakneck speed and noticed the spear aimed at his unarmoured chest at exactly the same time. The point of his bloodied sword caught the man in his shoulder with such force he reared back, lessening the impact of the spear that had cut through his clothes cleanly and drawn blood. Viciously, Prithvi thrust his sword into the exposed left armpit and watched the life die out of glittering eyes set above a thick black beard, as crimson blood frothed at a mouth thrown open in an agonized scream.

With the cavalry joining the fray, it was over in minutes. They cut down and subdued the remaining aggressors, chasing down those who attempted to flee. Once the lot of them was rounded up, the men were made to kneel on the ground.

'You dare lay a hand on the talarakshas!' their leader barked, glaring at Kanha who had almost unhorsed him. His horse had bolted and he had been dragged behind still tangled in the reins. 'The king will hear of this!' He was a big man, powerfully built and a livid scar marred one cheek.

'The talarakshas are supposed to protect the subjects of the king,' the mahamantri told the man calmly, 'from scum like the dacoits who roam the countryside and not take pride in being scum themselves. And I am sure the king will not be very pleased to know that you attacked his son, Prithviraj Chauhan-III, the crown prince of the realm.'

Jaws dropped to the ground and the captives stared at each other trembling in fear, the last of the alcoholic fumes dissipating as the gravity of the situation impressed itself upon them. How had it come to this? One moment they were riding high on the thrill of the chase. That little bitch had been so spirited! Now they were going to die. The thoughts made their stomach heave and the bowels churn out their contents in a sickening rush.

The captain alone remained sullen and defiant. He had explained everything to the guards. The girl's mother was a *vesha*, who had not paid the taxes due to them, whining about how she was unable to work because of illness. What would become of them if they listened to every creative sob story told by those miserable liars? Why, the kingdom would be poverty-stricken and the ruler might as well roam the streets with a begging bowl in hand. He had said as much and the soldier had struck him, nearly breaking his jaw and jarring a tooth loose, leaving it wobbling.

He shook his head in disgust. All this fuss over a common whore! The woman had to be taught a lesson, nobody defied the talarakshas, nobody! So they had grabbed her daughter while she wailed and rolled on the floor like a bitch in heat, tearing at her hair and beating her chest like one demented. Proud and beautiful the girl had been. She would have fetched a good price but the alcohol had upset his judgement. He cursed and muttered under his breath.

The captain stopped only when he looked up to see the yuvaraj standing erect before him. 'You have not only failed in your duties but abused your position, bringing dishonour to this land where we have always prided ourselves on protecting women, children and the weak.' His voice was cold and dispassionate. 'For your disgraceful conduct, unbecoming of a representative of the king of the Chahamanas, I hereby sentence you to death!'

The troops clicked their heels together and raised their swords, waiting for the royal command. Condemned to die, some among the kneeling men moaned, others begged for clemency, their leader spat out his loosened tooth along with a gob of spit and blood, aiming carefully for Prithvi's feet. His was the first head that rolled.

Still as a statue, Prithviraj did not look away as his sentence was carried out. Swords raised and lowered in circular arcs, the dull thwacks of blade meeting flesh, bone crunching, as severed heads, sometimes hacked from necks flew free from the shoulders and hit the ground, rolling a little before coming to rest. The bodies dropped from the kneeling position, twisting and convulsing, blood spraying in hot, sticky showers that rained down on the executioners. And finally, all that remained was the crumpled and lifeless remains of the talarakshas, keepers of law and order, reduced to silhouettes under the moonlight.

She was watching too. Somehow, even with his back to her, Prithvi knew it. When the fighting broke out, she had looked at him with gratitude so profound it had made his heart seize before fleeing to the cover offered by the trees. Looking at her, out of the sides of his eyes, he saw that she was indeed watching, her gaze empty of feeling, staring so hard he knew that she wanted to imprint every detail of the scene in her memory. Poor little thing! How she must have suffered . . .

'They are not coming back,' Prithvi turned to address her, but she was no longer there. Looking down he saw that she lay prostrate at his feet.

They spent the night at an imperial guest house. The girl had passed out and Prithvi had held her on the long ride back. He still remembered how she had felt in his arms. It had been difficult to let go when the hands reached out for her, separating them in the lodging. Her panicked moans of protest, which faded away when he promised her that she was safe.

Prithvi hadn't been hurt that badly after his first real fight, but Uncle Kanha insisted that a vaidya examine his royal person minutely. The wound he had taken to the chest was barely a scratch but they were all acting as though he was at death's door and it irritated Prithvi no end. Where was the mahamantri? At least he did not fret and fuss like a woman.

When the process was completed to Kanha's satisfaction, he breathed a sigh of relief. Had the damage to the person of the crown prince been any worse, he knew his head would have rolled too on the orders of his brother and Karpuradevi would have been happy to strike the killing blow herself.

Prithvi waited tersely for the lecture on the rashness of his actions in ordering the execution of the talarakshas to rescue a stray, the need to control his wildly impulsive nature and the rest of the nonsense the pandit was always harping on.

'I have seldom been prouder of you, Prithvi,' Uncle Kanha said instead, placing a hand on his shoulder. 'On this day, you proved yourself a man and a brave, kind one at that.'

Prithvi was so taken aback that he was momentarily speechless. 'Why, you are getting old and soft, Uncle Kanha! For a moment there, I thought you were going to insist on hugging me like mother and then I would have been forced to draw my sword again.' His smile was boyish and infectious. It had been a while since he had smiled like that and Kanha knew that his words had pleased him though he would never admit to it.

'There is no danger of that happening,' he retorted drily, 'especially since I was raised by Rani Kanchanadevi who as you know abhors unseemly display of tenderness. So we can keep our weapons sheathed, especially since they have seen enough action for the day.'

'She is little more than a child, Uncle Kanha,' Prithvi was serious again. 'How could they bring themselves to hurt her? Foul beasts like that should not have been born in the first place.'

Kanha scratched his beard thoughtfully; he wished he had called for some wine. It had been a long day. 'Unfortunately, you will find that it is all too common for people in positions of power to misuse their office and betray the trust reposed in them. Which is why it is most impressive that despite your privileged status, you risked life and limb to help someone in need. It is what a true Kshatriya, worthy of the name, would do.

'The talarakshas are referred to as the *kantakas* by the people because they are the thorns in this kingdom. But some do a good job with the limited resources at their disposal, genuinely doing what they can to protect the people. Many have been killed by dacoits though they fight bravely. We invest a lot in the troops in our armed forces and I am afraid we tend to scrimp and be miserly with the coins when it comes to the talarakshas, who are usually equipped with second-hand weapons and uniforms. Theirs is a hard job and most do the best they can. As always, it is the few like the ones we saw today who give everybody in their position a bad name.'

Prithvi frowned when he heard that, his brow crinkling the way it did when wrestling with a vexing problem. 'You don't have to bother your head about the umpteen frustrations of running a kingdom smoothly just yet, Prithvi. There will be time enough in the future. For now, it will suffice for you to focus on more important things like your studies.'

His nephew nodded and smiled again, 'I was confident that you were going to berate me for my hot-headedness and recklessness back there.'

'Being aware of your shortcomings is the first step towards correcting them,' came the reply. 'I think you will learn from that little imbroglio which nearly saw you terminate a long and glorious reign as king even before it began in the heat of a heated moment. There is no need for me to point out that it was mighty careless of you.'

Prithvi frowned at that. 'It wasn't quite that risky, Uncle Kanha. I was fully aware that our crack troops couldn't be too far off, especially since it is their job to make sure that their prince doesn't endanger his safety even when he does. Besides, I had two of the most acclaimed warriors in the land fighting by my side.'

'You cannot count on someone to catch you when you fall all the time, Prithvi . . .'

'I know that, Uncle Kanha. I am sure you will be happy to know that I am extremely sure-footed. Now if you carry on preaching, you are going to sound more like my mother and less like Kanchanadevi's son and that would make her come after you from the afterlife, so I am going to leave now to focus on truly important things such as finding a decent meal before I starve to death.'

Kanha watched him leave. In the space of a short journey, his boy had become a man. Even so, who did Prithvi think he was fooling? If Prithvi's accelerated departure had truly been on account of hunger pangs and not because he wanted to find the lovely girl he had rescued, Kanha would gladly eat his own sword!

'Our boy certainly has an eye for beauty,' Kadambavas began. 'Did you see that little slip of a girl after they got her cleaned up? She is remarkably good-looking. If that were not bad enough, she has a good heart. I had a talk with her and our stray is completely without guile. But I have no doubt all that will change, given what has happened to her and the scant regard society has for the likes of her.'

'What is her story?' Kanha enquired. 'Is it true what the talarakshas said about her mother being a vesha?' He frowned. Karpuradevi would not be happy to hear that her precious boy had put himself in danger for the sake of the daughter of a whore, especially if she were young, comely and already worshipped the ground Prithvi walked on.

'I am afraid so,' Kadambavas said grimly, 'but her father was a man of some prominence. From what I gathered, he used his influence to settle them comfortably in Sambhar and the girl had begun her training as a *ganika*. Apparently, she has been trained in the arts and shows exceptional talent.'

Kanha did not have to be told the rest of the story. 'Their patron must have been a man of advanced years and when he passed away, his immediate family probably made sure that all funds were cut off for these two. And set the talarakshas on them as well. That girl is lucky, Prithvi arrived like a god and saved her from a life of shame and infamy, which would have made death seem infinitely preferable.'

'I am not so sure about that. Some people are singled out for a life of torment. She may have been granted temporary respite from the evil that befell her, but I can't help thinking that in the long run, it will catch up with her and when it does, it will be even worse for she would have tasted both pleasure and hope, only to have it all taken away from her.' Kadambavas was a cynical man and he was genuinely sorry that his pessimism was always justified.

'Save your philosophy for when I have had a few glasses to drink,' Kanha cut through his thoughts impatiently. 'Is the news about the Chalukyan king true?'

'I received confirmation not too long ago,' Kadambavas was nodding. 'Ajaypal, the tyrant extraordinaire, is no more. He was knifed by his own troops. They say that he treated his own men worse than his enemies, persecuting them mercilessly and punishing the smallest lapses with capital punishment.

Of course, when it comes to a menace like Ajaypal, especially in these parts where we have so little regard for him, we can count on the details being embellished a little. They are already making him out to be thrice the monster he actually was by claiming he had Jain monks skinned alive, violated every woman who crossed his path, including his sainted mother, and insisted that he be served human flesh to break his fast.'

'I am glad you are able to mine this kind of material for humour, but tell me about his successor . . .'

Kadambavas refused to bite. 'Why don't you tell me instead?'

'It has to be his son, Bhimdev-II. He is of age and every bit as bloodthirsty as his father. The last I heard he was plotting to get rid of his unstable father with the help of his overeager supporters but that is what the tired old reports usually say.'

'Very good, Kanha, you are almost as well-informed as the pandit and the prince. Bhimdev acted quickly. He had himself installed and had everybody remotely involved with his father's murder arrested and executed without any further ado. He got quite carried away in his enthusiasm to see justice done and eradicated each and every threat to his reign. Or so they say. Now they are all running scared and even those who may have been less than thrilled with his ascent are fighting each other for the chance to kiss his backside.

'The new king of the Chalukyas is cunning and ruthless to make up for his moral turpitude. But you probably know him best, from your stint in Gurjardesa . . .'

'Unfortunately, we knew each other as children and later we studied together,' Kanha fell silent, debating exactly how much he ought to reveal. He liked Kadambavas well enough and they had learned to work seamlessly as a team. Despite his relative youth, he had been singled out by Sallakshanapal and trained to replace him. Someshwar leaned on both of them heavily and his queen trusted the mahamantri with her life.

Even Prithvi seemed to get on exceedingly well with the man. But Kanha couldn't help thinking that the mahamantri was just a little too clever, which may not necessarily be in the best interests of those around him.

As for Bhimdev, Kanha remembered a loathsome boy who used to sneak into the harem to watch the ladies bathe or change. Later, he boasted that the enormous risks he took were well worth it. Kanchanadevi had caught him once, hauled him up in front of everybody and whacked his bum with a stick.

Bhimdev never forgot the slight and had spread a vicious rumour that she was Maharaj Kumarpal's concubine and that he and Someshwar were by-blows of that illicit passion. Kanha had punched him out for that and broken his nose. They had to pull him away because he had come close to throttling the boor to death.

He sighed. All that had been a long time ago and it was quite possible that he had turned over a new leaf and may be amenable to letting bygones be bygones. However, it would be far likelier if Bhimdev chose to provoke trouble with the Chauhans, whose extensive territories had long been coveted by his predecessors.

'I take it that there is no love lost between you too . . .' Kadambavas, who had been watching him closely, interrupted his thoughts. 'But there will be plenty of time to discuss all that later. In the meantime, let us get something to eat and drink. Remind me to have a word with the pandit about teaching the prince to resist the tears and other charming blandishments of women before it gets him into any more trouble!'

The prince had given orders for the girl's care. He sent the vaidya to make sure that her injuries were carefully attended to, especially her torn and bleeding feet, that she be washed, dressed and given something to eat. When he went to check on her, the girl from the road who had been more animal than human was barely recognizable. Clad in flowing skirts of some gauzy material and an embroidered blouse, she wore the *chungi* tucked in at her waist, the other end worn pleated across her shoulder. Her ringlets had been combed out and braided. Prithvi had to stop himself from staring. Back on the road, he had failed to appreciate exactly how beautiful she was. Even without the use of cosmetic aid or ornaments, she looked beautiful. The girl was looking at him shyly from beneath long lashes that framed a pair of captivating eyes that would torment him in his dreams for a long time. 'You saved my life,' she said simply. 'I will spend not only this lifetime but subsequent ones as well trying to repay you for what you did today.'

Prithvi could not think of a reply. Her voice had a lilting, musical quality to it and he liked how it felt like a caress. 'My mother was less fortunate,' she was saying, staring into space and he saw the empty look on her face again. 'She always was a fighter and she fought to her last breath. None of our neighbours lifted a finger to help her. And she had helped them all when we had money. It was her nature; if she heard that somebody was ill, mother would send nutritious home-cooked meals and personal remedies. I have never known her to turn away anybody who came to our home for help whether it was for clothes, healing potions or a few coins.'

Prithvi knew that her mother had been a vesha. The pandit had warned him about women like that, insisting that they were toxic beings who should be given a wide berth. He said that having anything to do with them, including accepting their favours or just about any service, would pollute a person past redemption. 'If that were not bad enough, those debauched creatures are carriers of vermin far worse than themselves, which can infect a man with unspeakable diseases. I have known many who have sinned with these foul creatures. The rot sets in their bodies and their male organs turn black with decay before falling off entirely and they go to their deaths robbed of their senses and drooling like imbeciles.' The pandit had told them with ghoulish relish to drive his point home.

Prithvi had promised himself never to go anywhere in the vicinity of such dangerous beings whom the pandit had said were comely on the outside to disguise the poison they carried in their veins. Yet, he couldn't help thinking that the vesha seemed to have had a kind nature. Surely that counted for something? Whichever way he looked at it, Prithvi found it impossible to look down upon the woman who had given birth to this beautiful girl.

'They carried me away on their horses. I struggled as hard as I could.' Prithvi listened as she went on tonelessly, needing to unburden herself of a portion of the emotional baggage she would carry for life. 'Mother came chasing after us. While there was life left to her, I knew she would never give up and let them take me away. They knew it too and found it amusing, going just slow enough to allow her to keep up. But soon they grew bored and one of them stayed behind to make sure that she stopped following us. He came back soon and he made sure to wipe his sword on my skirt. I looked over my shoulder for a long time. Again and again, I turned. But she was no longer there.'

She swallowed and Prithvi was by her side holding her tight while she cried into his chest. He wished he hadn't executed the talarakshas, if only so they could be killed all over again for doing this to her. 'Don't cry,' he begged her. 'I am sorry all these things happened to you. But I solemnly swear that nobody will ever hurt you again.' The prince remembered the miners. He had done what he could but it had been next to nothing.

How could there be so much suffering in this world? And why was there so little anybody could do about it?

When she looked up at him, there was gratitude in her eyes and so much trust he would have willingly braved the fires of hell to keep her safe. 'You will accompany us to Pushkar,' he told her reassuringly, glad to note that that she had stopped crying. 'I was told that you are being trained as a dancer. Pandit Padmanabh will make arrangements for you to continue your training and you need not fear. It will be my personal responsibility to make sure that you lack for nothing.' Once he was released from his term of incarceration at the gurukul, which wasn't too far away now, he would take her back with him to Ajmer. It felt right that she remain close to him always. There was a reason fate had brought them together.

'It was my good fortune that the god I worshipped came before me today, when I needed him the most and saved me. As long as he is close to me, I will lack for nothing,' she whispered to him, perfectly in sync with his thoughts.

When people said things like that, about him being an incarnation of Vishnu or Arjuna reborn to rid aryavarta of the mlecchas, Prithvi tended to reply with cruel flippancy but he could not bring himself to burst a bubble that clearly gave her so much happiness. It made him feel good too, so he decided to shrug off her nonsense about god with polite modesty.

'You haven't told me your name . . .'

'My name is Yogita, sire!'

It was a pretty name and it suited her well. Yogita . . . Poor girl! She had lost so much and yet her spirit was bright and beautiful, so full of hope reposed in a life that had been nothing but cruel to her. If only he could have somehow saved her before she had to go through so much pain. Even so, he was gladder than he could say that their paths had crossed. They stayed that way for a long time, neither of them wanting to leave, wishing that they could remain this way forever. In that moment, the youngsters wanted nothing more than to simply be there for each other always.

Prithvi hoped fervently that the fates were listening and would grant him this one wish.

12

Yogita liked walking the several hundred yards past the foot of the Nag Pahar or the Snake Mountain as it was referred to, along the curve of its spur and then taking the path to the charming little hollow behind the waterfall. It was her favourite place in the world. Along the curving cliff face, there were many caves and over the last few years she had explored many of these with Prithvi.

Running deep into the heart of the hill was a natural cavern with pillars hewn in the sides and steps cut into the rock to allow pilgrims access to the ancient shrine dedicated to Mahadev. Devotees brought flowers and coconuts for the three-eyed god. They would place the offerings before him and pour their hearts out, hoping he would listen. Yogita liked to think that Shiva did care about them. They were all his children after all and she added her prayers to the countless other voices that called out to him.

Whenever she visited, it was her practice to sit at the feet of the lingam and recite some of the prayers her mother had taught her. Yogita implored Lord Shiva to bless Prithvi and grant him nothing but victory and a long life. 'Make him indestructible like you,' she murmured with fervent devotion. 'Keep him safe from harm always. Let his name live forever more.' As for herself, she asked for nothing. Only Prithviraj Chauhan mattered to her.

When her worship was over, Yogita stood up to leave. Beyond the cavern, she made a relatively easy climb to reach the stream and sat on a ledge of rock polished smooth by the elements. Wrapping a thin shawl over her head and shoulders she waited contently for her lord, which was how she always thought of him.

The prince had been as good as his word. She had been accepted into a reputable community of dancers and her days were spent in study and peace. Everybody was kind to her and she couldn't have asked for more. It was all thanks to the generosity of her lord, she knew. He was the reason for her existence and her very being. The rest of her life would be consecrated in his service.

The object of her thoughts was near. Yogita could feel his presence and his intoxicating natural scent. Her lord came and placed his hands over her eyes playfully, making her squeal with delight as he took his place beside her. It had been a while since they met and Prithvi was pleased to look upon that dear face. Especially after the summons he had received from his mother which had led to an extremely unpleasant conversation.

They sat in comfortable silence. Prithvi was engrossed in his thoughts. They were dark and filled with tumultuous passion but with Yogita by his side, he could examine them while deriving a measure of warmth and tranquillity from her soothing presence. His thoughts turned to his previous meeting with Karpuradevi, which had left him with a bad taste in his mouth.

The moment his mother had laid eyes on him, she had grabbed him in a tight embrace making him feel stiff and uncomfortable. Sensing this, she withdrew and insisted that he have dinner with her, hoping no doubt to emulate his grandmother. They dined on rich meat and a rice dish. Prithvi found he did not have much of an appetite and was irritated when she heaped roasted pumpkin on his plate. Had she forgotten that he could not abide the damn things?

Since he was too grown up to fling it aside, he let it sit there where it goaded him into greater heights of irritation. 'There are some things we needed to discuss and we hardly ever get the time to simply sit down and talk,' she began.

Whose fault was that? Prithvi was tempted to spit the question out but he held his tongue. His mother was looking harried. She had needed to use a lot of cosmetics to hide the lines of worry on her face and her once thick head of hair had become increasingly sparse and hiding the bald patches behind artful floral arrangements did not make for a very pretty sight. It was obvious that the cares of government had taken a rough toll on her.

'It is about your father!' Karpuradevi seemed unable to keep still and she was wringing her hands. 'And his new wife who is about your age.' It usually was about the king and Prithvi found it ironical that while his mother's complaints ran into the tens of thousands, his father had never once mentioned mother to him. Instead he would murmur a few platitudes and Prithvi would listen politely while both waited impatiently for their tiresome non-conversations to end.

Father *had* looked bad this time, when he had made the trip to visit him in his palace and half-heartedly paid his respects. The king seldom bothered with training exercises these days and a steady diet of intoxicants had led to his becoming increasingly obese; the liver spots visible on his balding head made him look a lot older than his years.

His new queen was a different story, preening at his side. The description of her fabled beauty that they had heard in Pushkar did not do her justice, Prithvi had to concede. She was truly exquisite and the signs of her pregnancy were just beginning to show. She flaunted it proudly, looking radiant with happiness.

Rani Ketaki was dressed to the nines in a beautifully embroidered garment of gold cloth depicting Ram and Sita.

A golden diadem was perched on her hair held up with golden pins in an elaborate hairstyle and festooned with pearls. She was one of those charming creatures full of perennial good cheer, who made it a point to engage him in conversation and enquire about his health and well-being. His father had far too many wives as well as concubines and Prithvi seldom bothered with their names but to his surprise he found himself responding to this one and her spectacularly sunny disposition.

Prithvi decided that he liked her better than some of his father's more insouciant companions but it was clear that mother loathed her young rival. His father though had looked absolutely besotted with his new bride and had one hand placed possessively on her belly. Like a young man in the first flush of love, eager to impress his beloved, he had recently assumed the title of 'Pratapalankeshwara' and had embarked on a flurry of projects. Work was currently underway at breakneck speed on five temples.

Prithvi knew that the situation with the Chalukyas had steadily deteriorated. Ajaypal's successor was even less kindly disposed to them than his father had been. Pandit Padmanabh and Kadambavas were working feverishly to ensure a diplomatic solution. Prithvi personally felt that the Chalukyas had to be cut down to size and Maharaj Someshwar felt the same way. However, it was embarrassingly obvious there were few who felt confident about a victory with Someshwar at the helm. But the king was lusting for a major win to enhance his legacy and his new bride was most encouraging of his efforts.

'Your father is making an absolute fool of himself,' Karpuradevi was saying in a venomous tone that made him wince. 'With his new pet and if that were not enough, her entire extended family has moved here to enjoy our hospitality. They have been here for months and show no sign of leaving, encouraging him towards greater heights of folly. What is worse, they are ruthless and ambitious and already making mischief for you and me.' His mother was working herself up into a rage.

'I think you are reading too much into this, Mother. There have been others before her and Father will get bored sooner rather than later . . .' Prithvi began when his mother interrupted him in a shrill voice. 'This one is different. This girl makes your father feel as though his youth and virility has been restored to him. The young queen is pregnant and your father is over the moon with joy. What if it is a boy? Don't you see?'

Karpuradevi's bosom was heaving. The humiliation was more than she could bear. Someshwar had issued an urgent summons to her, insisting that she meet him immediately in his private chambers. It had been years since he had sent for her, and she had gone to him taking particular care with her appearance. But as it turned out, Someshwar merely wanted to show her that his royal sceptre was still capable of reaching its full capacity for arousal, thanks to the little filly he had taken into his bed. The affront had been more than she could bear. But Prithvi couldn't possibly know these things and she certainly wasn't going to tell him. Yet, she had to find a way to make Prithvi understand the precariousness of their position.

Prithvi shrugged. 'What are you suggesting, Mother? So what if it is a boy? I am still Father's heir and the crown prince. Besides, my training is almost complete and soon, I will establish my military prowess. Why are you working yourself up into such a lather?'

As for the situation with the Chalukyas, he had no intention of discussing it with his mother, but he secretly hoped that Father would get a chance to prove himself. Prithvi could understand his frustration with being lumped together with Vigraharaj's 'weak and incompetent successors'.

Karpuradevi was getting frustrated too. She was not getting through to her boy, who looked irritable and distracted. For years, her enemies had been spreading infamous calumny about her relationship with Kanha. Some whispered that Prithvi was not his father's son. It made her want to tear her hair out in frustration and fury. After all the sacrifices she had made for this kingdom, how dare they impugn her virtue and accuse her of being unfaithful to her husband?

She had wanted to reassure Prithvi before the slander reached his ears but she simply could not bring herself to repeat those poisonous accusations against her. It was painfully obvious that she and Prithvi had grown distant and he no longer loved her as much as he used to. Instead, his affections were reserved for a tarnished bit of goods he had picked up on the wayside. The entire incident had made her blood boil. She would have liked to slap Kanha and Kadambavas for the foolhardy machismo and presumptuousness they displayed in assuming they knew something she didn't about making *her* son a good king.

Karpuradevi tried to calm herself. At least Prithvi still treated her with respect. If ever he asked her whether the rumours were true, she would kill herself that very instant.

Prithvi was looking at her strangely and Karpuradevi tried to bring her chaotic thoughts into some semblance of order. 'You are being dense, son, and refusing to acknowledge the gravity of this situation! You are yuvaraj for now but a beautiful young girl who is not above using her body to get closer to the throne, will not hesitate to stoop to despicable levels to snatch the crown for her own boy!'

'What are you suggesting we do, Mother? To the best of my knowledge neither of us is capable of even dreaming of hurting a young girl and her unborn child, so I think it is best we terminate this unpleasant conversation.' His voice was harsh and Karpuradevi was deeply hurt. Did he think she had no principles? If only he knew the full extent of the sacrifices she had made for him!

'I merely wanted you to be aware of the situation and be vigilant. The mahamantri and I have decided to increase the security for you at Pushkar. Where your safety is concerned, I will take no risks and spare no expense.' She stopped when she saw the disgust writ large on his features.

'Thank you for the concern, Mother, but there is no need for such drastic measures. I am perfectly capable of taking care of myself and have no need for nursemaids.'

Karpuradevi felt her own temper flare. She would wager that he did not speak so rudely to that dancing girl. 'All I can say is that a mother knows what is best for her son. And you must beware of calculating little bitches who will do anything, including taking advantage of your sympathetic nature, to bring a member of the royal family under their thumb. They are usually trained in dens of inequity to keep a man chained to their affections. I just don't understand why men are so foolish! If only I had been a man . . .'

'But you are not, Mother, and I am. Please try to remember that.' His face was a mask of fury and bidding her a chilly farewell, he had left.

Prithvi had been in a foul mood ever since. But he felt better now. 'It is good to see you, Yogita. If it were not for you, sometimes I would fear for my very sanity.'

She knew nothing of the Chalukyas or his mother's concerns and Prithvi was content to leave it at that. He was tired of people trying to educate him with their incessant chatter. It was nice to be with someone who did not have foolish expectations from him.

Both of them lived for these meetings. Sensing his mood, Yogita did her best to buoy his spirits keeping up a steady stream of chatter about her training and told him amusing little anecdotes or charming tales from the Puranas, which she knew he was partial to. Prithvi listened to her musical voice and tried to forget briefly the endless intrigue that being a prince involved.

Sitting there with Yogita for company, Prithvi wondered at the lingering unease that was preventing him from being perfectly happy. He couldn't shake the feeling that something wasn't quite right. Perhaps his mother's bodyguards, whom he had given the slip, had followed him there?

Abruptly, he got to his feet. 'You should go back at once. I will wait here for a bit. Take good care of yourself until we meet again.'

'You are always in my thoughts and prayers, my lord! Set your mind at ease. Everything will work out for the best. You will see!' With a last loving look, she turned to do his bidding. Prithvi watched over her departure, and she turned to wave at him before the darkness swallowed her up. The steps leading up from the Mahadev temple would take her straight back to within a short distance of the abode of her teacher. It was her practice to take the scenic route while coming to meet him and depart using the other exit, he knew.

Prithvi did not pray much but on that day he ordered the guardian deities in the imperious manner he wasn't aware he had to watch over her and keep her safe. It was an echo of her prayers for his well-being. It did not make him feel better. On that night his mother was constantly in his thoughts. The feeling of trepidation that had plagued him all along, built in intensity.

He cursed under his breath, his hand going automatically to the hilt of his sword.

Every instinct he possessed was sounding the alarm and above the ringing clangour in his head, he heard his mother's anguished wail, '*Prithviraj!*' The warning saved his life.

They attacked without warning in keeping with their training as assassins. Stealthily, they emerged out of the darkness, at one with it, shadows that moved across the rocky terrain with deathly intent, closing the gap between them and the young prince soundlessly and quickly.

Prithvi reacted out of pure reflex, spinning on his heel, raising his sword and slashing viciously, scattering the first wave. Almost immediately they regrouped, ready to attack again. Fortunately, though he had dismissed his mother's concerns, he had remembered her words and taken care to fasten his armour under his clothes. And he never went anywhere without his sword. Sick with worry over Yogita's safety, Prithvi raised his blade as his assailants surged out from the darkness again. Taking the offensive, which was not at all what they had expected from a young boy who was outnumbered seven to one, he rushed to meet them, forcing them to retreat under the onslaught of a vicious parry. It was a moonless night and his attackers had been trained to do their dirty business under the cover of darkness, giving them a distinct advantage.

One lunged at him, getting under his guard and Prithvi slashed at him, instinctively relying on the judgement of his ears and his gut instinct, moving with lightning speed, dancing in tune with the song of steel. A second swordsman made his move and managed a glancing blow that Prithvi barely managed to deflect. Once more his thoughts turned to Yogita, then his mind went blank and every one of his senses focused solely on meeting attack after attack as they descended closing off all escape.

And then Padhri Ray leapt into the fray. Plunging his blade into the throat of one, he kicked the feet out from under another before pulling out his sword and finishing him off. Kanak and Nahar were with him. The former was hacking at the backs of their knees, severing the hamstrings. Nahar had dropped two of them with blows to their exposed heads. And just like that, the tide had turned in their favour. The dying cries of the fallen men shattered the silence as Prithviraj and his companions worked in tandem to inflict mortal blows on the cowards who attacked from behind. Death was too good for their likes.

Padhri and Kanak were laughing in grisly merriment, well pleased with the prowess they had displayed against trained killers. 'We have to make sure she is safe!' Prithvi cried out.

'She is safe,' Jaya's voice came out of the darkness. 'Hari and I followed her till she reached her destination. They were not after her, Prithvi.'

A big smile of relief spread across Prithvi's face and he clapped Jaya affectionately on the shoulders, amazed that they had come for him. 'How did you lot find me?'

'We are your boon companions, Prithvi,' it was Kanak who answered, 'your safety is of paramount importance to us. We know that you thought you had given the bodyguards assigned to the task by your mother the slip, but actually they managed to follow at a discreet distance. Tonight though, Jaya, who loves you more than anybody else, noticed that they lay lifeless, carelessly half-concealed behind some trees, and he alerted us. We usually keep vigil till you return, so we made haste to reach you!'

'I owe you all my life,' Prithvi said quietly. 'How can I ever repay you?'

'You were doing very well on your own,' Jaya hastened to assure him. 'It was hard finding our way in the dark and I was worried about the delay.'

'I told him that trained assassins or not, it would be no small feat to lay a finger on Prithviraj Chauhan but you know how Jaya frets,' Padhri added. 'But we wouldn't have reached you in time if not for Jaya.' He clapped the little poet's shoulder with gusto and Jaya fell in a crumpled heap, cursing loudly.

Padhri hauled him back to his feet, dusting him off with great affection. 'When you recount tonight's adventure in your next poem, be sure to mention that I am no longer fat, but big and muscular like Bhima, with a truly great heart and a way with the ladies.'

Extremely pleased with themselves, they made their way back to the gurukul, chattering merrily and singing battle songs as if they had succeeded in single-handedly wiping out the armies of the Mussulmen. Prithvi was quiet. Though his companions had meant well, they had done too thorough a job of killing his enemies.

Now they would never know for certain who was behind this cowardly attack and his mother would work herself up into a hysterical frenzy. After his recent adventures, they wouldn't let him take a shit without assigning two guards to look over his shoulder and report back on the colour, consistency and scent of his bodily wastes, let alone keep his rendezvous with Yogita private, if it had ever been that. He sighed.

Prithvi hadn't told any of them about Yogita. She belonged to him alone and he had intended to keep it that way. Their time together was sacrosanct and he thought he had moved heaven and earth to keep it that way. After all that expended effort, it boggled the mind that his friends had been wise to his nocturnal outings all along.

He knew that they meant well but it galled him no end that they too had clapped their lustful gaze on Yogita. How could any of them be impervious to her flawless beauty? Had they passed their usual coarse comments about her ripe breasts or dreamt of running their fingers through her lustrous hair? Prithvi knew he was being horribly unfair to his friends especially after they had just saved his life. With gargantuan effort, he stopped this disturbing train of thought in its tracks.

Prithvi glanced at them—big and bluff Padhri, Nahar who made him laugh, faithful Kanak whose heart had always been bigger than his phenomenal talent, loyal Jaya who truly loved him like no other and dear Hari, of course. His younger brother caught and held his gaze frankly. Prithvi felt the great affection his brother had always borne him and impulsively they hugged.

It had been foolish of him to think that his life was his own but Yogita had been right. Everything *had* worked out. And he was grateful. Mostly.

Prithvi and his companions ought to have got into a lot more trouble for their escapade than they actually did. Pandit Padmanabh questioned them exhaustively one by one. 'It is by god's grace that not a single hair on your head has been harmed. That and the love of your mother,' he told the prince meaningfully, when it was Prithvi's turn. 'We will expend all our resources to finding out the nefarious person or persons behind this outrage and they will face the king's justice. Make no mistake!' He went on in this vein for a long time while Prithvi felt his thoughts wander. He had no doubt what Mother would say. She would insist that it was Rani Ketaki's minions.

Prithvi had a sneaking suspicion that the truth of the matter would be far from simple. Given the situation with the Chalukyas and just about every other neighbouring kingdom they had clashed with, he was sure they did not want for enemies and with war looming, it was hardly surprising that they all felt the need to resort to cheap, underhand tactics. *Let them come,* he thought to himself with an iron resolve, *I am not afraid of them and they are welcome to die by my hand!*

His face grew animated and the pandit was pleased that his speech was making such a tremendous impact. 'I understand that a crown prince of the realm may be strong-minded and will come and go as he pleases but for your own safety, I hope you will cooperate.' Prithvi felt his temper flare, but softened when Padmanabh added, 'While in my care, if anything untoward happened, your parents will have me skinned alive and strung up by the testicles. May I say that despite my many gifts, a high or even moderate tolerance for pain is not one of them . . .'

Respectfully, Prithvi folded his palms together, and the pandit waited triumphantly for the apology he was sure was coming. But he was disappointed because all he got from the prince was, 'I understand how you feel, panditji. We all care deeply about the well-being of our testicles.' *Irrespective of whether they are used or not.* And Prithviraj Chauhan left with his head held high.

The number of guards stationed around Prithvi tripled and he decided to make the best of it, sending some of them to escort Yogita to their usual visiting place whenever he wanted to meet her. Life would have gone on at the same sedate, snail's pace but then they received news which sent shockwaves rippling through their world. Maharaj Bhimdev had declared war and was marching towards them. Chittor, Pali and Jalore, which had been under their control since the time of Vigraharaj, had already been re-captured.

The garrisons stationed there had been slaughtered to the last man and their heads had been arranged in a grotesque mound outside the city gates where the carrion birds stripped the flesh clean, leaving only skulls behind.

Pandit Padmanabh sent for Prithvi and his companions. They were all needed at Ajmer. The army was to march after he had blessed the troops. The standing army as well as the militias, allied forces as well as the mercenaries had gathered ready for battle, answering to the summons of Maharaj Someshwar. Prithvi and his companions intended to request the king to allow them to fight, to avenge their fallen men. As they rode towards the capital city, they could feel the excitement in the air and hear the outrage of the people who were baying for blood.

The army arrived from various parts of the kingdom, rivers of men pooling into the sea. Battalions of the heavy infantry were gathered, smartly turned out and fully equipped. They held their spears and shields in their hands. In the front ranks were the younger men, their shields decorated with embellishments of shining copper. The veterans came behind them, their shields and sword hilts decorated with silver, and they carried them with pride.

All of them were engaged in training exercises as their officers drilled them mercilessly, practising manoeuvres and strategies of offence and defence. The clash and clang of their weapons made a frightful noise. Mothers and young wives were struck with terror when the waves of sound crashed over them and they lit lamps and broke coconuts at their preferred shrines praying for the safe return of their men.

The cavalry divisions were from the nobler classes of society and their armour, shields and weapons were engraved with gold and precious stones. They rode magnificently groomed steeds and made a truly impressive sight. The camel and elephant battalions were present too.

The king's own excitement level seemed to be at fever pitch. The prospect of war had given him his second wind and he was determined to distinguish himself. He would show his detractors! As the arrangements were underway, he insisted on involving himself with every single detail, going over the battle plans obsessively.

He sent for Prithvi so that they could have a quick word in private. The prince had no wish to lose this opportunity and put forward his request immediately. 'Father! May I please have the honour of fighting by your side?'

Someshwar shook his head and Prithvi felt his spirits flag. 'I know that you are chafing at the bit, my boy, but you haven't reached your majority as yet and besides, the subjects will feel better if you are safe and sound back here.'

Prithvi frowned. Of course, he would be 'safe and sound' along with the women and children, old and infirm. An awkward silence fell between them and lengthened. Someshwar saw the disappointment on his face. He remembered the early battles he had fought beside Maharaj Kumarpal. A particular memory stood out, his moment of glory when he had leaped from his elephant to Mallikarjun's and severed his neck after snatching the man's sword. He had taken life before but not like that. And he never forgot the feeling as he stood there, a veritable giant among men, bathed in the blood of his heroic adversary while all around his troops had cheered and saluted him, fighting with each other for the chance to touch his feet.

There were those who had begrudged him his victory and had tried to take his triumph away, crediting others for the kill and even after all these years, his gorge rose with the unfairness of it all. But he would not dwell upon all that, not when his moment of glory was so close to hand.

Turning his attention back to his son, he said, 'I know that you are a valiant warrior and I could not be prouder, but believe me when you have left the gurukul for good and find yourself in the thick of battle, a part of you will long in vain for the peace and quiet of a simpler life.'

The prince looked at his father, who noticed that they had exactly the same birthmark just below the ear. This was the closest they had come to really talking. How come they hadn't done this before? His father looked him in the eye. 'I know about the attack on you. Kadambavas has been instructed by me to find out the names of the miscreants behind this foul deed and bring them to justice. My intuition tells me that it was the cowardly Bhimdev who was behind the attack. He pretended to offer us a hand of friendship but he has been plotting behind our backs all this time. If there is anybody who can find out the truth it is Kadambavas. You are my heir and aside from the mahamantri, the only one I trust to take care of the kingdom in my absence.'

'The kingdom is in safe hands, Father.' Prithvi held himself erect, 'Victory will be yours!'

Someshwar smiled at his son. Everybody was right about him. He was an incredibly fine specimen of manhood and more importantly, he was blessed with abundant courage and a noble heart. This godlike youth had sprung forth from his loins! The knowledge filled him with pride and a strange sadness. If the gods were good, perhaps his son would make amends for the mistakes that were his.

'I may not come back, son, but know that you are a credit to the name of your illustrious ancestors. And you must do everything in your power to enhance the prestige of the Chahamanas, so that history will remember the glory of our race. Long after you and I are gone.'

It was time for Someshwar to leave. Prithvi touched his feet with genuine respect and his father blessed him with all his heart. It was the last time they would speak. Funnily enough, it had also been the first time.

The army was leaving in stately procession followed by a vast and sprawling entourage of slaves, cooks, flautists, acrobats, entertainers, healers, mendicants who sold talismans of gods and goddesses swearing that their trinkets could ward off death and disability, snake charmers, dancers, musicians, perfumers, magicians, fortune tellers and just about every type of camp follower.

Kadambavas was deep in conversation with the pandit as they watched the troops depart from the ramparts of the fort. 'It is hard to believe that it has come to this,' the pandit began. 'You led me to believe that by your ingenious skills of diplomacy you had arranged for talks with the Chalukyas so you could negotiate with them and ask them to pay a tribute in exchange for taking back control of the territories captured during the reign of Vigraharaj. What happened to all that?'

'The talks took place at Sambhar,' Kadambavas replied. 'Bhimdev agreed to send two of his brothers and their sons for the meeting. Kanha and two of Rani Ketaki's relatives were to represent Maharaj Someshwar. Everything was going smoothly and they seemed perfectly amenable to my suggestions, which I admit was rather suspicious, and we just had to thrash out the smaller points.

'In keeping with diplomatic tradition, we had arranged a hunt. There was fine wine aplenty and some of the most nubile dancers you have laid eyes upon brought in from the southern coast. Everybody was in the best of spirits . . .'

'Please don't tell me that our conciliatory overtures came apart because of some drunken brawl . . .' the pandit said dramatically, even though he was well aware that it was exactly what had happened.

Kadambavas was quick to clarify. 'Our guests were drinking. Kanha and I had decided to have our wine watered down just to keep a clear head. It may have been a deliberate attempt to provoke or merely drunken babble but Bhimdev's idiotic brother brought up those tired old rumours about Maharani Kanchanadevi's chastity though we all know that Someshwar and Kanha were born here. Rani Ketaki's relatives took umbrage at that, shouting that they were confusing the virtuous Kanchanadevi with Maharani Karpuradevi, openly questioning the paternity of Prithviraj-III.

'I have never seen Kanha lose his temper so badly. None of us were carrying arms at dinner, but he grabbed a fruit knife and slew Rani Ketaki's kith and kin faster than we could blink let alone respond. Thinking they were under attack, Bhimdev's delegates jumped into the fray and fighting broke out between their armed guards and ours. You know the rest, not many survived that night.'

'But I am pleased to note that you got out safe and sound, Kadambavas,' the pandit interjected smoothly. 'Perhaps the Chalukyan king had hoped for just such a scenario when he sent those louts on a diplomatic mission, thus managing to kill two birds with one stone. And it reflected badly on us that the people who were supposed to be on our side couldn't guard their tongues against foul half-truths. How fares Kanha?'

'Needless to say, Maharaj Someshwar was furious with him for not taking better care of his wife's relatives. The young queen was most distraught and given the advanced state of her pregnancy, the king was worried. It was all very sentimental and exceedingly touching. Kanha being who he is wanted to make a clean breast of everything but I dissuaded him most strongly against such a course of action.'

Pandit Padmanabh smiled to himself. It was not a secret that Rani Ketaki's father, the raptorial Chandana, was angling for the position of mahamantri and it was he who had shouted down Kadambavas and insisted that his relatives be part of the diplomatic mission. With all of them despatched to Yama's abode, the canny old man had retreated with his tail between his legs, at least till the situation with the Chalukyas was resolved.

'Do enlighten me about the assassination plot, won't you?' he requested softly.

Kadambavas revealed nothing on his face, but he was surprised. Drastic measures had been taken to ensure the greatest secrecy. But the pandit's intricate web of spies among the ascetics, nuns, monks, musicians, dancers and courtesans clearly missed nothing and reported back to him.

He remembered the beautiful courtesan who had been brought in for the night's entertainment. She was without doubt the most gorgeous woman he had laid eyes upon. The blood had throbbed in his veins with raw excitement when he took in her swan-like neck, shapely shoulders, her firm breasts and smooth, shapely thighs. How tearful she had been when he discovered her later that night, cowering in her tent, how she had pressed herself against him in fright, begging for an escort to take her back in safety to her own place! Kadambavas had felt the slightest frisson of suspicion, but he had not been able to resist her.

'Kanha and I questioned some of the members of the Chalukyan delegation as well as their troops who had survived,' the mahamantri began, filled with fresh respect for the pandit's strict observation of celibacy. 'They were tight-lipped but we have certain techniques to loosen their tongues. We learnt that the entire exercise had been planned to lull us into a false sense of security while Bhimdev moved his armies into position for his invasion of Sapadalaksha. Many of our clandestine informers were slaughtered and their remains disposed of in secrecy so we wouldn't even realize they had gone missing. They most certainly had inside information. Worse, they had hired assassins to kill the king as well as the prince. Our men managed to hunt down and kill the ones sent after Maharaj Someshwar, a long way from Ajmer, but we were too late to prevent the attempt on the prince's life.'

'Prithviraj enjoys the favour of the gods,' the pandit said thoughtfully, 'but I am afraid that till we have succeeded in identifying those within our own ranks who would seek to betray the realm, we cannot afford to relax our guard. This plot runs deep and there are so many pieces still missing from the puzzle. Time is against us, we need to unmask the traitors in our midst and we must do it quickly.'

The man's dolorous tone was getting to Kadambavas. He was not superstitious but the implications of their conversation did not bode well for the men who were making their way to the banks of the Chambal where the enemy had massed. People spoke highly of his sagacity and many were openly suspicious of the mahamantri's seemingly magical ability to divine things but he was perfectly aware that he was no magician. Not even a Chanakya.

He set a lot of store in gathering intelligence and he believed he had a reliable network of informers. However, in this particular instance, his clandestine agents had let him down woefully, revealing the many leaks that would take a long time to plug. Which is why he had pushed for a diplomatic solution and blamed himself for its spectacular failure. Now they had been dragged into a war they could ill afford to lose and Bhimdev, who had proved himself a dangerous enemy, seemed to be firmly in control.

Kadambavas saw the soldiers disappearing into the horizon, the last echo of their marching and the galloping hooves swallowed up by the vastness of the distance between them. The soldiers looked tiny, like toys that could easily be stamped upon by giant feet.

13

As they marched, Kanha found himself worrying endlessly. Karpuradevi had been out of her mind with fear ever since the attack on Prithvi. She was convinced that Rani Ketaki and her family had been behind the whole thing and he could do little to set her mind at ease.

Not that he was without his own suspicions in the matter. It bothered him that Bhimdev had outmanoeuvred Kadambavas. It seemed to indicate that the Chalukyan king had the backing of powerful allies who had not yet revealed themselves. He had been pondering over it endlessly, sifting through the maze of possibilities, till his head began to pound in protest.

They set up camp not far from Chambal. Senapati Bhuvanakamala, who had taken over the control of the military from Sinhabala shortly after the installation of Someshwar, sent patrols into the surrounding countryside to study the movements of the opposing forces and to keep watch for surprise attacks. Guards were posted all around the perimeter.

The horns sounded shortly after Someshwar's tent had been pitched; the officials were summoned. As befitting his status as the king of the Chahamanas, Someshwar's temporary accommodation was made of the finest fabrics, embroidered in crimson, silver and gold. Carved wooden poles were used to prop up the structure and every inch of the floor was covered by fine mats and imported carpets procured from lands in the west. Heavy curtains separated the king's sleeping and bathing chambers from the main section, where he would meet with his war council.

As they gathered around, a light meal with watered-down wine was served. The atmosphere was tense. Maharaj Someshwar's new father-in-law, Chandana—who had recently been elevated to the rank of a general, though his experience in combat according to Kadambavas was limited to stabbing people in the back—adopted a belligerent air. He was openly hostile to Kanha. Chandana did not dare openly accuse the king's brother of murdering his relatives but he stopped just short of it.

For his part, Kanha was content to ignore that pompous prick of a man and only wished he could tell him that he had killed his useless kin with his own hands and they had all died blubbering and begging for their lives like the cowards they were. The king, meanwhile, was happy to pretend that they were one big happy family because any other version was sure to give him a giant headache.

Enthusiastically, Someshwar outlined his plan for the battle: 'I have listened to the reports of the scouts who were sent ahead to stake the enemy camp for days and returned with valuable information. Their camp is in a sorry state at sundown and a semblance of order is restored only when the sun has truly begun its ascent. Discipline appears to be very lax. Their animals are tethered and hobbled to prevent them from straying away and the rest of the camp is in a state of disarray. If we attack just before dawn, we will have the element of surprise and in addition to that we can take advantage of the chaos and confusion as the soldiers scramble to fasten their own armour while the slaves struggle to get the mounts bridled and ready for war. The superiority of our men will be evident and we will make mincemeat of them.'

He paused for dramatic effect looking around at his war council as though daring them to find a fault with his flawless plan. Chandana rose ponderously to his feet, his jowls wobbling and his reptilian eyes glittering as he applauded loudly and commended the king on his military genius.

Senapati Bhuvana was examining his fingernails with great attention when Kanha glanced over at him for support. The other generals were nodding along as they shovelled food into their mouths and called for more wine. The king took it as a sign of endorsement of his views and was looking mightily pleased with himself.

Taking a deep breath, Kanha spoke, 'It is a very good plan, maharaj, but if I may speak, I would like to submit a few points for your examination.' Chandana snorted and his cronies muttered angrily under their breath. Kanha ignored the lot of them with regal distaste, holding his ground.

His brother glared at him, 'Say what you must quickly and let us get on with it. We need a good night's rest before we make our decisive move. Bhimdev will think we are footsore and weary, not up to making a surprise attack, and we need to disabuse him of his notions.'

Kanha composed his features and tried to find a magical pitch that would convince the king. 'The Chalukyans have chosen this spot with care believing their position to be defensible. And they may be right. The river runs fast and its volume has swelled after the recent rains. The banks are steep and silt-laden. Our cavalry as well as heavy infantry will find the going rough in the water and on the sodden banks. The mobility of our troops will be severely compromised and if they were to push forward with their cavalry, we may be forced back into the river and no man's land.'

Silence fell as the council collectively held its breath. Someshwar seemed extremely put out. 'I have not overlooked a single detail, Kanha. We have experienced guides who have assured us that there are shallow points in the river where it can be easily forded. Once we are clear, at best they will manage to have their infantry lined up and we will use our assault troops to drive them back while the cavalry will protect our flanks. As I have already said, every eventuality has been taken into consideration and duly covered.

'Now if Kanha is finished with the nitpicking, let us retire for the night, tomorrow is a big day. We will smash our enemies in the battle of Chambal and at its conclusion you are all invited back here for a hearty celebration.'

As they trooped out of the tent, having received their orders, a few of the members looked at Kanha in commiseration. They no doubt truly believed that they were being extremely helpful and adequately compensating for their ineffectiveness back at the war council. As always, Kanha wondered about the supreme incompetence of men who rose to power and occupied positions of great responsibility.

His thoughts turned towards Kadambavas and he found himself wishing that the mahamantri was there. They had grown closer not because their regard for each other had improved but through the effect of shared secrets and spilled blood. The man had a veritable genius for cleaning up a mess and they could have used his talents in this situation, which was rapidly deteriorating into a shambles.

Kanha noticed the charming members of the entertainment troupe as they made their way to the king's tent. Chandana ushered them inside looking every bit like the pimp he was. The celebrations had already begun it would seem and prematurely at that. Senapati Bhuvana caught his eye and signalled for Kanha to join him. For a moment he was tempted to ignore the man but since he had nothing but a restless night to look forward to, he retraced his footsteps and followed the senapati into his tent.

Bhuvana did not bother with any small talk. 'The situation is far more dangerous than even you realize,' he said, his voice terse and urgent. Kanha did not respond, waiting in silence for the man to elaborate. He could hear the frogs croaking on the banks of the river and the chitter-chatter of insects.

'Don't you think it is a little suspicious that security isn't as tight as it ought to be on their side of the river? They seem to have posted only a token number of guards on duty. They have been here for a few days, which means they too must have some knowledge about the points where a crossing can be effected and yet they have left them largely unmanned.'

Kanha nodded. It had struck him as odd too. You did not have to be a military genius to figure out that the Chalukyans were planning a nasty little surprise for them and Someshwar was being very obliging by accepting an enemy's invitation with open arms.

'Closer to the camp they are on high alert, with teams of sentries and archers on patrol duty. They have lit fires at the guard stations to make sure that they are on the lookout for a stealth attack.'

'Looks like Bhimdev has taken every eventuality into consideration and covered it!' Kanha commented drily. 'Tell me, have your men discovered if Bhimdev is getting some additional help from allies that we need to know about? He seems a little too sure of himself.'

'That is what I wanted to speak to you about,' Bhuvana growled, his face distorted with outrage. 'Their allies are none other than the Chauhans!'

Kanha stared at him in shock, not comprehending and then the truth struck him with the force of a sledge hammer. He was a dunderhead for not having seen it sooner! Every family had its share of bad apples and for as long as he could remember, in these parts the Chauhans of Nadol were believed to be as bad as they came.

Given their family's history of fratricide, he had always felt it was a pity that Simharaj, grandson of the famous Vakpati-I, had not got rid of his quarrelsome younger brother, Lakshman. Instead he had allowed him to leave in high dudgeon and establish a separate kingdom in Nadol. Aside from the strategically important Mandore, it was a piddling excuse for an empire at best and a treacherous nest of vipers at worst.

The Chauhans of Sapadalaksha had always outshone the inferior branch of the family with the result that the Chauhans of Saptashata, as they liked to refer to themselves, had been every bit as jealous as the Kauravas had been of the Pandavas.

Bhuvana cleared his throat. 'They have been hand in glove with the Chalukyas ever since Mularaj-I entered into an allegiance with them. Your ancestor Durlabharaja-II taught Mahendra Chauhan of Nadol a lesson for his treachery and they have clearly been biding their time to exact their revenge. It seems that Bhimdev has revived this old alliance with Kumarasimha.'

The senapati paused and swallowed as though he were preparing to say something unpleasant. He looked a little green at the gills and Kanha had a sinking feeling in the pit of his stomach. Bhuvana spoke so softly that he had to strain his ears to listen. 'My men have indicated that Rani Ketaki's relatives may be in cahoots with our enemies. The jyotishis insist that she is carrying a boy and her father is determined to rule in his stead. Meanwhile, if heaven forbid, anything untoward were to happen to either the king or the prince . . . Kumarasimha intends to place his son Kelhanadeva on the throne of the Chahamanas.'

Kanha was feeling a little queasy. Plots within plots within plots. Never had he felt the absence of his mother so sorely. Kanchanadevi had thrived on this sort of thing, relishing the excuse to bare her fangs and unsheathe her sharpened claws.

Bhuvana's stomach was making unpleasant noises. How the man had been put in charge of the military escaped him.

'You understand that it is impossible for me to act in such a delicate manner,' he said, mopping his perspiring brows. 'In fact, you did not hear anything from me and since I have acted in accordance with my conscience it is best that you leave and do as you see fit.'

In a daze, Kanha stumbled into his tent. Quickly, he scrawled a message on a palm leaf with his silver stylus, filling the grooves with a special mixture of powdered charcoal and vegetable juice prepared by the pandit to make it easier to read. As he waited impatiently for it to dry, he thought of how reluctant he had been to learn the code Kadambavas had been hell-bent on teaching him so they could communicate in secret. He was a simple man and all this was beyond his ken and yet he was in the thick of things. Kanha could practically hear his mother hissing at him from the other side of life, urging him to get on with it.

Once the *talapatra* was ready, he concealed it in a silken pouch tucked into his clothing and stepped out casually as though he were out for a stroll in a park, hoping he did not look too conspicuous. He kept on walking till he reached the perimeter of the camp. The sentries were alert but they let him pass when they realized who he was.

At the remotest outpost, he spotted the man Kadambavas had told him about and concealing himself behind a tree, he waited for an opportune moment to catch his attention, since he was not alone. A sharpish chap, the man indicated that he needed to relieve himself after taking note of Kanha's presence. He sauntered over to where the king's brother was waiting for him.

Without a word, he accepted the talapatra and rejoined his companions. Kanha trudged back to his tent. The mahamantri had assured him that he had a relay system in place to make sure that urgent messages reached him quickly. And he hoped that Kadambavas had a contingency plan as well to avert the disaster that was staring them all in the face. There was nothing more for him to do now but to wait and see what the morrow had in store for all of them.

Kanha lay awake as the hours rolled by listening to the sounds of merriment from his brother's tent. Sensing his restlessness, his attendant sent him a companion to warm his bed and calm him down. He had chosen well, knowing his master's preferences. Kanha was moved by the old pimp's thoughtfulness. If fate had decreed that he die in battle tomorrow, thanks to the stupidity of his sibling, he saw no reason to let his last night on earth be a complete waste.

14

The battle of Chambal was a rout. A complete and unmitigated disaster. They had walked, nay rushed, into an ambush. Their clumsy attempt to make the crossing in secret did not fool the rows of sentries who had been keeping vigilance on the far side of the bank and they raised the alarm. The Chalukyan archers took up position and showered down a steady stream of arrows, finding their marks by the light of torches they had placed on the trees and lit as soon as the alarm was sounded. In minutes, the waters of the river turned red with the blood of the fallen Chahamanas troops.

Javelins and spears were loosed on them in a relentless stream. The horses lost their footing and many were lamed. The piteous neighing of the beasts further demoralized the troops. All would have been lost if not for the elephants.

Kanha gave orders for them to be used as a bridge at the points they had chosen to get the infantry across with ease, while the mounted archers gave them cover. The temperamental pachyderms seemed calmer in the water and the mahouts had little difficulty getting them to keep still. 'Forward!' he shouted and his men were galvanized into action, managing to reach the other side. Behind them they heard the booming of the drums, it drowned out the sounds of dying.

Searching frantically for the king, Kanha saw only the confusing mill of soldiers running frantically, brandishing their weapons. 'Throw them back,' somebody was shouting, 'give the fish something tasty to eat!'

The squadrons of the Chalukyas were massed for the attack and the men charged with their spears lowered till all around there was nothing to see but the tangled bodies of men, cutting and hacking at whoever appeared within range.

Kanha spotted his brother then. He too had made the crossing successfully. Mounted on his charger, he was leading the offensive and his sword was drenched in blood. To Kanha's horror, none of his personal bodyguards were visible. He was bleeding profusely from a wound he had taken above his collarbone. The golden diadem he was wearing marked him clearly as dawn broke and every single enemy soldier worth his salt surged towards him. The charger came under attack and the poor beast was cut and stabbed at a dozen places. As it collapsed, his brother was trapped underneath.

Kanha was fighting for dear life surrounded on all sides by enemy soldiers. A giant raised his axe but Kanha thrust his spear into his throat and lopped off another's arm. As he struggled to his feet, determined to reach his brother, Kanha heard shouting, 'Maharaj Someshwar is dead!'

He refused to believe it. Fighting like one demented, he mauled his way past the crush of battling men to the spot where he had last seen his brother. The charger lay dead. Somebody had already gotten their hands on the bridle. There was a lot of blood and it was hard to tell whether it was the horse's or the king's. And then he saw it, protruding from beneath the horse a limb hacked off almost at the thigh. It had belonged to his brother. The late Maharaj Someshwar.

A howl rose above the sounds of battle. An unearthly, inhuman keening filled with the demented rage of a madman. At the time, Kanha did not know that the animalistic baying emanated from his own being, torn from the very depths of his mourning soul.

Cries of 'Maharaj Someshwar is dead' were carried across the ranks, which were thrown into instant disarray. With their morale shattered, the troops were forced back by the enemy soldiers who fought with fresh impetus. Amidst scattered resistance, many fled in droves against the onslaught. It would have all been over had it not been for Mahamantri Kadambavas.

The canny tactician had held the troops from Dillika led by the valiant Govindraj, descendent of the Tomars and regent of the Chahamanas, in reserve. They had stayed put at Mathura till they received the mahamantri's summons after which they proceeded with great haste to attack the Chalukyans and the Chauhans of Nadol from the rear.

Govindraj led the vanguard himself, hammering into the ranks and penetrating so deep, he broke their spine under his impetus. His fresh cavalry galloped along enemy lines, harrying the troops and unloosing a storm of spear and sword.

In the meantime, Kanha had rallied the scattered squadrons of the Chahamanas and they regrouped, rediscovering their courage when the king's brother roared exhortations in his bull voice, 'If you are truly men born to your virtuous mothers, fight! For vengeance and for glory! See what they have done to your king! They must not go unpunished! Show them the quality of your mettle and make them regret the day they were whelped by whores!'

Galvanized into action and their fury stoked to boiling point, the resurgent warriors attacked with killing fury, throwing back the advance of the enemy. The battle of Chambal would have remained a stalemate, but Govindraj was relentless and his rear guard had already been given explicit instructions.

While the battle raged ahead of them, they succeeded in filling the ditches dug around the enemy camp with incendiary material and set fire to it. As the tents went up in flames, with all their equipment, reserve weapons, livestock and even women, the Chalukyan soldiers tried in vain to combat the raging inferno. Bhimdev had no choice but to flee the battlefield with his men, taking with him Maharaj Someshwar's mutilated remains.

Late in the evening, the opposing camps sent their emissaries to negotiate a truce. A lot of words were exchanged and the haggling seemed to go on forever. Finally, Bhimdev agreed to return the body of Maharaj Someshwar in exchange for the right to hold on to Chittor, Pali and Jalore. As a 'goodwill gesture', he was persuaded to pay a fair sum of gold as reparation for the damages of war and return the golden image of the family deity that had been affixed to the pommel of Someshwar's saddle.

Needless to say both sides were bitterly unhappy with how the battle of Chambal had turned out. At the end of it, there was no grand celebration. Hasty preparations for the long march home were made, and the troops trudged back, their hearts sick with the losses that had been sustained. And to perform the last rites of their fallen king and the other dead soldiers.

15

Pandit Padmanabh had decided to stay on in Ajmer for the duration of the war to help the mahamantri rule the kingdom. It was he who broke the news to Prithviraj, huffing and puffing all the way up the stairs to the tallest battlement, where the prince was usually found, feeding the pigeons or staring into the distance thinking the thoughts and dreaming the dreams only he knew about.

One look at the pandit's face and Prithviraj knew that the news wasn't good. His teacher shook his head in answer to the question in his eyes. From early reports, they knew that the battle of Chambal had not gone well for them.

To his credit, he did not lose his composure. Instead Prithviraj gazed at the Aravalli hills flanking his beloved city, seeming to imbibe some of their silent strength. He remembered how badly his father had wanted to win, how desperately eager he had been to prove himself. But defeat, ignominy and death on a battlefield was what he got. *It will not be my lot in life,* Prithvi swore to himself, *I will seduce the goddess of victory and keep her by my side.*

There was a delicate matter to be broached to the prince and the pandit had been the chosen envoy. 'From the time of your birth, it was obvious that you are born to rule. And yet haste as they say makes waste. Besides, our history is littered with examples of how terribly things could go wrong when princes with tremendous potential are placed on the throne before they are well and truly ready.'

Prithvi did not bother to reply and merely waited for his teacher to say his piece.

'Your studies are not yet complete and since you are a minor, it will be in the best interests of the kingdom if a regency council ruled till you are ready to take your place as the rightful king of the Chahamanas.'

He saw the sudden rage flash across his features like a streak of lightning. 'I suppose my mother will act as the regent, till it is officially recognized that I am a man fully grown and a warrior.' The prince did not wait for confirmation, 'There will be a day of reckoning for the Chauhans of Nadol and the Chalukyans under Bhimdev. They have gone too far. What news of my Uncle Kanha and Govindraj? I hear that it was Govindraj who prevented the annihilation of our forces. At the completion of my father's funeral rites, it is my wish to thank him personally.'

'That is most gracious of you, yuvaraj. As for your Uncle Kanha, he is stricken with grief but he fought like a lion and succeeded in retrieving the body of the king from his enemies.' *Your uncle is a good man and the only mistake Kanchanadevi ever made in her life was to push out her sons from between her legs in the wrong order*. The pandit left out that part, saying instead, 'We shall leave for Pushkar after the period of mourning has passed and resume lessons.'

For the briefest moment, he saw anticipation writ large across the prince's face but when he replied, Prithviraj's face was expressionless. 'As you wish, panditji! Now I must visit my mother and offer my condolences. And thank her for taking up the burden of regency.'

It was only after the prince had made his departure that the pandit allowed himself to wrinkle his nose. The expression brought to mind a man who had just got a whiff of an overflowing chamber pot. 'Whatever is the world coming to when the king of the Chahamanas allows himself to become enamoured of roadside vermin and a despoiled one at that?' he muttered aloud. Surely his charge knew that she had been held in captivity for days and was most certainly used every which way a man or many men could use a woman?

It was awful that it had fallen to him to take care of such an unseemly situation. The queen regent would have rooted out the problem of the girl with the brutality but none of the finesse that had been so characteristic of her mother-in-law. Kadambavas, on the other hand, would have no doubt figured out an ingenuous way to extricate the prince from her sticky web without breaking a strand. Perhaps it was time to talk to the mahamantri and figure out how to deal with the girl once and for all.

The mahamantri was deep in conversation with the queen regent. For the moment at least, she was hiding her grief very well. Like Kanchanadevi, she refused to wear the white sari to mark her as a widow. Kanchanadevi had abhorred the practice. 'It is bad enough that a woman of my stature and intelligence has to deal with idiotic males whose brains are far smaller than the point of a needle in order to run a kingdom. The job would be ten times harder if they saw a grieving widow clad in miserable white, whom they will be tempted to use as a loincloth. Which is why I have always comported myself in a manner befitting a queen and any man who even looks at me with anything less than the utmost respect is a dead man!' she had always said.

Karpuradevi was determined to live by the same credo. She wore austere garments and unostentatious jewellery, covering her head with a veil, but refused to play the part of an inauspicious woman. She simply did not have the time or inclination to wail and weep, bemoaning the loss of her husband by tearing at her hair and beating her breasts. Currently, she was in the process of interrogating the mahamantri about the fallout from the battle of Chambal.

'The orders issued by the queen regent have already been successfully carried out. You will be pleased to note that Kanha has personally sent me a message clarifying that the enemies of the throne did not survive the battle and the march back home. Their injuries from the battle took a sudden turn for the worse,' Kadambavas was saying, 'despite the lamentable occurrences that have claimed the life of Maharaj Someshwar, we may derive some satisfaction that a deplorable situation was contained before it got well and truly out of hand.'

Karpuradevi had to concur. 'I must talk to Prithvi and see how he is taking the news of his father's death. They were never very close but even so it is a sad day when a boy is deprived of his father prematurely. And it is to be hoped that he will not be difficult in the days to come, while we work tirelessly to strengthen the kingdom prior to his ascent. In the meantime, we must have all in readiness for the funeral rites. There is so much to be done, I can barely think straight!'

'You must calm yourself, my queen, and not concern yourself with these matters. Preparations are already underway. I have sent a team of vaidyas and pandits handpicked by Padmanabh to meet the procession and begin the purification rituals so that the young prince may be spared the trauma of seeing his father's condition.'

The queen appreciated his delicacy but she knew that when he said 'young prince', he actually meant her. It annoyed her when men assumed that she would faint and fall to the ground every single time she was confronted by news of a violent or unpleasant nature. The reports had been perfectly clear and concise if grisly. Maharaj Someshwar had sustained grievous injuries in the course of an ill-advised attack. He had been crushed under his horse and the enemy soldiers had fallen on him like wild animals, hacking his body to pieces and dragging away the parts to be given as a trophy to Bhimdev.

She was sorry that Someshwar had come to such a bad end but even his mother would have agreed that he had it coming with his foolhardy recklessness and childish disregard for the council and those who knew better. It was easy to see where Prithvi got his own mulish streak.

Karpuradevi took a deep breath. 'There is much that needs to be done. News of my lord's passing would have spread everywhere by now. We have managed to deal with the Chalukyas and their treacherous allies for now but their movements will have to be carefully monitored in the event of further attacks. There will be others as well looking to get their hands on Sapadalaksha territory. It is hard to predict where or when our enemies will strike, but we must be alert and prepared for anything. No one must be allowed to weaken the realm!'

'My informers will gather intelligence from within and without our borders. They will report on the mood of your subjects and the movements of our allies as well as any battle plans of hostile forces.' Kadambavas had hastened to reassure her.

The tiniest of frowns marred her features. Kadambavas knew what she was thinking. It had been a breakdown of intelligence that had led to this whole mess in the first place. She would never admit that ultimately everything had worked out entirely to her satisfaction.

'We cannot afford any mistakes,' she said, stating the obvious in the mahamantri's opinion. 'Our enemies must not be allowed to think that with a young boy on the throne of the Chahamanas, our realm is ripe for the picking.'

Prithviraj walked in just in time to hear the tail end of her comment. He had bypassed the guards posted outside the queen's private audience chamber, already asserting his authority. Kadambavas closed his eyes for a moment. He hated getting caught up in whatever power struggle was happening between them. It were these internal conflicts that usually brought down entire realms and undid all the results men like the pandit, Kanha and himself worked so hard to achieve.

The future king looked at his mother in cool appraisal. 'I am sorry for your loss, Mother. It must be a terrible blow to you and a time of great sorrow. Yet you have shouldered this burden without breaking down and taken on the responsibility of dealing with my inheritance. I acknowledge you as the queen regent.' His tone struck just the right note conveying respect, sympathy and sorrow, yet somehow he seemed to be pronouncing a scathing indictment on her failure as a wife and mother. Karpuradevi felt like she had been slapped in the face.

Her bosom heaved mightily but before she could respond they heard the shouts of the guards as Ketaki tore into the room like a dust storm straight out of the desert, a roiling mass of destruction. She was wailing, screaming incoherently, tearing at her hair and shouting curses fit to make the ears bleed. Barrelling past Prithvi, she pointed an accusing finger at Karpuradevi and spat at her feet. 'You had them all killed! My husband, my father, my cousins . . . All of this was planned by you and carried out by that blood-traitor lover of yours! Do you know the things they say about you? Don't think you will get away with this! The gods will make you pay . . .'

The young queen, no older than Prithvi, was completely out of control. She was clutching her gravid belly and was in a state of dishabille, her garments torn and her hair a wild tangled mess.

'I loved my husband! He was my king and god! You cared nothing for him. It did not matter to you in the least whether he lived or died. Now you would kill me too like you killed him and the others. Even his unborn son and true he . . .' she could not go on because she was choking on her tears.

Prithvi could barely hear her over the ringing in his ears. From what he could gather, her father and relatives had been killed and she felt the queen regent was to blame. And she probably wasn't far wrong. If his mother harboured the remotest suspicion that her relatives were involved in the assassination plot against him, there was no saying what she might have done. Especially since his loving mother had long been waiting for the right pretext to get rid of Rani Ketaki and her family, who had dared to get so close to the king.

Suddenly the younger queen threw herself at him, scrambling to get her arms past her stomach and around his feet. 'For the love of god, have mercy, my prince! I am not afraid of death. Gladly would I have joined my husband on the flames if it had not been for the child I carry. Please don't let her harm my baby! My child is innocent. He does not deserve to die.'

Gently, he placed his hands on her shoulders and raised the girl to her feet. 'A young mother and child need never have any reason to fear me. You will not be harmed and neither will your child, who is my father's son and my brother. That is a promise!'

He looked at his mother as he said the words. And she read the warning in that powerful gaze. Clear as day.

Maharaj Someshwar's funeral was a solemn and exceedingly grand affair. His mandaleshwars, *dandanayakas*, jagirs, samants and well-wishers from the length and breadth of the Chahamanas kingdom arrived in droves to pay their respects. Prithvi, Hari and Uncle Kanha took their position by the side of the enormous funeral pyre built for the king's last journey as the priests led by the pandit chanted the prayers and incantations that were part of the last purification rites and rituals.

Pandit Padmanabh had instructed them that these final rites were crucial as it was a holy process of expiation that would release the *atma* or soul from any unsightly stains, thereby restoring it to its original pure state. And when the body was cleansed in Agni's flames, the atma would merge with Paramasiva and a mortal would finally achieve moksha from the unforgiving cycle of birth and rebirth.

Prithvi supposed it was one way of making the king's heir feel better about the fact that his father was gone. At least, the monotonous chanting was drawing to a close. Or so it was to be hoped. He was beginning to think that the priests could keep it up till the very end of time or till he tore out his ears and flung them at their heads.

He followed the pandit's instructions mechanically, wanting it all to be over, so that life could return to some semblance of normalcy. With his own hands, he lit the pyre with the torch that had been handed to him. Uncle Kanha led him behind the enclosure as the flames caught, aided by the generous libations of oil and ghee poured over the fire, rising higher and higher till it was an almighty conflagration, crackling louder than the roaring of the priests.

The heat was unbearable and Prithvi felt Hari flinch by his side. There were palls of thick funerary smoke as Yama's consort Dhumorna arrived, cavorting with the flames as she ushered the soul to her lord's domain. Uncle Kanha stood on the other side and he held himself stiffly, seemingly tensed about something.

Prithvi blinked as a procession appeared on the other side. They were his father's many wives and concubines, he supposed. Had so many volunteered to perform Sati? And then he saw her at the head of the procession: the young girl no older than him. His father's favourite wife, who had given him back his youth, rejuvenated his spirit and made him so happy during his last days. The mother of his unborn baby, who had been adored all her short life. The beautiful girl whom he had promised would come to no harm.

Rani Ketaki looked so ethereal and lovely, the onlookers found it hard to breathe. Her steps were small and shaky and the glassy cast to her eyes said it all. His mother was a stickler for appearances. After all, it would be most unseemly if the procession carefully chosen by her went to their deaths, kicking and screaming bloody murder. On the other hand, if given a healthy dose of kushumba, they instantly became pliant as lambs while being led to the slaughter house.

She was close to the flames now. Prithvi stepped forward unthinkingly with arms outstretched. *No mother*! *This is too monstrous*! *With her family gone, she couldn't possibly do us any harm*! But Uncle Kanha grabbed him by the shoulders in a grip of steel.

For the first time in the course of their long relationship, Prithvi turned a gaze full of rage at him that hurt a lot worse than the wounds he had taken in battle, but Kanha wouldn't back down. 'Please, Prithvi! It is done now. If you disrupt the proceedings, it will be an inauspicious beginning to your reign,' he was pleading with him. Seeing that his anger refused to be assuaged, Kanha let him go. When the prince turned, it was already too late. He could no longer see her.

The flames rose even higher, delirious from gorging on the flesh of the living. It seemed that the procession was endless as they all walked into Agni's outstretched embrace. Bedecked in exquisite silks, adorned in their finest jewellery with carefully made-up faces, they all had the same unsteady gait, glassy cast to the eye and non-seeing stare as they entered his father's pyre. The fire devoured them all, cackling as it did so, not sparing even the screams of its victims, swallowing them whole.

A lone tear ran down Prithvi's hot cheek but it dried up almost immediately.

Karpuradevi saw and felt her son's anguish and she knew he would never forgive her. The queen wanted to go to him, take her baby into her arms and comfort him. She would have settled for a single look from him. But her son seemed to find the sight of her repulsive and would not turn her way. Instead he stared as though hypnotized at the flames.

Don't you understand, my son! It had to be done. Her brat would have always been a threat to you. Those fine noblemen standing all around, pretending to be your faithful vassals, could have rallied to your rival's side and sought to depose you and rule in his name.

You are good and kind but in this world there will always be those who will use those very things to their advantage and seek to put you on a funeral pyre. I am the mother of a king and those fine principles you have are a luxury a queen cannot afford to have. Someday, you will understand that everything I did was for your own good. Think more kindly of your mother then. Remember that she loved you!

It was the anguished voice of her heart. And it fell on deaf ears.

16

Prithviraj had been in the foulest of moods. No matter how hard he trained, rode or ran he found that his rage refused to dissipate. He considered running away with Yogita but even that thought made him feel bleaker than ever. For a moment, he was tempted to have his mother imprisoned and flogged. Padhri thought it would be a good time for them to sidestep the pandit's stern rule prohibiting the consumption of liquor. At the time, Prithvi thought it was the most brilliant thing his friend had uttered in his life.

The next morning though, when he woke up he found himself near naked on a training field, his head in a pool of vomit, purple bruises all over his body and a head that was fit to bursting with pain. His companions were in identical states, even Jaya and Hari. Once the vaidya, a man named Narana, had taken care of their assorted injuries, he spoke to them for the better part of the day on the evils of alcohol consumption, assuring them that they would die pissing blood if they drank the poisonous stuff ever again. A messenger came to him bearing an urgent summons from his mother and wound up with a face full of the foul potion the vaidya was forcing him to drink to help with his hangover.

By then, Prithvi was heartily sick of every single person in his life. On an impulse, he decided to keep his word to the pandit and thank the hero of the battle of Chambal for stellar services rendered. It had turned out to be a good move, which resulted in him finding himself far away from the turmoil of Ajmer and comfortably ensconced at the royal residence in Dillika.

The mandaleshwar Govindraj was much younger than his Uncle Kanha and Kadambavas. He was a good-looking man and carried the trappings of his noble birth with ease. His manner was pleasant and easy-going. There was a certain serenity to the man that Prithvi found himself drawn to. He had hated listening to the condolences of thousands of people on the tragic demise of his father, but it was different with Govindraj. He was earnest, sincere and kept things light by sharing an amusing anecdote about his relationship with Someshwar. When the invitation to visit had been extended, Prithvi accepted with alacrity.

On the ride thither, he and his friends had been thoroughly charmed by their host and his city both. Govindraj had told them about the origin of Dillika. 'A long time ago, one of the ancestors of the Tomars by the name of Kalhan beheld a strange sight. A fierce hound was chasing a hare when it turned around suddenly with the savagery of a predator, attacked its pursuer and chased it away. Knowing that it was an omen of great portent, he called his wise men. They told him that the place was sacred for beneath the surface rested the hood of Sesha, who bore Vishnu during his *yoganidra* as well as the weight of the world. Hence, it was decided to build the city at that very spot. It has been prophesized that Dillika will always be a seat of great power in the known world.'

Jaya was nodding along in his most scholarly manner. 'It is true! Can't you all feel the vibrations and the primeval energy that is pulsing underneath? They say that in the age of epics, Dillika was none other than Indraprastha, the capital city of the Pandavas, raised by the grace of Krishna and built by Maya, the brilliant architect of the asuras.'

'It is decided then,' Kanak asserted, 'You should shift to Dilli, Prithvi, and make it the new capital of the Chahamanas! The sheer abundance of feminine pulchritude in these parts makes it worth considering, wouldn't you say?'

Prithvi had been sorely tempted. But Jaya said, 'The people here don't like it when you refer to their beautiful city as "Dilli"! And they tend not to take kindly to outsiders who ogle at their women openly and refuse to treat them like sisters. Moreover . . .' Kanak hit him on the head then, nearly knocking him off his seat. They all roared with laughter, including Prithvi. Sometimes Jaya seemed to ask for it. Gracious as ever, Govindraj fell back to make sure the sensitive poet was unhurt.

Their host proved himself to be exceedingly thoughtful, arranging for singing minstrels, dancers, contortionists, magicians and storytellers to keep his young and rambunctious company entertained. Prithvi found it all to be most diverting but the prince liked their conversations best of all.

'I am glad to see that your spirits have lifted,' Govindraj commented as he entered the prince's luxuriously appointed private chambers. Prithvi's smile widened. His stay at Dillika had provided him with the respite he needed. 'It is nice here,' Prithvi said. 'But I must get back to Pushkar. The pandit must be having conniptions by now.' *And I miss Yogita. When she is not by my side, I am incomplete.*

Govindraj nodded in understanding. He guessed that something was weighing on the future king's mind and waited patiently for Prithvi to unburden himself. 'I have been thinking,' he began, 'that I would have liked to have been there when Mahmud of Ghazni terrorized the countryside. What a formidable antagonist he must have been! An opponent worthy of Arjuna himself!'

His host shook his head. 'Be very careful what you wish for, maharaj . . . There are monsters aplenty in our world without wishing for the worst of them to wander in our midst. Besides, you must already know that a new power has emerged from the ashes of the Ghaznavid empire. From what I have heard from the Mussulmen traders, who were interrogated by my men, the Ghurs make the scourge of our aryavarta look like a purring kitten by comparison . . .'

Prithvi was intrigued. 'Tell me about the Ghurs . . .' he asked eagerly, morbid fascination writ large on his features.

'There appears to have been a blood feud between the Ghurs and the Ghaznavids going back many decades. Ghur was a feudal territory of Sultan Mahmud, but his successors were considered weak and this prompted them to make a bid for independence. The insurrection appears to have been dealt with an iron hand and Bahram Shah of Ghazni had two Ghur princes poisoned. That was the tipping point and their brother whose name is really hard to pronounce . . . What was it again?' Govindraj's forehead was creased in thought. 'Alauddin Husayn, I think, retaliated with vengeance.'

Prithvi was hanging on to every word and seemed to have been transported to another place where it was all unfolding before his very eyes.

'He sacked Ghazni, which at one time was apparently revered as the "bride of cities",' Govindraj continued, caught up in the lad's youthful enthusiasm. 'I should think so since it was paved in gold with the riches he plundered from our lands and temples. Mahmud's capital city burned for seven days and seven nights. The flames sparked by the wrath of a bereaved brother spared nothing of the fine palaces, baths, places of worship and public buildings. He made the captured citizens watch as their homes burned and many put out their eyes unable to watch the horror unfold . . .

'Then the man who was given the honorific "Jahansuz", meaning "Incendiary Destroyer of the World" or something, slaughtered the men, raped the women and sold the children into slavery. In other words, it seems the sins of the beastly

Ghaznavids finally caught up with them, as did the curses of the victims!'

'Equating men like that to beasts is an insult to our four-legged friends,' Prithvi opined. Govindraj could practically see the wheels turning in his head as the scion of the Chahamanas resolved to be magnanimous in victory, treating his enemies with clemency. However, he had been in enough wars to know that they tended to break down the barriers of decency erected by civilization, allowing bloodlust to come boiling to the surface. Still, it was to be hoped that Prithvi would succeed in doing the right thing when the killing frenzy was upon him.

'What happened after that? What became of Ulaudin Husayn,' Prithvi tried unsuccessfully to wrap his lips around the name, 'the one they called "The Burner of the World"?'

'I am not sure of what became of him but his nephew is the Sultan of Ghur now.' Govindraj tried to recollect the things he had been told. 'He also has a mleccha name that is hard to pronounce . . . Ghiyasuddin. But the man we have to concern ourselves with is his brother Shihabuddin. Our people refer to him as Mahmud of Ghur since he seems to be made in the same mould. But unlike the former who has been dead for more than a century, this one is alive, kicking and seems determined to raise all manner of hell.'

Govindraj paused, gathering his thoughts. 'Shihabuddin is fiercely loyal to his older brother and is a ruthless warrior. After every conquest, he sends the finest of his plunder to his sibling and the sultan. As a reward for his services, he has been named the governor of Ghazni. The two of them have an understanding. Ghiyas will focus on eliminating their enemies to the West while Shihab will turn his attention to the East and the remains of the Shahi kingdom still under control of a surviving member of the former Ghaznavid empire.'

'Then it is only a matter of time before Shihabuddin turns up in aryavarta. He will never be able to resist the treasures of our land, overflowing as it is with milk and honey,' Prithvi said this the certainty of one who had seen the veils of time part to reveal the future. 'We stand on the threshold of a crucial moment in time, an epoch-making moment. Fate has thrown up a similar combination of circumstances from the past that has proved to be the catalyst for great glory. But when history repeats itself, the results themselves will not be the same.

'It is a brilliant opportunity for us to blot the stain on our honour and reclaim our pride. We will fight him together, you and I! What a battle it is going to be! They will sing our praises forever! Can't you just feel it in your bones?'

And at that moment, Govindraj felt it too. The chill of presentiment, hardening into a heavy weight that settled at the very bottom of his heart. Gathering his courage, he clenched his fist and placed it over his chest. 'We will ride together to whatever fate has in store for us! May the name of Prithviraj Chauhan live forever!'

Back in Pushkar, the pandit was not having conniptions but he had just concluded a rather unpleasant conversation with a personage he found most odious. The only solace to be had from the prince's rebellious streak was that he had been given a little time and space to take care of the little bitch who had got her filthy paws on the future king of the realm. And not a moment too soon! Word had reached him that the impetuous youngster was on his way back.

The time had come for him to get it all over and done with quickly. Already the affair had been allowed to go on for far too long. It would never do if the wench succeeded in getting herself impregnated and presenting them with a sordid bundle of shame to flaunt her hold over their king. He remembered how brazen she had been. Karpuradevi would have his hide if such an unspeakable monstrosity were allowed to come to pass. Which was why he had taken such a harsh stand with her.

He mopped his balding pate and forehead, which were perspiring freely. He still remembered the way she had held herself, fierce and proud. How boldly she had looked him in the eye and the fearless way in which she had accepted the sentence he had handed out!

'Have you no shame?' he had asked her finally, frustrated that his stern injunctions had not reduced her to a quivering mess and a puddle of tears. 'You are not fit to be in polite society and you dare to presume that you will someday be the consort of a king! And don't think for a moment that we will allow you to complete the formalities that will let you embark on a career as a ganika. A creature such as yourself cannot be allowed to join their cultured ranks and rub shoulders with the cream of aryavarta. If you had any honour at all, you would have killed yourself the first chance you got!'

'I thank you for the kindness and forbearance you have shown me for the duration of my time here. Right up to this meeting, my sojourn here has been the happiest in my accursed life and for that you will always have my gratitude.' She had replied with quiet dignity and grace. 'As to your proposal, I accept wholeheartedly for it is what I had intended to do all along.'

Holding herself erect, she made ready to leave though he had not given her permission to do so. The little hussy had looked him in the eye and said, 'I have been guilty of much wrongdoing and the gods will judge me for the same, but I will never lower my eyes in shame nor kill myself over the cruelty and sins of others!' Then with her head held high, she had flounced out of his chambers. Like a queen.

If the prince were to ever find out what he had done . . . But what was done was done. Besides, his loyalty was to the throne and he had done his part to ensure the well-being of the one destined to sit on it for what would hopefully be a long and glorious reign. Sometimes even the best of sovereigns needed to be protected from the worst of their impulses.

On arriving at Pushkar, Prithvi stopped only to pay his respects to the pandit before leaving to meet Yogita in their usual spot. She was waiting for him and Prithvi stood there for a few minutes just to drink his fill of her. How beautiful she looked as she sat there, with her feet swinging just above the stream bed! Dark-skinned and raven-haired, the graceful curves of her body and silken limbs reminding him of a beautiful fawn he had once seen on a hunt. Her eyes were just as large and mournful. When he looked into them and saw the ineffable sadness, he felt her grief in his own heart and wanted nothing more than to take her in his arms and soothe the pain away.

Sensing his presence, Yogita turned and a beatific smile lit up her face. Prithvi hastened to her side. There was so much he had to tell her. She listened intently while he told her about his father's passing, his mother's treatment of Rani Ketaki and his visit to Dillika. 'I am to take my rightful place on the Chahamanas throne before the year is out,' Prithvi told her in his king's voice. 'You must come with me to Ajmer. It is a beautiful little valley ringed by the Aravalli mountains. And we will be together always.'

She smiled at him. 'This aryavarta will finally have the leader it needs in you! You are going to be the best of kings!'

Prithvi acknowledged the praise with a tilt of his head. 'I have been trained for it by Guru Bharadwaj and Pandit Padmanabh. The latter insists that I am his masterpiece!' He didn't notice that her smile had become a little strained. 'My first task will be to secure the borders of the empire. With my mother on the regency council, our enemies will feel daring enough to test the might of the Chauhans and I have to convince them otherwise. Once I have taken care of the rebels and avenged my father by crushing Bhimdev, I will be ready to take on a dangerous and worthy foe!'

'What do you mean? Tell me about this enemy . . .'

'Shihabuddin of Ghur comes from a rough, mountainous land famed for its iron ore deposits, hunting dogs and horses.' He had insisted on speaking to the mleccha traders himself during his stay at Dillika so he could be well-informed about his rival's movements. 'They rose to power by defeating the successors of Mahmud of Ghazni and razing his capital city to the ground. Now he turns his roving eye to the East and the fabulous bounties that our beautiful land has to offer. This time, when he dares to show his face in these parts, we will not be caught with our pants down and I will defeat him so soundly in battle that he will flee to the bowels of the wild lands that spat him out and never come back. As for the cowards who are afraid of the barbarians and inclined to flee, I will have them killed!'

His voice throbbed with passion and an irresistible force that would brook no opposition and yet Yogita had never been more afraid for him. Fate had plans for all of them and from her experience, it was a cruel and capricious creature that gave with one hand and took it away with the other, ever jealous of the happiness of others.

This person from Ghur seemed to be one of fate's tools employed in the cause of snuffing out what little joy was left in the world. 'He must be a cruel man indeed if he managed to outperform that accursed Mahmud of Ghazni in terms of atrocity. From now on, I will pray that his enemies will succeed in killing him before he comes to our borders. If they don't, I pray that he is struck down by an incurable illness or a bolt of lightning.'

Prithvi laughed aloud, sometimes she was such a girl! 'It is destined that our paths will cross as will our swords. I will fight him and emerge as the victor. Then we will remember this day and laugh at your groundless fears together.'

She stayed silent and sad. Prithvi stared at her. For the first time in his life, he felt a frisson of pure terror.

Yogita took a deep breath. She would have been content to stay at his feet forever—this handsome young man who was the kindest person she had ever known. The all-powerful forces that governed over everyone in existence had not acceded to her wish though. It was best that she broke the news to him quickly.

'I was taken in to continue my training in the courtly arts out of respect for your wishes, but my teachers and priests have made their decision. It has been discovered that I do not have the needed credentials and qualifications to dance before the gods on religious occasions. They say that my background makes me unworthy. Therefore, in a few days' time, I will be inducted among the *Yogini Sampradayas,* take holy orders and devote myself to the ascetic way of life.' Her cheeks were wet with tears as the words spilled out of her in a rush though she tried to control her runaway emotions.

Prithvi was dumbfounded, though he should have seen this coming. 'My mother has something to with this! If she has threatened you in any way, I will . . .'

'No, sire!' she was crying now. 'The queen has nothing to do with this. It is a decision that I wholeheartedly accept. If you take me with you to Ajmer, it will be just the thing your enemies need to create a scandal. I would rather die than bring shame upon your name!'

'I will never let you go . . .' Every word was uttered with a vehement intensity that scared her and seeing the fear in her eyes, he grabbed her by the wrists. With a sudden movement, he hauled her up in a wrenching motion that made her gasp. The physical proximity and his raw forcefulness made her heart pound as he pushed her up against the wall of a rock, bringing his face close to hers: so close that their lips were a mere heartbeat away.

His touch inflamed her senses and she felt herself enslaved by the flames of the desire he felt for her, the recognition of which sent her into a frenzy of excitement. Nothing had prepared her for the power of the forbidden passion that cascaded over her, a tidal wave of ecstasy obliterating all thought but the need to merge herself with him. But foreboding flooded her heart, breaking free of the restraints that sought to constrain it, bringing sobering despair close on its heels. Breaking free of the hold he had over her, she refused to give in. To his need or hers.

'I love you more than the gods, more than life itself,' she said, finding her courage, 'for the rest of my life my thoughts and prayers will be devoted solely to you. But after what happened to me during all those days spent in captivity, what remains of my honour is the most precious thing I own and it will not be sacrificed so you can keep me as a concubine.'

Her words landed on his ears like thunderbolts lacerating his very soul. He had refused to acknowledge the things that had been done to her after she was kidnapped. His mind had always refused to process it. She may have accepted the past and made her peace with it. She may have the fortitude to let him go. But he couldn't do it and for the first time in his life, he felt unworthy, like the cowards he had promised to kill. At that moment, he hated her.

She saw the hatred in his eyes and cried out loud as her heart shattered, never to be whole again. Extricating herself from his rough embrace, she touched his cheek gently, memorizing every single detail of that countenance, imprinting it on her soul. 'Farewell, Prithviraj Chauhan!' It was the first time she had used his name. 'Do not forget me or the great love I bear you.' And then she walked away, without waiting for his reply, without looking back. Not once.

'I will never let you go! You are mine and my will cannot be denied! Once I become the king, *yogini* or not, I will have you dragged to my side in chains if that is what it takes . . .' His stentorian voiced boomed against the rock face, echoing off its sides.

Yogita gave absolutely no indication that she had heard his hurtful words, which clearly implied that he too believed that she was his to do with as he pleased, and it hurt her more than anything else she had endured. Even so, a tiny part of her hoped that he would keep his word. That he would keep her chained to his side and never let her go.

17

Prithvi pored over the reports, hardly able to contain his excitement. The pandit was amazed at the reaction. He himself had an unholy terror of barbarian invaders who brought the dogs of war to this very aryavarta and sought to destroy temples and priests with fire and steel. He shuddered at the prospect. Ever since he had heard about this latest threat, he had been praying to Shiva to stop making love to Shakti, open his third eye and incinerate the lot of them. It would make things so much easier for his devout followers.

'And so it begins. Shihabuddin of Ghur has invaded Multan successfully after subduing the Karmatiyas. Wasn't that a part of the Shahi kingdom, which was invaded by Mahmud of Ghazni? Aren't they Mussulmen?' Prithvi frowned as he tried to remember.

'That is correct,' the pandit said pedantically. 'However, that region seems to change its religion the way we change our clothes. It was home to the Mussulmen before the Buddhists took over. Then a great majority of its people were Hindus but now the Mussulmen have repopulated the land, though a substantial number of Hindus and Buddhists continue to live there.'

'The man moves fast. He has also captured Uchch, where some still practise the teaching of Gautama Buddha, where the Mussulmen comprise the majority. It just proves what I have always known. The first time around, Mahmud of

Ghazni justified his bloodthirstiness and rapacious plundering by claiming that he was acting on the orders of his god but Shihabuddin cannot claim the same if he is attacking his brothers of the same faith!'

'Wait and watch! Soon he will be calling for the infidels to convert to his faith. And when they refuse, he will seek to tear down their walls, burning and plundering like his predecessor. Soon people will be intimidated enough to surrender to his outrageous terms but once they throw open their doors, he is still going to sack them.

'Religion is as good an excuse to go to war as any other . . .' the pedagogue droned on. 'Now he has turned his attention to Nadol. Kumarasimha, the blood traitor, has sent emissaries seeking the help of the Chauhans of Sapadalaksha. The nerve of that man! He stabs the father in the back and has the unmitigated gall to come begging to the son for help!'

'Kumarasimha does not have much of a choice, does he?' Prithvi said thoughtfully. 'After the battle of Chambal, when the truce was negotiated, Bhimdev was asked to pay an indemnity and he agreed albeit grudgingly. But later, he made Kumarasimha cough up the entire amount, laying the blame for their defeat at the feet of his former allies. The Chauhans of Nadol were humiliated and left without resources. They simply cannot mount a viable defence against an impending invasion and such a formidable opponent.'

'Serves them right too . . .'

'I disagree!' Prithvi asserted. 'By going to their aid, there are certain benefits to be had. It is a good way to break up the pestilential alliance between the Chalukyans and the Chauhans of Nadol. In addition to that, we will get a chance to see Shihabuddin's battle tactics and turn him back before he gains the slightest foothold in aryavarta.'

The pandit thought it was a horrendous notion. Prithvi was a fine warrior but he was as yet a boy who hadn't even finished his studies whereas Shihabuddin was a veteran who had sharpened his claws on the dead bodies of the Ghaznavids. However, he said with a great deal of tact, 'The regency council will never agree to this.'

Prithviraj's voice became chilly at once. 'It behoves them to act in accordance with their king's will. Which is why we must leave at once for Ajmer so that they get the opportunity to hear my thoughts on the matter.'

Padmanabh felt an urgent need to excuse himself and go to the privy. 'Maharaj, the queen will never agree to this proposal.'

'Then the regent would have forced my hand! And I will have to release her from the services she has rendered to the throne. At this juncture, I must ask where the loyalties of my revered teacher lie?' His voice was ominous and the pandit did not hesitate. 'I serve Prithviraj Chauhan, rightful king of the Chahamanas.'

'It is simply impossible!' Karpuradevi said firmly. 'We cannot go to the aid of Kumarasimha and the Chauhans of Nadol. Is it necessary for me to remind you that his treachery resulted in the death of your father?'

The queen regent did not know why her son found it necessary to vex her so. It was bad enough that there were those who held her responsible for the disaster at Chambal though she had been against it from the very beginning. Some had gone so far as to say that Kanha had engineered the whole crisis to steal the throne from under his brother's nose the way he had his wife. Bloody ingrates, the lot of them! And now her son was insisting that they expend valuable men and material on a war they did not need.

'I am fully aware of their perfidy and it is my intention to make them pay. But Shihabuddin is not a foe to be taken lightly and cannot be allowed to make incursions into aryavarta. I owe it to the blood of my ancestors not to rest till the mleccha menace is wiped out! And we are not rendering this service out of the goodness of our hearts. Nadol and Mandore will become absorbed into our realms and Kumarasimha will be taken prisoner while his son Kelhanadeva will be appointed as the mandaleshwar. When faced with the risk of annihilation, they will have no choice but to agree to our terms,' Prithvi told her in controlled tones.

The reason Mahmud of Ghazni had got away with so many depredations were people like his mother. Prithvi was sure of it. If only his grandmother was alive! Kanchanadevi of Patan had known how to leave sentiment and stupidity out of decision-making.

Karpuradevi glanced at the members of the regency council. Prithvi did the same. The Brahmin Sodh who had accompanied his father from Gurjardesa seemed to be mildly interested in the proceedings that were a refreshing change for the *sandhivigrahika*. To the best of his knowledge all he did was eat and then make the immediate vicinity around him uninhabitable by constantly belching and farting.

Prithvi suspected that Senapati Bhuvana had got the job because he was related to Achaldev, who just happened to be the queen regent's father. The man was so cautious and spent so much time deliberating the umpteen ways things could go wrong that it was a wonder he got anything done at all.

The pandit, Uncle Kanha and, of course, Mahamantri Kadambavas rounded out the council. 'I am with Maharaj Prithviraj on this,' it was Kanha who had spoken. 'This Mahmud of Ghur is far too dangerous an adversary from what I hear for us to indulge in our petty disputes and internecine fighting that he can easily use to his advantage. Blaming Kumarasimha for my brother's death and using it as an excuse to look the other way while the greedy grabber of Ghur makes incursions into aryavarta is not in our best interests in the long run. He will be emboldened enough to strike again and again.

'It will be a repeat of what happened with Mahmud of Ghazni. Nobody went to their neighbour's aid, blinded by their hatred over real and imagined slights, choosing to laugh at their neighbour's misfortune when the mleccha tore down their citadels and temples. And then, of course, they were singing a different tune when he landed up on their doorsteps and gave them exactly the same dose of his infamous inhumanity!'

Prithvi nodded in acknowledgement of his support. He turned to the mahamantri, who cleared his throat before speaking. 'Everybody here knows that I loathe the Turushkas and it goes without saying that the threat posed by Shihabuddin is a real one. Even so I cannot condone entering into an alliance with blood traitors for it is an unforgivable crime. Let them burn and it is to be hoped that Patan burns as well.

'This will give us time to deal with the Chandels and Bhadanaks. Something is afoot and my informers tell me that we can expect an uprising from within our own borders. We need to tackle the enemies closer to home before we go to save our enemies from their enemies.'

Kadambavas spoke with the cool voice of reason, making Prithvi sound like the rash, impetuous youngster that he was. It made him furious but a display of temper would merely assure this lot that they were perfectly justified in not taking him seriously. In future, they would know better than to do that. He would make sure of it. The king's word was the law after all.

Kadambavas tracked him down. He had known exactly where to find the perturbed prince. Calling for his horse, the mahamantri went after him. It was a wild ride across the sprawling and wild terrain. Sensing the presence of the minister,

Prithvi tore through the countryside seeming to have taken wing and was well on the way to disappearing into the vivid blue of the horizon that stretched endlessly ahead of them.

The mahamantri jumped into the wild exhilaration of the chase. He too was something of a nonpareil when it came to riding. And so they raced; Prithvi allowed Kadambavas to bridge the gap, allowing him to come closer, thinking he had a chance and then he would pull ahead well out of reach.

When he finally stopped, the horses were well and truly blown. Sweat slathered their muzzles and they were snorting and huffing from the strain. They let them drink some water from a pond nearby and Prithvi had brought some treats for them. As the noble beasts munched contently, Kadambavas tried to gauge the mood of the prince. He seemed calmer but he knew that could change in a heartbeat.

'You will get your war with the *Yavana* and his demon hordes. It will be an epic clash and I know you will prevail. And I am not saying this to make it up to you since you feel betrayed. But if you think about it carefully without feeling so ill-used and angst-ridden, you will realize that the right decision was made.'

'We will have to agree to disagree about that,' Prithvi wouldn't give him an inch. 'All of you insist on treating me like a callow little boy who has only actually played at war without ever being in one. At the same time, you tie my hands and force me behind mother's skirt every time I want to take the plunge!'

Kadambavas had to agree that the boy had a point but he would be damned if he were going to serve up their young king on a silver platter to a barbarian after he had been groomed so carefully.

However, for a brief moment doubt assailed him as Kanha's words came back to him, 'I know that you don't want our king locking horns with such a mighty adversary before he has even cut his teeth in a real war but this is nevertheless a mistake.

We have set a dangerous precedent by not going to the aid of our people and blood relatives at that. Now more than ever, all the people of aryavarta need to present a united front before a common enemy that may just prove to be the deadliest threat to our sovereignty since Mahmud of Ghazni. On the morrow, when Prithvi asks the Kshatriyas to rally together under his banner, they will perversely point to this day and hold it against him, though it was us who thwarted his will.'

Damn the man! The mahamantri shook off his misgivings and addressed the prince, 'There is another matter of exceeding importance that must be brought to your notice!'

'Is it about Nagarjun?' Prithvi asked him. He seemed pleased at the shocked look on the minister's face. 'I thought it best to keep myself abreast of his movements given the present situation. Besides, lesser men have been known to succumb to temptation when the incentive was a crown and a throne.'

'But how did you know about the whereabouts of Maharaj Vigraharaj's younger son, who was only a minor at the time of your father's ascent to the throne?' the minister enquired, though he could hazard a guess.

'My grandmother felt my namesake and the slayer of Amaragangeya had been remiss in sparing Vigraharaj's other son. Prithviraj-II had sent the boy to a secret location somewhere in the vicinity of Meerut so he could be far from the court and its attendant intrigues. Shortly before her death, she managed to identify the location and passed the information to me, saying that she wanted me to handle the situation as I saw fit.'

Not for the first time, Kadambavas thought that had they handed the realm of the Chahamanas to the remarkable Kanchanadevi, she would have built an empire that stretched to the very ends of the earth and ensured that every inch of the realm was superbly administered. He would have appreciated her even more if she had seen fit to eliminate the threat instead of making it a learning exercise for her grandson.

'How will you handle it, maharaj?' Kadambavas enquired delicately.

'Nagarjun has holed himself up in the fortress of Guduganva with the support of a few traitorous chiefs who did not have much faith in their new king. Clearly they like taking instructions from the queen regent even less. Currently, they are trying to work on securing the support of the Chandels or the Bhadanaks to press their claim.'

'We will send a few divisions chosen by General Skand. I am told that his men acquitted themselves very well in the battle of Chambal. Govindraj speaks most highly of him. They will blockade the fort immediately and commence siege operations. The rest of the troops will march after my coronation. I will lead the men. They need to know that they are led by a warrior who will take exactly the same risks they do. Together, we will root out the pretender as well as the traitors and then they will face the king's justice.'

Leaping astride his steed, the king tugged on the reins and quicker than thought he was racing back towards the palace. It had been a long day for Prithvi. And he needed something to help him relax and unwind. The mahamantri hoped the prince would find the little sport he had arranged for him most gratifying. He was confident the prince would appreciate it more than the inexperienced fumbling or whatever it was he had done with the stray.

It was nearing midnight when Prithvi returned from the training field. His companions had joined him and they had gone a few rounds together. By the time they were done they looked like pigs who had been rutting in the mud and filth. Jaya, who had been content to sit on the side and cheer them, assured them it was the price paid by those who sought to establish themselves as heroes in the battles to come. Padhri tossed him into a trough of water.

Prithvi's attendants scrubbed the grime off his body and massaged it with fragrant oils. As he lay soaking in his bath, he contemplated why he had pushed so hard to hasten his ascent to the throne.

After his last conversation with Yogita, rage and grief had fought each other for the honour of driving him to madness and nearly succeeded. At the time, finding that life had lost its savour for him, Prithvi wanted to leave them all behind—Yogita, his mother, ministers, companions and disappear into the snow-clad mountains that loomed over aryavarta in the north.

Some said it was Shiva's abode and none could make it to the lofty summit that was supposed to be the highest in the three worlds. Prithvi wanted to make the attempt. Once he made it to the summit, he would have a few words with Shiva and tell him exactly what he thought of the gods who demanded so much from the mortals and then callously tossed them to the raging currents of capricious fate, to struggle and make their way as best as they could. Once he'd said his piece, it was his plan to go see the mysterious lands that lay on the other side.

Nahar had told them that there were girls there with skin the colour of gold, faces more lustrous than the moon and bodies so beautiful no man could resist them. It was said that their hands were so soft and skilled that they could open the gates of *swarga* with the power of their touch alone. That the dew in their lips was sweeter than honey. It all sounded very good to Prithvi. If he were smart, he would hand over the kingdom to Nagarjun, wish the usurper and his mother the joy of each other and simply ride away never to return.

Instead Prithvi was going to fight him to death over a throne he wasn't sure he wanted. But he knew it was a lie the moment the thought took shape in his head. This was his birthright and the foundation upon which he would make his bid for glory and immortality. Those who dared try to take it away from him would pay for it with their lives and more.

His thoughts were still whirling frantically as he made his way towards the bedchamber, wondering where his attendants were and why the idiots hadn't seen fit to light a solitary lamp. Something stirred in the darkness and Prithvi responded at once. He leaped at the shadowy form, pinning down the assassin with his weight and reaching for the heavy lamp holder with his other hand. He was strangely calm as he made ready to inflict the killing blow.

A low moan, soft and sensuous, reached his ears and his captive, who was completely naked under him, struggled to break free. Even as she writhed beneath him, Prithvi felt the silky smoothness of her body as she clung to him with all her strength. His heart was hammering in his chest as he flipped her over, breathing in the fragrance of her long hair. Prithvi felt himself hardening with excitement. Her lips and fingers moved over his body with sensuous playfulness and it felt like a thousand silken butterflies fluttering against his heated skin.

He let the lamp drop to the floor. 'Let me light that for you,' she murmured throatily, 'believe me it is always better when one is not groping in the dark.'

By the soft, golden light of the lamplight she looked like a goddess, a wanton one with a wicked glint in her eyes. And her body looked every bit as good as it felt. On that night, he was happy to be a student again, submitting to the expertise of his tutor, who led him through the moves in the dance of love, in a rhythm as old as time. Together, they unlocked the portal to pure pleasure and frolicked within till dawn broke.

In the harsh daylight, Prithvi looked upon the face that lay asleep in the crook of his arm, sublime even in sweet repose. And yet all he could think was that it didn't belong to Yogita and he couldn't bear to look upon it for another moment.

18

The fort of Guduganva was blessed with a commanding position. Built on an artificially elevated mound, created with rich earth dug up from the foot of the site, it was visible for miles around. Built for the express purpose of withstanding a siege, the walls were thick and high, with raised parapets, battlements and high watchtowers. Massive gates reinforced with iron had protruding sharpened spikes to protect against the onslaught of war elephants, which were used as battering rams. The gates sealed the impressive arched entryway that could be approached only if the drawbridge was lowered.

They had dug a moat around the fort, filling it with the aid of a small, natural spring. Anyone who sought to ford it would provide the crocodiles that lurked thither with an adequate repast. A thicket of wicked-looking acacia and thorny bushes had been planted outside rather like the defences at Ajmer and it was said that not even the tiniest of birds could navigate past that treacherous terrain. With the exception of these, the surrounding area was arid without much tree cover, barring a few skinny palm trees and thorny scrub.

Prithvi was leaving no stone unturned to crush the rebellion. Relays of messengers kept him informed about the siege. 'I want them to feel the pressure constantly. At no point should they feel safe in there, because they are not! We will hound them night and day, forcing them to ride out and confront us! They think the fort they stole from me is impregnable but we'll tear the walls down with our bare hands if that is what it takes!'

Skand proved his competence by cutting off all supplies from outside and preventing any movement around the fort. He had consulted with the veterans who had served under Maharaj Vigraharaj and they told him about secret subterranean passages leading in and out of Guduganva. He sent his troops to try and force their way in. Nagarjun's chief supporter Devabhatta had been a smart man before he made the fool's move to turn traitor. Anticipating this move by the Chahamanas, he had sealed the exits.

'Now that is a defensive game they are playing. So keen are they to keep us out that they have well and truly trapped themselves!' Skand was undeterred, knowing that patience was the most important weapon required by the besiegers. Now the rebels would have no choice but to rely on help from the Chandels or the Bhadanaks. However, he had made sure that no messages went in or out of the fort, having his best archers take shifts to prevent them from releasing birds and guards to prevent the lone brave heart from slipping out across enemy lines.

While it was true that the Chandels as well as the Bhadanaks hated the Chauhans of Sapadalaksha with a vengeance, they loved their precious backsides more and wouldn't risk a direct confrontation with the large force Maharaj Prithviraj had assembled.

When the wind was right, he set fire to the prickly jungle that was supposed to act as a natural defence against them. His men waited at a comfortable distance while the rebels fought the choking clouds of smoke and emptied buckets of precious water they could not afford to waste to soak the wooded beams that had been used in the watchtowers and parapets to prevent them from catching fire.

The old guard had been sceptical of Prithvi's novel concept to send out an advance guard to harass the rebels but the effectiveness of this measure silenced them quick enough.

When Prithvi heard that the defenders had been on starvation rations for months now and the siege was inching towards a confrontation, he decided to go all out for the principle engagement. He gave his assembled troops the order to head for Guduganva. The infantry, cavalry, elephant and camel corps marched at once.

The king ordered them to carry enough provisions for themselves and their animals. In addition to this, a thousand camels carried additional supplies. Uncle Kanha felt his chest puff up with pride when he saw the boy he had bounced on his knee, slip into his role as the king as if it were the most natural thing in the world. Watching him give instructions and bantering with his men, Kanha couldn't help thinking that Someshwar would have parted with an arm or leg to possess that kind of charisma.

Skand and his men were mightily pleased to see their king. They were relieved by fresh troops and Prithvi ordered a feast prepared for them in honour of their untiring labour over the past few months. Later that night, a war council was held in his tent.

'They will be forced to make a break for it if only to help Nagarjun escape and make contact with our enemies. That must not be allowed to happen. This uprising has gone on for long enough and it ends now. We cannot allow him to make any more trouble for us. Not one of the rebels will leave this place alive!' Prithvi seemed to be very much in control. And his youthful aggression and determination got even the veterans fired up.

'Devabhatta will lead the forces. They cannot risk Nagarjun's life. They cannot hold out much longer. The siege has taken its toll on them as has sickness and morale must be very low indeed. They know that Yama rides with Maharaj Prithviraj,' Skand added. 'It is my belief that Nagarjun and a few will sneak out like rats while Devabhatta engages our main forces.'

'I will lead the men myself, unlike that coward who prefers to sacrifice his people and troops so that he can run away and hide!' Prithvi's words were greeted with thunderous applause and Jaya seemed to have gone into raptures.

If Kadambavas had been here, he would have been hard pressed to stop himself from snorting aloud, Kanha felt. He had always thought that the bards were the bane of their way of life with their grandiose notions of how the Kshatriyas ought to adhere to a rigid code of chivalry. 'It makes for great poetry that would delight the heart of overwrought women but on the battlefield, it is the surest way to get a man killed,' the mahamantri was fond of saying.

Kanha had to agree. But something told him that Prithvi's approach might just turn out to be effective.

In the weeks leading up to the final charge of the doomed, Prithvi received some news that sent him careening into one of his black rages. He stormed into Uncle Kanha's tent, scattering the guards and causing him to spill the contents of his goblet.

'Have you heard?' he bellowed, his eyes blazing.

Unfortunately Kanha had, thanks to the mahamantri who had been courteous enough to give him a little heads-up. The rabid raider from Ghur whom Prithvi had taken such a shine to had turned out to be somewhat less formidable than the monster from Ghazni.

As expected, Shihabuddin had an easy time of it with the Chauhans of Nadol. Kumarasimha's unhappy career had come to an ignominious end when the Yavana invader slaughtered his forces, relieving him of his head and having it displayed from atop the battlements. Encouraged by the easy victory, he had turned his attention to Bhimdev of Patan.

'Bhimdev has crossed swords with Shihabuddin. They met at Kasindra and with the help of Marwar, the Chalukyans inflicted a crushing defeat on him, forcing the Turushkas to beat a hasty retreat. He is boasting that they will never set foot on aryavarta again, thanks to him. If that does not make your blood boil, I don't know what does! We have my mother and the regency council to thank for denying me a victory over the mlecchas.'

'I say good riddance!' Kanha replied calmly. 'If a jumped-up excuse for a warrior like Bhimdev can prevail over him then he certainly is no Ravana for Rama to bother himself with. There will be other enemies worthier of the name, though why you seem hell-bent on seeking their ilk out is beyond me.'

'You have said it yourself, Uncle Kanha.' The worst of Prithvi's temper tantrum seemed behind him. 'Rama needed a Ravana to become the hero he was supposed to be. And when I first heard about the destroyer from Ghur, something told me that he was the one I have spent the better part of my life training to destroy! But all the hours I have spent practising will not be for naught. This setback just makes me more determined than ever to prove what I am capable of. I will build the biggest realm this aryavarta has seen and I will not stop till I have dissolved the borders that separate us and keep us at each other's throats, robbing us of peace and prosperity!'

Fierce intent radiated from him in waves. 'Nagarjun is wasting my time. He is nothing but an ant and I am going to stomp on him like one. And then we will pursue the enemies of Chahamanas. Bhimdev's ill-deserved success will make the crushing defeat I plan to inflict on him all the more bitter and he will die with the taste of it on his lips! Then together, we will begin our quest to expand this empire built by our ancestors from the snow-clad mountains of the north to the great ocean in the south.'

He paced, restless as a caged beast, eager to unleash its barely repressed fury. Suddenly Kanha was afraid. Prithvi did not notice. 'You know I will follow you to the ends of the earth,' he said quietly. 'But for now, I suggest your focus remains fixed on bringing this siege to a successful conclusion.'

'Oh! There can be no doubt on that score, Uncle Kanha, Nagarjun is a dead man,' Prithvi said with great confidence. 'It was Devabhatta who gave him claws and is the backbone of this revolt. I will take care of him and this insurrection will be ground to dust. I have sent an emissary to the rebels asking them to hand over Nagarjun and surrender immediately if they want their lives and a royal pardon. But they are too deeply embroiled in this scheme and will not back down. They will leave me with no choice but to cut them down without mercy. These are our men, Uncle Kanha, and it galls me that it has come to this!'

He paced some more and then turned to Kanha with a sudden smile. 'You were right about what it means to be a king, Uncle Kanha. But now that I am one, it behoves me to be a good one. In order to make that happen, I need to be victorious in battle and to ensure that I am fully prepared to do what it takes. Which is why this battle is already won! As well as the ones I will embark on after this one.'

Having vented his spleen, the young king left as suddenly as he had come. Perhaps he did not want to hear what Kanha had intended to say, sensing that it might just throw a pall over his visions of the future in which he always emerged triumphant. Fate enjoyed pissing over such grandiloquent schemes, Kanha had wanted to tell him but perhaps it was best if some words were left unsaid. Besides, Prithvi's unshakeable faith in his beliefs was imbued with the power to make them a reality, he felt.

Kanha refilled his goblet and chugged it down with a single gulp. War was no longer a sport he enjoyed. In fact he hated it and had little patience with those who sought it in their misguided quest for glory, leaving nothing but a trail of blood and bodies behind. They must be doing something wrong if a child who had been so full of potential suddenly wanted nothing more than the monsters of his nightmares to be made real, just so he could have the pleasure of slaying them.

Kanha contemplated his empty goblet. It reminded him of himself. He had told Kadambavas and the pandit to leave the girl alone. Love, even young love, was never so strong that it did not curdle sooner or later, he had told them insisting that Prithvi would grow out of his misguided infatuation. Even if he didn't, she would just be one of many in a harem that would be filled to bursting with beauties from every part of aryavarta and beyond.

But, of course, they hadn't listened, choosing to interfere with his childish passion and now Prithvi believed himself truly broken-hearted and miserable. A wounded animal with nothing but more of the same to offer his subjects. And people wondered why he had no wish to take a bride and bring children into this dark world they had created.

The drums sounded from within the fort as the defenders signalled their intention to attack: one last desperate attempt to stave off the inevitable. The drawbridge was lowered slowly as the pulley was worked and the roller set in motion, revealing the ranks of the infantry standing poised to meet them. They knew what awaited them and they stood determined to make their lives cost dear for the enemies who stood ready to claim it. Devabhatta had them form a solid phalanx with their shields held in front of them and the spears lowered as they advanced in a steady march, like an armoured beast with spines of steel.

So it was true then! Prithvi mused as he took in their formation. The royal physician, Narana, had given him a little something for his nerves and he felt like he was floating outside himself, seeing everything with heightened clarity. There had been reports that the starving rebels had butchered their animals to eke out their dwindling rations. Skand's advance guard said that they had been subsisting on rats and had been reduced to skin and bone. Fevers ravaged them, leaving a swathe of death in their midst. Without the means to perform the funeral rites, the bodies were isolated in warehouses where they decomposed in the heat, spreading the risk of more infection, their very presence demoralizing the survivors.

Prithvi held back the cavalry and signalled for the heavy infantry to smash the defenders. Within moments, the fighting became furious as the archers from their positions in the loop holes, high on the ramparts let loose their arrows in a torrential flow. Prithvi sent in the elephant corps and mounted on the backs of the pachyderms, his best archers tried to pick off their counterparts while providing cover for the foot soldiers.

The horses were growing restless, raking the ground with their hooves, and Prithvi at the head of the cavalry paused on the verge of giving the signal for the attack. He could see the perspiring faces of his men, their limbs tense and stiff as they readied themselves for the clash, the glint of their enemies' weapons and shields blinding them. This was the moment when confronted with imminent death that the will to survive would assert itself. This was the moment when they felt more intensely alive than ever before. And it was the moment when Prithvi felt himself resurrected.

With a cry, Prithvi charged and his men followed. The crash of that almighty impact seemed to penetrate to the very heavens above. Under the fury of the brutal assault, the enemy lines began to waver and Devabhatta's penetrating cry rang out, 'Fight for your lives! For the honour of your women and children! Fight to prevail against the tyrant and send the little prince back to his immoral mother!'

That was when things became truly violent. Prithvi's men advanced looking for openings, thrusting their weapons looking to wound, hacking and slicing as they fought to kill. Prithvi had decreed that no quarter should be given to the rebels. The masses of the enemy began to thin and sensing victory, they moved in for the grisly finish.

The ground was slippery with blood, lopped off body parts and expelled bodily wastes. *Hardly the stuff of poetry*, Prithvi couldn't help thinking, *more suited to the privy*. And he laughed aloud, urging his men to make a quick end of it. He caught a glimpse of Padhri and Kanak and wondered if his own face was contorted with the same savage glee.

Exhausted by their ordeal, the rebel soldiers began to give way under the relentlessness of the onslaught as wave upon wave of attackers fell on them, sweeping them away in overwhelming numbers. Knowing that the worst had happened, some of the defenders flung themselves off the battlements and into the moat below.

By sundown, the battle was won. But Prithvi knew that it wouldn't be over till Nagarjun was in chains. He looked over at General Skand who shook his head. Devabhatta was in their hands and the men were keen to begin celebrating but Prithvi issued orders insisting that his rival claimant to the throne be found. He had asked Uncle Kanha to secure the fort and take command of the prisoners before reporting back to see what could be done about the vexing disappearance of Nagarjun.

That night as he ate a light meal with Uncle Kanha and General Skand, Prithvi was trying to decide on a course of action. The exhilaration of his victory over the rebels had been replaced with blinding fury that Nagarjun had made a clean escape. He had sent for the vaidya and demanded more of his blessed potion to take the edge off.

Skand was giving his exceedingly disheartening report and Prithvi was doing his best to rein in his frustration and anger that despite his express orders, the idiots had let Nagarjun give them the slip.

'The many hidden passages leading out of the fort had been sealed or so we thought. My men attempted to force their way in but it proved impossible. I asked them to stand guard over the exits just in case. However, Devabhatta had one only partially sealed in order to fashion an escape route should the need arise.'

His manner was exceedingly calm in the face of his king's mounting rage. 'Nagarjun was escorted by a unit of crack troops and they fought their way past the guards. My men were all killed and hence the rebels got a head start. However, they won't be able to make it far with their camels in such a weakened state. My guess is that Nagarjun remains in a hidden location not too far from here. Despite scouring the countryside, my men have not been able to unearth any information about this secret refuge. Devabhatta will have to be persuaded most strongly to let us know the whereabouts of the traitor.'

'Have him brought before me,' Prithvi barked the order. Skand nodded to his men, who hastened to do their king's bidding.

'He is not going to break under torture,' Uncle Kanha warned him softly. 'The man seems impervious to pain. They said that he did not even scream when they pulled out his fingernails and broke his fingers. You can inflict all the hurt in the world on him and he is still not going to budge.'

'Who said anything about hurting him?' was all Prithvi said before retreating into silence.

They brought Devabhatta to him in chains. Two men held him by the elbows, since he could not stand on account of his kneecaps being broken. Kanha had been right about the old man; he had aged like a fine oak, his body still firm and muscular. Even his hair was iron grey. Despite his injuries and current predicament, he held himself upright with pride and steady resolve. *It was just too bad that he was going to die like a dog*, Prithvi thought with real regret.

He instructed his men to remove his chains and give him some water to drink. Once the veteran was seated as comfortably as could be managed under the circumstances, Prithvi looked at him in silence for a long while, his gaze steady and piercing. 'I admire your courage, general, I truly do, but we seem to have arrived at an impasse and I fear it cannot be allowed to continue.'

Devabhatta tilted his head courteously in acknowledgement of the compliment and coughed up a little blood as he struggled to get the words out. 'Do your worst, but I will never betray the true king of the Chahamanas.'

'Your loyalty is truly commendable but it is too bad that it is wasted on the likes of Nagarjun who shamelessly left his men to die for him while he himself fled like the despicable coward he is. But that wasn't all he left behind, was it?'

'If you are speaking about Maharaj Vigraharaj's stores of treasure that his loyal servants have safeguarded in the name of his true heir, all I can say is that you do not have the right to lay a finger on it, especially since the blood of the greatest king of the Chahamanas stains your hands.'

'Are you accusing me of using treacherous means to slay a blood relative? Have a care how you speak, old man. I meet my enemies in fair combat and the man who says otherwise must be prepared to lose the foul tongue that uttered such lies,'

Prithvi snarled at him, his senses swimming as the man's words buzzed around him, taunting and pricking him.

'It may not have been your hand that struck him dead, but the sins of your father and grandmother have incurred a debt that you will one day pay for in heavy coin,' he spat out the words.

'You seek to bamboozle with your words,' Prithvi replied, 'but I wasn't talking about the victor's spoils. The wise say that a man's worth cannot be measured in coin but by the virtue of the women who brighten his home and heart.'

Alarm flickered in the man's eyes for the first time. The very air in their tent was thick with the menace of the terrible threat. At his side, Uncle Kanha tensed. Even Skand gave a little start. Neither of them had seen this coming, especially since Prithviraj had insisted that women, children and the infirm should not be ill-treated in any way. As for the noble ladies in question, they had been placed in comfortable lodgings and Prithvi had personally assured them that they would be well taken care of.

'You will never escape the wrath of the gods if you dishonour Maharaj Nagarjun's mother or wife in any way!' Devabhatta stammered, horror stamped on his features.

'Their fate is entirely in your hands, general, as well as any honour or dishonour that may or may not be their chosen lot. You will lead my men to the rat hole where the bastard is hiding,' Prithvi told him, his eyes blazing with demoniacal intent as he leaned closer so that Devabhatta would feel the full impact of his words. 'Otherwise those poor ladies whose only crime is to be associated with a weakling, who would abandon them to the tender mercies of the king he has betrayed, will have to face the consequences of Nagarjun's treachery.'

'Even you wouldn't stoop so low as to hurt the women in your care . . .' his voice was strangled and suddenly he looked his age, as though he felt the weight of his years and the pain of every battle scar that adorned his body.

'Would you dare to test me? Know then, that I have never disrespected a man as much as I disrespect that fool, Nagarjun, who presumes he has what it takes to rule. He simply isn't worth the many lives that have been lost on both sides. There will be no more blood spilled on account of him. Make no mistake, it ends now and I will do whatever it takes to make it happen.'

Devabhatta wilted under the heat of that scorching gaze and Prithvi knew that he had won. The general was a broken man. Tears ran down his cheeks as he told them where Nagarjun could be found. 'That you even contemplated violating a woman's honour in order to prevail over an enemy tells me that it was the right choice to fight to the death to prevent the likes of you from ascending to the throne of the Chahamanas. This is an accursed day, for a heartless tyrant has triumphed and it signals the beginning of the doom that is going to consume this aryavarta!'

Skand signalled to the guards and smote the handle of his spear on the back of Devabhatta's head, but still he shouted to Prithvi, who watched him stone-faced, 'You will spend an eternity in a thousand hells tormented by the knowledge that the downfall of our land and its people was the inevitable result of your execrable actions!' The blows rained down on his head, cutting his words off as blood flooded his mouth a few instants before he collapsed.

Prithvi looked at his prostate form and then nodded to Skand. 'Do not fail me this time!' The general bowed and made his way out of the tent. His men dragged out the comatose form of Devabhatta. As they watched, Prithvi turned to Kanha. 'This is what it takes to win, uncle! And I am going to keep winning, for as long as I am alive!' he said the words with a sad little smile.

General Skand took a unit of his best men to the hunting lodge, tucked discreetly within a thick jungle a few hours' ride from where they were camped. They surrounded the place within minutes, making short work of the defenders.

Nagarjun was dragged out by the soldiers who were not inclined to treat him kindly. He was blubbering in terror, his jowls quivering as they dragged him, kicking and screaming to carry out the king's justice. They took only his severed head to present to the king, leaving his body propped against a tree, with his entrails on his lap.

A great cheer rang out across the ranks of the gathered troops when Skand and his men returned holding up the head of Nagarjun. A rhythmic chant was taken up in murmurs at first, becoming progressively stronger as the men put their hearts and the full power of their lungs behind it, till the chant became a roar, and the heavens resounded with cries of *'Prithviraj! Prithviraj! Prithviraj!'*

19

They rode back to Ajmer. Accompanying them were the heads of the rebels which Jaya had suggested be displayed on the battlements of the fort as a gentle reminder of the fate that awaited those who dared betray their king. Prithvi promptly put him in charge of the enterprise. Their companions made it a point to pause occasionally by the carts loaded with their macabre burden while Jaya shouted at the men under his command to do something about the crows that swarmed over them, hoping for a choice morsel.

The troops were in high spirits as they marched back. Prithvi had expressly forbidden them from looting, wanton destruction and raping the women. 'That sort of thing would reduce my own men to the level of the despicable mleccha hordes I have sworn to annihilate!' were his very words which though stirring had proved to be of little solace to the men deprived of the excesses they had been looking forward to. But he had made up for it by being very generous with the vast booty they had recovered from the fort.

The new king personally rewarded his troops with generous dispensations for those who had distinguished themselves while suppressing the revolt. General Skand received rich presents and was elevated to the post of senapati. Bhuvanakamala was relieved from the post. His mother would be furious but that was the idea.

Hence, on their way back, the troops sang songs about the valour of their new king on and off the battlefield. 'They worship the ground he walks on,' Jaya enthused to Uncle Kanha as he rode by, seizing the opportunity to leave his onerous chore behind and escape the buzzing of the flies and the unspeakable stench for a few moments. Maharaj Prithviraj was riding at the head of the column with Skand.

Kanha nodded, glancing back at the heads and the smears of crow shit splattered across Jaya's robes. 'That is true. This is a momentous occasion and a resounding victory for one so young. It would have been interesting to see if Maharaj Prithviraj would have followed through on that terrible threat though. For a moment there, I thought that Devabhatta was going to call his bluff.'

'He couldn't have even if he had wanted to . . .' Jaya said mysteriously.

'What is that supposed to mean?'

'Nagarjun's mother and young wife were treated with every respect and consideration by our king. Deep down he has always been a kind and gentle soul,' Jaya said staunchly. 'They were placed under the care of the guards in a comfortable tent. However, both consumed poison they had carried concealed on their persons. We found their bodies when Skand was on his way to capture Nagarjun. When told, Prithvi actually cried.'

Kanha had heard about their unfortunate deaths and Jaya's version of events was touching but he could not help but wonder why the two women had not taken the poison *before* they were captured, if they were unwilling to let Prithviraj decide their fates. It was hard to ascertain the truth when it came to these things.

All he knew was that he had been present during the interrogation of the late Devabhatta. His head like Nagarjun's had been given pride of place in the cart behind them and their heads bobbed along beside each other. Like the general, Kanha had believed that Prithviraj Chauhan meant it when he had said that he was perfectly willing to sacrifice a mother's life and a wife's honour to get what he wanted. Prithvi had also meant it when he said he admired Devabhatta's courage but that had not given him pause when he gave the order for his immediate execution.

Sensing his scepticism, Jaya spoke again. 'All that matters is that the revolt of Nagarjun and its bloody conclusion makes for a fine yarn. Why should we care about what really happened and what didn't when there is absolutely no way of knowing for certain? Doubts and endless questioning serve only to detract from the enjoyment of a beautiful story that not only entertains but elucidates as well, irrespective of whether virtue or vice carries the day!'

Kanha had to concede that Jaya, whom he found somewhat annoying, had a point. Perhaps ultimately all that mattered was that the story got told. The little man who seemed to be perched rather precariously on his horse rushed back to chase off a crow that had helped itself to one of Nagarjun's eyeballs. As if it mattered in the least! What was the point of fussing over the dead? Surely death at its worst could not pose half the terrors that life did?

The people of Ajmer had prepared a rousing welcome for the young hero. There were thousands of men and women on the streets, throwing flower petals before the returning troops. Some watched from the roofs of their houses, or held up their little ones, asking the handsome young king to bless them.

Karpuradevi was waiting at the palace when Prithviraj made a triumphant return. The roar of approbation from his people warmed her heart. His reign had begun in a burst of glory and she couldn't have been prouder. News of his dauntless courage had spread like wildfire. They recounted tales of how he had led the charge himself, wielding the sword and his bow with unmatched skill, leaving thousands of corpses in his wake.

She herself hadn't been too happy about the grisly garland of severed heads, ripe and bursting with maggots and assorted vermin, that was to be displayed on the fort. His people thought it was too marvellous for words. It always appalled her that men and women had such an appetite for brutality. The queen mother wanted to perform the *aarati* herself, the way she had always insisted while he was still a boy to ward off the evil eye.

Now all that remained was for her to find him a nice girl or girls to marry who would love him the way she herself did, soothe him when he was in a temper and bear him strong heirs to ensure an unbroken succession to the throne of the Chahamanas. Only then would her duty as a mother be fully discharged. Even Kanchanadevi wouldn't have faulted the way she ensured that the throne was secured for Prithvi. And unlike Kanchanadevi's son, her boy would be remembered as the greatest warrior of the age.

Prithvi did not look unhappy to see her though it had to be admitted that he seemed far more enthused at the prospect of conversing with Kadambavas. The mahamantri garlanded the king. 'You are a credit to the illustrious line of the Chauhans, maharaj! May you live forever.'

He had arranged a grand celebration to mark the momentous occasion of Prithvi's victory and coins had been issued to commemorate the feat. There was much feasting and entertainment. Prithvi participated in the festivities gaily enough, exchanging pleasantries with the guests. Only those who knew him well would have realized that his heart was not in the revelry.

The most famed dancer of the age—a beauty with fine dark hair and body made purely for sin—failed to arouse his interest. After they had eaten, she performed for them, her body bathed in the golden glow of the lamps, her movements smooth, sinuous and sensuous as she simulated the frenetic, primeval rhythms of lovemaking at its most uninhibited. All the gathered men had their eyes glued on her. They were openly panting at the shattering climax, which left the dancer bathed in sweat and her diaphanous garments clinging to the curves of her body. But even her heated exertions failed to get a rise out of the young king.

'You don't seem too exuberant for one who has proved his mettle on the battlefield and crushed his enemies, maharaj!' Kadambavas observed over the din of the rousing applause in the aftermath of the sensuous performance. The mahamantri hoped she would do even better, later that night, in the more intimate confines of the king's sleeping chambers, where he had arranged for her to be present.

'I remember feeling euphoric at some point,' Prithviraj replied thoughtfully, 'as well as intensely alive, supremely confident and invincible as a god. Food tastes better when you feel that way and the consummation of desire is far more satisfying. But pleasure that intense can hardly be sustained, can it? Eventually, it wears off and you are left with nothing save emptiness and a bitter taste in your mouth.'

'Emptiness isn't the worst thing in the world,' Kadambavas informed him, 'it leaves you plenty of room to fill up with more food, wine and women. Think of it as that feeling of immense pleasure you get when your bowels have well and truly been voided . . .'

The mahamantri decided that he needed to have another chat with Narana, the royal vaidya, about the king's unsettling bouts of melancholia. The last thing the realm needed was a ruler who refused to allow his broken heart to mend, preferring to leave it to fester and infect the rest of him.

Pandit Padmanabh was present and he was most effusive in his praise which the king accepted graciously without a trace of the irritation he was actually feeling. Then he turned to acknowledge the other ministers who were most anxious to have a word with him.

While Prithvi was thus engaged, the pandit whispered furiously in the mahamantri's ear. 'I have trained him to show restraint with regard to indulging his baser appetites when it comes to intoxicants and women, but you seek to unravel all my hard work with your infernal meddling!'

'On the contrary, panditji,' he replied serenely. 'I am merely building on the solid foundation you have laid. Abstinence is not very effective and when its practice is enforced, a virile young man may just implode with the force of thwarted, repressed and unfulfilled desires. On the other hand, if a man were to sample the pleasures life has to offer in moderate doses, he will be able to achieve his potential to the fullest!'

If Kadambavas had been so inclined, he would have lambasted him for ignoring his suggestion while dealing with the stray their king had adopted for his own use. That had been another mess which he had cleaned up using his own initiative. The girl had been beautiful after all and he had better ideas about how her talents may best be employed.

The pandit, meanwhile, had no choice but to content himself with a reproving glare directed at the mahamantri. He insisted that Prithvi visit him at Pushkar to cleanse himself in medicated baths and imbibe his healing potions to rid him of the bad vapours that were polluting his royal person. To nobody's surprise, Prithvi did not seem too enthused about such a course of action.

The king's companions did not seem afflicted with the extreme mood swings that plagued him. They cornered him and wished to know what his next move was going to be. Prithvi thought of snow-clad mountains and the endless sea, of disappearing into the horizon on his horse. Out loud he said, 'We will stay put at Ajmer for a bit. There is no doubt that there are certain mind-numbing affairs that require my attention. Once that is taken care of, I intend to mount my horse and visit the parts of the realm it wanders into. You lot can accompany me as well and we will have ourselves a fine adventure.'

In his head, there was the sound of thundering hooves as they charged into bodies and the entangled mass looking like a single, grotesque organism that sought desperately to tear itself apart. On the morrow, he would familiarize himself with the reports of the informers regarding the movement of the Chandels and Bhadanaks. Based on their intelligence, he would no doubt be able to formulate a plan of action.

'We will, if your horse were to wander into charming bordellos, houses of ill-repute, parlours adorned by courtesans, dens of dancers . . .' Padhri said with a lascivious wink at Jaya. 'Our little poet needs to experience erotica first-hand in order to spice up the colourful saga of Prithviraj Chauhan and his brave companions.'

'Leave Jaya alone,' Kanak scolded. 'If the need should ever arrive for us to perform a virgin sacrifice, we won't have to look far . . . An adventure does sound good but hopefully there is good fighting to be had soon.'

'You are bound to get your wish, Kanak,' Nahar said. 'It is only a matter of time before the Chandels and Bhadanaks give us adequate reason to go to war and the Chalukyans can also be counted on for some good sport. They say that Shihabuddin of Ghur is rallying his troops for another raiding expedition to aryavarta.'

Prithvi nodded and laughed along, even as he made a mental note to ask his spies about the latest activities of Shihabuddin. Without warning, his thoughts turned to Yogita. Suddenly, he wanted nothing more than to see her again. Catching Hari's eye, he motioned for his brother to step out for a bit so they could converse in private.

'Have you found out her whereabouts?' Prithvi enquired, trying to keep the eagerness out of his voice.

'It hasn't been easy,' Hari informed him. 'The Yogini Sampradayas are supposed to devote their lives to prayer, meditation and service. They work with the poorer sections of the populace, helping women and children suffering from ailments, who cannot afford the services of the vaidyas. It is mostly a thankless job and they hardly stay put in one place.' He did not mention that she was a little too young to handle the demands made of a yogini. Only those women who did not have much to live for tended to make it their vocation while they waited for Yama's noose to tighten around their necks.

Prithvi felt his heart grow heavier with every word that was being uttered. Not being with her, not even knowing her whereabouts was a torment that could scarcely be borne. Hari looked at his brother's face and wondered if he should tell him that she seemed to have disappeared into thin air.

None of the informers could even confirm that she had been inducted into the order of the Yogini Sampradayas. One of the men had told Hari that he wasn't sure but believed that she was in Kannauj and her appearance and deportment had been more in keeping with a concubine rather than an ascetic. The man had been ordered to get more information but he was yet to return. Hari decided to wait till he heard something concrete.

'Mother is very worried about you,' Hari, ever the dutiful son and brother, felt compelled to tell him. 'She feels that marriage and children will complete your happiness.'

'Do you think our mother and father were ever happy together?' his big brother asked him.

Hari shook his head. 'Their marriage was not exactly a source of joy for either. We both know that. But neither of them regretted having you! If their union had such happy results for aryavarta, it couldn't have been all bad.'

'They had you too, brother, and in my opinion, that was the best thing they ever did.' Hari was taken aback but seemed pleased. Thrown together nearly all their lives, they had shared everything but try as he might, Hari could not begin to understand the effect this girl had on his brother. He was reminded of the prophecy they had heard at the Harshnath temple all those years ago.

'Let her go . . .' Hari said softly, 'be happy for the time you had together. If she is no longer meant to be a part of your life then so be it.'

This was the first time Hari had presumed to tell his brother and the king what he ought to do. It made his hackles rise and he refused to articulate the words that sprang to his lips, desperate to be understood. *I don't expect any of you to understand. On that fateful day, I saved a blameless soul's life and in doing so, became responsible for her fate. As a warrior king, I am a harbinger of death and destruction for the ostensible purpose of preserving the peace. Yet on that day, I was able to right a wrong and it gave me hope—that even if something beautiful is broken past recognition, maybe there is a chance that it will someday be made whole again.*

Even so, Prithvi supposed his sibling was right but it did not matter in the least. He did not want to let his Yogita go and couldn't even if he wanted to.

20

Prithvi woke up with a splitting headache. He wasn't very happy to see one of Pandit Padmanabh's assistants waiting for him outside his private chambers. The man was perched uncomfortably on the edge of a seat with a cloth pressed to his nose, as if he was afraid to inhale the smell of intoxicants and the musky odour of sex that pervaded the atmosphere. He sprang to his feet at the sight of the naked king.

'Maharaj! My name is Maladev. Your teacher, the sainted Pandit Padmanabh, has sent me to attend to your personal needs and any physical ailments that you may be suffering from . . .' he gesticulated as if he were speaking to a befuddled child.

Prithvi had a good mind to throw the man out on his pompous backside but he was most persistent. He had come armed with his own staff and they had drawn a hot bath for him 'to sweat out the noxious vapours' and fed him a specially concocted infusion of herbs and ginger sweetened with honey 'to clear the clouds in his head'.

To Prithvi's surprise, their remedy for his debauches of the previous night was most effective. At least, he no longer felt like chopping off his own head to stop it from throbbing. They helped him dress and the king felt fully capable of dealing with the pressures of governance. He reminded himself to thank the pandit for the annoying but useful creature Maladev.

He spent the better part of the week dealing with the thousand things that needed his immediate attention, including the governance of his provinces, administrative and military matters, reassigning officials and the complaints of his subjects. The last especially was most tiresome; he hadn't known that his people were so given to whining endlessly about the minutiae of the mundane. The king had a good mind to delegate this thankless task to the pandit or Jaya. In order to deal with the pressure, he set aside a portion of the day for military exercises and riding, convinced that he would lose his mind if he did not land a few blows and throw a dozen punches.

Kanak, Padhri and Nahar had been elevated to the post of dandanayakas with their own battalions to command. They competed with each other to prove that their division was the best and in the process succeeded in increasing the quality of their assault troops a hundredfold. Hari, meanwhile, had joined his council of ministers, training under Uncle Kanha and Kadambavas. The bards of the royal court were happy to include Jaya in their midst and he was pleased to be associated with some of the greatest artists and scholars in the land.

Prithvi studied the intelligence that the spies had collected and summoned his council to decide on their course of action against the Bhadanaks. It was Senapati Skand who spoke first. 'We have incontrovertible proof from the prisoners we interrogated during the siege of Guduganva that the Bhadanaks had sent a garrison of their troops to be stationed at the fort in order to give aid to the pretender and work against our interests.'

'What do we know of their current movements?' Prithvi asked even though he knew the answer to that.

'They continue to make incursions into our borders on the northeast of Sapadalaksha territory,' Skand replied. 'There were a few skirmishes and my troops stationed over there have thrown them back but they need to be taught a lesson. It appears that they are deliberately provoking trouble with the Chahamanas so that they can draw you out to a battlefield of their choosing. Currently their troops have been summoned to Bayana.'

'Your uncle, Maharaj Vigraharaj-IV, met them in battle during his reign and meted out a humiliating defeat to them,' the mahamantri began. 'He made the region a Chauhan feudatory and forced them to pay heavy tribute. Realizing that they would be beggared soon without two coins to scratch together, let alone an army, they rebelled and established their independence during the short-lived reign of Amaragangeya. Ever since they have continued to be a thorn.'

'Well then, the matter is settled! All that remains for us to do is to pluck the thorn and cast it aside. We will march against Tribhuvanagiri, their fool of a king, and meet his forces at Bayana.' Prithvi ruled firmly, feeling a faint stirring of excitement. He remembered how profoundly good it had felt to feel alive when death ran roughshod in their midst.

'The key will be to eliminate their fabled elephant corps,' Skand informed them. 'With your permission, maharaj, I will put together a strong division to neutralize this threat.'

'Let the preparations begin. We will set forth at the end of this month. This time, I intend to do a thorough job of wiping out the Bhadanaks. By the time we are done with them, there will be nothing left of them or their kingdom. They will be sorry that they ever crossed the Chahamanas of Sapadalaksha!'

Preparations for the upcoming battle took up nearly all of Prithvi's time. Messengers hurried to the mandaleshwars and the jagirs, carrying the king's demands for fully equipped fighting units. The samants, his high-ranking nobles, came forward to offer their services. Some of the soldiers served the kingdom and received their fee and equipment from the government.

Others were hired mercenaries, professional soldiers who wore their own uniforms and carried their weapons of choice. A third category included recruits who were of fighting age.

Skand organized the varying divisions, assigning them to suitable units and putting them through a gruelling routine of military exercises and manoeuvres, in addition to making sure that they were well equipped with armour, shields and weapons.

Prithvi made arrangements for the administration of his kingdom during the battle. Mahamantri Kadambavas and Pandit Padmanabh would stay behind. His mother had insisted that he hand over the reins of the kingdom to her but Prithvi wouldn't hear of it. 'The king thanks you for your services, mother,' he told her stiffly. 'But need I remind you that Sallakshanapal and Bhuvanakamala have gone into retirement voluntarily now that their tenure has ended?'

'Kadambavas and Padmanabh seldom see eye to eye, and they are too busy in their game of upmanship to run the kingdom efficiently. The onerous chore of keeping them in line and extracting the best from both is something I have become proficient in. You cannot deny that during your minority . . .'

Prithvi interrupted her tirade. 'My days as a "minor" are over and done with. You must be aware by now that the ministers here are unwilling to take their orders from anybody other than their king. It was the main reason Devabhatta and his faction joined the rebels. It was different when my grandmother helped out during Father's reign. She commanded the respect of the council and was known for her inability to put a wrong foot forward.'

He stopped when he saw the hurt in her eyes and tried to stifle his exasperation. Surely she was aware of exactly how unpopular she was with the ministers? It would be really tiresome if she were to kick up a big fuss and become emotionally distraught before his military expedition, so he tried to mollify her.

'Why do you want to kill yourself with the cares of governance?' he began in his most charming and conciliatory tone. 'It would be helpful to me if you would devote yourself to the repair and renovation of the temples and other public edifices. I am also told that the charitable institutions that are supposed to cater to the requirements of the poor have become pockets of blatant corruption. You are the only one who is trustworthy and capable enough to deal with this situation. What do you say, Mother? Can I count on your support?'

Since she was his mother, who had personally wiped his royal bottom, Karpuradevi knew that she was being blatantly manipulated. But even so she could not resist when he appealed to her like that. Having acquiesced to his demand, she swore to herself that every one of her resources would continue to be expended with the intention of ensuring his well-being. Whether he acknowledged it or not, her son needed her now more than ever and she was determined to be there for him. Even if it meant that he would hate her for it.

Prithviraj met the holy man on the banks of the Anasaghar lake. He was relaxing in the king's pavilion and listening to a travelling troupe of flautists, who were so talented that even the birds stopped trilling to pay heed to the divine music. 'Hearing you play, even a dying man is likely to forget his troubles,' he complimented them warmly, handing their leader a big bag of gold coins.

One of the guards came to him. 'There is a Mussulman waiting to see you, maharaj! His name is . . .' it came out as garbled gibberish, 'and he requests a private audience with the king. They say that he is a holy man, sire, and that he has performed many miracles.' He sounded both suspicious and awestruck at the same time.

Prithviraj was feeling benevolent, still awash in the ecstasy induced by the musicians, and granted the request of the visitor. As the guard went to fetch the man, he remembered the miracle-performing Mussulmen from one of the reports submitted by the informers. They said that the foreigner was from a land called Khorasan that belonged to the Persian empire, which had in the days of yore been filled with riches even more abundant than aryavarta.

This holy man was cut from a different cloth than the mleccha hordes they were used to with their fierce, warlike ways and their propensity for butchery and large-scale rapine in the name of their god. They called him 'Garib Navas' because he cherished the poor, was the very epitome of compassion and so kind even the talarakshas had been known to pour out their hearts while seated at his feet and leave his humble residence gentle as lambs.

As the enigmatic foreigner walked towards the pavilion, Prithviraj saw that he was clad in rough-spun robes of cotton, had weathered skin, was slender and yet seemed possessed of a robust energy. But as he drew closer, his most arresting feature became readily apparent: his eyes. A gentler pair would be hard to find.

Once pleasantries were exchanged, Prithvi bade him to sit and signalled for refreshments to be served. The man accepted gratefully and began talking in a voice that radiated warmth. 'My name is Muinuddin Chishti and I am an Arab by birth. It is not quite the same as the Turushkas, though the people here fail to see the difference.'

Prithvi didn't either but he was intrigued and curious to know more. The man liked to talk and did not seem to mind sharing intimate details about himself. 'I have travelled across half the world—Bukhara, Samarkhand, Baghdad, Multan and Lahore—trying to understand why people do the terrible things they do. My family has been on the run for many generations now, persecuted by the Arabs, Turks, Persians and the Pashtuns on account of our ideological and theological differences with those in power. I was at Multan studying with the wise men of the city when Shihabuddin of Ghur arrived on the borders, bringing with him a wave of destruction and it was time for me to leave again. They told me about the wise men who live on the banks of the river Ganges and so I came in search of them, hoping they will help me understand.'

'But why exactly were you persecuted if you worship the same god?' Prithvi wanted to know.

'My ancestors belonged to the same Hashim clan as Mohammad, the Prophet. After the death of the Prophet and his successor, those with warlike tendencies came to power and they did not like those of the clan who did not have similarly destructive urges,' the holy man replied. 'It is a great pity that the new wave of followers began to interpret the teachings of the Prophet in keeping with their own ambitions and petty interests.

'Those who knew Mohammad said that he was the kindest and most compassionate man who had ever lived. All he wanted was for people to live in peace, bound together by their love for the true god. The Prophet believed that all men and women are created as equals, made in the image of the lord, and he simply could not condone violence and senseless destruction.'

The king tried not to laugh out loud at that. Still he supposed he was being hypocritical given that the Kshatriya clan he belonged to might just be viewed in the same light as the marauder from Ghazni or Shihabuddin of Ghur by those whom they had oppressed. Besides, like the holy man, a lot of people who had sought to make their homes in Sapadalaksha were Mussulmen and he was curious to know about their one god, who was so powerful, and his Prophet, who seemed to have been a genuinely noble soul like Chishti himself.

'I am sure you understand my confusion,' he began but the man held up his hand in a placating gesture, eager to explain.

'After the Prophet's death, the Ummayids came to power. They built a powerful empire and insisted that the conquered people convert to the true faith. And this set a dangerous precedent. Mohammad's followers took jihad to mean a holy war. However, the Prophet had been referring to the struggle within every individual as he is pulled in opposing directions by the forces of light and darkness.'

Prithvi nodded in understanding. He certainly knew what that was like!

'They have reduced the teachings of Mohammad to a war cry and they have forgotten his message of love, peace and compassion. But the Sufis—who emerged as a mystical sect from amongst the followers of Ali, the son-in-law of the Prophet—have not forgotten.'

'Even among us Hindus, we have the Saivites and Vaishnavites as well as other sects. At various points in our history, there have been differences of opinion that accelerated into active conflict. Your situation sounds a little similar . . .' Prithvi commented. 'And you say that you come from a long way off! Isn't it remarkable how alike people are even when they are so different?'

Chishti nodded in agreement. 'The Sufis practise humility, charity and truthfulness. We believe in giving of ourselves the way a flower would give its fragrance or the lamp its light. But even here, the threat of violence and imminent destruction looms over the land. Shihabuddin approaches with his militant and misguided ideals. He has claimed Peshawar and Lahore in his name . . .'

Prithvi looked up in surprise, even his informers had not apprised him of the situation. 'Peshawar and Lahore were under a Ghaznavid ruler and a Mussulman. How does Shihabuddin justify the deaths of fellow followers of your faith?'

'When men chase after power and glory, they find all sorts of excuses to justify their inhumane conduct and in their minds, at least, are fully convinced that they are entirely in the right. The ruler of Peshawar and Lahore was a man named Khusrao Malik and Shihabuddin managed to take his son as a hostage. When Malik offered a truce to negotiate for his son's release during the siege of Sialkot, Shihabuddin pretended to agree, but when his opponent arrived for the meeting he was captured. Later, both father and son were slain.'

Prithviraj was deeply disturbed when he heard the story. The invader from Ghur was a fanatical monster without any scruples or redeeming qualities. 'Now that he is comfortably ensconced in the fort of Lahore, he will begin lusting after the lands of aryavarta. His initial forays, though thwarted, appear to have merely whetted his appetite. But you are not here to give me intelligence. May I ask after the purpose of this visit?'

The holy man took his time to answer. Prithviraj felt the peace and light inherent in the great soul seated next to him and felt his own heart grow warm from the proximity. 'Not all the Mussulmen, as you refer to us, seek to plunder, destroy or forcibly convert. Some of us come in peace to live out our days in this wondrous land that has opened its arms to us.

'I myself have experienced nothing but friendship and hospitality from the people of this land but there are others who have not been so lucky. They are blamed for the actions of Mahmud of Ghazni and made to pay the price for his atrocious conduct, often by the keepers of law and order. As it is, they are struggling to make ends meet and the Turushka tax makes it exceedingly hard for them. I come to beg for mercy on their behalf.'

'My ancestors barring a few exceptions have followed a policy of not only tolerance but acceptance of people belonging to other faiths,' Prithviraj assured him. 'The peaceable Jain monks and Buddhists will attest to that fact. I have chosen to emulate their example and you have my word that Mussulmen who come in peace and seek only to make an honest living will not be persecuted.'

The Sufi saint's eyes twinkled at him. 'I do not doubt it but those who hold positions of great power in your administration may not feel the same way.'

Prithviraj realized that he was referring to the mahamantri. 'You have *my* word!' he repeated. 'As for the Turushka tax, I have to be practical here. If it were to be waived then the deficit would result in increased taxes for my people and they would blame the Mussulmen for this inconvenience and harbour ill-will towards them, which in turn would lead to further persecution of your people. This way, the peace will be preserved and your people can count on the friendship of their neighbours.'

'I thank you for your forbearance and the goodness of your heart. It is always gratifying when those in power are just. The power of love, kindness and mercy is no small thing and they are the sparks of light in a dark world. May Allah keep you safe, my son!'

Prithviraj was deeply moved. As Muinuddin Chishti made ready to depart, he stopped him. 'When Shihabuddin and I are engaged in an almighty clash, will your prayers be for my victory or his? I know that you will answer me honestly.'

The saint's eyes were no longer twinkling. 'Those who give themselves over to violence and embrace its destructive power can never hope to win, irrespective of the side they represent. By its very nature, war cannot yield victory or happiness, in its wake there is never anything but sorrow and suffering. Therefore, I will pray for both your souls and hope with all my heart that salvation remains within your reach.'

21

Prithviraj and his army reached the plains of Bayana shortly before sunset. As the servants made camp and unloaded the baggage trains, the king caught a glimpse of his opponents. They had made camp on the other side, beneath a range of hills that loomed over them, their polished weapons glinting as they caught the fading rays of the sun.

The war council was convened. Prithviraj missed the sagacity and infinite calm of Uncle Kanha, whom he had left behind in Ajmer to take care of things in his absence. After his talk with the Sufi mystic, Prithviraj had decided that it was high time the talarakshas were muzzled. They had been running wild under the mahamantri and Kanha was just the man to bring them to heel.

Senapati Skand, Hari and his companions crowded into the tent. His commander-in-chief had already briefed him on the possible means they could use to counter the famed elephant corps of the Bhadanaks that so heavily outnumbered their own. Their scouts reported that 1200 war elephants would be brought to bear against their 500. They discussed their options and the king outlined the plan of attack for the battle that would commence at dawn.

They retired to their tents and tried to rest amidst the squealing of the pigs that the king had insisted be transported to the battlefield. The soldiers would have been glad to skewer the damn things that ate their own excrement and stank up the place for miles around.

When dawn broke, the elephant corps of the Bhadanaks dominating the plains of Bayana confronted the Chauhan army. They stood at the very forefront of the attack line, separated from each other by the foot soldiers, whose job on that day would be twofold—protect the limbs and sensitive underbelly of the pachyderms while killing as many of the enemy as they could manage.

Prithviraj had to admit that the battle elephants looked truly formidable, arrayed with their ornamented head pieces of pure gold and great clanging bells worn on massive necklaces. Wickedly curved tusks had been sharpened. The king knew they could easily pierce the thickest armour, hook the victim by the soft midriff, raise him high in the air before smashing him to the ground, crushing the spine and breaking almost every bone in the body. It was the preferred killing move of the giants.

The mahouts with their iron-tipped goads, the *ankush*, sat with their feet held in position by the stirrup behind the waving ears of the elephants. Gilded howdahs rested on its back and the archers sat within its protective confines, ready to inflict massive damage through arrowslit loopholes.

Prithviraj held back his own similarly impressive elephant corps. The great beasts that looked like impregnable fortresses in the first wash of dawn could move surprisingly fast despite their bulk. They were extremely intelligent and responsive to commands. However, they were far more temperamental than the horses and did not have the same mobility and manoeuvrability. Prithvi loved the gentle giants and steeled himself for what must be done.

He had ordered Maladev, the nursemaid sent by Pandit Padmanabh, to stay behind in Ajmer preferring to take only vaidya Narana. A small dose of kushumba and Prithvi was wonderfully calm yet alert. The infantry would be crushed underfoot if tested against the elephant corps, so the king had them lined up on either side of his cavalry.

Skand had made the cavalry as well as the infantry practise opening up their ranks, creating a passage for the elephants to blunder through and then the archers to turn and attack from the rear. They had practised with their own war elephants; those who were too slow were thrown from their mounts and suffered terrible injuries while a few of the most unfortunate among them were crushed beneath those massive feet. Prithviraj had their funeral rites performed with full honours and provided compensation for the families.

His men were still haunted by the memory, the king knew. But they were brave and stood firm at his back, ready to follow him to the gates of hell and beyond.

Astride his charger, at the head of the vanguard, Prithviraj gave his battle cry, his voice carrying to the ends of the ranks. Behind him the mighty war drum boomed, cymbals clashed and conches blared, the pulse of every man who heard it thrumming in response.

Tribhuvanagiri was practically salivating when he saw the cavalry coming at his invincible elephants and he gave the order to attack. His young adversary would sup on bitter defeat within an hour! The horses raced towards them and just as the Bhadanaks braced for the explosive impact, Prithviraj gave the signal and the horsemen executed a wide turn with jarring suddenness, perfectly synchronized and brilliantly executed.

Befuddled, the mahouts tried to slow the charge of the elephants. In the meantime, the infantry had marched forward from either side in a solid wedge, the shieldsmen closing ranks and forming a solid wall, affording protection to the men within and the burden they were dragging, squirming into the battlefield.

The soldiers at the forefront of the wedge were carrying torches and as they paused to light them, the panicked pigs were released. They wore leather harnesses coated with grease, holding in place little sacks stuffed with cotton and twigs, soaked in oil and fastened to their backs. From an opening in the centre of the wedge, their backs afire, and prodded by smaller goads, they fled pell-mell into the rush of the oncoming elephants as the foot soldiers beat a retreat.

The elephant corps scattered in all directions driven to mad panic by the smell of smoke and the heat of the flaming missiles that got in their midst, throwing them into ruinous disarray. Thousands of Tribhuvanagiri's men were crushed under their bulks. All around was complete and utter chaos.

Even the horses balked at the sight and smell of the incendiary objects that got between their legs and reared back violently tossing their riders. Tribhuvanagiri tried to rally his men from the golden howdah he was seated on, as his own mahout struggled to calm the panicked beast. Already some of the mahouts had their mallets in hand and were driving their spiked goads into the sweet spot behind the ears.

Meanwhile, the cavalry had rushed back into the fray. They attacked the mahouts or aimed well-placed blows to the trunk and ankles of the elephants. The ropes securing the howdah in place were also targeted. All around them, men fell to their deaths as their unstable, makeshift shelters atop the great beasts collapsed in a heap. Incendiary arrows were loosed at the beasts and the silken mats on their backs caught fire. All around was the smell of burning flesh and fresh excrement, the sound of trumpeting elephants, whinnying horses, squealing pigs, foul curses, anguished cries of those in mortal pain and the pounding of drums.

The bowmen mounted on their own elephant corps surged forward to finish things off. The king had ordered the flautists to accompany them to the battlefield so that their music could soothe the pachyderms while all around them the battle raged. During Nagarjun's revolt, it was the elephant corps that decimated pockets of resistance among the troops. They were needed to perform the same service here.

Prithviraj singled out Tribhuvanagiri's mount and took off in hot pursuit, his charger responding to his command instantly, while his crack troops followed close on his heel. At full gallop, he fired arrows from his great war bow, picking off the mahout first. The elephant's rage was uncontrollable and it mowed down all who got in the way indiscriminately. Prithvi wheeled away and his horse responded, charging away from the murderous behemoth.

Atop the howdah, Tribhuvanagiri had taken a javelin to his side and an arrow protruded from his neck. Only one of his attendants was alive. Desperate to save the bleeding king, every soldier worth the name threw himself into the fray. Members of his cavalry tried to get close enough to help while the Chahamanas troops did everything to stop them. And then the attendant lost his head. He pulled out his sword and plunged it deep into the elephant's neck, sending spasms ratcheting across the beast's hind legs. The next moment, the mighty beast had hit the ground claiming lives even in its death throes.

Moments before they dragged Tribhuvanagiri from the howdah, he had pulled out the arrow sticking out of his neck and jammed the sharp point into his throat. Even so, he died only after they began hacking away at him and his mount both.

The victory cries of Prithviraj's men rang out as the sun blazed over them. They had prevailed on every single front and their jubilation was a sight to behold as they leaped high in the air, prancing among the multitude of corpses that lay in all directions.

Prithviraj did not celebrate. He raised his sword in acknowledgement of the familiar chanting of his name and his horse reared up on its hind legs. This image of their god-king silhouetted against the splendour of the sun was the one his men carried in their hearts while there was life left to them. As for the object of their great love, he had spurred his horse on towards the camp. Not for the first time, he wished he could leave it all behind. But thinking like that was a child's game and the king had a thousand things that needed his immediate attention.

It was a stupendous victory for the young king of the Chahamanas and his fame spread all over aryavarta. His annihilation of the Bhadanaks yielded riches to rival Kubera's fortune. Tribhuvanagiri's treasury was emptied and mountains of gold, silver and copper coins, along with bushels of precious stones and priceless artefacts, were carried to Ajmer on the backs of the remainder of the late king's fabled elephant corps.

To mark his triumph, there were celebrations for ten days and nights. Cows were gifted to the Brahmins and bards were rewarded with bags fat with coins. As for the troops, they were sumptuously feasted and served the finest vintages in a manner befitting visiting royalty for ten days and nights. The most renowned singers, musicians and dancers from across the realm performed for them. Their king felt that his men deserved nothing but the best and served them everything their hearts desired. Every banquet witnessed wildly indulgent drinking and debauched orgies that went on till dawn.

And then one night a goddess appeared before the mighty monarch, Prithviraj Chauhan. She was extraordinarily beautiful with hair the colour of midnight, adorned with a crown of precious stones, and eyes that sparkled with the light of all the stars that bedeck the heavens. Taking him by the hand and leading him deep into the woods to the temple of gold, where she was worshipped, she threw open its treasure vault, bestowing on him riches enough for several lifetimes. 'You are my beloved, the keeper of my heart that I had vowed to give to none but the noblest hero in the three worlds. For as long as I watch over my lord, he shall remain undefeated in battle and none but the three-eyed god will be able to match his prowess. Endowed with my gifts, he will prevail over the monsters both mortal and immortal that plague this land!'

'So did the king consummate his union with the gorgeous goddess?' Padhri wanted to know. 'And how come there is no mention of Padhri Ray, slayer of ten thousand?' They were forcing their protesting stomachs to accommodate the rich viands and fine wines during the course of yet another evening of revelry.

'If you had not interrupted me so rudely,' Jaya replied huffily, 'you would have heard about Padhri Ray, the fat bastard who soiled his small clothes at the sight of the ten-thousand-strong elephant corps of the Bhadanaks.'

Padhri grabbed the bard by the neck and, pulling off his fine-jewelled turban, flung it on the floor, where it lay dangerously close to a puddle of vomit. 'Oh! Leave him alone!' Kanak intervened. 'Everyone knows that you slew the ten thousand, those poor unfortunate souls who happened to be in the vicinity when you soiled your small clothes.'

'Your little songs seem to have captured the fancy of the people, Jaya,' Nahar slurred, ogling the bevy of beauties who were swaying hypnotically in front of them. 'They genuinely believe that our king is wed to the goddess of victory. Most worship the ground he walks on! Speaking of the great hero, how come he isn't here today?'

'His mother and Pandit Padmanabh cornered him into a meeting. He usually loses his appetite after one of those . . .' Kanak remarked.

'I know what it is all about!' Jaya said mysteriously and refused to say a word even after Padhri offered to disembowel him to extract the information. He relented only when Kanak retrieved his fine turban and dusted it off before handing it back to him.

'His mother has found the ideal bride for the king and she wants the nuptials to be concluded immediately. The queen mother says that she will breathe easier if there is a heir to the throne,' Jaya whispered to them.

'Do you know who the bride is?' Nahar asked. 'To the best of my knowledge, every princess, hell, every girl in the land and her mother wants him.'

'Except the ones I bed, of course!' Padhri insisted.

'Especially the ones you bed!' Kanak told him. 'They can abide your company only if they close their eyes and pretend you are the king.'

'The bride is a Paramar princess named Padmavati,' Jaya said in hushed tones.

'Well, I'll tell you one thing for nothing,' Padhri leaned forward. 'The king's divine bride is not going to like this one bit!'

Prithviraj did not like it one bit. He hated it when his mother and the pandit teamed up against him. 'This girl is perfect for you,' his mother was insisting. 'She is beautiful, pleasantly plump, always a sure sign of good health, and most importantly, has wide child-bearing hips.' The Paramar princess was a clever girl, who had learned to read and write, but Karpuradevi did not mention that to her son. It was never healthy when a man realized that his wife was exactly like his mother.

'She will bear you strong sons who will brighten the last few years left to me with the patter of their little feet and musical laughter.' Karpuradevi continued, 'Is it so wrong of me to want to see my grandchildren before I die?'

The pandit was bobbing his head vigorously just in case his wholehearted endorsement of the queen's words wasn't ridiculously obvious. He looked reproachfully at the king, his eyes chiding him for the cruel treatment of his caring mother.

My father married you, I am sure they told him roughly the same things about you and look where it got him. Prithviraj was itching to say the words aloud.

'Mother, I have already told you that it is my intention to turn my attention to the Chandels,' he said instead. 'They have always been an inimical presence and now is as good a time as any to tackle them. With the Bhadanaks and the Chandels taken out of the equation, their territories annexed to Sapadalaksha, I will be able to march against the Chalukyas,' Prithviraj said impatiently.

He was determined to destroy his enemies close at hand before taking the attack to Shihabuddin of Ghur. Prithviraj was sure that those who dared to harp on his unwillingness or inability to produce heirs were thrown to the famed hounds of Ghur.

'Pulverizing the Chandels is an excellent course of action, maharaj,' the pandit piped up. 'However, wars are not won on the battlefield alone. By making powerful alliances through marriage you will be able to bring various kingdoms into the realm of the Chahamanas and useful allies can only enhance your position. A worthy successor to the throne will also put paid to the plotting of those who dream of seizing it.'

'It is best to have children when you are young and virile,' Karpuradevi interjected, 'and the seed is at its most potent.'

Prithviraj was glad he hadn't eaten. His mother's talk of the quality of his seminal discharge was making him nauseated. And he resented being treated like a stallion being put to stud. He had no doubt that this wasn't the last conversation he would be having on the subject since in all likelihood his mahamantri was playing the pimp himself and had assembled an army of suitable girls with 'wide, child-bearing hips' for him to marry and make babies with. *Yogita had tiny hips that he could have easily encircled with his palms*. He forced the thought from his mind.

'My mind is made up. We will talk about this after my conquest of the Chandels. Why don't the two of you proceed to the feast? I will have a word with the mahamantri about our next expedition and will join you there in a bit.'

The queen mother would have liked to have a word with the mahamantri as well. She would tell him exactly what she thought of the hussies he exposed her son to. Her biggest worry was that Prithviraj had inherited his father's weakness for women along with his crown.

As Prithviraj began to walk away, she turned to the pandit and spoke softly to him but just loud enough for her son to hear. 'That Bhimdev is such a debauched old man. Padmavati is young enough to be his granddaughter but he has been pestering Maharaj Daravarsh Paramar for her hand. My informers tell me that the princess is most distraught and frequents the temple every day, praying that Maharaj Prithviraj will help her escape the clutches of that depraved Chalukyan.'

Pretending not to have heard her, the king walked away in the commanding manner that was so characteristic of him. But the queen mother was later informed that during his discussion with the mahamantri on state matters, the subject of his marriage had cropped up and the king had conveyed that he was not entirely averse to marrying the Paramar princess.

Needless to say his capitulation warmed the cockles of her heart and she couldn't resist saying to the pandit and the mahamantri, 'All boys, even the valiant kings among them, can achieve their full potential only as long as they pay attention to the words of their mothers. For there is no power in the three worlds to rival a mother's love.'

Maharaj Prithviraj found his wedding a most tedious affair. There were a lot of formalities to be observed and he was told to perform as many charitable acts as possible before his wedding.

Pandit Padmanabh, with his army of priests and astrologers, spent hours finalizing the most auspicious time to conduct the nuptials and even the precise moment when he was expected to consummate the union. There were so many purification rites and rituals to ward off the evil eye that Prithviraj lost his temper with the lot of them.

Karpuradevi seemed determined to empty the treasury he had so painstakingly filled to the brim, by buying up all the flowers, jewels, silks and sweetmeats in the land for the wedding procession and conducting lavish ceremonies every step of the way to Abu. 'The Paramars are very happy with this match and the bride's family will be sending enough gold, silver and valuable ornaments to fill our coffers,' the pandit told him, 'in addition to several hundred heads of cattle, fine Arabian horses, battle elephants and many more costly presents as well as an army of valuable attendants to carry them all back.'

That did not make Prithviraj feel better though, for one who was irritated beyond measure, he bore it all with a pleasant demeanour that came across as entirely natural. When the day of the wedding dawned, his thoughts were full of Yogita. His heart told him that their story wasn't over yet and he held on to that heartening thought. And it lifted his spirits considerably.

The Paramars had arranged a grand ceremony. When the king was escorted into the marriage pavilion, he was attacked by a gaggle of giggling girls who refused to let him see the bride's face. Prithviraj played along, making a big show of bribing them with expensive presents his mother had picked out, which made them squeal in a manner reminiscent of the pigs he had released against the elephant corps of Bhadanak.

The little ones crowded around him, jostling for his attention. Prithvi lifted up a small girl who was dutifully carrying out her assigned task of dropping rose petals at his feet and carried her all the way to the pavilion. She blushed and the crowd roared with laughter. 'He has always wanted a daughter,' Jaya murmured to his companions.

'Don't let the pandit or the queen mother hear you. They will have your tongue for it!' Kanak warned.

Later the assembled guests swore that the king was the most handsome and charming man alive.

When they finally unveiled the bride, he almost wished they hadn't. She was wearing a crimson sari heavily embroidered with gold thread and so much jewellery that the finest archers in his ranks would have had a hard time finding the weak spot in that impenetrable armour of solid gold. Her face was barely visible under the cosmetic goop he had never liked, with black collyrium drawn thickly over her eyes, reminding him of the time he had given Padhri a black eye. The red dye over her lips made it look like they were bleeding.

She stood timidly by his side, bearing the weight of her ornaments and the heavy garlands they were to exchange as the solemn ceremony got underway with the priests screaming their lengthy mantras at the top of their lungs. Daravarsh Paramar performed the *kanyadan* and gave away the bride. They tied her sari to Prithviraj's robes and they walked around the sacred fire three times, taking exactly seven steps to complete the circuit—the *sapt padi*. And finally he tied the weighty *mangalsutra* around her neck before they exchanged garlands and he marvelled at her ability to bear the tremendous weight on her neck. The deed was finally done and they were married.

The assembled gathering agreed that it had been a beautiful ceremony and that the union of Prithviraj Chauhan and the Paramar princess would prove most beneficial to the realm.

Prithviraj reclined on his nuptial bed, which had been strewn with rose petals, fiddling aimlessly with the strands of jasmine that festooned the chamber. There was a pitcher of wine, bowls of fruits and sweetmeats within reach. A gauzy curtain separated the bedchamber from the room beyond where the bride was being prepared for her wedding night.

The new bride was finally divested of the heavy sari, jewellery and the many garlands. Her maids poured jugs of heated water over her head, perfumed with fragrant sandalwood. They dried her hair over a beautiful bronze Sambrani holder placed over heated coals and dressed her in a sheer sari that would inflame her husband. The fragrant tresses were artfully arranged and adorned with strands of fresh flowers. When Padmavati was ready, she was led into the bedchamber and the women withdrew discreetly.

She walked stiffly towards him with eyes downcast and the colour high in her cheeks. The king saw that without the garish bridal paint, she was quite lovely. He couldn't help but notice that she seemed to be trembling as if she were preparing for the worst ordeal of her life. Gingerly, she seated herself on the edge of the bed, still refusing to look at him.

The king was used to women who were expert in the art of lovemaking and were pleased to flaunt their skills for their mutual pleasure. He had no foreknowledge about how exactly he was supposed to handle a virgin bride. Mutual awkwardness dragged on for what felt like years and finally the bride burst into tears, unable to stand it. Gently, Prithvi placed his hand over her shoulder, remembering another girl who had disappeared into his past. She too had needed to be comforted.

His bride flinched when he touched her. 'I am not going to hurt you . . .' she relaxed a little on hearing the kindness in that voice.

'I am so sorry. They said that I must give you pleasure but I don't know how.' The words were tumbling out of her in a rush.

'All I can think is there is going to be blood on the sheets. They said it is very painful the first time a girl's maidenhood is claimed by her husband but I should bear it with a smile and then I'll get used to it. But I have been so scared . . . They said that the blood will be proof of my worthiness, that this marriage has been consumed, no connonesome . . . and duly witnessed. What am I going to do?'

Prithviraj had to stifle the laughter that bubbled to his lips. The pandit had told him about that particularly odious morning-after ritual, where the sheets from their bedchamber would be examined and displayed from the ramparts of the palace to assure the populace that the king had successfully screwed his virgin bride. His teacher had stressed repeatedly that if they consummated their union in the auspicious time frame delineated for the purpose, a veritable lion among men would be borne by his new bride. Sometimes, the revered panditji genuinely tested the extent of his forbearance.

'You should just go to sleep,' Prithviraj replied to her query. 'It has been a really long day and I think you can use the rest.' He couldn't say about other men but tears did not really get things going for him. Or a frightened girl who had the air of one expecting to be mauled by a tiger.

'But what about the blood?' Padmavati queried fearfully. 'They will come to check in the morning and everybody will know that I did not do my duty. And then they may say . . .' she couldn't seem to complete the sentence.

'We don't want that, do we?' he told her with a mischievous glint in his eye. 'If they want blood, then they will get some!' Her eyes became huge as he grabbed the fruit knife and slit his palm ever so casually. She placed her hands over her mouth and continued to watch without daring to breathe as he held it over the sheet, nonchalant as you please, staining it red with his blood. Then he licked off the rest, before helping himself to some wine.

'Now everybody will be happy! And you can go to sleep without worrying about blood and pain,' Prithviraj assured her.

Padmavati looked at him in shocked silence and then her face relaxed into the sunniest smile he had ever seen. It was a wondrous thing to behold. She seemed to have no words to express her gratitude but she touched his feet with both hands and when he raised her by the shoulders, she leaned in and kissed his forehead. Alarmed by her boldness, she fled to the farthest corner of the bed and disappeared under the covers.

Prithviraj stayed awake for a little longer, thinking about the massive treasure troves he had amassed that had prompted people to say that he enjoyed the favour of a goddess. Yet none of it had felt as good as a clumsy kiss that had been wet with gratitude. He smiled when he thought of what the pandit, his mother and mahamantri would say if he were to inform them that from this point onwards his life would be devoted to gathering kisses.

He drank his wine and listened to the stillness of the night before his thoughts returned to the problems posed by the Chandels and Shihabuddin of Ghur. He wondered if Yogita was happy wherever she was. Had Uncle Kanha managed to curtail the excesses of the talarakshas? He was still mulling over the things that weighed on his mind, slithering around like snakes, when sleep claimed him.

Eventually the marriage of Prithviraj Chauhan and Padmavati was duly consummated, for real. 'It was nowhere as awful as I thought it was going to be,' she had told him on that memorable occasion, brushing away a strand of hair that was glued to her sweat-stained forehead. 'When they told me that you displayed the skulls of your enemies on the walls of your fortress, I was petrified. People are so stupid to believe such lies. If they knew you like I do they would never accuse you of such horrific deeds.'

'Such filthy lies!' Prithvi assured her. 'The truth is I punished the rebels by having their male members chopped off and stuffed in their mouth right before they were impaled on sharp sticks and displayed on the battlefield.'

He burst out laughing when he saw the shocked expression on her face. The king had grown very fond of his bride who had proved herself to be sweet, charming and exceedingly talkative once she had survived the imagined horrors of her wedding night. He knew that not all the women he had taken his pleasures from would attest to the same, but with Padmavati he was always gentle. And she rewarded him with her undying love and friendship.

Within a few months of their return to Ajmer, the bride had sweet tidings and the entire kingdom rejoiced, adding their prayers to hers, hoping for a bouncing boy before the year was out. The king, however, wanted a girl who would be as loving as her mother. Needless to say, the pandit and Karpuradevi were horrified. Thousands of pujas were performed to the gods asking them to intercede and give Maharaj Prithviraj what he needed. Not what he wanted.

Not that it stopped the king from constantly reiterating his wish for a daughter just to gall her, Karpuradevi felt. It was during this blissful period that Govindraj, mandaleshwar of Dillika, sought an audience with the king. Prithviraj had him escorted to his private chambers at once. When Govindraj entered, the king was shocked to see his deathly pallor and insisted that he revive himself with a preferred inebriant.

Govindraj accepted though it was obvious that he did so only to please his king. 'I offer you my heartiest congratulations on your recent victories in the battlefield as well as off it. May I say that this is only the beginning and it is my belief that you will scale greater heights and your fame will spread far and wide across the very annals of time.'

The king smiled in acknowledgement of the praise. 'Those words mean a lot, especially when they come from the lips of a man as noble and valiant as yourself. But tell me, old friend, what troubles you and how may I redress the wrong that has clearly been done?'

Govindraj took a deep breath, 'Have you heard of Alha and Udal? They belong to the Banaphar clan and are generals of Paramardi Deva, the Chandel king.'

The king nodded. 'Their exploits are known to me. Needless to say, I have no fondness for the pair, seeing that they are to blame for subjecting my people to the cruel excesses of their ilk every time they infringe on our borders with their bands of hooligans.'

'They sing a different tune in the Chandel strongholds of Mahoba, Khajuraho, Bundelkhand and Jeyabhukti,' Govindraj said bitterly. 'They claim that the Chahamanas and their vassals are tearing apart the very fabric of aryavarta with their expansionistic ambitions and it is up to their local heroes like Alha and Udal to stop us. In the name of freedom, the Chandels have sworn to teach the tyrants of Delhi and Ajmer a lesson.'

Prithviraj frowned. *Are they calling me a tyrant now? Do they think I am made of the same mettle as Mahmud of Ghazni or Shihabuddin of Ghur? How dare they! My people, on the other hand, hail me as the protector of aryavarta and beloved of the goddess of victory, thereby attributing my hard-earned wins to divine intervention! How is it that no matter what I do, people want to either spit in my face or kiss my backside, both of which are equally repellent?* His guest was still speaking and Prithvi gave himself a mental shake.

'The Chandel prince, Brahma, despicable coward that he is, sent his dogs Alha and Udal to abduct my daughter on his behalf so he could marry her by force. I called for my troops and we gave chase at once!' He paused and sipped a bit of wine before gathering his emotions and continuing.

'She was only a girl! And the poor little thing has always been frightened of horses. But she is of my blood and fierce of spirit. My daughter struggled furiously and that brute Alha hit her to subdue her but she wouldn't stop fighting to free herself from his wretched paws. In the heat of the battle, amidst the storm of spears and arrows, I watched it happen with my own eyes . . .'

His voice was so choked with grief and pain that Prithvi himself had to fight to swallow the lump in his throat as Govindraj forced himself to go on. 'She broke free from his vice-like grip and in doing so lost her balance . . . I watched as she was crushed beneath the wheels of the chariot and held her in my arms as she breathed her last. They slaughtered the rest of my men who gave chase. All I ask . . .'

'You don't have to ask, old friend!' the king interrupted. 'I remember Krishnakumari, who was like a sister to me. We will declare war on the Chandels and avenge the death of one who was worth more than that entire kingdom of rakshasas put together.'

Govindraj was so grateful he couldn't find the words to express it. The king commiserated with the mandaleshwar over his loss, sharing charming little anecdotes he remembered of Krishnakumari from his visit to Delhi and doing what he could to ease a bereaved father's grief. When Govindraj had retired, he summoned his council and announced that they were going to war. Again.

22

Prithviraj conferred with his mahamantri, Govindraj, Skand and Uncle Kanha regarding the battle plans. They spent days going over the information painstakingly gleaned from their spies. The kingdom of the Chandels was a rich and powerful one and their famed troops would not be easy to subdue. It was an important undertaking in Maharaj Prithviraj's military career and he was determined not to leave anything to chance.

Kadambavas had asked to join his king on the battlefield, insisting that he had trained the council of ministers so well that they could actually run the kingdom blindfolded. His uncle did not wish to miss out on the action either.

'It is fitting only for women and children to stay put while the men fight,' Kanha had said. 'I don't want my skills to get rusty. It is the surest way to join the ranks of the old and the infirm. Besides, I am sure that I can teach those strutting peacocks—the king's companions—and every soldier in the army a thing or two.' Prithvi knew that it was only his deep affection that kept his uncle from including him as well.

He had acquiesced. En route to Jeyabhukti, they took it in turns to speak to him and caution him about the hidden dangers posed by his latest campaign. 'The pandit must have given you his usual lecture on the history of the Chandels, isn't that right?' Kanha began. 'As I recall, he tends to equate them to dogs who carved out a kingdom on the leftovers of their imperial masters.'

Prithvi laughed. 'He used exactly those words to describe them!' The Chandels had been the feudatories of the mighty Pratiharas. Yashovarma, the founder of their line, had taken advantage of their declining power to grab the powerful forts of Kalinjar and Gwalior, establishing his own kingdom in Bundelkhand. His descendants had expanded the kingdom so that it extended all the way from the river Chambal in the north to the Narmada in the south.

'One of the kings in their line, Vidyadhara, successfully repelled the attack of Mahmud of Ghazni, adding great lustre to the hitherto lacklustre reputation of the Chandels. They still brag that they alone have the distinction of impeding Mahmud's advance into aryavarta. Ever since, the Chandels have been coasting along borne on a single glorious moment from the past,' Prithviraj remarked, surprised that he could remember the pandit's pedantic words from his childhood.

'Their temples at Khajuraho and Kandariya Mahadev temple are famous and people flock to them from all over the land. A dancer from Khajuraho is well known to me . . .' Prithvi was surprised to see the rapturous look on his uncle's face, 'and believe me they are among the finest exponents of art and lovemaking in the three worlds!'

He grinned at his nephew conspiratorially, which prompted him to ask, 'Did you care for this dancer, Uncle Kanha? Do you miss her?'

Uncle Kanha shrugged. 'On the journey of life, you meet a lot of people. Some make more of an impact than others. You never know who is going to be with you to the very end and who is destined to leave you halfway. It is not in your hands. In the end, you just have to be grateful for whatever time you had with those who matter in some way or the other.'

'How is it possible for you to always maintain that imperturbable air of equanimity, Uncle Kanha? But I know what you will say . . . that you were raised by Kanchanadevi.' He grinned as he said that and looked very much like the boy he still was at heart, not at all like a monarch and a father-to-be.

'How fares your young wife? The queen mother chose well. Padmavati has a good heart and I like that your being the king of the Chahamanas has nothing to do with the fact that she clearly thinks the world of you.'

'Is that right? Just before we left, I got the impression that she didn't think quite so highly of me and went as far as to say I was truly my mother's son,' Prithvi replied, his eyes softening at the memory.

'Padma wanted to see a real battle as she called it,' he grinned. 'Needless to say, Mother put paid to her grand plan of accompanying me, saying that the battlefield was not the place for ladies of fine birth, especially when carrying the heir of the Chahamanas. They got into quite the squabble over it, with my wife insisting that her mother-in-law is a tyrant. Both feel I take the other's part and I was delighted to head for the road, leaving behind the horrific power struggles of the harem that usually make the bloodiest of battles seem tame in comparison!'

'The young queen probably felt that her presence would prevent you from adding to the long line of lovely ladies Kadambavas has so assiduously been filling your harem with.'

'And here I was wondering why she liked my mahamantri exactly as much as she loves my mother!' Prithvi replied, ignoring the derision in Uncle Kanha's voice. The mahamantri and his uncle had a bizarrely complicated relationship and he adopted the same stance with those two that he had taken with his mother and wife. Wild horses couldn't force him to interfere with the stormy dynamics that defined the relationship between either pair.

Kadambavas seemed a little preoccupied. 'My informers have told me that Paramardi has appealed to his neighbour

Maharaj Jaichand of Kannauj for help. It is a worrisome turn of affairs because the Gahadwala ruler seems to be jealous of your growing influence and power. I am not sure it bodes well for us that our enemies are sleeping together.'

'I have never even met this Jaichand,' Prithviraj remarked, 'but recently, somebody told me that we are cousins on our mothers' side. From what I hear, he is a proud and prickly man who feels entitled to glory and respect though he is unwilling to allow his deeds to do the talking and dirty his hands with things like military conquest! But has he acceded to Paramardi's request?'

'His troops have not been mobilized in Kannauj, I am told,' Kadambavas replied. 'But that does not mean we cannot expect a stealth attack with a surrounding manoeuvre that could prove disastrous for us. It is what I would do.'

Prithvi did not doubt it for a moment. 'Let Jaichand of Kannauj do his worst! The way I see it, this is a great opportunity for us to kill two birds with one stone.'

After all this time, Prithviraj was still capable of shocking him! The king seemed to relish the prospect of imminent danger—nine out of ten men would not have responded with so much enthusiasm when confronted with the distinct possibility of being caught between two great enemies. And his attack plan was so simple it was pure genius—lower the horns, stomp the hooves and charge!

It had proved effective thus far, but Kadambavas worried about the day when their young king would go too far. Already, he seemed to think he was invincible and that nobody could ever prevail over him. To the best of his knowledge, the fates singled out men like that, seducing them by letting them think that they enjoyed the favour of the gods, allowing them to savour the taste of victory in a steady succession, right before they took it all away.

The mahamantri wondered if the king's melancholia was catching. It was not like him to brood this way. They were prepared for anything and yet he could not shake the feeling that there was a terrible calamity lurking ahead and nothing in their arsenal to deal with the fallout.

The armies of the Chahamanas and the Chandels were to meet on the battlefield of Urai. Prithviraj led his men while the famed hero of the land, Alha, commanded the enemy troops. Paramardi had chosen to remain safely within the walls of his supposedly impregnable fortress city of Kalinjar.

It was Jaya who had told his king a little something about the commander. 'His people love Alha because he is one of them, as is his brother-in-arms, Udal. They were both of modest means and belonged to the Banaphar clan. But they rose through the ranks simply on account of their extraordinary skills. Apart from being exemplary fighters, they are also brave, generous to a fault and loyal. Their detractors have sneered at their low birth and uncultured ways but the truth is that Alha and Udal rigidly adhere to the code of the Kshatriyas even more so than most true-born Kshatriyas.'

'If you love them so much, why don't you go join them and compose songs in their honour?' Padhri growled. Kanak and Nahar were scowling too. Prithviraj could tell why Jaya's comments rankled. His companions were all of noble birth and clearly resented the implication that they had risen to their positions of power for reasons other than that of pure merit. Jaya ignored the jibe.

Prithviraj left them to it and sent for his charger, deciding to go for a short ride so he could mull over things he had learned before drawing up battle plans and issuing instructions to his men. A sudden weight settled on his heart. It was as if there was a sudden shift in the winds of fortune that did not bode well for the future.

23

Later, when everything was in readiness for the clash with the Chandels, Prithviraj found himself tossing restlessly in his tent, unable to sleep. A king had many enemies, both within and without, he reminded himself, and it would never do if he were to allow himself to be lulled into a false sense of security because his subjects and soldiers gave unstintingly of their adulation. Prithvi thought back on his conversation with the Sufi mystic following which he had asked his Uncle Kanha to bring the talarakshas under his command. It had been one of the smartest decisions he had made, which in turn resulted in the fomenting of new friendships. A king could never have too many of those . . .

Prithviraj thought about his encounter with Chandradeva, chief of the Khokars, who had been taken captive on the orders of Kanha. They were accused of harassing the Mussulmen who had been living on the fringes of Sapadalaksha territory since the time of Mahmud of Ghazni. It was a delicate situation and Kanha had consulted with the king.

Prithviraj had asked his uncle to personally ensure that the chief and his men were treated with respect till he found the time to address them directly.

'It was my impression that the Khokars were honourable men who were the living embodiment of the high ideals and the bravery of the Shahis. The same Shahis who shed their last drop of blood fighting the Turushkas in order to keep the women and children safe from their advances.'

'We are honourable men, sire,' Chandradeva said with quiet dignity. 'Anybody who dares suggest otherwise is a liar. We too have taken an oath to devote our lives to rooting out the Turushkas. They have had to contend with us every time they plan their cowardly attacks.'

'Is that right? Then how is it that the Khokars who have long fought the raiding Turushkas are currently in the business of harassing innocent traders, their women and children?' the king queried. His voice was soft but steely.

Chandradeva flushed. 'My men got carried away in the heat of battle. But we will not allow the Mussulmen to sully aryavarta with their polluted presence. Not after they trampled our faith, burnt our temples and raped our women. If they think that we will forget the past and not make them answer for their crimes . . .'

'You don't think it is ironical that *you* are retaliating by trampling on *their* faith, burning *their* places of worship and raping *their* women? Is there really a difference between the two of you? They too claim that their actions cannot be held against them because they have the sanction of their god, you know . . .'

'We are nothing like those heartless mlecchas,' Chandradeva flared up at once, forgetting that he was in the presence of his king, forgetting even himself in the heat of his fanatical passion. 'My father served Maharaj Vigraharaj most loyally, and for generations we have fought to wipe out the menace posed by the Turushkas towards our land, women and children. I fought with my men against the new Mahmud from Ghur, the one who has refused to learn a lesson, though the Chalukyas defeated him once when he had advanced into Punjab and Sind.'

He paused, the thought of his homeland overrun by the Turushkas too much for him to bear. Prithviraj's informers had told him as much but they had reported that his forays into Punjab and Sind had been raiding parties and he had retreated as quickly as he had come.

'The invader has returned to his heavily fortified military bases at Peshawar and Lahore. The defences are impregnable. He watches your every move, sire, and unlike Mahmud of Ghazni, this man wants to invade all of aryavarta and establish the rule of the Mussulmen.'

Prithviraj had been told that Shihabuddin was preparing for war. That he had hired slaves known as the 'Mamluks', who were trained since childhood to fight and remain impervious to pain in battle. It was not known where exactly he would strike but naturally, by dint of his recent victories, Ajmer would be a tempting target. Prithviraj was looking forward to the encounter and was pleased to note that his enemy was taking him very seriously indeed.

'The new Mahmud of Ghur is the reason we have been struggling so hard to rid this sacred land of every single Mussulman out there, who presumes he has a right to be here,' the Khokar chief interrupted his thoughts, anxious to exonerate himself. 'You said it yourself, sire, that we will fight till the last drop of blood has been shed and the very last breath taken. They say that you too have taken an oath to drive out those savages from our aryavarta. Take us with you on this noble quest, sire, so we can help you fulfil this glorious mission you have undertaken!'

'I am glad to hear you say that,' Prithviraj said warmly, 'but if you wish to serve in this undertaking and be a part of my mission to vanquish Shihabuddin of Ghur, it is important that you give me every assurance of your loyalty. Among my men, blind obedience to the will of their king is an attribute that is prized highly and insurgents shall be rooted out without mercy. Law and order is taken seriously in my realm and I cannot have my subjects meting out their version of justice in whatever misguided way they see fit.'

'We are warriors, sire, and proud to call ourselves your men!' he said passionately. 'You have our word that we will be faithful to you unto death and obedient as you please. Some of my men have been a little too zealous in the pursuit of our chosen cause but if you can find it in your heart to be merciful, I swear to you that you will never have cause to regret it.'

'The worst of the offenders, the overly zealous ones you just mentioned, have been singled out by my men and will remain incarcerated,' Prithviraj ruled. 'As for the rest of you, I order you to present yourselves to General Skand, who will assign you billets in the royal army. He acts in my name and you will follow his every instruction to the last letter. If there is the slightest hint of insubordination . . .'

The king did not bother to complete the sentence and Chandradeva bowed. He did not reiterate his undying loyalty but Prithviraj knew that the man was grateful. Having them incarcerated with the rest of the low-lives would have been a crushing blow to the honour of the Khokars. The king hoped that the debt would be repaid with worthy deeds.

Kanha hadn't been entirely sure though. 'I have little patience with rabid dogs, who can somehow find it in their hearts to justify raping little children. Yet these hoodlums have the support of your subjects and if we punish them for the crime of murdering the Turushkas, even the peaceable traders among them, I fear there will be communal riots tearing apart the very fabric of this realm. Men like Kadambavas and the pandit are to be blamed for fostering hatred in the hearts of hitherto tolerant people.'

Prithviraj nodded. 'It is a tricky situation and I thought long and hard about it. We can use the services of the Khokars when we tackle Shihabuddin and the Turushkas but in the meantime, instead of terrorizing innocent people it is best that they devote themselves to eradicating our enemies. Skand will keep them in line.'

Uncle Kanha looked at him and wondered when exactly his nephew had grown up and become such a good king. His mother would have been proud. And he was too.

The king interrupted his thoughts. 'Did you not find Chandradeva's revelation that his father served Vigraharaj most interesting? I am sure we too can find gainful employment for their unusual talents. Men like the Khokars are dangerous because they are fanatical followers of their faith. However, they can serve a useful purpose once we have figured out a way to muzzle their more bloodthirsty impulses or at the very least, direct them towards those who are more deserving of defeat!'

Prithvi was thinking about the Khokars and their role in the battle to be fought on the morrow when a lone shadow detached itself from the darkness pooled at the entrance of his tent. His guards were probably dead, he realized. The king's hand moved imperceptibly to the jewelled handle of his dagger . . . He relaxed when he saw the sensuous movements of the perfumed courtesan who came towards him. Kadambavas had sent her no doubt to make sure that he was well rested for the battle tomorrow.

'Sire! It is me! I hope you have not forgotten . . .' an achingly familiar voice came out of the darkness just before she stepped into the dim glow cast by the lamp.

How could I ever forget? Prithvi still heard her voice and saw that hauntingly beautiful face every single day of his life. He remembered her laughter and the way she looked at him when they used to talk for hours about nothing in particular. He had forgotten nothing. Not even the words she had uttered while insisting that she wouldn't dishonour herself by becoming his concubine.

Now years later, she had come into his tent, a painted and professional purveyor of her countless charms. Even as recognition of her calling brought with it an unreasonable rage, a part of him was nevertheless glad to see her. The sudden urge to slap her hard was at war with a strong need to crush her to his chest.

She seemed apprehensive and was watching his face closely. Yogita had not been this bold back when he had known her. 'How did you manage to get past the guards?' he asked her coldly.

'I had to find you and warn you,' she spoke hesitantly, taken aback by his hostility. 'Dressed as a boy with my hair tucked under my turban, I ordered a detachment of the bodyguards assigned to the protection of my person, to help me circle the main army and get through to you.'

'How did you get past my guards?' he asked her again.

'I was waiting and watching for the opportune moment to present itself. Then we saw the beautiful woman making her way to your tent with the seal of the mahamantri. My men subdued her and I borrowed the seal and her clothes. It was of utmost importance that you be warned.'

'Which one of my enemies' harems have you graced with your presence?' Prithviraj asked her.

Hurt flashed across her eyes and he was sorry despite himself. But within an instant, it was replaced by a rage so fierce that Prithvi quailed in the face of it. 'For the second time in my life, I was abducted by the talarakshas, the guard dogs of the Sapadalaksha realm,' she spat out, 'whose king seems utterly incapable of protecting his subjects. They sold me to some traders who were headed to Kannauj. And if Maharaj Jaichand's mantri had not found me, who knows what would have happened? You rescued me from such a fate once but there seems to be no escaping my destiny.' Bitterness soaked her every word.

Yogita took a few moments to study his face and he stared back giving nothing away. 'A few months after I became a part of Maharaj Jaichand's harem, a Chahamanas spy contacted me and said that I must keep him informed of the movements of the king. That he spoke in your name. It was his practice to question me every once in a while but I had nothing of value to share. Besides, though Maharaj Jaichand has been most kind . . .'

Yogita broke off when she saw the anger on his face, seeming to boil over from every pore of his being. 'Please listen to me!' she begged. 'I am not privy to any secrets of the state. My position has always been too lowly for me to be of any value as a spy. But when I found out that the Gahadwalas were planning to ally themselves with the Chandels for a surprise attack, I had to do my best to warn you. Though I tried, it was impossible for me to locate your man on my own. They said that a lot of the informers had been killed to keep this information secret and I assumed the worst, hence . . .' her voice trailed off.

She had risked her life to come across enemy lines to make sure that he received fair warning. And the worst of it was that such sacrifice hadn't even been necessary, given the information they were privy to. Just like that he found his anger melting away and he pulled her to him. She hugged him back fervently, wanting to memorize the feel of his hair, the strong, masculine scent of his skin, the musky odour of the overwhelming desire he felt for her.

Yogita had been wracked with torment for a long time now. In fact, she knew of no other state of being. But ever since she had learned that Maharaj Jaichand planned to collude with the Chandels to destroy Prithviraj Chauhan, her suffering had worsened. The king of the Gahadwalas was a stern man and rather temperamental. For some reason, he had taken a fancy to her, which had led to her position being considerably enhanced. In return, she had looked after his needs with all the devotion that could be mustered by an unwilling heart.

She had not been able to forgive herself for betraying the only man she ever loved by giving herself to Maharaj Jaichand. Yet now that she was in Prithviraj's hands, she hated herself for being unfaithful to the man who was the closest thing to the husband she would never have.

Oblivious to her despair, Prithvi's lips had found the pulse beating at her neck and he was caressing her when she pushed him away. Stunned, he reached for her. Why wouldn't she give herself to him? Especially since her fine scruples had not stopped her from taking to concubinage like a duck to water . . . He hated himself for thinking that way about her, but there it was.

'You are mine.' It was a plea. 'If you ever cared for me in the slightest, you will stay here and let me love you the way I have always wanted to. On the morrow, I ride to meet my foes and by the time the sun sets tomorrow, the crows might be fighting for the remains of my body. I am not afraid to die on a battlefield. A true warrior can do a lot worse. But I am afraid of a life where you are lost to me . . . it is the one thing I cannot face!'

Her cheeks were wet with tears and her heart torn apart in two by the conflicting emotions that waged war inside. By making the choice to save his life, by betraying Maharaj Jaichand, she had thrown away her own. And the lives of the men in her command. Guilt flooded through her being, burning like acid.

'I am your woman,' she told him, 'my heart has always belonged to you. But Maharaj Jaichand has been good to me and I have repaid him with treachery. This sinner does not deserve either of you.'

Prithvi's voice was hoarse with pain. 'You are no sinner! I promised to keep you safe from harm but failed to keep my word . . .'

'Don't say that, sire! You gave me my life back,' she said softly, 'and the time we had together was the only part of my life that made me truly happy. I have treasured every single moment and relived them a thousand times. It was the only thing that kept me going and for that, I am truly grateful. When Yama comes for me, I'll go happily, knowing that my heart's desire to see you one last time has been granted.'

He held her as she sank to her feet, gathering her close to him as they lay together on the rug, comforting each other as best as they could. This was not the ideal situation for either of them but Prithvi was filled with relief and gladder than he could say that she had risked so much to make her way to him. Now that they were together again, nothing else mattered. She would return with him to Ajmer and he would make sure that she lacked for nothing. As for the men who were responsible for what she had been put through, there would be hell to pay. And if his mother was involved . . . Yogita whimpered and he forced himself to calm down.

Her lids were heavy as she lay in his strong arms, but Yogita refused to shut them, wanting to prolong that moment of exquisite bliss, making it last for as long as it was possible.

There could be no turning back for her. Yogita had known it all along. By now, her perfidy would have been reported to the king. She had asked Maharaj Jaichand to allow her to accompany him and his stealth troops to their secret location near Urai. She was sure that he would refuse.

To her surprise, he hadn't. 'You have never asked me for anything before and I will grant your request. The battlefield is no place for a flower so you shall travel farther inland with an escort and pay a visit to the beautiful temples this land is famed for.' It had been most thoughtful for a man as taciturn and stern as he was. Her heart turned at the thought of how he would react when he found out what she had done. She had slipped out from the camp they had set up for her, having selected a handful of men who were pliant and amenable to her will.

The rest had given chase but in the fighting that followed most had been killed and she had ridden on, never once looking back, with the few who had kept up with her. All of them were honourable men, some with families and children. Her dastardly actions had cut their lives short. They told her that a lone guard had escaped and he would have reached the king by now.

His rage would be a terrible thing to behold. But Maharaj Jaichand was a cautious man and he played the game of chance only if victory was assured. She knew him so well. By now, he would have made the decision to return to Kannauj, leaving behind a token force to honour his pact with the Chandels. Yogita hoped that someday he would find it in his heart to forgive her.

She hoped that Prithviraj would forgive her too and realize that she had been left with no choice. It was her hope that he would understand that she had done all this out of the great love she bore him. That she would go on loving him no matter where the tides of fortune saw fit to dump her.

Later, Prithviraj did not know how long she had been in his arms or the precise moment they had fallen asleep. When he came to, it was still dark outside. Yogita lay beside him. But something was terribly wrong. She was stiff and cold. He could not hear her breathing. Gently he shook her by the shoulder, praying for a response. But there wasn't, though he tried to revive her repeatedly.

The king laid her on his own bedding, covering her with his robe. Taking her cold, unresponsive hand in his, he sat by her side till the sun rose. She looked peaceful, almost as if she were asleep and would wake any moment. There was a trickle of blood near her lips that had turned a faint shade of blue from whatever it was she had taken, when she made the unforgiveable decision to leave him.

Prithviraj sent for his brother, Jaya and Narana. Though it was still early, the vaidya appeared before him looking fresh and alert. The king liked the physician. He was always so sympathetic. Narana gave the impression that he took his vocation seriously, that it was his mission in life to ease human suffering and pain whenever he chanced upon it. More importantly, at times such as these, he did what he was told without asking questions.

Jaya came in and his eyes bulged when he saw the lifeless beauty stretched in front of him. Even Hari seemed horror-struck. 'I want the two of you to perform her last rites. Just make sure that . . .' He could not go on. They nodded in mute understanding. Prithvi left at once.

He could not bear to be there any more. She had returned to his life without warning and departed just as quickly. He remembered how she had felt in his arms a few hours ago. And now her life had been snuffed out just like that. How ephemeral human existence was and how utterly pointless it all seemed!

But there was a battle to be fought and he was genuinely grateful for the distraction.

'What happened to her?' Jaya asked the physician once the king had made his abrupt departure. He looked at her supine form, aghast that the girl who had liked to hum and skip, who had loved Prithviraj even more than he did was no more. Surely the king had not done this to her?

'Poison!' Narana replied. He was a man of few words.

'Was she in pain? Did she suffer in the end?' He did not see how it mattered now but she had been so fragile in life, so in need of protection.

The vaidya hesitated. 'She was and she did. But I don't think the poison was to be blamed for that. A woman in this profession may have her fill of pleasure but happiness will always be denied to her.'

The vast army of the Chandels stretched out across the plains of Urai. Alha had arranged them in battle formation, with the infantry lined up in the centre and the horsemen on the wings. The troops carried silver quivers, gold-tipped arrows and spears, swords with jewelled pommels that glinted in the distance.

Alha, commander of the Chandel forces, rode towards them on a richly caparisoned horse with Udal by his side. Kadambavas had performed one of his miracles of diplomacy and both sides had agreed to a parley. Prithvi gathered the reins of his horse, spurring him towards the midway point between the armies. General Skand accompanied him. He was a worried man. The mahamantri had told him that the king was in one of his black moods and the vaidya had given him a heavier dose of a little something, which might yield some unexpected results.

It was Alha who spoke first. 'What happened was an accident. It is the Kshatriyan way to claim a bride by dint of force and we merely wished to claim Princess Krishnakumari for our Prince Brahma. If I could give my life to bring her back to the realm of the living, so that she might be reunited with her father, I would do so.'

'That is a fine sentiment,' Prithviraj replied, his tone barely masking his belligerence, 'even if that lofty statement has no real value, given that it is simply impossible to execute.'

'I ask only that we be allowed to pay reparations to Govindraj of Dillika,' Alha said calmly, refusing to be baited, 'so that the people of this land are not made to pay for the tragedy that they had no part in.'

'Are your allies, the Gahadwalas, in agreement with this decision?' Prithviraj queried.

Alha was unflappable. 'I speak with the voice of Maharaj Paramardi.'

'Be that as it may, my terms are these: in addition to the reparations made to the mandaleshwar of Dillika, I demand an unconditional surrender. If my terms are met, no blood need be shed here. Paramardi will be my feudatory and he will receive the respect due his rank. Jeyabhukti will be merged with Sapadalaksha. Together, we will tackle the enemies of aryavarta.'

'I cannot accede to that,' Alha said. 'We are perfectly willing to join a coalition against invaders and we will accept your leadership in a venture of that nature, but we will not surrender our freedom when threatened to do so. Don't ask it of us, sire!'

'In essence you are accusing me of being the aggressor who has politicized a young girl's death and brought war to your doorstep, while you are merely striving to preserve the peace and pimping for Brahma!' Prithviraj's eyes flashed fire and his voice was rising. Behind him General Skand braced for the impact from the collision he was steering them towards. 'In reality you have repeatedly destroyed the peace with your ill-advised incursions into Sapadalaksha territory, setting fire to harvest crops, destroying homes, wreaking havoc with trade and terrorizing my subjects. Accept me as your rightful king and you will enjoy my magnanimity. However, if you persist in refusing, then prepare to fight to defend your home and honour. Because I will do battle unto death, so let your king watch perched safely in his stone nest as his kingdom burns!'

Prithviraj spurred his horse and rode back with General Skand close behind him. Behind them there were wild cries of panic as the ranks of the enemy boiled to life. The king did not look back but Skand could not resist a peek. Balls of flame seemed to be dropping from the very heavens, creating havoc in the lines as the troops milled about in confusion. For a second, Skand stared at his king who was laughing maniacally at the spectacle, wondering if he really were a god capable of channelling Agni's power and weaponizing it.

'That would be my brave Khokar troops,' Prithvi chortled, his eyes seemed aflame as they reflected the great balls of fire. 'They were told to ambush the stealth troops of Kannauj who were lying in wait with orders to take us by surprise. Being blessed with initiative, Chandradeva has found a creative way to use the catapults that had come into their possession during the struggle against the Mussulmen. Those things are capable of hurling chunks of huge rocks over great distances and had done a lot of damage to their own fortresses.'

He laughed again, 'Severed heads dipped in pitch and set on fire make for wonderful incendiary missiles, don't you think?' Skand shivered when he heard the sound of raw pain masquerading as mirth. 'It is too bad that Jaichand had absconded. That man had left mere hours before the Khokars fell on his men! He has great instincts when it comes to preserving his own hide. Cowards usually do!'

The counterattack wasn't long in the coming and it was a blistering one. Alha and Udal reassembled their troops, striving to form a solid square to attempt a direct, valiant clash. They nearly succeeded but the Khokars drove them relentlessly from behind, making mincemeat of the defenders, driving them forward to be smashed against the solid wall of Prithviraj's troops, who were also surging towards the Chandels.

But Alha and Udal refused to let them have an easy time of it. Their voices boomed over the war horns as they rallied their men, imbuing them with fresh heart and ferocious intent as they threw back the soldiers who swarmed over them like bees in a hive. They knew that they would receive no mercy and asked for none, determined to drag as many of the Chahamanas troops as possible into the very bowels of hell.

Nahar confronted Udal, and the latter swung a mighty battle-axe that cleanly sliced through the helmet claiming a chunk of his scalp and leaving him blinded as copious amounts of blood gushed over his head and face. It would have all been over then, if Padhri and Kanha had not appeared to stave off the attack. Alha was deadlier by far, making short work of his enemies who came at him in an endless rush, inciting his own men to perform feats of valour. On any other day, they might have prevailed but it was not to be for the gods appeared to be frowning on their enterprise.

Prithviraj Chauhan was a man possessed, seeming to be everywhere at once, materializing wherever the fighting was fiercest. With reckless courage and utter disregard for his own safety, he appeared to be courting death with the ardour and persistence of an infatuated lover. Those who saw him on the blood-soaked plain of Urai swore that he appeared to embody the wildest and most feral of Lord Vishnu's incarnations—the Narasimha avatar. Half-man and half-leonine beast, he was an unstoppable force of pure destruction, tearing apart wave after wave of the attackers, littering the ground with corpses. All in his vicinity shrank back in terror and grizzled veterans inured to the horrors of war fainted in fright at the sight of the wrath-filled apparition.

Inspired by his example, his men fought like lions, convinced they were led by an invincible god. The king's eyes were glazed and he roared like the predator he had become. He issued a challenge to the commander of the Chandels. 'Fight me if you dare, Alha of the Banaphars! If you are truly your father's son and not the by-blow of shameless whoring, cross swords with me and claim the honour of death by the hand of Prithviraj Chauhan!'

Alha rose to the challenge, his face contorted with fury. Blood was soaking the left side of his face from a head wound as he turned his horse to meet his antagonist. Even before his manoeuvre was complete, Alha hurled his spear in a single, fluid movement. His aim was true and the point tore through the king's breastplate, painfully grazing his chest and nearly unhorsing him with the tremendous force of the impact. The Chahamanas troops held their breath but miraculously Prithviraj held his seat and they whooped in delight as he unsheathed his sword even as his mount charged forward. At full tilt, he drove the point into Alha's throat, who died even before Prithviraj had yanked his weapon back in mid thrust.

The valiant hero slid down from the horse which was drenched with his blood, his feet caught in the stirrup and his head dragging against the hard earth as the beast sought to flee. Enraged, the Chandel soldiers converged on his killer, spurred on by Udal. 'The man who brings me the head of the tyrant Prithviraj Chauhan shall have all the wealth and women he can wish for! Kill him like the cur he is and claim your reward!'

They hacked at the limbs of his horse but Prithvi leaped nimbly aside, unmindful of the pain that ratcheted across his chest, his sword making short work of those who rushed at him, buying time for his own men who were fighting desperately to reach him as he whirled around in a death-defying dance.

Prithviraj saw the great battle-axe a moment too late to stop it. Deflected ever so slightly by his belatedly raised shield, which nevertheless saved his life, it smashed into the side of his head. Prithviraj fell on his side, his mouth filled with blood and filth. Howling in fury, Udal raised the axe high above his head for the fatal blow but Govindraj had broken through and his thrown spear had taken Udal in the shoulder, throwing him off balance.

Screaming wildly for his men to rally around their king, he threw himself on Prithvi while Kanak and Padhri attacked Udal from behind, hacking off his upraised arms. Prithvi got to his feet, hurling Govindraj aside. Later, he would have no recollection of what happened next.

The ghosts from his painful past seemed to be controlling his spirit, urging him to vent his fury and pain on the hapless, maimed creature that fate had seen fit to place in his path. He gave himself over to the bloodlust, revelling in its terrible power to bestow the gift of death. In his frenzy, he raised his sword and lowered it in a vicious rhythm enjoying the feel of it severing through skin and bone and gristle. Over and over again, he repeated the sinuous movements, feeling the ebullient boy he had once been die a thousand deaths, and still could not stop.

When Prithviraj finally came to, Udal was unrecognizable, his body reduced to jellied remains and a bloodied mess unfit even for the carrion birds to feast upon. All around, his men were cheering their tremendous victory over the Chandels and had taken up a familiar chant—'*Prithviraj! Prithviraj! Prithviraj!*'

The mighty king of the Chahamanas, beloved of the goddess of victory, wept but his tears ran into the blood that caked his face as his companions led him back to the camp so he could sleep it off.

Uncle Kanha who had watched the macabre spectacle of Udal's grisly end had retired from the battlefield, unwilling to participate in the raucous celebrations and debauched revelry that would no doubt follow. He was seated on a mound watching one of the soldiers relieving a fallen man of his silver quiver and going over his person for other valuables, when Jaya found him.

'He cannot be judged by the same standards as ordinary men,' Jaya said stoutly. 'Maharaj Prithviraj had been through a terrible ordeal and yet he led his troops, withstanding a great deal of pain from frightful injuries, pushing himself beyond human endurance to emerge victorious. He is not like the other conquerors and he does not permit his men to loot or rape unlike so many others who would insist that it is the victor's prerogative to do so. The gods will not hold this against him.'

'Won't they?' Kanha seemed to be in mourning. 'He desecrated the body of a man who had been valiant and honourable in life, who deserved respect in death and the right to his dignity . . .'

'Yogita had been a part of Maharaj Jaichand's harem,' Jaya said in hushed tones, fully convinced that his idol's behaviour was perfectly understandable. Sensing that Kanha was unmoved, he elaborated. 'She escaped at great personal risk to warn our king. And then she consumed poison. He held her in his arms when she passed away. Sometimes, grief may drive a man to do things he wouldn't otherwise.'

Kanha had no wish to continue the conversation. 'The worst deeds usually have the best of justifications and it has seldom amounted to much in terms of exonerating one for unforgiveable crimes.'

He rose to his feet and walked away, marvelling at the bard's penchant for melodramatic flourishes irrespective of the time and place. When he entered his tent, Kadambavas was waiting for him, sipping from a goblet with a relaxed air. Kanha swallowed his irritation and sat down. At least, the mahamantri had the redeeming quality of not romanticizing the foibles in human nature that made the world such a dark and dreary place.

'Today's events were a small price to pay, all things considering,' Kadambavas remarked evenly, 'though it is to be wished that their paths had never crossed in the first place. What are the odds you reckon of a common little thing managing to disrupt the equilibrium of a king? Sometimes I think the gods have a perverse sense of humour.'

'The pandit told me that she had taken holy orders, yet somehow she appears to have landed in Maharaj Jaichand's harem. You wouldn't know anything about that now, would you?'

'I am not surprised! The stray was extraordinarily good-looking if you remember . . .' Of course Kadambavas would give nothing away. 'Had she remained in her chosen vocation, I have no doubt that she would have been abducted and sold into a brothel, but as it turned out she seems to have been singled out by fate to be the bane of kings. It is most unfortunate that a creature like that was born in the first place.'

Kanha tried to keep his temper in check. 'All it takes is for a single dishonourable act of the sort we witnessed today to ruin an unblemished record of chivalry or to destroy every single achievement that came before. You are a fool to imagine that what happened today marks the conclusion of the fateful events that were set in motion long ago when a chance encounter saw the king rescue that poor girl. Maharaj Prithviraj is relentless if nothing else and he will not rest till he has got to the bottom of this unfortunate affair and taken those involved to task.'

'Our king is resilient if nothing else,' Kadambavas said reassuringly. 'Besides, I have no doubt that there will be other matters to distract Maharaj Prithviraj from his unseemly grief and a misguided desire for vengeance against those who have served the best interests of the realm.

'I am expecting glad tidings from our young queen any moment now and it is time the king distracted himself with the blood sport the Chalukyas can always be counted upon to provide. You will see, there is no cause for so much angst. Maharaj Prithviraj Chauhan's finest moments are still ahead of him.'

Kanha shook his head. 'Why was it so difficult for you and the pandit to leave that poor girl alone? She would have merely been yet another addition to the king's harem. Why did you have to make that blameless girl suffer? It was a senseless crime and one deserving of punishment . . .'

'As always you seem convinced that the pandit and I are responsible for all things rotten in this realm, forgetting that we merely obey the orders of the royal family, be it the king or the queen mother. But what is the point of assigning blame? It serves no purpose besides sowing seeds of dissent among us.

'There is no need for all this talk of gloom and doom, especially on the happy occasion of the king's victory over the Chandels. Why don't you leave matters of intrigue to the little bard and spend tonight in the company of a graceful young girl or two?'

Kanha couldn't believe the nerve of the man as he accepted the goblet that was pressed into his hand. He thought of the prophecy Jaya had told him from what was practically another lifetime. About how a girl would be the death of Prithviraj and Kadambavas both. Superstitious dread filled his being and it took a whole lot of inebriants and amorous pursuits to help him shake it off.

24

Prithviraj had been in a world of pain, his body covered with a vast assortment of cuts, scratches and the scars of battle. The wound he had taken to the chest throbbed and was covered with a thick bandage. It was a reminder that he had no business being alive after everything he had done to court death. Perhaps he was immortal. The thought made him inexplicably sad.

His youth seemed far behind and the king felt ancient. Intense experiences that many would not know over the entire duration of a lifetime felt crammed into every single day of his existence. Perhaps he wasn't meant to grow old, infirm and die in his sleep. It was the only heartening thought he could find in the bleak landscape his mind had become.

It had been a week since he had defeated the Chandels. Prithviraj had wanted to go after King Paramardi and his son Brahma and besiege Kalinjar. However, Kadambavas, Kanha, Skand and even Govindraj were against such a course of action.

'No fort is impregnable,' he had snarled at them. 'We will storm Kalinjar and hang the Chandel king from the tallest flagstaff.'

'It is a hill fort, maharaj,' Kadambavas told him, 'and enjoys certain insurmountable natural fortifications. Besides, we do not have the time for a lengthy siege. There are other pressing concerns for us to deal with.'

'We have broken the spine of the Chandels for good and established our might!' Uncle Kanha said his piece. 'Anything more will be overkill at this point.'

Govindraj merely nodded in acknowledgment. It was Kadambavas who spoke again, 'The Chalukyas are moving towards Nagore, hoping to seize it while you are occupied here. We must hasten back.'

'Skand will hasten back with all the men he needs. Hari and the dandanayakas will accompany him with their divisions.' His senapati bowed. 'We have unfinished business to take care of in these parts and we will join them after its successful conclusion.'

Kanha and Govindraj were looking at him curiously. Prithvi nodded to his mahamantri, granting him permission to elucidate. Kadambavas cleared his throat, 'With Alha and Udal gone, Paramardi has not only been declawed but is bereft of his right and left arm as well. Malkhan and Sulkhan, belonging to the same Banaphar clan, are holed up with their impotent monarch in Kalinjar. The entire kingdom of the Chandels with its fabled wealth is at our mercy and ripe for the picking.'

There was ghoulish relish on the face of the mahamantri. Kanha scowled, not bothering to mask his disdain. As for Prithviraj, his face may well have been carved in stone. An uncomfortable silence fell over the little company gathered in the king's tent. They remembered the king's words to Alha, *let your king watch perched safely in his stone nest as his kingdom burns*!

Was the king going to turn his army loose on the kingdom of Chandels, allowing them to run roughshod over the land like a pack of marauding wild animals? He could do it but would he find it in his heart to issue a death sentence for an entire realm? The soldiers of the Chahamanas were brave, loyal and disciplined. But if the king actually turned over an entire kingdom to them to do with as they pleased, they would quickly devolve into packs of ravening beasts, looting, destroying property, raping and setting fire to everything in sight! It would be a catastrophe of inhumane proportions equal to the savagery of Mahmud of Ghazni. Kanha, Skand and Govindraj were aghast. Even his companions had fallen silent.

Only Kanha dared speak up, 'We are Kshatriyas and we settle our differences on the battlefield. With their king and his troops stationed in Kalinjar, the generals Alha and Udal dead and the rest of their army either dead or captured, the citizens of this land are defenceless and deserving of our protection.'

'It is good to know that you have such a fine opinion of your nephew whom you raised with your own hands,' Prithviraj's voice was sardonic. 'Those who believe in their hearts that your king is a depraved tyrant may leave now with their men. As for those whose trust I have the privilege to enjoy, we will depart at the first light of dawn. Mahoba, Khajuraho, Chhattarpur, Rajghar await our attention!'

As the council trooped out, Kadambavas winked at Kanha who had to resist the urge to punch him. Prithviraj gestured for Govindraj to stay back. 'I haven't thanked you for saving my life, old friend!' he began. 'You shielded me with your own body. Devotion like that cannot be repaid but I am indebted to you for your actions and will find a way to repay you.'

'I did nothing more or less than what my sense of duty demanded, Maharaj Prithviraj,' Govindraj said quietly. 'When my little girl died before my eyes, I experienced grief and hatred like never before and I swore that vengeance would be mine. It would not have been possible without your help, maharaj, and I am grateful. Honestly, I can ask nothing more from you. May the departed spirit of my daughter watch over you always and protect you from harm.'

'How does it feel?' Prithviraj asked him, a strange look in his eyes.

'Maharaj?'

'Vengeance . . . How does it feel, now that you have had your revenge against the men responsible for claiming Krishnakumari's life?'

'I thought there would be satisfaction to be had in watching them die, overtaken by the consequences of their actions,' Govindraj's voice was troubled, 'but I felt nothing, not even in the heat of battle. Krishna's passing left a void which I sought to fill with blood, but it remains empty because she is never going to come back. Nothing is going to change that. And as it turns out, that is the only truth and I have to learn to live with it.'

'They came to a terrible end, given that they have been lauded for their innate nobility. Ultimately though, it was a moment's miscalculation that came to define their very existence. Are you saying that it was all a mistake?' Prithviraj asked curiously, as though he were trying to put his finger on a truth that was eluding him.

'That is not what I am saying, maharaj,' Govindraj said with a sad smile, 'some would say that I have blood on my hands, that my actions led to the undoing of a kingdom. But perhaps it was inevitable, already determined by fate. All I know is that even armed with foreknowledge, I would have still made the decision to avenge my daughter's death and sought your help. Ultimately, we are little more than birds and despite the endless flapping of our wings it is the power of the wind that directs the course we must take.'

'So Alha and Udal were going to die anyway irrespective of what they or their killers did or didn't do?'

'In all likelihood, but perhaps if they had shown mercy or compassion, even a little consideration towards a hapless girl they had in their power, they too would have received the same in the end.' Govindraj's voice broke. 'I am saying that as long as we don't let the anger and hatred snuff out the sparks of goodness that no man is without, there is hope for us and everybody else as well.'

They sat in silence for a few moments. A messenger rushed in breathless, his bow slung crookedly over drooping shoulders. He could barely stand erect and was covered in dust and grime—evidence of extremely hard riding. 'Maharani Padmavati has delivered a strong and healthy baby boy, sire!' he blurted out. 'The queen mother herself sent me with the glad tidings. She wanted me to find out what you intend to name the prince and I am to return at once.'

Prithviraj glanced at his mandaleshwar and found his own large grin mirrored on his face. 'My son's name will be Govindraj Chauhan. You may leave after you have had food, wine from my personal stores, rest and your weight in gold.' The messenger smiled through his fatigue, touched the new father's feet and withdrew.

Kanha strode into the tent just then, determined to have it out with his nephew but stopped when he saw the joyful looks on both their faces. In fact, for the first time in his entire life, Prithviraj Chauhan was looking a little shy. It was Govindraj who told him the news. 'Maharaj Prithviraj is the proud father of a lion cub! May he live forever!'

Kanha was dumbstruck and it was Prithvi who spoke. 'Well, he is not the girl I wanted but perhaps my boy will amount to a lot more than his father.'

His uncle embraced him and when Kadambavas walked in to discuss the recent profligacy of the king directed towards a lowly messenger, he saw Kanha lifting the king bodily and swinging him around as though he were still a boy.

Prithviraj postponed their departure by three whole days, declaring bountiful celebrations to mark the birth of his son. There was plenty of feasting but for a change, the revels did not involve excessive drinking, dancing girls or orgiastic excesses. Instead, the king had General Skand arrange a series of competitions to test the skills of his men.

The finest horsemen, charioteers, swordsmen, wrestlers, archers, runners, acrobats were given prizes and other feats of athleticism and daredevilry were richly rewarded. Those who had distinguished themselves with feats of bravery and risked their own lives to save others during the course of their military campaigns were recognized and generously compensated. Prithviraj announced that those who had fallen in battle would not be forgotten and that their families would receive an annual stipend.

His men banged their spears, raised their shields and took up the familiar chant but this time the cries of *Prithviraj! Prithviraj! Prithviraj!* were interspersed with '*Govindraj!*' and that word amidst the deafening din of their weapons made their king's heart soar. Prithviraj was even tempted to return with the messenger to Ajmer. He wanted to see Padmavati, hug her to pieces and cover her with jewellery. If it hadn't been for her, he would have forgotten entirely what it was like to be happy.

When they marched, the high spirits of the king and his men were tangible. Skand and Hariraj headed towards Nagore with their troops to counter the Chalukyan threat while the rest began their tour of the kingdom of the Chandels. Prithviraj sent emissaries to reassure the populace that they would come to no harm provided they accepted him as an overlord.

In honour of his son's birth, he released the prisoners of war and allowed them to return to their families. To his gratification, many of them chose to stay and joined his army, disillusioned with Paramardi who remained in hiding, leaving his subjects to face the music. Prithviraj's clemency further convinced them that he was chosen by the gods and that aiding his enterprise to deal with the Turushkas once and for all had divine sanction.

At every one of their stops, the reigning council of ministers welcomed them with open arms, showered their conqueror with hospitality and paid generous tributes. Many of Paramardi's jagirs and mandaleshwars swore allegiance to Prithviraj Chauhan, gifting him with gold, silver and precious stones. Young girls of noble birth were offered to the king in marriage and he could not refuse.

Prithviraj appreciated the trained troops he was presented with to supplement the ranks of his forces. Many young men of fighting age also volunteered to join his army and Uncle Kanha took them under his wing.

In the famous temple of Khajuraho, the priests said pujas in his name, blessing his mission to drive out the Turushkas once and for all. The conquest of Jeyabhukti was the crowning achievement in his already stellar military career. As they marched towards Nagore, the Chalukyans already under tremendous pressure brought to bear by General Skand effected a full retreat, alarmed at the prospect of facing the full might of the Chahamanas army and their invincible king.

Thus, when the king turned back towards Ajmer, it was at the head of a mighty army many times the size of the one he had set out with. He had two more major victories to his credit and booty sufficient to line his coffers. The citizens had turned out in full strength to greet the conquering hero but Prithviraj was bursting with impatience to see his wife and son. The thought of being reunited with them filled him with so much joy, a tiny part of him was scared stiff.

25

Karpuradevi was waiting to perform the customary aarati with her own hands. With his stupendous victories over the pretender, Bhadanaks, Chandels and Chalukyas, her son had proved himself to be the greatest emperor in the entire history of aryavarta and it was only the beginning. He was born to triumph over the evil in any form and had been chosen by the gods to save aryavarta from the Mussulmen.

Prithviraj was impatient to see the strong-willed hussy he had married and the handsome boy she had borne him. So Karpuradevi was pleased when he stayed long enough to present her with choice pieces of rare and exotic jewellery he had gathered during his recent conquests. Then he left with indecent but understandable haste to the harem where she had insisted Padmavati remain confined.

The new mother had thrown quite the tantrum when denied her wish to welcome her husband, the conquering hero, but Karpuradevi had been firm. She was appalled with the young queen's tendency to give herself so many airs. In her youth, she herself had been obedient to the will of her mother-in-law, acknowledging that she was older and wiser.

Meanwhile, in the harem, Padmavati was so happy to see her husband that she forgot entirely the long list of complaints she had compiled against his mother. The young queen thawed further when he nearly buried her under the weight of all the jewellery he presented her with.

The little prince was asleep in his crib and his parents admired him, palms linked together, convinced that even baby Krishna would not have possessed a tenth of their little boy's infinite charms or talents.

'He looks every bit as handsome as you,' Padma said, 'and we have to make sure that he grows up to be a fine warrior like his father, with the godlike ability to turn his enemies to dust.'

Prithviraj was silent. His son was tiny. Why, he could easily fit on the palm of his hand! 'If all goes well, my boy's inheritance will be a single, unified aryavarta, blessed with peace and prosperity, free from threats both inside and outside. I want him to devote his time and attention to building fine monuments that will outlive us and patronizing the fine arts. His days will be filled with the satisfaction of having helped create priceless works of art. People from the three worlds will visit this very aryavarta to see heaven on mother earth. This is my dream for him.'

Padma was touched that he had given it so much thought but she found his vision more than a little unsatisfactory. It sounded exceedingly boring. Nobody worshipped or lauded men of peace. The mighty warriors, on the other hand, were the ones who aroused adulation in the hearts of everyone and went on to cover themselves in glory, winning fame and immortality in the process. It was what she secretly wanted for her little Govindraj. It would be interesting to see if the gods acceded to her wish or her husband's.

In the meantime, there were matters of tremendous gravity she wished to discuss with him. But the little prince had woken up and was bawling loudly for his mother's breast. He had ejected his bodily wastes and the air was rank with the odour. Govindraj screamed lustily in protest when his nursemaids carried him away to clean him up and relented only when he was returned to his mother's arms.

Taking advantage of the blessed silence while her son nursed, Padma spoke up. 'I hear that you have taken wives enough to fill five more harems.'

'It is a good start,' Prithvi told her seriously. 'They say Lord Krishna had 16,100 wives and I want to make sure that I have at least a few thousand more wives than he did.' He ducked and the silk cushion sailed over his head.

'Shortly before our marriage, my father said that a good wife should not be jealous of her husband's other wives. That I ought to do my people proud by being docile, obedient and a source of infinite comfort, never once questioning your decisions,' Padma said solemnly.

'That is sage counsel indeed. Your father clearly did something right besides having you,' Prithvi joked, knowing fully well that she hated when he spoke disrespectfully of her father. 'Am I to take it that you are going to get along with my other wives the way you get on with my mother?'

She frowned at his frivolity. 'I did not say anything about getting on with them. But you have my word that I will not have any of them poisoned!'

He stiffened ever so slightly when Padma said that. His young queen did not notice the sudden change in his demeanour. The little prince needed to be burped and she was preoccupied with him and her expectations for his glorious future. *If Karpuradevi's son had turned out so well, surely her son would be even more heroic and successful? If the gods were kind, he would not only inherit a unified aryavarta but go on to conquer the rest of the world as well.*

Prithviraj was fascinated by the boy's antics and enjoyed watching him grow. Govindraj was able to turn over and hold up his head within days and was running when babies his age were still struggling with the challenges posed by crawling. He enjoyed spending time with his son and was proud that he was the only one who could calm the baby in the midst of a full-blown tantrum by singing battle songs to him. He was growing like a weed before his very eyes and time seemed to be flying by.

He resented every moment when he was called away from his wife and son. Becoming a father did not excuse the king from his duties and there was always some serious matter of state that demanded his undivided attention. Even so, he was grateful for this golden period of peace in his life and knew that he was fortunate to be blessed with so much abundance.

He commissioned works by the leading artists and builders of the day and hoped he would live long enough to see the completed works, wondering why he was doing so. It was an ill omen, he knew, which meant he went on thinking his dark thoughts even at the height of his happiness.

Kadambavas and General Skand kept him apprised of the movements of Shihabuddin. Uncle Kanha chipped in with his valuable suggestions while the pandit, though in failing health, sent him lengthy epistles full of well-meaning advise he always meant to read but never got around to.

'Mahmud of Ghur has his tentacles deep in the provinces of Punjab and Sindh,' Skand reported. 'While we were locked in conflict with the Chandels, he managed to bring those regions in the northwest entirely under his control. Ajmer and Delhi are most certainly his next targets and furious preparations are underway for the clash.'

'It has been almost three years now and Shihabuddin must be ready for war against us. Thankfully, we too have been readying for this clash for many years now,' Kadambavas said, his visage so grim he reminded Prithviraj of the Khokar chief. 'By the time, he makes his move, we will be ready to give him a fitting reply.'

Prithviraj nodded. He had been right to study this dangerous adversary from the day he had first heard of him. Now they would need to intensify their efforts and force the invaders to return to the mountainous regions and the caves spattered with bat droppings that had been their original homes. *While the Chahamanas rule in Sapadalaksha, the invaders will never be able to gain a foothold in aryavarta.* He swore it to himself over and over again.

'Send emissaries to all our neighbours,' he ordered, 'inform them about the impending invasion. It is their fight as much as ours and the least they can do is show their support with money and troops. The honourable ones among them will join our cause.'

Kadambavas cleared his throat, his way of indicating that the king was going to hate his suggestion but must make himself amenable for the greater good of the realm. But he would soften him up first, Prithvi knew. 'I have already taken the initiative to send my best diplomats and their teams to enlist support for our cause from the other kingdoms who are most likely to be amenable. The response has been most heartening, sire,' Kadambavas began.

Kanha looked up. *For all his faults, Kadambavas was certainly no shirker when it came to performing his duties in a manner that was beyond exemplary,* he had to concede albeit somewhat grudgingly.

'The Paramars of Malwa are our allies and relatives by your marriage to Maharani Padmavati and have promised their support. We have found the Guhilots of Mewar most obliging as well. The Kacchwaha, Dahima and Mohil chiefs have also thrown in their lot with us.' Kadambavas paused for a moment, letting it sink in.

'I am going to assume that the Chauhans who had formerly ruled at Nadol were less enthusiastic about throwing in their lot with us . . .' Kanha remarked drily. The king scowled at the memory. He had not forgiven either his mother or Kadambavas for overruling his decision when they had formed the regency council during his minority to support the Chauhans of Nadol when Shihabuddin had attacked and driven them from their homes. Now they would prefer to join their hated adversary and watch Sapadalaksha burn than help their own kin.

'How can we blame them? When they came to us for help, we spat on their faces, now it is their turn to do the same . . . We have only ourselves to blame.' By that, of course, he meant his mother, Kadambavas and the pandit.

'The Bhatis have also been rather unforgiving. They moved to Jaisalmer after the capital city of Lodrava was sacked by Shihabuddin of Ghur. Their spokesperson was unequivocal in his refusal, claiming that since the Chahamanas did not see fit to render aid in their time of need, they see no reason to join us in this expedition and shed the blood of their people to ensure that our lands are safe. Maharaj Jaichand of Kannauj will not be helping us either nor will the Chalukyas of Patan,' Skand added

'Myopic morons, the lot of them,' Kanha growled. 'They hope to see Sapadalaksha destroyed by the invader, not realizing that it will be their turn sooner rather than later and the unfortunate ones among them who aren't killed outright will be enslaved for generations by the Mussulmen.'

Kadambavas was looking at him coldly. 'There is no sense in dwelling upon the so-called bad decisions of the past. The people of aryavarta have always been divided by their petty differences and that is not going to change overnight or even in the future for that matter. We have to work with what we have got.

'When the Chauhans of Nadol were crushed, the strategically important city of Phalodi came under our control. On my recommendation, Udag of the Sankhalas, who has always been on friendly terms with us, serves as Maharaj

Prithviraj's mandaleshwar and has raised a strong army and promised to fight by our side.'

'Mercifully, not all of maharaj's relatives are holding a grudge. The Johiyas of Maroth, Maharaj Vigraharaj's family on his mother's side, have agreed to join the coalition under your leadership,' Skand informed him.

Prithviraj nodded and waited for Kadambavas to spit it out. Right on cue, he began, 'The bonds of friendship which we have so painstakingly forged would become even stronger through marital ties and your loyal allies have offered the hands of their daughters. At this time, it would help if you were to personally visit your vassals and the kingdoms that constitute your coalitions. Many young men of fighting age will be inspired to join us in this endeavour.'

The king sighed in resignation. He wondered if the mahamantri had considered the complicated logistics involved in finding a means to keep the hundreds of wives and concubines he had provided for him sexually satisfied. By politicizing his sex life, he seemed hell-bent on destroying it. Now that Padma had dutifully provided him with an heir, the pressure had eased a bit. For that at least he supposed he ought to be grateful.

'I have a war to prepare for,' Prithviraj said firmly, 'and it is best that I remain here. However, since you deem it important, you may go ahead with the marriage ceremonies but as Maharani Padmavati informed me, where she comes from if the groom is otherwise occupied, the nuptials are performed with his sword standing in. It seems like an extremely practical solution to me.

'As for the young men who need a bit of persuasion from their king to join the resistance to face the greatest threat since Mahmud of Ghazni, I do not want them in my army!'

The council was dispersing when the king ordered his mahamantri to stay back. 'I thank you for the effort you have put in to bring together this coalition. Having been preoccupied with this enterprise, you were probably too busy to do what was asked of you by your king years ago on the battlefield of Urai.'

'I haven't been derelict in my duty, sire!' the mahamantri replied. 'A report was given to you following a thorough investigation even though the circumstances were far from ideal and it is a matter of exceeding delicacy. Most of our spies in the kingdom of the Gahadwalas were found out and killed. The survivors are too afraid. We have had to replace nearly all of them.

'On our side, I have nothing but speculation and absolutely nothing by way of concrete evidence. It has been murmured that some among the talarakshas have blamed that orphaned girl for the death of their comrades. They took their revenge by abducting and selling her to some traders from Kannauj.'

'The contents of the report are familiar to me and I have already expressed my dissatisfaction with the scanty information. Would you be suggesting that absolutely no new facts have emerged despite your best efforts?' Prithviraj enquired.

'The talarakshas are no longer under my care, maharaj, and it is not my place to interrogate Kanha's charges.'

'What if I were to tell you that my personal investigation into the matter has revealed that my mother and the mahamantri were involved in the unfortunate demise of the orphan girl, as you refer to her as? Would you confess to the same if the allegations were true?' Prithviraj asked politely.

The mahamantri looked him straight in the eye. 'I cannot answer for anybody else, maharaj, but I have always been loyal to the king of the Chahamanas and have never acted against his interest. When my life is over, I will be able to give the dark lord of dharma an untarnished account of my services.'

The king let him go. He suspected that even if he were to have the man tortured to within an inch of his life that was all he would ever get out of him. Mahamantri Kadambavas was made of cast iron after all.

Prithviraj was expecting an urgent summons from the queen mother and she did not disappoint. He put off the meeting for as long as he could to spite her, before dragging himself over to her private chambers. Karpuradevi rose to greet him and he noticed that her hair which had turned completely silver suited her and she was starting to resemble his grandmother Kanchanadevi.

The queen mother seemed happy to see him. She embraced him and whispered in his ear, 'I hope you will forgive a mother for doing not what she wants but must in the interest of her son who means more to her than life itself.'

Then without warning, she stepped back and slapped him hard across the face. The king of the Chahamanas had seldom been less prepared for anything in his life. He stepped back in shock, far more hurt than he cared to admit. He stared at his mother who was crying and breathing heavily, through a haze of his own tears.

'Despite what you think, my entire life has been dedicated solely to doing what is best for you! Prithviraj Chauhan-III has been a credit to his mother and this land. My son is the greatest warrior this world has seen and I couldn't be prouder. You are the only one standing between the reckless, burning ambition of the Turushkas and the very existence of our aryavarta. I will not let you throw your destiny away because of this foolish obsession over a girl chance-met on the road, who is dead and long gone.'

Prithviraj reared back as if she had struck him again. The queen mother felt the wrath that had been the scourge of his enemies uncoil within him, gathering force, ready to strike her with all the power that could be mustered by his pain. But she was his mother and she was not afraid. Whether he was to acknowledge it or not, his own courage was inherited solely from her and she was relentless in her attack.

'There is so much that is good and beautiful in your life,' Karpuradevi snapped at him, transformed into something he did not even recognize. 'The goddess of fortune has blessed you with plenty—a thriving kingdom, success over your enemies, a loving wife and an heir. Every one of the men in your service is loyal and would gladly die for you. Yet you treat them all with unseemly suspicion, dismissing the love they bear you with callous disregard for its tremendous worth. And it is all because you want to embrace your forbidden passion for that girl like the spoilt child you cannot afford to be!'

'If I were to find out for a certainty that you were involved . . .' Prithviraj began. To his horror, he sounded surly.

'What will you do, Prithviraj?' she asked, eyes blazing. 'Will you have me killed? Will you entertain your terrible suspicions and kill the mahamantri as well? There will always be some self-serving serpent keen to pour poison in your ears about your loved ones. Will you destroy your companions on the strength of spurious statements? Strike Kanha's head off? How dare you even entertain such thoughts? Are you arrogant enough to think that your achievements are the result of your actions alone?'

Prithviraj shook his head, feeling as though he were struggling to free himself from a sticky web of self-deception. Every one of her barbed words found its mark and through the inflicted wounds and pain, he felt the haze of confusion that had enveloped him lift slowly. 'Mother! I loved her. To you she is just a stray, chance-met on the road, but she meant everything to me and I owe it to her memory . . .'

'To do what? Torment yourself by clinging to the misery her loss afflicted you with instead of embracing the many joys that adorn your very existence? You are a king, Prithviraj Chauhan, and don't you dare forget it! You owe all who have sacrificed their entire lives to make your reign a glorious one and every one of the subjects who worship the ground you walk on a tremendous debt. You will do well to devote your entire being towards discharging it with interest.'

Never had Prithviraj felt so crushed and so deeply ashamed. The queen mother softened when she saw the state he was in. 'It is all right to feel scared of the awesome burden you carry, Prithvi! But the love you claim to nurse for this dead girl is merely an excuse to self-destruct so you don't have to keep on delivering the impossibly high expectations people have from you.

'That is all this persistent melancholy is about. Don't fool yourself. There was never a future for you with this poor girl. Epic love stories have no place in real life. They are nothing more than the products of the fevered imagination of bards, who have deeply frustrated libidos since all women worth the name would rather lie with warriors who perform actual feats of valour instead of just singing about it.'

Prithviraj continued to look shell-shocked but his lips curved upwards. Karpuradevi exhaled slowly. 'I will make it a point to tell Jaya your thoughts on the bards!'

'Don't you dare dismiss the entire thing as a joke, Prithviraj Chauhan!' she said with mock severity. 'Promise me that you will make your peace with the memory of Yogita and let her rest in peace. The path ahead is a dangerous one but if anybody has what it takes to negotiate the lurking horrors, it is you!'

Prithviraj looked at his mother in the eye and for the first time, Karpuradevi saw the only thing she had ever wanted from every man in her life—unconditional respect. 'I promise, Mother! It will be hard but if I were to forget, you are there to knock some sense into my head, though I would be grateful if you didn't do it literally!' He rubbed his cheek with a grimace, still unable to believe that it had happened.

Karpuradevi laughed again and embraced her little boy. She was more pleased than she cared to admit that the king of the Chahamanas, scourge of his enemies who had been blessed with the courage of a thousand lions, flinched away from her touch in momentary fright before sinking into her arms.

26

The largest army ever gathered in the history of aryavarta, a confederacy of Kshatriyan kingdoms led by Prithviraj Chauhan, marched towards Tabarindah, a fortress on the border of Punjab, near Sirhind. After years of intensive preparation and endless raids, Shihabuddin had finally made his move and seized the fort. Prithviraj had decided that they would fight to reclaim it.

They had received an urgent message from Chandraraj, Govindraj's son and the king's mandaleshwar, stationed in Sirhind. The messenger he had sent begging them for succour, painted a truly horrific picture. 'The sultan of Ghur has captured Tabarindah and has stationed a large garrison comprising 1200 cavalrymen under the command of Ziauddin Tulaki. It was a lightning strike, sire! These Turushkas have massive war horses with their hooves clad in iron and they can cover large distances almost as if they were winged creatures!'

Skand frowned when he heard that and Prithviraj noticed out of the corner of his eye. It had long been a pet peeve of his. The general had complained repeatedly about the quality of the horses they imported from Arabia. Most were weakened or lamed from the journey and were no match for the Turushka horses that seemed to be fleet as the wind if the reports were to be believed.

'My grandfather told me repeatedly that Mahmud of Ghazni's successes were solely on account of the superior breed of steeds they fielded, enabling them to maintain a blistering pace.' It was a familiar refrain from the senapati. 'Moreover, the Turushka soldiers eat the flesh of their horses and drink its blood to enhance their own strength, speed and stamina.'

They had all laughed at his tendency to harp on the issue and his outlandish notion to fashion the same iron shoes for the horses like the barbarians, teasing him about his hankering for horse meat in the hope of performing like a well-girded stallion. Skand hadn't been amused then and he wasn't now. None of them were laughing. But then again the Turushkas as well as their demonic steeds had an unholy terror of their elephant corps and now that they fielded a large number of the well-trained pachyderms that they had appropriated after the conquest of Bhadanak, they would have a distinct advantage, the king felt.

The messenger was clearly at the end of his endurance and he had refused all offers of sustenance till he had made his report, pausing only to sip almost apologetically from a water skin. 'The attacks are every bit as bad as we have been led to believe. They advanced upon Tabarindah like rakshasas or pisachas reincarnated from another age, destroying everything in their paths. Entire towns have been set ablaze as they stopped arbitrarily to make camp. Not one of them has honour. They seize men, women and children, the ones that have survived the repeated violations of their modesty . . .'

The man choked on the words that described deeds so foul he could barely give utterance to them. 'The demon hordes are entirely indiscriminate when it comes to acts of rape. Nobody is spared on the basis of gender, age or even infirmity. Some of the men swear that they have seen these unnatural monsters copulating with their horses! Lord Chandraraj begs for your immediate assistance, maharaj!'

Prithviraj had not hesitated and issued marching orders at once. He had put together a cavalry that was 2,00,000 strong, 3000 elephants and an infantry corps numbering 2,50,000. The colourful flags, standards and insignia of the men along with their metallic weapons gave them the appearance of an endless sea monster that made its way forward inexorably to consume its enemies with jaws of iron and steel.

The king glanced across the undulating lines of his formidable army. Uncle Kanha was issuing instructions to his division, steady as the rock he had always been. Mahamantri Kadambavas's restless eyes seemed to be scanning the landscape ahead. Prithviraj fancied he could practically see the wheels turning in the man's head as his mind sifted through every possible move the enemy was likely to make and the best way to counter it.

Govindraj was an ocean of calm in the middle of an army bustling with furious activity. He was a good man and a trusted friend. Prithvi had always admired the mandaleshwar's air of tranquillity even in the heat of battle, it was what made him a hero.

Padhri was always boisterous before a massive battle and he was singing a bawdy song lustily, urging his troops to join in, while they looked on partly amused and partly askance at his levity. Nahar was polishing his weapons, seemingly oblivious to the antics of his brother but Prithvi knew that he tended to keep an eye on him. Kanak, ever alert, felt his gaze and raised a clenched fist and placed it over his heart. The king raised his spear in acknowledgment.

Prithviraj could not find Jaya but he knew that he would be close, attentive to his king's needs, protective about his friends though he was the smallest and weakest in the group. A keen observer of human nature, he had been the heart and soul of their group, always able to instil confidence, soothe frazzled nerves and bolster courage with a few well-chosen words.

Senapati Skand moved like a whirlwind seeming to be everywhere at once, issuing instructions in an endless stream, competent and very much in command. Prithviraj remembered what his mother had said. All the achievements he had been lauded for would have been impossible without these men and yet the credit had always gone solely to him. On the other hand, if he were to fail, the ignominy would be solely his as well. He wondered if he would be remembered as the hero or the fool . . . Only time would tell. And perhaps it wouldn't matter in the least when his life force had been extinguished and all that remained of him were the ashes.

Prithviraj noticed the vaidya close at hand and nodded at him. He tended to become morbid just before a battle and Narana had always helped with that. Soon, his trepidation would vanish, leaving behind nothing but euphoria and an unshakable confidence in its wake.

Shihabuddin of Ghur awaited them at Tarain, with the main Ghurid army not too far from Thaneshwar, Prithviraj learnt, intercepting them before they reached Tabarindah. He was annoyed. The vast army he had assembled was proving to be a cumbersome beast and their progress was unwieldy and a lot slower than he would have liked.

They encountered refugees who were fleeing in droves, trying to put as much distance between themselves and the Turushkas. Clad in rags, carrying their paltry possessions in small bundles, all of them had horror stories to tell—of houses being burnt with entire families inside, rape, mutilation, torture and random executions. Some of them carried their dead children in their arms, holding them up for the king and his men to see. They were wailing in anguish, calling down the wrath of the gods to avenge them.

It was a heart-rending sight and the king was shaking with rage. Presented with the evidence of the sultan's cruelty, his men responded in kind and by the time they came within sight of the enemy, their anger had come to a boil.

On the vast, undulating plain of Tarain, the assembled Turushkas with their mighty squadrons of cavalry were splendidly arrayed, attired and armed. They wore a coat of mail, the metal scales fastened together with small rings. It resembled the glistening scales of a fish. Their helmets were remarkable things made of iron, which they wore over a kind of loose turban. Flexible mail was attached to the sides of the helmet and it fell lightly to the shoulder like a curtain covering most of the face and neck.

Prithviraj noticed his adversary at the very centre with the rest of his army arranged in neat rows on either side. Sultan Shihabuddin was easily identifiable by his superior accoutrements and the elite bodyguards who surrounded him. He was wearing trousers and long-sleeved robes of a silken material, embroidered with gold threads and solid gold bands running down the sides. His chest was protected by a breastplate and a magnificent, crested helmet rested on his head.

Every one of the demonic steeds they had heard so much about was clad in armour with pieces of embossed metal protecting the forehead and ornamented plates protecting the neck and torso. The horsemen carried recurved bows, quivers strapped to the saddles, war hammers, lances, pikes, swords, javelins and axes.

'It's them!' Prithviraj roared, feeling the first stirrings of battle lust, accentuated by the effect of the drug in his bloodstream as it rushed through his veins, humming a requiem for victory. 'Show them no mercy and remember that you will receive none! Tear them into pieces and don't stop till you have annihilated the last one, drenching this very aryavarta with their life blood! No more tears will be shed on this land because of the atrocities they have perpetrated against our gods, men, women and children! Fight for revenge, honour and glory! Charge!'

All through the ranks, the commanders of the various divisions echoed the sentiment of their king and took up his cry. 'Remember, what they have done to this aryavarta and our people! Remember! Fight them and give them a taste of your valour! Crush them like the vermin they are!'

The war horns sounded and their enemies responded by blowing on their trumpets and pounding on large brass kettledrums, resulting in a din that turned bowels liquid with fear, making hearts palpitate in a heady mix of anticipation and mortal fear. The signal to attack was sounded repeatedly on both sides. They would be pitting the might of their cavalries against each other.

Armed riders set off towards each other in an avalanche of motion, tearing up entire chunks of earth under their hooves and the ground trembled under the ferocious onslaught. Spears lowered, they were on top of each other in a concentrated, headlong rush and hundreds fell dead in that almighty clash, unseated from their horses, limbs akimbo, trampled to a bloody mush by the stamping hooves.

The air was filled with the neighing and snorting of war horses, the clash of shields, the hiss of discharged arrows and the metallic slicing of swords, assorted war cries, guttural swearing and shouted cuss words, interspersed with howls of agony from the wounded and the dying.

With overwhelming strength of numbers and a full-frontal attack that had served them in good stead so many times in the past, Prithviraj's men tore through the centre of the enemy, seeming to nearly swallow it whole, cutting it off from the divisions on the sides, leaving them trapped and vulnerable.

Caught like animals in a net of steel, the Mussulmen fought furiously looking for a way out, sustaining terrible losses in the process. Prithviraj's cavalry, on the other hand, managed to hold its lines, and the ranks remained intact as they slaughtered their hated adversaries in droves, refusing to give an inch.

Prithviraj could taste victory and he roared in exultation, wielding his bow and arrow, aiming for the eyes, scoring a hit every single time. On that day, his touch was golden and he could make no mistakes as he shouted to his men, urging them to kill every last one of the Mussulmen.

His adversary, the sultan, could not believe how embarrassingly one-sided this engagement was turning out to be. He could feel the despair of his men as they stared impending death in the eye unable to muster any kind of resistance, succumbing in endless numbers. But Shihabuddin of Ghur had never lacked for courage and he was incapable of acquiescing to defeat.

Raising his sword high in the air, he tugged on the reins and led a furious charge. His elite guards rode hard, trying to catch up with him, inspired by his daring refusal to kowtow to his enemies. Shihabuddin espied a noble warrior, wielding his weapon with eerie grace, leaving dozens of corpses in his wake, and made directly for him. Govindraj of Dillika saw the hurled lance and was powerless to deflect it. He gritted his teeth for the impact and felt them shatter as pain exploded in his skull.

A lesser man would have surrendered to the agony but Govindraj had already made his countermove. His enemy had leaned forward from the force of the throw and the point of the mandaleshwar's spear took him high in the arm, nearly unseating him. Seeing the sultan collapse, blood fountaining over his horse in a grisly shower, his guards fought like demons to throw back the rush of soldiers. One of them, a young lad, leapt onto his lord's horse and propping his bleeding, comatose form against his own, spurred the great war horse, turning it around and fleeing for the hills.

Govindraj wiped the blood from his face for a better look, dizzy as waves of pain ratcheted across his body. As his consciousness drained away, he saw the lifeless body of the sultan slumped in his saddle and was immeasurably glad just before the darkness claimed him.

Shihabuddin's troops stationed at the wings were trying their best to reach the overwhelmed centre that had nearly collapsed. Desperately, they attempted diversionary manoeuvres seeking to draw the cavalry away from their besieged sultan but soon they were fighting for their own lives as the Kshatriyas refused to take the bait. Instead, they regrouped for yet another tremendous frontal attack with the sole purpose of effecting a complete annihilation.

The scene of carnage was a horrendous one, with dead soldiers and beasts lying on the field for as far as the eye could see. Suddenly cries of 'the sultan is dead!' reached the ears of the Mussulmen and wails of distress tore forth from their lungs. The knowledge broke the back of their resistance. Utterly demoralized, they fled pell-mell from the battlefield.

Their generals, trying to restore some semblance of order, gave the command to fire at the retreating backs of the cowards who had given up before the retreat was signalled. The watching Kshatriyas laughed aloud at the scene, which closely resembled a farce as the Mussulmen began to chase their own men, sharp arrows picking off the runners one by one.

Prithviraj's men were clutching their stomachs and laughing themselves sick at the sorry spectacle as the surviving commanders rallied the straggling bits and pieces that was all that remained of the army of the mighty Turushkas, beating a more orderly retreat, which nevertheless reeked to the high heavens of ignominy.

The Chahamanas troops gave chase for a while but the cheering and celebration of their tremendous victory, comparable with the great battle of Kurukshetra, had already begun in earnest. Quickly, they turned back not willing to miss out on the unfolding revelry. Even the officers were joining in, shouting for wine. Discipline was lax everywhere and the soldiers were going through the bodies of the fallen men, sifting through blood and mutilated flesh for anything of value.

Maharaj Prithviraj was in a daze, unable to process the things that were happening around him and his ears were still ringing from the din of the battle, preventing him from hearing the muted cries of his heated mind or the clangour of his thoughts, which were trying in vain to tell him something.

The last thing he remembered was the sight of Govindraj going down. To his surprise, he found himself staring at the bloodied mess that was his mandaleshwar's face and leaned over for a better look. He had slid down from his horse and lay crumpled on the battlefield. The king gathered him in his arms and saw that he was hanging on by a thread, taking in his presence through eyes that were nearly swollen shut.

Govindraj opened his mouth and was urgently trying to say something but only gurgling sounds emerged as blood gushed forth copiously. He spat it out and tried again. 'I killed him, sire! The demon from Ghur is dead! May his soul, abandoned by his god, rot forever more in the hells of Yama!' And having expended the superhuman effort required to give utterance to those fateful words, he passed out.

'Are you absolutely sure?' the king asked him but there was no reply.

The mahamantri had sent his men to look for Maharaj Prithviraj and they zeroed in on the pair. Gently, they extricated Govindraj from his arms, while others helped him to his feet. The soaring exultation Prithviraj had experienced when his army had torn the Turushkas to bloody shreds was dissipating faster than he could hold on to it and all that remained was crushing disappointment and abounding emptiness. Shihabuddin of Ghur's life had been his to take. Now he would never get another chance. The absurdity of his reaction made him cackle with laughter.

All around, there were the sounds of raucous celebration. Forgetting all about decorum and discipline, his men gathered around their king. A particularly gigantic specimen lifted Prithviraj on his shoulder and began to prance around in a victory dance. Every single soldier even the grievously wounded ones, were shouting at the top of their lungs—'*Prithviraj! Prithviraj! Prithviraj!*'

The king's companions led the victory celebrations, dancing on the fallen bodies of the corpses, checking to see if there was life left to any of the wretched creatures at their feet, making a little game of it. The wounded enemy soldiers were dragged out and various appendages were hacked off and their agony prolonged till death arrived belatedly for them.

None of them wanted to leave the mightiest scene of triumph that aryavarta had ever witnessed. Casks of wine and food were brought to the triumphant soldiers. They ate and drank with bloodied hands, savouring life as they floated on a sea of death.

Prithviraj felt his spirit tear itself free from his body, which was floundering on a sea of confusion and chaos. It would have been nice to soar away but it was hard to do so with wings sticky with blood and regret. Instead he hovered over the scene of battle, seeing it all from a great distance.

He could have sworn that he saw Shihabuddin of Ghur wounded and dangerous, his crested helmet turning to meet his gaze, implacable and twice as deadly as he leaped up to pluck him out of the sky and wring his neck. But he was dead. *Dead. Dead. Dead.*

Jaya helped Kanha and Skand find the king. He was seated on a corpse with his face buried in his hands. They led him away as quickly as possible even as the merrymaking began the slide towards unspeakable debauchery. The mahamantri was waiting in the royal tent as they handed over the king to his attendants. Prithviraj seemed unhurt and only mildly disoriented.

They waited outside as they took care of him, washing away the remnants of battle, applying soothing salves and helping him into fresh clothes. They stood outside in silence listening to the great, gut-wrenching sobs of the emperor of aryavarta as he wailed like a soul in mortal distress. Prithviraj Chauhan's racking sobs went on and on as he wept like he had never before. Kadambavas sent for Narana, who rushed to the king's side and administered a sleeping potion to him. Even then he fell into a troubled sleep, tormented by nightmares.

Kanha and Skand looked absolutely petrified. Even Kadambavas seemed shaken by the vehemence of the king's reaction in the face of absolute victory. It was Jaya who explained in solemn tones, 'He has achieved the pinnacle of glory! For the rest of his life there will be no high as sublime as this one. He has touched the very heavens with the greatness of his deeds. Now there is nowhere to go but down till his soul makes its last journey towards immortality!'

The three men stared at each other in genuine incomprehension. How could the greatest moment of their lives feel like such a terrible portent of disaster? Something was terribly wrong and they would be damned if they knew what it was.

27

The king had set up court at Thaneshwar. He received delegates from all over aryavarta as the congratulatory messages poured in from every quarter along with rich tributes and even more proposals for marriage. Amidst all the glad-handing, Prithviraj could not shake the lingering feeling of unease that clung to him, like a speck of dust in his eye.

He had sent a force with Hari at the head to deal with the garrison Shihabuddin had left behind in his tearing hurry to embrace the death he deserved. The stubborn bastards were staying put at Tabarindah and refusing to surrender. Prithvi had told his brother to wipe them out. He was confident that with that last pocket of resistance stamped out, aryavarta would truly be freed from the Turushka menace. As an afterthought, he sent Chandradeva and his Khokar troops to render aid to his brother.

With that business sorted out, he was ready to return to Ajmer, Padma and his son, little Govindraj. According to a messenger from his capital, his son had expressed concerns that since his father had conquered everything there was to conquer, there would be nothing left for him.

Everybody laughed at that and the king smiled as well. But the words filled him with trepidation. They were marching back towards Ajmer and had camped for the night when Jaya informed him that Kanak was severely ill. Post the stupendous, historic win at Tarain, he had been indulging himself a little too much. He had been complaining about a stomach ailment that had taken a turn for the worse.

When the king visited him in his tent, he was doubled over in pain and delirious with fever. He tried to sit up when his childhood friend approached him. 'You must forgive me for not rising, maharaj! But as you can see, I am shitting my life away.' He tried to laugh at his own wit, but wound up coughing violently instead.

The king sent his own vaidya to attend to Kanak. But there wasn't anything to be done and Narana only managed to make his last moments less painful. His passing cast a pall over their mood and it was a sombre crowd that returned to Ajmer.

Karpuradevi was waiting with her customary aarati but as she lifted the tray, her hands shook and she dropped it with a clatter, splattering red vermillion on the king's feet. The queen mother said nothing then, but her heart filled with a nameless dread that refused to relinquish its hold on her. From that moment onwards, she devoted her time to prayer and charity, begging the gods to bestow the benefits of every meritorious act she had performed in this life and the ones before to her son.

For Prithviraj Chauhan, life returned to a semblance of normalcy as he busied himself with the humdrum monotony of looking after his kingdom. Padma kept his spirits up with her natural ebullience and Govindraj was a blessing he was truly grateful for. The little prince insisted on being taken for long horse rides with his father, and the citizens gathered in droves to catch a glimpse of them. Karpuradevi worried endlessly about the evil eye cast by the envious and instructed Padma on how best to ward it off. Her daughter-in-law listened with half an ear, convinced that dotage had claimed the matriarch.

One day, Prithviraj had an important visitor. It was Chandradeva. Somewhat surprised that the leader had seen fit to come personally, the king had him admitted to his presence.

One look at his face and it was obvious that he came bearing dire tidings.

'Shihabuddin of Ghur is not dead!' Those were the first words the Khokar chief uttered. He was not one to bother with pleasantries.

'Impossible!' the king remembered his disappointment on finding out that he was dead but not by his hand. 'Govindraj told me that he had killed him.'

'We intercepted a messenger who was trying to carry the news into Tabarindah,' Chandradeva informed him. 'He confessed it all under torture. One of his personal bodyguards rushed the sultan away from the battlefield and they did everything possible to keep him alive. The foul creature we captured swore that their sultan defeated death and is now invincible. Even as we speak, he is gathering a large army to march against us, again. Just before we plucked his tongue out, he swore that aryavarta will burn and Shihabuddin has sworn to build a new kingdom on the ashes of your own!'

Prithviraj sat in silence for a few moments, 'Is there anything else I should know?'

'The rakshasa of Ghur has taken his defeat badly and has retreated to his capital at Ghazni to get his strength back. We were told that he has sworn not to touch meat, alcohol or women till he has claimed the life of Prithviraj Chauhan in battle and established his kingdom here.

'That is not all . . . he arrested all those who had fled from the battlefield and had them fed to starving swines. This is the worst form of barbarian punishment, the messenger said, as it prevents their souls from entering the paradise of their god since all things porcine are considered polluted and those of their faith are forbidden all contact with these creatures.'

He shook his head contemptuously. 'Needless to say we fed his remains to the pigs so he too could join his fellow traitors who are burning in hell.'

'It is unlikely that Shihabuddin of Ghur will show his face here again, but if he does, we will be ready. And this time, I will kill him myself. In the meantime, how goes the siege?' Prithviraj said, his voice flat.

'Commander Hari has not had much success. He is content to sit outside the walls, busying himself with feasting and frolicking with the camp followers! When I protested, he suggested I bring you the information we managed to glean from that spy personally,' his pursed lips had become a thin line.

The king frowned at that. He appreciated the man's honesty but it was hugely annoying that Hari had proved himself incapable. In his reports, he had said that the siege would be a protracted one but he would prevail. Eventually. Prithviraj hoped Hari would succeed before his hair turned white and his last tooth had fallen out. Perhaps he should have sent Skand instead.

As for Govindraj, he should have got his bloody facts straight before claiming he had killed a dangerous adversary, who now roamed free thanks to his stupidity. If he had been around, Prithvi would have broken the rest of his teeth. Some of the anger needed to be directed in his own direction, the king knew. He had been careless and it was a luxury a man in his position could not afford.

The Khokar chief took in his troubled countenance and ventured an opinion. 'It had been too easy, sire, but we must not be disheartened by the resurgence of a terrible threat we had falsely assumed was quashed. We will stand firm against them no matter how many times they come back bearing fire and destruction. In the end, we will prevail, sire! We have to.'

His voice sounded desperate and the king recognized the hopelessness that Chandradeva refused to acknowledge. He remembered his meeting with Muinuddin Chishti and the last words that wise man had said to him . . . *Those who give themselves over to violence and embrace its destructive power can never hope to win, irrespective of the side they represent. By its very nature, war cannot yield victory or happiness, in its wake there is never anything but sorrow and suffering. Therefore, I will pray for both your souls and hope with all my heart that salvation remains within your reach.*

In that instant, he recognized the truth with blinding clarity and when he spoke it appeared that he had slipped into a trance. 'You and I have been trained in the art of war, Chandra, and we are finely honed weapons of destruction, expending our terrible skills on causes we are taught are truly worthy. But it is all a lie. There is no cause that justifies violence and no conquest has any meaning when the price is suffering and the infliction of pain. In the end, I am no different from Shihabuddin of Ghur. I too destroyed my enemies without caring about those who were sacrificed along the way.'

'Don't say that, sire!' the chief insisted, his voice choking with tears. 'You call yourself a weapon of destruction but you are nothing like that accursed villain. This aryavarta has not known a better king or a nobler one! Why, sire, I was little more than a rabid dog watching and participating when my men raped Turushka women and killed their children. But you showed us the right way, taught us the importance of never hurting the innocent, and in doing so you saved our very souls, cleansing it of the sins that had stained it. We worship you as a god, Maharaj Prithviraj, and you must triumph in order for good to prevail over evil.'

The king smiled at him sadly. 'Your words give me succour, Chandra, and I am grateful. They will comfort me when death claims me for its own. Shihabuddin and I have set in motion a chain of events that must culminate in a cataclysmic tragedy and it looms over us all. My only fear is that if I am to die without claiming his life, then this endless cycle of blind hatred and killing will be perpetuated for an eternity.'

He shuddered as if the thought was one that he simply could not bear. 'If that were to happen then you must chase him to the ends of the earth if necessary to put him down as well. With both of us gone, the legacy we leave behind will be one of hope and maybe our successors will know better than to emulate Prithviraj Chauhan or Shihabuddin of Ghur. Perhaps future generations will learn from our folly and strive forever to establish peace on mother earth.'

Chandradeva was crying but his voice was steady when he addressed his king. 'You have my word, sire! It is my privilege to serve the best of kings and it is an honour to serve as an instrument of your will.'

The king seemed calmer now and the Khokar chief was pleased to note that there was fresh strength and purpose on his noble features, radiant as the sun. 'Forget about the siege, Chandra. There is an ineluctable tide that bears us along and some things will always be beyond our control. In the meantime, return to your family, wife and children. If you don't have anyone, find someone and spend your days leading to the ultimate conflict, trying to extract all the happiness that life has to offer. If there is one thing I have learned, it is that the moments of simple joy are always worth more than entire lifetimes crammed with all the so-called victories we are fated to experience and endure.'

His mahamantri was looking grave. Kanha and Skand seemed impassive as ever. Looking at the three of them, Prithviraj wondered how it was that so many capable people had managed to be so monumentally stupid in the aftermath of Tarain. 'How is everyone taking the news of Shihabuddin's survival and plans to attack again?'

'Surprisingly well, sire!' Kadambavas assured him. 'The coalition we put together is behind you and others want to join in as well. All in all, we can count on the support of 150 vassals. This time we will have as many as 3,00,000 horses and 3000 elephants to the sultan's 1,20,000 men. This army Shihabuddin is assembling includes hired Afghans and Persian swords in addition to his own Turushkas. He must be truly desperate.

'In other heartening news, I am told that Shihabuddin's own borders are not secure and one Khwarizm Shah has massed for an attack on his northern frontiers. He will have to deal with them before he can even think of marching on us.'

The senapati seemed deep in thought. 'We have to remain on our guard and not take anything for granted. The fanaticism of the Turushkas is unlike any other threat we have encountered. They are calling it a holy war and the preparations are beyond heavy. Moreover, there are threats to our undertaking from within the fabric of this very aryavarta.'

They all fell silent. *Traitors in their very midst.* The king could easily hazard a guess as to who they might be.

'He will deny it to his last breath, but my informers in Kannauj tell me that Maharaj Jaichand may be in talks with Shihabuddin of Ghur and may be willing to help him in his endeavours to crush you,' Kadambavas reported.

'Jaichand may well hate our king and is no doubt rooting for us to die in battle, but I nevertheless find it hard to believe that the great grandson of Govind Chandra of Kannauj, who died bravely while fighting the Turushka aggressors in the time of Ghazni, would willingly offer aid to a Mussulman, and one who is hated so vehemently in this very aryavarta. His very own family and subjects will spit on his face!' Kanha averred.

'Which is why any help he gives the enemy will be done under conditions of anonymity and secrecy,' Skand retorted drily. 'Be that as it may, Jaichand is bitterly envious of Maharaj Prithviraj and never loses an opportunity to belittle him. He has organized a huge sacrifice to have himself named the foremost emperor of aryavarta and has spent a fortune to gain support for himself and undermine our cause.'

'Let him do his worst. If the best he can do is sit on his flabby backside and chant mantras, hoping to repudiate the achievements of one who earned them on a battlefield, we have no reason to fear him or his shameless tactics. Nor will I dignify them with a response!' Prithviraj said with a sudden ferocity for one who had been planning not to respond at all.

'But that is not all, maharaj,' Skand went on glancing at Kadambavas. 'Jaichand arranged a swayamvara for his beautiful daughter, Samyukta, whom many have compared to an apsara, and in a blatant move to insult, he had a statue of you planted at the entrance to the hall. He claimed that you are not fit to be included in a gathering of kings and were better suited for guard duty.'

'How dare he? Call the troops! Let us march at once and burn his kingdom down!' the king said flippantly. 'It would allow Shihabuddin to ram his entire phalanx up our . . .'

'Maharaj! What I was trying to say is that his daughter garlanded the statue and declared before the entire assembly that she will marry none but you. Needless to say, Jaichand is furious and has banished her to a palace on the banks of the Ganga. Perhaps you would consider . . .' Skand stopped as if the rest was self-explanatory.

Kanha and Kadambavas stared at him, united for once in their disbelief of what he was suggesting. 'I did not know that you had such a romantic soul . . .' Kanha said drily.

'Are you suggesting that the king marry his enemy's daughter in the face of his opposition? We would be risking open war! And we can't risk getting caught between two enemies . . .' Kadambavas was adamant.

'It would be a risky move,' Skand said, 'but this rivalry between two major kingdoms in aryavarta, especially when there is such a powerful enemy barking on our doorstep, can't bode well for us. If the king were to wed the princess from Kannauj, surely with time and the appearance of grandchildren, Jaichand will thaw enough to lend us his support.'

'Enough, senapati!' Prithviraj said firmly, 'I refuse to have anything at all to do with Jaichand's daughter. A treacherous viper's young one even if it is comely is still a treacherous viper. It is unfortunate that we are unable to resolve our differences and unite in a common cause but there is nothing to be done at this juncture. The next man to suggest that I carry away the princess of Kannauj from under her father's nose and make her my wife will be rewarded with a thousand lashes. Apsara indeed! Why, I'd rather wed an unwashed donkey instead!'

28

The queen mother was most insistent. Together with her old crony the pandit, she insisted that her son visit the Jinamata temple at Bulandshahr and take a dip in the Ganga to counter the baleful influences that surrounded him. There was no resisting a two-pronged attack of this nature and Maharaj Prithviraj took his companions, Padhri and Nahar, with him. He was hoping they could recapture a slice of a simpler time.

Senapati Skand instructed Padhri and Nahar to take some of the best men from their division to guard the king. And so they set out. It was the happiest they had all been for a long time. They left behind the dignity of their exalted positions in Ajmer and teased each other mercilessly, laughing so hard the guards were hard pressed to keep a straight face.

Padhri was one of the most respected men in the kingdom and said it wasn't half as satisfying as farting underwater. As always, he turned around and offered to crack my skull if I put that nasty jibe into my 'Prithviraja Vijaya' and I had to explain to him that nobody cared about yet another smelly warrior in the king's entourage. He kicked my horse then and the poor beast reared up, almost killing me.

Even the king laughed as I struggled to regain my seat, although he was the only one who bothered to see if I had survived the brutal assault. Padhri and Nahar were engaged in a keen discussion on whether the bald pricks of the foreign enemy enhanced one's sex life or made it more painful. We missed Kanak sorely.

Destiny led her to us some distance from the Jinamata temple. She and the rest of her company were across the river. It was obvious that they had come a long way and their horses were blown. They were the strangest group of women we had ever seen. About half a dozen in strength, they were all young and beautiful, dark as the fabled blue lotus. They wore their long hair gathered in plaits, which came down to their waists.

Not an inch of their bodies was visible. They wore embroidered leggings and an upper garment of a sort I had never seen before. Full-sleeved with an embroidered bodice that was gathered at the bust and fell in flowing swirls to the knees. They carried short swords, waterskins and small shields. One even carried a bow.

Even among those beauties, Samyukta stood out. When she caught a glimpse of Maharaj Prithviraj, she smiled in pure delight, and teeth that were perfect as pearls were revealed but it was the feeling behind it that would have lit up the darkest of places. Her face was round as the moon and of delicate colouring and features. Even with the wind whipping her clothes into disarray, it was obvious that her body was sculpted to perfection. And when the king looked into those magnificent brown eyes, which glowed with an inner light, he was utterly lost.

Seeing us gave them a fresh lease of life and they signalled to us urgently. They had captured the king's fancy at any rate. We made arrangements for a boat to ferry them across and they seemed nervous and excitable, urging us to hurry, looking over their shoulders all the time.

We soon saw why. It appeared that the entire army of Kannauj was at their heels. Our archers tried to provide them with cover but two of the women belonging to Samyukta's guard fell dead. Already they had sent for the elephants to be lowered into the water as a makeshift bridge to allow them easy access. The others shielded the princess with their own bodies and they made it across in one piece.

The king lifted her up gently and placed her in front of him on his saddle. From that moment on, they were lost to everything else and seemed aware only of each other. Behind them a terrible battle raged. Shouts of fury, the clash of arms, arrows zigzagging all around, finding their marks with meaty thumps, horses neighing, men dying, women screaming— Prithviraj and Samyukta were oblivious to it all.

It was love of the sort neither had experienced before, not to be confused with passion, desire, affection or infatuation, that rarest of incandescent feelings which few among the mortals are chosen to experience. Both were consumed by it, filled to the brim with irresistible need and a profound, almost sacred joy that they had found each other. The danger that surrounded them on all sides made their love all the more poignant for it was heightened by the terrible fear that they might lose each other.

This was the love that bards sang about, the thing that people hoped for and prayed they might find one day. The thing that too many lived and died for. And die they did. So many of our men and theirs fell that day. Sacrificed on the altar of the terrible love, that ineluctable force of nature that swept Prithviraj Chauhan and Samyukta away. And all of us who knew and loved them so much as well. It was the final gift of the merciless goddess who had loved him. Its invincible power would destroy a great king and the unified aryavarta he had come close to achieving.

Only a handful of us survived the journey back into the borders of the Chahamanas kingdom. Padhri and Nahar fell. I never understood why I alone, the least impressive of our little company famed for physical prowess, managed to outlive them all. *Prithviraj wept openly for them during the grand funeral rites he had performed in their honour. Princess Samyukta stood by his side, sharing his grief and everything else. Her quiet dignity and strength was a palpable thing and the king clung to it for dear life.*

It was only in her ingenuous arms that he forgot his pain, the demons from his past and the terrors of an uncertain future. And so he remained there, unwilling to let go. His only solace was the comfort of her loving embrace. He willingly drowned in the depths of her eyes, which understood the dark secrets of his soul and loved him all the more for it. Even defeat would be bearable to the unconquered hero as long as she was by his side.

They loved each other with a wild and reckless abandon, pouring the depths of their intense passion into each other, like ghee over flames that burned higher and higher, bathing them with its radiance and divine splendour, burning their souls and fusing them together with its unbearable heat. They revelled in each other, sundering the bonds of this world, harkening to the beauty and mysterious forces that called them from beyond. Ultimately, they loved each other so fiercely because deep down was the sobering knowledge that neither cared to admit: if their sublime romance lacked one thing, it was permanence.

While the king and his lover remained ensconced in each other's arms, uncaring of the tumult in the world around them, matters of great import were unfolding. Mahamantri Kadambavas was a cautious man, given easily to suspicion. He had seen much of human nature and had a dim view of it on the best of days. Not being a believer in love or coincidence, he began to investigate.

The bold and beautiful company of female guards who had accompanied the princess from Kannauj were watched closely. Even so the mahamantri nearly missed the plot and with it, so much more. The cleverest of the lot had been most resourceful and discreet. She had been carrying on a liaison with one of the guards assigned to the watchtower. One night, he and the rest of his company fell dead, poisoned by loving hands that had thoughtfully brought them spiced wine.

By the time the alarm was sounded, a small unit of Jaichand's crack troops had entered the fort. Fighting broke out and by the time the mahamantri and the senapati found out that it was a diversion, it was almost too late.

The beautiful assassins had been told to strike at an opportune moment. Their targets were Maharaj Prithviraj and the young prince. In the melee and ensuing confusion that followed it was hard to find out precisely what happened. Many of the eye-witnesses were dead. And the only way to shed light on the events of that night of horror was to piece together the fragmentary evidence and fill in the gaps with guess work.

Kanha and Kadambavas had broken into the harem to stop the warrior maidens and protect the royal family. They succeeded insofar that the king and his son escaped the cowardly attempt on their lives.

When the fighting broke out, Maharaj Prithviraj rushed out, naked as the day he was born, sword in hand. Two of the assailants fell by his hand. Kanha and Kadambavas prevailed over the rest. But they were not long for this world either. Women did not fight fair and their daggers had been poisoned. The king could only watch helplessly as his beloved Uncle Kanha and invaluable Mahamantri Kadambavas died in a pool of their own vomit, which had turned black from the poison.

Senapati Skand arrived to give the king his report. The survivors of the ambush and the one who had let them in had been captured. By orders of the king, the soldiers were to be dismembered. As for the warrior maiden, her punishment was so terribly inhuman, I cannot put it down but her screams rang out across the barracks for three days before death claimed her accursed soul. None of us shed tears for her plight.

When the king returned to his chamber, heartsick with grief, he had no inkling that the tragedies of that fell night were far from over. Princess Samyukta lay in the state of dishabille he had left her in. The ivory hilt of the dagger that had been plunged into her chest was visible between her perfect breasts.

Maharani Padma, who was standing by the side of the body, turned as he approached, sick with shock and grief. 'I did promise I wouldn't have your whores poisoned . . .' she said. It took three of the guards to pull him off her, and even so he nearly throttled his wife. They never spoke to each other again.

Torn apart by bereavement, Maharaj Prithviraj was prostrate with grief. The vaidya was in constant attendance. I went to see my friend too and my heart broke at the sight of what the mighty monarch had been reduced to, drugged out of his skull and drooling like an imbecile, so far gone in his pain that it would prove nigh impossible for him to return to sanity. Later, when death came for him under such lamentable circumstances, my only solace was that Prithviraj Chauhan had already died. At the precise moment when he was separated for good from his Samyukta.

Everybody blamed the princess from Kannauj for what happened. Hariraj made me promise that I would not mention her in my 'Prithviraja Vijaya'. He wanted her very memory expunged from the recorded history of the greatest of the Chahamanas kings. I obeyed. For he rules now and bravery is not my forte.

And yet, I cannot find it in my heart to consign my true account of their tragic love story to the flames. It is not what my king would have wanted and so I will leave it concealed in my chambers. If it is meant to be found, it will be.

Their love was real and though the price proved too high for them and this very aryavarta, I have no doubt that if given the choice, even in light of everything that happened, Prithviraj Chauhan would still choose love. And Samyukta. Every single time.

29

For the second time, the battlefield of Tarain witnessed two mighty armies camped on each side. All efforts towards finding a diplomatic solution had fallen apart. It was hardly surprising since the sultan wanted his opponent to apostatize or fight to the death. On the other hand, Maharaj Prithviraj was perfectly willing to spare his sworn enemy's life provided he was willing to retreat to his own land.

Despite their bravado, Prithviraj and his men were suffering from an acute case of apprehension. They ate and drank a lot more than they wanted to, determined to create an atmosphere of buoyancy and a spirit of upbeat confidence. Their musicians and trained bed-slaves lulled them into a slumber heavy with unease, rife with nightmares and haunted by unseen spectres.

As for Shihabuddin of Ghur, he was taking no chances. Under the cover of darkness, he sent a unit of his soldiers who had been specifically trained for night attacks. They fell on the unprepared camp, making short work of sleeping soldiers and setting numerous tents on fire. It was a massacre reminiscent of the time the cowardly Ashwathamma had crept into the camp of the Pandavas, making sure that none of the sleeping heroes ever woke up again, using knives and fire to hasten their demise.

The killers melted away into the shadows almost as quickly as they had materialized, leaving terror and untold damage in their wake. Prithviraj slept through it all, under the influence of a particularly concentrated dose administered to him by Narana. His dependency had become more acute and he needed a heavier dosage to achieve the mental equanimity that was becoming increasingly elusive for him.

Senapati Skand and Govindraj worked through the night trying to restore some semblance of order. Dawn was just breaking when the enemy attacked. Even though the Turushkas were in a state of disarray, they dared not risk a direct charge. Instead, they relied on the superior mobility of their divisions and the flexibility of their lines, which would confound their adversaries. Shihabuddin sent the first four divisions comprising 7000 each of his elite corps—the mounted archers. They harried the lines of an army arranged for a frontal crash, to crush their opponents with the bulk, seeming to come at them from all sides.

Shock troops drew in close enough to shoot their arrows in a torrential outpouring. Using their deadly recurved bows, their aim was unerring and well-placed arrows found their mark, the sharp point disappearing into eyeballs bulging with terror. Released with tremendous force, some of the arrows tore right through the armour of the king's men as if they were little more than paper.

Having unloosed their terrible missiles, they withdrew, forcing their disoriented opponents, who were flummoxed by this unfamiliar military strategy, to give chase, exposing themselves to those terrible arrows. The endless skirmishing sapped the strength and morale of Prithviraj's men and they struck out in blind panic.

Maharaj Prithviraj rode into battle then and the soldiers rallied to his side, fighting with fresh heart. Their horses even caught up with the superior and far faster steeds of their adversaries and were able to inflict some damage.

Then Govindraj of Dillika fell. His helmet had fallen and his skull shattered on impact with the ground. He was identifiable by the missing teeth in his mouth, which was frozen in a silent cry of agony. Prithviraj Chauhan went berserk. 'I will see you on the other side, old friend,' he roared, 'with enough of these heartless rakshasas to fill the furthest bowels of hell!'

When Prithviraj had finally woken up that dawn with a funerary dirge playing in his head, he had refused the services of his vaidya. 'No more poison for me, Narana, thank you! On a day like today, it won't make much of a difference.' He could feel the clammy breath of death on the back of his neck and it was far more exhilarating than anything life had to offer.

On that day, he fought like never before, digging deep into seemingly inexhaustible reserves of potent energy. Arrows poured forth from his bow in an endless fusillade. A raging river of blood soaked the battlefield of Tarain and his foes spilled their lifeblood into it at the urging of his arrows. But it was all to no avail.

Never before had their armour or sword arm felt so damnably heavy. The greatest army in the history of aryavarta raised for the express purpose of stopping the Mussulmen faltered, poised on the brink of abject defeat and worse. The goddess of victory had given their king her love but he had betrayed her for a wanton temptress and in her rage, she had abandoned them all. They cursed the name of the whore who had brought Prithviraj Chauhan so low.

For a while their superior numbers staved off the inevitable. And then Shihabuddin of Ghur gave the order for his fifth division of heavy cavalry to charge and they rushed into the fray, raging bulls released from their pen to tear apart all who stood in their path. They slammed into the ranks of the army, a solid wall of steel and their lines collapsed, wiped clean with their own blood. As the sun began its downward descent, the battle was over. It was the end.

Prithviraj was slumped on his saddle, weak from loss of blood, wounded in so many places it was a miracle he wasn't already dead. His mount wouldn't give up on him though and made a mad dash to take him to safety. Despite the desperate effort, Shihabuddin's cavalry caught up with him near Sirhind and they took the king captive. He was weak with pain but fought them vehemently hoping they would kill him. But the sultan's men had their orders and they didn't dare claim his life.

The defeated king was in chains but other than that, they hadn't treated him too badly. Their physicians had attended to his wounds and cleaned him up. He had been given fresh water to drink and food had been proffered but he had declined. *One does not have an appetite when one has been vanquished*, he thought and laughed out loud. His guard stared at him with the air of one who fully expected the dangerous beast in his care to bite.

Mercifully, the victor did not keep him waiting long. Prithviraj could not help noticing that he looked remarkably unremarkable for a bloodthirsty conqueror. For a man who had not touched meat or wine for over a year, he had a slightly protuberant belly and he was pleased to note that the heat was getting to the sultan as evinced by a small heat boil on the very tip of his nose. Prithviraj tried not to stare at it.

They gazed at each other for a long time. 'My men were right about you,' the sultan told him finally with the aid of an interpreter. 'They say you have the look of the devil in your eyes. It makes them frightened and they wished to put out the unholy light in their depths with firebrands.'

Prithviraj had nothing to say and contented himself with a glare. 'You are fearless, I'll say that for you,' Shihabuddin said in frank admiration. 'By the grace of Allah, your life has been spared and perhaps it is his will that you live to a ripe old age, granted the blessing of bouncing your grandchildren on your knee.'

His adversary smiled at the incongruent and highly improbable image. 'For men like you and I, that is an impossible dream. It is one that we don't care for much, at any rate.'

'Even so, you don't have to die today or tomorrow. I will return your kingdom to you and if you have no wish to convert to the worship of the one true god, preferring to be exempt from his grace and spend an eternity in torment, I will not insist that you convert. However, in return for my magnanimity, I ask for nothing but loyal service from my devoted vassal.'

'That is a lot more merciful than what I was led to expect from you,' Prithviraj began conversationally, 'and for that you have my gratitude. However, I cannot give what you ask for. While there is life in my body and breath in my lungs, I will keep on defying and resisting the rule of our invaders, who seem unable to stop themselves from destroying our temples, looting the land and raping defenceless women. The humiliation of defeat is something I can accept but it would be impossible to live with myself if I betray my land and my people. Shihabuddin of Ghur will never sleep easy while Prithviraj Chauhan remains alive for he will be seeking to kill him and if left alive it is only a matter of time before he succeeds.'

Molten rage suffused his features and the sultan glared at him, seeing his own implacable will reflected in the scorching gaze of his prisoner. 'Then you leave me with no choice but to grant you the mercy of death at the hands of my executioner.'

'So be it! May your victory over me bring you more joy than my victory over you did me!'

The sultan was present for the execution of Prithviraj Chauhan. The man was not afraid and he even joked with the guards who led him to his death. It was a frightful waste and

Shihabuddin was genuinely sorry to see that noble head roll in the dust. If only he hadn't been so blastedly stubborn . . . Still, it had to be admitted that Prithviraj Chauhan had been a worthy adversary. Despite himself, the sultan was saddened that this formidable warrior's story had ended so abruptly.

Epilogue

Sleep did not come easily to the sultan these days. Not even when he spent long hours in prayer to help settle the turmoil in his mind. It had been a gruelling campaign but he was pleased with the results. The Khokars had risen in rebellion in Lahore and he had returned from Ghazni to deal with them personally.

The scene of the battle had been a familiar one—endless carnage to be followed by utter devastation, looting, raping and destruction. He had tried to stop it but his generals had looked at him as though he had lost his mind. The men must not be denied their due, they had insisted, and these filthy infidels need to understand that when they rebel against the sultan, who is god's representative, the retribution will be severe.

Shihabuddin rubbed his temples wearily. He could feel the light smattering of heat boils on his forehead and remembered how Prithviraj had taken note of one fourteen years ago. That stubborn man had refused to submit, all the way to the very end, staunchly refusing to be party to his sins against this land. Not that his recalcitrance, bolstered by his reckless courage and noble ideals, had done him or his land much good.

With the fall of Prithviraj Chauhan, Shihabuddin's men had advanced unimpeded into the very heart of aryavarta like a ravaging wildfire. Following his victory at Tarain, the sultan had marched towards Ajmer, handed control to Govindraj, the minor son of Prithviraj Chauhan, and left one of his Mamluk

Turks to oversee things. However, Hariraj was every bit as stubborn as his brother and had captured the capital city of his ancestors with the help of one Skand who had been Prithviraj's commander-in-chief.

Qutb-Din-Aibek, regional governor by order of the sultan, put paid to Hari's efforts to restore the glory of his ancestors. Having been vanquished in battle, Hariraj consigned himself to the flames. Jaichand of Kannauj had been killed in the Battle of Chandwar. Within a decade, a big chunk of northern and central India came under the sway of the sultan.

Leaving his newly forged empire in the hands of Aibek, he had returned to Ghazni. The sultan's forces, led by his Turkish generals, brought Dillika, Meerut, Aligarh and wide swathes of the Ganga–Yamuna–Doab plain under the Ghurid control. The Chalukyan capital of Anhilwara Patan was sacked. Those were tumultuous times and the political landscape underwent drastic changes.

Many rulers surrendered in exchange for keeping control of their territories but later reneged on their promises or rose in revolt. Even his able generals had fought among themselves for overall control and Shihabuddin had to return and sort out the mess. *There is something in the very air of this land,* the sultan mused, *it foments distrust and dissent, making the wisest of men behave with utmost foolishness.*

It had been two years since his sainted brother, Ghiyasuddin, had left this world leaving the entire realm to his care. Now it was his responsibility to deal with the constant crisis that was central Asia as well as the hotbed of conflict in Prithviraj's aryavarta. Having crushed the rebellion of the Khokars with an iron fist, he hoped that they would all simmer down and give him some peace.

In the end, Prithviraj Chauhan had been right. His stupendous victories had not brought him much joy. On most days, it was a luxury if he could attend to his ablutions without

being dragged away from the privy to attend to some urgent matter. The sultan wondered why he was feeling so morose after his recent victory.

It was a dark and sultry night. He was camped on the banks of the river Jhelum. Once he returned to Ghazni, he would go on a long pilgrimage, giving alms to the needy and spend his time in prayer, drawing ever closer to the infinite presence of Allah. In fact, why must he wait?

He knelt on the little prayer mat and closed his eyes. He did not open them when pandemonium broke out across the little camp and the sounds of a pitched battle destroyed the calm of the night. When the daggers of the Khokars led by their chief, was plunged into his body, Shihabuddin of Ghur did not even cry out. 'Consider this a personal gift from Maharaj Prithviraj Chauhan!' one among them said. And as he fell, he heard them chant a familiar refrain . . .

Prithviraj! Prithviraj! Prithviraj!

References

Ali, D. 2004. *Courtly culture and political life in early medieval India*. New York: Cambridge University Press.

Chandra, S. 2006. *Medieval India: From Sultanate to the Mughals* (Revised ed.). New Delhi: Har Anand Publications.

Chatterjee, P. 2010. *Empire and nation: Selected essays*. New York: Columbia University Press.

Farooqui, S.A. 2011. *A comprehensive history of medieval India: Twelfth to the mid-eighteenth century*. New Delhi: Dorling Kindersley (India).

Keay, J. 2000. *India: A history*. New Delhi: HarperCollins.

Mehta, J.L. 1986. *Advanced studies in the history of medieval India*. Vol. 1: 1000–1526 A.D. New Delhi: Sterling Publishers.

Middleton, J. (Ed.). 2015. *World monarchies and dynasties*. Vol. 1–3. New York: Routledge.

Naravane, M.S. 1999. *The Rajputs of Rajputana: A glimpse of medieval Rajasthan*. New Delhi: A.P.H. Publishing Corporation.

Nizami, K.A. 1999. The Ghurids. In M.S. Asimov & C.E. Bosworth (Eds.), *History of civilizations of central Asia*. pp. 177–190. New Delhi: Motilal Banarsidass.

Roy, K. 2015. *Warfare in pre-British India: 1500 BCE to 1740 CE*. New York: Routledge.

Sanyal, U. 2016. Tourists, pilgrims and saints: The shrine of Mu'in al-Din Chisti of Ajmer. In C.E. Henderson & M. Weisgrau (Eds.), *Raj rhapsodies: Tourism, heritage and the seduction of history*. New York: Routledge.

Sharma, D. 2015. *Early Chauhan dynasties*. Jodhpur–Ahmedabad: Books Treasure.

Somani, R.V. 1981. *Prithviraj Chauhan and his times*. Jaipur: Publication Scheme.

Syed, M.H., Akhtar, S.S., & Usmani, B.D. (Eds.). 2011. A concise history of Islam. New Delhi: Vij Books India.

Talbot, C. 2016. *The last Hindu emperor: Prithviraj Chauhan and the Indian past 1200–2000*. Cambridge: Cambridge University Press.

Tandle, Dr. S. 2014. *Indian History*. Solapur: Laxmi Book Publication.